To Debbie Spiegelman

Table of Contents

Prologue.

The book was begun in depths of humility, and ended likewise with the murmur, 'God be merciful to me, a sinner.' It is a book for sinners, and for lovers of humanity. I apologize to them for the sins of the book and that it loves much but not enough.

—Carl Sandburg, The American Songbag

This bricolage was begun a bit differently. Your author / editor / redactor was innocently listening to a Great Book while ambling through the woods and getting both exercise and culture when a tall, skinny, contentious young woman appeared in her head and began interrupting the great classic with her own decidedly silly yet touchingly earnest opinions. Your scribe shook her head and tried to concentrate on the fine words of literature.

But then this personage was back, and with friends in tow. And enemies. Promises to write down their stories had to be made. Some of these characters were insistent about starting a story but then refusing to finish it. They had to be cajoled and appeased through certain acts of theft. Whether these acts have improved this book, the Public, including you, Dear Reader, will decide.

An authorial fiddling friend dropped by the other day to visit the chaos and play some tunes. He happened to read through a few pages of this perambulation. He felt it needed less obvious Oogling and Wikapeeing and more demands upon its gentle readers to open up their own Botkins, Lomaxes, and other works of folklorists and grad students ensconced at their universities or on the roadsides, writing theses and dissertations that no one reads and earning doctorates to continue doing more of the blessed same.

"Let your readers search the Web themselves," he said, "since everything can be found there and it's all true, even if it never happened. All this extraneous information gets in the way," he admonished, "and no one has time to read long books."

He added:

"Don't use big words, so everyone can read it."

- "Put in plenty of sex and violence."
- "Make it short. People have other things to do, you know."

My elegant pal also suggested that attempts to sound erudite were somewhat embarrassing to any reader who knew anything about any of the subjects mentioned in this history. Therefore, this work refrains from all such embellishment, pretense, and scholarship, let alone literary or musical profundity.

And then he added: "Slap this puppy up on Amazon and make yourself a quick buck. Give 'em a story. And don't forget to write yourself some good reviews."

I must murmur Carl Sandburg's prayer and his apology, though he had little cause for the latter.

Poems.

1. To the Book

May some readers take a
look, at this goofy little
book, and not despise its cowed
reliance, on a literary
giant.

2. To Donna Cody

Adamantine Donna Cody
Won't put up with any toady.
Not that many would toady to her since she is a bit nuts.
And tends to get into some obsessive and obscure musical ruts.

3. To Mabel

A dedicated Christian
You take no guff
And let the world know
When you've had enough.

4. To Dulcie Tobey

A woman fiddler,
Well, what do you know?
Where did she come from?
Where did she go?

5. To Sandy Panther

Love of money is a curse,
But to have none at all is usually worse.

6. To Sandy Panther, Rockandy, and Blue: Syllabics

If dogs think you're wonderful,
then you probably
are. Humans can't tell, poor things.

7. To the Rambler

O faithful one of glorious lineage
Today they'd sell you to high tech millionaires and call you
vintage.

8. The Wit and Wisdom of Sandy Panther

You can kill a chicken
By kissing it to death.
'Tween a hero and fool,
There's just a hair's breadth.

9. To Donna Cody

Duncan wants you to eat,
Mabel wants you to be neat,
Aunt Jane knew you couldn't be beat.
Rockandy finds you sweet.
Viv says your thinking is too full of self-deceit
But the future will lay praises at your feet.

10. To Donna Cody

To tie up so many folks in your skein
is a gift. May it grow denser as the years
grow more bitter.

11. The Rambler's Complaint: A Dialogue

R: You leave me to languish in heat and in rain.
DC: As to your fortune you need not complain.
R: You load me to bursting, then make me go.
DC: I fill you with gas and I keep your speed slow.
R: Dogs tear at my seats and slobber and snuff.
DC: You can bear it, O Rambler! You're strong enough!

Dramatis Personae: In Order of Their First Appearance.

Donna Cody – A lover of old-time music and a fiddle player.

Professor Jane Porter (Aunt Jane) – Donna Cody's aunt and benefactor, deceased.

Rockandy – Donna Cody's beloved hound dog.

Mabel Watkins – Aunt Jane's and Donna Cody's housekeeper and Duncan's mother.

Duncan Watkins – Mabel's son and general handyman, who cares for Donna Cody.

The Rambler – Aunt Jane's 1959 Rambler American sedan.

Dr. Johnson – Donna Cody's veterinarian, who tells her about C. C. Leggett.

C. C. Leggett – A fiddler extraordinaire and Donna Cody's first live mentor.

Edna Leggett – C. C. Leggett's very competent wife, who plays the little parlor organ.

Buster – The Leggetts' dog.

Veet, Pretty Eyes, and Daisy – The Leggetts' cows.

Dulcie Tobey – A woman fiddler who was popular in the 1930s, source of "Chickalielee Daisy-O" and other rare, sought-after tunes.

Marvin – A gas station attendant who befriends Donna Cody.

J. Q. Briggs – Marvin's employer.

Mrs. Mary Jane Stout – The deacon's wife. She is part of the church that Aunt Jane attended.

Darlene – A friend of Mrs. Stout.

The Goslings – Mrs. Stout's female followers.

Mrs. Cody – Donna Cody's mother.

Sandy Panther – Donna Cody's companion. A banjo player.

Bob – One of a number of folk singers.

Mr. Rotmensen – Proud owner of "Rotmensen's," a high-quality Dutch restaurant.

The Archivist – An anonymous person who helped the author.

The Librarian – Another anonymous person who helped the author.

Vera Love – A devout former singer. She and her husband rescue Donna Cody and Sandy Panther and inspire them.

Albert Love – Vera Love's devout husband, who drags Sandy Panther out of a dangerous fight.

The Balsam Evangelist – Vernon Lugner, who sells Donna Cody and Sandy Panther a dubious remedy.

Peter – A seductive leader of a strange commune.

Jimmy – A helpful member of the strange commune.

Joe – A singer-songwriter.

Vivian Smythe – A student of noises of all sorts.

Marcy Mellow – A singer who breaks hearts and doesn't care.

Christopher – A folk singer who died for love, supposedly.

The Old Town Rounders – Josh Coshinsky, Tom, Bob, and Guthrie. Like Donna Cody, they are aficionados of old-time music and an early part of its musical revival. They temporarily include Donna Cody and Sandy Panther in their band and name themselves **The Hokey Okey Dokies.**

Davis and Clayton – Two of a group of vicious dog breeders.

"Old Eph" (Ephraim) Jankey – A famous old-time fiddler who generously hosts pilgrims who want to learn from him.

Emma Jankey – Old Eph's wife.

Zeke Jankey – Old Eph's kind son.

Braxton Jankey – Old Eph's obnoxious son.

Frank – The proprietor of the Dew Drop Inn.

George – One member of a group of hunters; he owns a dog who has lost her gameness.

Blue – George's dog re-christened by Donna Cody and Sandy Panther.

Mandy Monroe – A fiddler and shantyboat dweller.

Mr. John – An officer of the Nob County Correctional Institute.

Miss Evans – A worker at the Nob County Correctional Institute.

Gina – A prisoner from the Nob County Correctional Institute.

Enoch – A kind farmer.

Erma – Enoch's wife.

Carden Wade Goodman – A prolific author, adventurer, folklorist, and professional Southerner.

Frances Augustinia Goodman – Carden Wade Goodman's wife, who is also a talented writer.

Othar Roman – A banjo player extraordinaire.

Dora Richards – A famous country singer who has decided to get back to her roots. Her family is well known to folklorists for its talented singers and huge body of song from generations past.

Fred Jones – Dora's former manager.

Rosie, Lala – Mabel's sisters.

Preacher Watkins – Mabel's father.

Lamar – A boy who attempted to molest Mabel in her youth. He turns out to be surprisingly connected to another character as well.

The Richards – Dora's family. The children are, in order of age (first boys): Likens, John, Paris, Vidam, Henry, and Philip. The girls are Clara, Maritrue, Susie, Dory, Phoebe, Anna, and Sally.

Horace Richards – Dora's father.

Elizabeth Richards – Dora's mother.

Likens Richards – Dora's brother, a very talented singer.

Maritrue Richards – Dora's sister, who leads Donna Cody to Solly's Cave.

Solly Richards – Dora's great-great-great-grandfather, who lived by Black Bird Rock and Solly's Cave.

Ricky – A police officer.

Auntie Rufe (Rufinia Joan Blechard) – Sandy's "aunt"—if not an actual relative, then certainly Acting Aunt. She is attached to a strange group of refugees of all sorts in Dog Lick Holler.

Old Mother – A crazy old lady at Dog Lick Holler who loves animals but can't stand Donna Cody.

Chapter 1: Donna Cody: Her Looks, Her Books, Her Records, and Her Dog, as Well as Her House and a Brief Mention of Her Aunt.

When springtime does come,
O won't we have fun,
We'll throw up our jobs
And we'll go on the bum.

—"Hallelujah, I'm a Bum!", traditional

Donna Cody was a little over six feet tall and skinny as a snake. She could sit on a chair, cross her legs, and tap her crossed-over leg's foot's heel on the floor while playing the fiddle, which was mostly all the time, unless she was playing a guitar or a mandolin or something else, in which case she still liked to cross her legs and tap her heel. She hunched over her instruments in ways that spoke of a painful future and a protracted relationship with a physical therapist. Her skin was the color of watered-down government powdered milk with some pale blue mottling the white. The veins on her hands were beginning to show through. Her fine blonde hair hovered like a wispy lenticular cloud above her small, narrow face, and her tiny round tortoise-rimmed spectacles that made her look wide-eyed all the time. She usually wore dungarees and a white shirt with a Peter Pan collar and maybe a large man's crew-neck sweater over it since she was often cold. She had sailed into her twenties with a shambling and oddly graceful oblivion to all the swirling fads around her.

She lived in a broad and comfortable if somewhat rundown sky-blue Craftsman with black trim. It sat on the edge of a small Ohio college town, in a wilderness of old snowball bushes and lilacs, laurel, forsythia, and wisteria. Inside, Donna Cody spent most of her time listening to LPs and reel-to-reel tapes over and over to catch that little hitch in the bowing or that roll up the fiddle's A string or that shuffle note in a C chord. She did not own a TV or a radio.

Donna Cody had inherited the house from her Aunt Jane, who hadn't looked related to her in the least since she had been round and short. A long-retired English professor (though perhaps "retired" wasn't the right word as she had left the university under dubious circumstances), she had been one of the few relatives who had taken a fancy to Donna Cody and kept up with her throughout childhood. This was probably due to Donna Cody's long letters to her, which Aunt Jane found interesting and endearing in their pedantry. When Aunt Jane died—at far too young an age, which is when many of us die—Donna Cody found herself with a small inheritance[1] and the small house in a small Midwest college town 500 and some miles away from her parents and siblings. This made her happy, in spite of her grief over Aunt Jane's demise.

Donna Cody had taken only a few of her aunt's things out of the house, but had put a good many things of her own into it. Aunt Jane's elegant oak bookcases were filled with titles like Ian Watt's *Rise of the Novel* or E.R. Curtius's *European Literature and the Latin Middle Ages*, as well as a lot of Sir Walter Scott.[2] Donna Cody's bookcases, on the other hand, followed the ubiquitous student model of boards with bricks stacked on the ends. The boards sagged dangerously, and the books leaned drunkenly, but at least each bookcase was clearly arranged by topic. A folklore wall contained the blessed and humane Benjamin Botkin, resting uncomfortably next to Richard Dorson, who was leaning even more inappropriately onto the majestic Zora Neale Hurston, and still more folklore bedfellows.[3]

---

[1] Jane Porter had instructed through a testamentary trust that Donna Cody receive a monthly stipend. An old friend of hers was the trustee. She had made sure these instructions were fulfilled.

[2] Donna Cody later cited the long footnotes in Sir Walter's novels as highly influential in her love and study of folklore. Her love of Edward Waverly always remained undiminished.

[3] These included Richard Chase, Norm Cohen, Josiah Combs, Alan Dundes, Archie Green, S. Green, Joe Hickerson, both Lomaxes, Stith Thompson,

Another section on this shelf housed books of carefully collected songs: *Red Hills and Cotton*; *White Spirituals of the Southern Uplands*; a variety of Baxter-Stamps hymnals; Cecil Sharp's two volumes of *English Folksongs from the Southern Appalachians,* Vance Randolph's four-volume set with swirling Thomas Hart Benton end papers, as well as Randolph's book *Pissing in the Snow.*[4]

Then there were the tune collections: Samuel Bayard's *Hill Country Tunes* and his *Dance to the Fiddle, Dance to the Fife*; Coles' *1000 Fiddle Tunes*, R. P. Christeson's two volumes of *The Old-Time Fiddler's Repertory.* And more.

A much smaller banjo section.[5] Some books about mandolins, guitars, and string bass. Pamphlets on how to make dulcimers, a huge corner with spreading shelves of folktales, and even a blues section.

Wooden crates held 78s and tapes, and these were arranged alphabetically. These included classics like the Harry Smith Collection, a stack of Texas Shorty singles, Carson Robinson's band with Lawrence Loy as caller, as well as his calling with Wilbur Waite's Pokeberry Promenaders, and a huge stack of "hillbilly" singles.[6]

Donna Cody was digging back further and further into recordings of

---

D.K. Wilgus, Charles Wolfe, and random copies of *The Journal of American Folklore.* And many more.

[4] In addition: Jean Ritchie's *Singing Family of the Cumberlands* illustrated by Maurice Sendak; Ruth Seeger's delicate *American Folk Songs for Children*; John Jacob Niles' *Ballad Book*, Leonhard Deutsch's *Folksongs of Florida*, and many more.

[5] She had Pete Seeger's *How to Play the 5-String Banjo*, even though she couldn't play the banjo at all.

[6] She was dubious about the singles, but she couldn't resist them. In addition, she had an interesting record called The Country Blues by Samuel Charters. She had not quite figured out the black roots that watered the old-time music tree—yet. She also had was starting to find out about collectors who would let you buy tapes of their records, some collections of "Golden Era" recordings from major record labels.

people who didn't call themselves musicians but just played. She wanted music that was played and sung by people who worked at other jobs than music for a living, for whom music was the air they breathed, and she wanted to be like them except that she didn't have to work for a living, which made for some conflicted thinking, so she didn't think about it too much.

Instruments lay about everywhere. Autoharps leaned together in a corner. Beside them sat a weird instrument with a piano-type keyboard that had apparently married a zither and become one flesh. Banjos strewn in another corner had also participated in strange unions with mandolins, guitars, and even tambourines. Fiddles with fallen-over soundposts, missing pegs, holes in their fronts, and hopelessly beat-up necks lay around in their own hospital ward, many of them crying out for the ICU. Someone had suggested that Donna Cody throw picks all over the room so that she'd have one whenever she needed one. Thus, flatpicks looked like little black, gray, tortoiseshell, and white holes on the old Oriental carpet, as if beckoning you to shrink and then dive down into yet stranger musical universes. They were handy until you tried to vacuum, but of course Donna Cody never vacuumed anything. Mabel, however, did, and she had a few things to say about those picks to anyone who cared to listen. (We will shortly hear of Mabel.)

Yes, it was a messy, crowded world before the Web came along, and you had to look far and wide to find what you wanted. The journey was comfortingly and maddeningly meandering, and it could take you anywhere. A librarian or Donna Cody's mother would have had fits before getting to work right away straightening it all out, as folks who don't believe in crooked paths will do. But Donna Cody spent most of her time taking things out, reading, listening, learning from them, and then rearranging them. Her own systematizing instincts, while not entirely reliable, were insistent. She read just enough to have strong opinions, but she had not yet read enough to realize she didn't know anything. And this is the real purpose of reading, isn't it?

Donna Cody might have become lonely if it had not been for her beloved mangy hound, Rockandy. She had found this creature at the pound. Rockandy had one brown eye and one blue eye. They weren't evenly horizontal above his nose. He had long black ears, a mournful hound face, and a speckled body like that of a Bluetick Coonhound. But his legs were long and skinny, and he tended to trip when he ran, which was often since he was, after all, a hound, and he liked chasing things. He could bay as loud as you could wish, and so he was Donna Cody's best friend and protector, though he had not been necessary in the second capacity so far.

Rockandy was getting past the first bloom of youth, just as Donna Cody was. The house was settling around them pretty comfortably, but it was the back-before times: no Internet, no Facebook, no email or Twitter or all the buzz and hum. Just landline phones and letters and a chiming old clock on the mantelpiece. Donna Cody tended to avoid the phone. She had some avid correspondence, mostly with the occasional professor or record collector who didn't mind some idiotic questions or who might know things like why the fiddle tune "Phoebe Ice" was found in Pennsylvania and West Virginia but nowhere else, or how George Pullen Jackson had traced Amish tunes back to the Middle Ages. She was too young to know what she was talking about, but she knew what she wanted to be talking about.

As comfortable as her life was, Donna Cody, still being young enough in spite of herself, was feeling stirrings. She was thinking of the Lomaxes camping on the side of the road as they traveled and recorded, of Cecil Sharpe and Maud Karpeles trekking though the Appalachian Mountains, of Ben Botkin going out to find his "living lore" with working folks. She dreamed of collecting and adding to the great cathedral of the music of the folk. Spring was nibbling at winter, and the house hovered over her just a little too much like a tomb, especially when, as she was sitting on the floor, a bookshelf toppled all four volumes of Vance Randolph's set of Ozark folk songs with the Thomas Hart Benton end paper pictures on top of her. Luckily, they weren't damaged. Rockandy woke up and came over and licked her nose.

"Rockandy," Donna Cody said, "I need to find these people who sing these songs and play these tunes. It's time to strike out and find the true and authentic folk before it's too late.[7] There have to be some still out there. We need to follow the highways and travel the byways and look for the music. And we'll need to take a tape recorder, too." (Remember, dear readers, that when Donna Cody was young, there were no MP3 players, no fancy phones, no tiny handheld thingamajigs. It was a dark and mysterious time.)

"Here I've been sitting," Donna Cody continued, while Rockandy lay on his back, feet in the air, as she rubbed his belly, "here I've sat, and I don't play music much with anyone else and I don't see much of anyone else. It is time to venture forth. They're not all dead."

Now it should be known that Donna Cody had a few friends besides Rockandy, two like good family. These were her neighbors: Mabel and her son, Duncan. Actually, they lived on the other lot. Aunt Jane had willed them their house, as she had willed Donna Cody hers.

Mabel had been Aunt Jane's housekeeper for many years, and both Mabel and her son Duncan helped Donna Cody out. Mabel was big, and like many of us of a certain size, she did not like to plop or flop. She wore

---

[7] This idea of saving it all before it's too late is known as "salvage ethnography." Academics argue that there's no such thing as "lost" because everything changes anyway and our ideas about something being lost are cultural stereotypes that we force upon others, etc. Thankfully for us, Donna Cody was all about salvaging.

a self-respecting girdle, a formidable bra, and, always, a dress. Never pants. She was a fortress of tough love before the term was invented to catch up with all those tough ladies. She thought Donna Cody was unfortunate in her looks. She wished her son knew Jesus a little better than he did and that he would stop wearing dungarees. She cleaned the house enough so that it was healthy and walkable: her goal was a clear path through each room. Cleaning had been a lot easier with Aunt Jane.

Duncan had taken on more and more of the outside yard and house work as he broadened at the shoulders and lengthened in the legs until he was almost as tall as Donna Cody and a good deal more muscular. He kept Aunt Jane's flowers weeded and trees pruned, he fixed drains and pipes, he cooked whenever Mabel let him. Both Mabel and Duncan loved Donna Cody, and she loved them. Duncan kept trying to feed Donna Cody, but she smiled, took a sip, or a bite, or a nibble and then pushed the food around a bit. She was easily distracted.

When Duncan found out that Donna Cody wanted to go looking for music, naturally he worried about how she would eat and how her car could possibly make it and whether she would be safe. The car was Aunt Jane's 1959 Rambler American sedan, and it was only a few years old. It was royal blue with a white roof, and it had a hole in the floor behind the front seat so that if you were a passenger in the back, you could watch the road going by underneath. (No one knew why the hole was there, especially in such a new car.) Exhaust fumes would drift in and out unless you put something over it. But the car's friendly headlamps and perpetually astonished-looking grille were endearing. Duncan was always tinkering with it. He had grown up some with that car and knew every inch of her.

Chapter 2: The First Quest. A Canine Encounter. Instructions in Farming and Fiddling.

Treat my daughter kindly, and do to her no harm,
And when I die I'll leave to you my little house and farm,
My horse, my plough, my sheep, my cow, my sheds and little barn
And all the little chickens in the garden.

—"The Little Chickens in the Garden," sung by Mrs. Guy Bosserman, Pineville, MO, on September 3, 1924, in Vance Randolph's *Ozark Folksongs*, Vol. IV

The story of Donna Cody's first trip is told all over now by old-time music players. You can probably find it on the Web somewhere. People credit it for tunes that have become staples, tunes that would have gently but irrevocably disappeared. After consulting many stories, I believe I have a reasonable account of this visit.

One early spring day, with little piles of snow still on the roadsides, Donna Cody loaded up the Rambler, directed Rockandy to the front passenger seat, got in, and started down the driveway; Duncan ran after her waving two freshly baked loaves of anadama bread. She came to a halt, took the bread, thanked Duncan, and told him to convey her gratitude to Mabel, since they were looking after things while she was gone. She even surprised herself and gave him a kiss on the cheek when he leaned in with the bread, which made him glow under his smooth brown skin. And then, she was off.

Donna Cody was hoping to find Calvin Cecil Leggett ("C. C." for short), a fiddler in the next state over that she had heard about from the vet one day when Rockandy was getting his shots. Donna Cody and the vet were friends since he was not only a vet but a guitar picker who "knew a few fiddlers." He had given her some vague directions: C. C. and his wife lived off the East County Road on a little farm, about 100 miles away. Or, as C. C. had told the vet: "Two far see's and one go by house on the road."[8] And if she got lost? Well, that's what folks did all the time, and the world was probably a better place for it.

Donna Cody and Rockandy were excited. They had the car windows partway down, the sun was shining warmly for such an early spring day, and the Rambler was rumbling away at 40 mph, faster than it had gone in a long time. Rockandy stuck his head out the window and snuffed at the air, his ears streaming behind him. Donna Cody sang "Goodbye Girls, I'm Going to Boston," even though she wasn't anywhere near Boston. Then she tapped her left-hand fingers curled around the steering wheel, thinking out the pattern of a fiddle tune. This habit had developed in the last year or so. One might doubt the safety of such a practice.

After a few hours of driving, some wrong turns, and furious honking from all the cars stuck behind her, Donna Cody turned off on East County Road and drove down to the end. Once she passed the first house it was easy to see the little yellow house with the chickens pecking around on the side.

"That must be it, Rockandy," she said a bit nervously. She had never just showed up at someone's domicile before. But the house was reassuring, with an immaculate mailbox and the name "Leggett" carefully printed on it, a small tidy barn in the back, snowdrops giving way to crocuses, and hopeful daffodils coming up behind them, lining a little dirt path that led up to a creamy white door with a screen door in front of it. Donna Cody shut off the Rambler, stepped out, and stretched. She let Rockandy out, and he bounded around but then uncharacteristically howled to announce their presence.

A black dog the size of a small bear leapt out from behind the house,

---

[8] For those of you who find this as confusing as your author did, this means that you drive to the horizon and then do it again and then past a house on the road. In the flat parts of the Midwest, apparently, this works.

barking and growling. Before Donna Cody even had time to think, that dog had bitten her on her calf. She let out a yell and jumped back into the Rambler, dragging the yipping and scrambling Rockandy in on top of her. He skittered over to the passenger seat and barked nonstop. A thin, slightly hunched-over old man came hobbling pretty quickly out the door and down the path, yelling "Here now!"

An old woman came out right behind him, yelling at the dog and the man and swinging a mop over her head as if she were going to clean the sky. Rockandy and the bear dog hurled insults back and forth. The chickens yelled at the top of their little lungs. The woman set down the mop and chained the dog to the fence, which looked as if it would give any second. The old man hobbled over to Donna Cody while she was telling Rockandy to calm down.

"What do you want?" said the old man. "You got the dog kinda riled."

"Sir, I am looking for Calvin Cecil Leggett," she said. "But right now, I believe I need a bandage." She opened the door and eased out slowly on her good leg. Some blood was coming out at a good clip as she rolled up her pant leg. The woman, coming up behind, saw it, and without a word ran back in the house, while the man matter-of-factly said, "That's me."

Mrs. Leggett came back with a bandage and some Mercurochrome, with assurances that this would prevent rabies. She cleaned Donna Cody's calf and wound a bandage around it. The bite wasn't too bad, just a nip. It just looked bad with all the blood.

"Thank you, Mrs. Leggett."

"You are very welcome," she said. "I don't know what got into Buster."

Donna Cody, feeling better, guilelessly announced her mission.

"Mr. Leggett," she said, "Dr. Johnson, my vet, told me about you and your fiddling. I would dearly love to play some tunes with you because I am learning to fiddle."

C. C. never blinked an eye, being a somewhat expressionless person, but politely said, "Well now, ma'am, I don't teach."

"But you play the old tunes, and I would love to hear how you play them," pleaded Donna Cody.

"Well, I can play 'em, I guess. My chores are about done, it being Saturday and all. I suppose we could sit down and play a little."

"But it's suppertime," interrupted his wife. "You come in now, hon, and we'll sit you down and get you something to eat. You look like you could use it. Then you can play your tunes, Calvin." It was obvious that she ran things.

Donna Cody thanked them both, handed C. C.'s wife (whose name was Edna) one of Duncan's anadama loaves, which made a great impression, she grabbed her fiddle and let Rockandy out with stern admonitions. He and Buster, after some prolonged sniffing and a little jumping around, decided they could get along. Buster's negotiations with Donna Cody took a bit longer but eventually resulted in a peaceful settlement.

Donna Cody helped Edna set the white enamel table while various edibles were whisked from the tiny old refrigerator and the stove. While this went on, Edna extracted information: How she had found them? Did her parents know where she was? Why was she all alone, & etc. Donna Cody explained about Dr. Johnson, noted that her parents were no longer in charge of her and that she was used to being on her own.

Edna shook her head. "You don't seem old enough to be out on your own, hon. But these days, that's what the young people do, I guess. There's been a couple of 'em come through, looking to record Calvin."

C. C., out in the back, sounded like he was putting things away with lots of clanging and banging. He finally shuffled in and washed his hands. Donna Cody was relieved.

As they sat down, she had to wonder if they had somehow known company was coming. After a quick blessing, they all dug into beef and potato hash, corn pudding, fried apples, piccalilli, dilly beans, and slices of Duncan's incomparable bread with a creamy lump of homemade butter to spread on them. They finished it all off with tomato soup cake.[9] Donna Cody was not a big eater, but in this case, she did her best because it was expected. Duncan would have rejoiced.

It was a businesslike affair. No one talked much except for Edna asking Donna Cody if she didn't want a little more of this and a little more of that. After the cake, Edna ladled some mugs of liquid from a big pot simmering on the back of the stove. A bunch of branches were sticking out of it, and it turned out to be sassafras tea, which Donna Cody found delicious.[10]

After the leftovers had been given to the dogs and Edna and Donna Cody had done the washing up, they went in the living room with their sassafras tea, while Donna Cody and C. C. took out their fiddles. Edna turned to a little pump organ. They all looked at each other, and waited awkwardly.

"What would you like to hear?" C. C. Leggett finally asked.

"Do you play that tune 'Soldier's Joy'?" asked Donna Cody.

"Well now, yes, I do," said C. C. Leggett, never lifting bow to fiddle.

Donna Cody saw she was going to have to push harder. "This is how I try to play it," she said. And she attempted a version she had learned from *Ryan's Mammoth Collection, 1050 Reels and Jigs (Hornpipes, Clogs, Walkarounds, Essences, Strathspeys, Highland Flings and Contra Dances, with Figures)*. But she had not played in front of other people much, at least not since

---

[9]Tomato Soup Cake, or "Mystery Cake," became popular during The Great Depression and through World War II, especially because you could leave out things like butter and milk and it would still work.

[10]Your author would like to advise you against drinking sassafras tea since it contains a carcinogen known as "safrole." But no one knew that then.

school, and so she was shy, making more mistakes than usual, which seems to be a natural law in playing music before others. Not only that, but without the page in front of her, she was forgetting parts of the tune.

C. C. and Edna listened politely. Donna Cody kept at it and got it down a little more. Then Edna played some chords behind her with a beautiful oompah, oompah, oompah. This confused Donna Cody, since the tune transformed into something a little bit different, but then she began to relax into those chords pumping and pushing her along. Then C. C. joined in, though he played the tune even more differently and got some rhythm into it that was mysterious and compelling. Donna Cody finally put her fiddle down to listen, but that made Edna and C. C. stop as well.

"Oh, no, please go on playing!" said Donna Cody. "I like what you're doing much better." So they did, and they sped up and whooshed right through the tune a few times.

"Can I go get my tape recorder?" asked Donna Cody.

Edna and C. C. looked at each other. "You're not going to make a record of it or anything, are you?" he asked.

"Oh no," said Donna Cody. "I wouldn't know how to begin. I want to listen to how you play so that I can learn."

"Well now, looks like you already know that tune," said C. C. "Don't you want to learn a new one?"

"But I don't know it the same way," said Donna Cody. "I have to learn off records or from books, and I want to learn from people."

"Nothin' wrong with records, but I know what you mean," said C. C. with the hint of a smile. "I can't read music myself. Wish I could. Well, then, go along and get your tape recorder."

Donna Cody lugged it back and recorded "Soldier's Joy." And kept recording as C. C. went on to some more tunes in D and then "Billy in the Lowground" and more tunes in C and then "Sugar in My Coffee-O" and more tunes in G. Edna sang "When the Roll Is Called up Yonder," with C. C. creaking out a tenor line behind her. They moved into tunes Donna Cody had never heard of—jumpy, fast little tunes, some of them in B-flat, which was a challenging key for her.

Donna Cody was enthralled. She recorded and then would try to play along, though she checked herself when she tried to cross her legs and tap her heel on the floor as usual; Buster's bite still hurt. But if this was the price she had to pay for these tunes, she would pay it gladly.

C. C. had what is known as an upbow style and moved his bowing hand in little circles, rocking between the strings. She wanted to learn how to do that. She watched him and copied the best she could, her long arms and elbows looking like giant buzzard wings. Her wispy hair got in her eyes, and her mouth hung open and twitched a little as she played. She was intent on C. C.'s fingerings. C. C., meanwhile, seeing her devotion, opened up and talked about how he had learned this tune from his Uncle Julius, that tune from the time he worked in a logging camp when things were tough, that one from a jukebox in L.A. when he was passing through.

It was hours later, dark outside, with all the bug noises of a spring night chirruping away when they put their fiddles down. Edna proposed that Donna Cody stay over for the night. Donna Cody, seeing that the house was tiny, proposed that she sleep in the Rambler. Edna immediately tut-tutted the idea of sleeping in a car.

"But where is the girl gonna sleep, Edna?" asked C. C.

"She can sleep in that little room in the barn," said Edna, who then turned and went out with purpose and intent in her eye.

"Well, Miss Cody, we can play some more tomorrow after church, I reckon."

Donna Cody said, "If you will teach me your tunes and feed me, I will help you take care of your chickens and cows and pull weeds. Can we do that for a week?" C. C. thought about it.

"Hmmm. Well, let's see how we all like it," he said.

Edna, carrying a pile of sheets and blankets, had bustled in at the end of this. "Now Calvin, you know *I* take care of the chickens. I'm sorry, Miss Cody, but no one else is going to touch them. Miss Cody, do you really know how to milk cows? I suppose you know how to weed?" Donna Cody had to confess that she actually had never learned either of these skills. C. C. and Edna looked at each other, looked back at her. C. C. looked at his fiddle.

"Oh, what the heck," he said. "We'll just see how it goes."

Chapter 3: Of Bovines and Bowing. The Magical Tune.

Cow and the sheep walking through the pasture,
Cow says, "Sheep, won't you walk a little faster. BAA!"
Sheep said, "Cow, I gotta sore toe."
Cow said, "Sheep, I did not know. BAA!"

—"Jimmy Sutton," as sung by the Highwoods Stringband

Donna Cody heard the bang on the door and groaned. It was Thursday morning. She was sore all over, especially her back, which was used to slumping over books and instruments, not hoeing, weeding, milking, or even washing up. She rubbed her eyes, shifted on the hard straw-filled tick mattress, stretched to a length that made her look like she was on Torquemada's rack, curled up again, sat up, nudged Rockandy with her toe, and threw off her covers. It was still dark, but it was cow milking time for Day 4. She hoped things would go better today. The Leggetts only had three gentle Guernsey cows, all a beautiful chocolate brown. They were named Veet, Pretty Eyes, and Daisy, but they all looked alike to Donna Cody. C. C. told her he always had names for each of his "girls."

"I know 'em by the head and by the udder. Then you can recognize 'em from both directions," he'd said, as he introduced Donna Cody to each one. She had found that so far, the only things that got C. C. talking much were fiddling or cows. There might have been some other things, but she hadn't run into them. He would cuddle one of the cats and talk about how he played a cornstalk fiddle when he was a boy, sawing across the stalk with a stick and humming the tune. He even showed Donna Cody how to make one, and she sawed on it a bit. He told her that he got his first fiddle when he was seven. His dad traded a wagon for it. Donna Cody got the idea that this was an astoundingly generous act and that the family had been pretty poor. He had played for dances, which was good money, but mostly he had had to work.

In the mornings, after giving the cows scoops of silage to munch on and keep them busy, Donna Cody would brush and wipe off the teats, then grab and squeeze down, trying not to pull. Her hands ached. She had thought farm life was going to be a little more idyllic, with plenty of time to sit on the porch and play.

"They may not know English, but they know what you're sayin'," said C. C. the first day, gesturing at his girls. "It's not what you say but how you say it." So Donna Cody had tried to sing and hum nice cow-themed material: "Streets of Laredo" and "Come a Cow Cow Yippy" and "The Old Cow She Crossed the Road," which is challenging since that tune shifts keys. It hadn't helped much. The girls had bucked their heads, rolled their eyes, and shifted their giant, threatening flanks. They had knocked her off her stool. They had knocked the pail over, usually after it was full. Yesterday, after knocking the pail over, Pretty Eyes, the sweetest one of all, had pushed her off the stool into the already spilled milk. The Leggetts were not pleased about all the lost milk, but Rockandy and Buster and the cats, being opportunistic, were very satisfied with Donna Cody's performance.

Now, four days later, things were going a little better. Donna Cody staggered in with the milk and then helped Edna fix breakfast and feed the dogs. After breakfast, she hoed and hand-weeded and held some greasy metal machinery for C. C. while he fixed it. It was getting nicer out as spring asserted itself, but they still hit some sleety rain, and Donna Cody was soon soaked through. C. C., in his coverall, was oblivious.

Rockandy followed her and Buster followed Rockandy. They had all become fast friends. Buster now liked to lay his giant black head in Donna Cody's lap, something Rockandy did his best to tolerate. Buster also liked to drool when he did this, but Donna Cody was charmed by the beast's turnaround and attempted amends for his former hostilities. The bite marks were slowly fading on her leg. Buster's adoration also cemented her growing friendship with the Leggetts.

After helping with supper and wash-up, C. C. and she would sit down with the tunes. Edna sometimes joined them for a while on her tiny parlor organ. Mostly, though, C. C. was all over Donna Cody's case. If he began a sentence with "Well…" she knew she was in trouble.

"Well, now, Donna. That's not quite how this goes," he'd say. (She had finally gotten them to stop calling her "Miss Cody.") She watched his stubby cracked fingers as she tried to stay clear of his breath (chewing tobacco), and strained to hear notes that weren't there for her. She knew they *were* there, but she knew that she had to listen to the tune repeatedly to hear them because she expected them to be somewhere else instead of where they were.

"I keep hearing this note that I can't see you making," she whined.

"Well now, that's the bowing," he said. "You need to let your bow get the notes. It's how you move the bow, is all. Now if you could hear Old Dulcie Tobey play that. I can only play a little bit like her, but I keep trying."

Dulcie Tobey was the fiddler he talked about the most, though there were many more. Donna Cody wrote their names down. Sometimes, they listened to C. C.'s records. He loved Kenny Baker and Tommy Jackson and other bluegrass fiddlers, but when he played back the tunes, they sounded different—and much better, to Donna Cody's mind. Their recordings were often fast, smooth, and slick, but C. C.'s playing was a little slower, which allowed her to hear the tune and all the bouncy shuffles that made it feel as if she were riding down rapids on a creek. But according to C. C., there were no official recordings of Dulcie Tobey. Donna Cody had never heard of her before, but C. C. said she was the fiddler everyone looked up to.

"She's dead now, right?"

"Well now, I believe so," he said, "but there's been rumors come up every few years about someone finding her in some holler or even in towns and that she plays better than ever. Too bad you kids with your tape machines and all couldn't have got ahold of her. Don't think she ever went up and recorded for the labels. And she didn't sing or nothin'."

"Hmm," murmured Donna Cody musingly, thinking of her books, her old LPs and 78's, and realizing what a river of song and tune and story lay secretly underneath all of them, a flood of people no one would ever know about, who never got into those books or on those tapes and records. All those dead fiddlers, players, voices. They were going away, and they would be drowned out by Top 40 hits and television advertisement jingles, and all the trivia pouring out from people who only cared about making a buck. She wanted to dive into that secret dark river, to escape from the relentless banality around her.

"She must be dead if she was already old years ago," Donna Cody said. "But why would she have to sing to get herself recorded?"

"Well, I think that's what the record companies wanted from a woman," C. C. said. " 'Course, my mama sang, but she wasn't about to go play out or nothing like that."

"Why not?"

"Wasn't something the women did. They was busy with the kids and all."

Donna Cody writhed in her seat but went on. "But Dulcie Tobey never did stay in one place long? Did anyone learn her tunes?"

"I reckon some of us tried. No one can play them like she could, though. And the kids today," C. C. said, in a sudden burst of talkativeness, "they don't care about the old tunes, 'cept a few like yourself. They all want to play rock and roll. Even the square dancers. Used to be, you could fiddle for dances around here at the granges. Now they all use records— if you can even find a square dance."

At this point, before things got too morose, Donna Cody knew it was time to jump in and ask if he knew any waltzes or tunes in A or how his bow worked when he played "The Girl I Left Behind Me."

By the end of the week, Donna Cody had learned five tunes by heart and recorded a lot more. Many of these tunes were not new to Donna Cody, but C. C. played them in his own jumpy way, and she wanted to learn them that way. Not only did he push the bow up when Donna Cody would have pulled it down, but he put in little trills that were new to her. He played two strings together so that the harmony string against the fingered melody string made a drone, like bagpipes. He said playing two strings together was a double stop, which was not exactly new to Donna Cody, but the ones he came up with were different from what she was used to.

"It rings!" Donna Cody exclaimed, and C. C. allowed himself his faint smile. He slid his little finger up to get a high note to match the next string for more ringing.

One tune above all was her favorite, and this was called "Chickalielee Daisy-O" and was in the key of D. Donna Cody loved this tune as if it were a wild animal that had come like a medieval unicorn (or Buster) to lay its head in her lap. It galumphed around like Buster, too—the first part being longer than the customary 16 bars—and then threw itself at you in the second part, in the short, lay-its-head-in-your-lap part. This was the way Donna Cody thought about fiddle tunes.

By the end of the week, both Donna Cody and the Leggetts were fond of each other and tired of each other as well. Along with her learned tunes, her taped tunes, and the wonderful "Chickalielee Daisy-O," Donna Cody had learned a little about how to milk cows, hoe weeds, clean up in good earnest, and even cook some, though mostly, she stirred things since Edna was not about to relinquish control of the kitchen, which was a good thing. She did have a feeling that they had gotten a lot of work out of her, but she had made three new friends, counting Buster. (She did not count the cows.) It was Saturday afternoon, and time for her and

Rockandy to go.

C. C. helped her pack up the Rambler, and Edna gave her a beautiful big round cornbread to take home in place of Duncan's anadama loaves, which had been toasted, spread with jam and butter, and even, at the end, turned into French toast. In addition, Donna Cody was given two quart jars of piccalilli, five small jars of jams—each a different jewel-like color—and some canned meat that scared her to death, but she didn't say anything except thank you. C. C. was not a hugging sort of person, but Edna was, and Buster slobbered all over her and Rockandy.

"Now don't be a stranger," said C. C., making a beginning of breaking into a smile. It took a lot to get him to smile, so this was a real honor.

Donna Cody promised to return, and she meant it. Rockandy jumped up on the passenger side of the front seat as Donna Cody held the door open for him. Then, she stepped in. Edna and C. C. stood on the porch, waving as she drove off. After that, they flopped on the couch to watch *Lawrence Welk* on TV. After all, it was Saturday and tomorrow would be the Day of Rest. They were getting started on it early.

Chapter 4: Donna Cody Defends the Oppressed.

Each day I'll do a golden deed
By helping those who are in need,
My life on earth is but a span,
And so I'll do the best I can.

—"A Beautiful Life" by William M. Golden / Golding[11]

Donna Cody hummed, "Chickalielee, chickalielee, chickalielee waaooo" to herself as she drove along. She had made up these words to help herself keep the tune firmly in mind. The Rambler didn't have a working radio, and she wouldn't have listened to it anyway unless she could have found a good country station. Her left-hand fingers tapped out note patterns on the steering wheel. Rockandy slept curled up on the front seat. Behind them, a long line of cars began to pile up. When someone tried to pass Donna Cody, she unconsciously veered toward the middle line and sped up a little, a not-uncommon failing of inexperienced drivers. Someone would finally pass her, roaring by with his or her middle finger extended, horn blaring. Donna Cody, lost in the intricacies of "Chickalielee Daisy-O," hummed and barely saw any of it as visions of C. C.'s fingers danced in her brain.

Luckily, however, she noticed the gas gauge, which actually worked thanks to Duncan, and so she finally pulled over to gas up in the middle of a tiny little town, under the sign of a red horse with wings. A long line of yelling people in honking cars passed by after her. The station, like the town, was a sleepy little place, nothing like the gleaming, chirping megalopolises we have now. An older man was yelling at a hollow-chested

---

[11]At some point, his surname changed from "Golding" to "Golden," perhaps when he was thinking about golden deeds. He apparently wrote most of his hymns in the state penitentiary, which would certainly inspire one to write about something better.

teenager and slapping him on the side of his head. This brute was clenching a stogie in his teeth and looked like Bluto from the Popeye cartoons with a big toothy mouth and black mustache and beard surrounding it, as well as wide shoulders and thick, scary forearms.

"You'll wear that uniform and like it!" he snarled.

"Aww, I'm wearing it, ain't I?" whined the boy. "But you're not paying me what you said you would."

SLAP! "Get out there and pump that young lady's car!" yelled the man. The boy jumped forward to get out of the way of any more slaps and skittered over to the pump. He began filling the tank and then went over to wash the Rambler's windshield. But Donna Cody was indignant, and she rolled down the window.

"You shouldn't be hitting him!" she screamed at Bluto. Rockandy stuck his head out the other window and growled a warning growl. The boy jumped, dropped his squeegee on the Rambler's hood, and under his breath said, "Oh, please shush, ma'am."

Bluto spun around and ran over. Donna Cody rolled up her window. Rockandy growled in earnest. The boy took the nozzle out and closed up Donna Cody's tank, but then Bluto smacked him across the face so that he fell to the ground. Donna Cody was so mad that she jumped out, and Rockandy jumped out after her, snapping and growling. Bluto backed away, while the boy lay there sobbing and trying to pretend he wasn't.

"Here's your four dollars, you stinking creep!" said Donna Cody. She threw them on the ground. Bluto edged over to grab them (watching Rockandy carefully), snatched them up, and started toward Donna Cody, yelling curses that it would not be edifying to repeat here.

A sudden bolt of lightning cracked the sky. People jumped and screamed. Far up on his stand the horse with red wings rattled as a gust of wind raced through, and then another bolt struck and hit the horse. In slow and terrible motion, he made a huge, mythic descent, crashing to the ground in a glorious slow-motion catastrophe. Donna Cody later swore she heard him whinny as if he were enjoying the whole thing. Rockandy yelped and barked as a rushing fountain of water burst up—a broken water main. Donna Cody ran toward the boy. Bluto yelled at her and waved his arms and danced with rage, as if the lightning and plunging horse were all her fault. Donna Cody and the boy huddled together waiting to be pummeled. But Bluto, with a narrowed evil gleam in his eye, ran to the front of the Rambler, threw open the hood, and did something. Rockandy ran after Bluto and chased him into the station, where he slammed the door and locked it. The boy tore away from Donna Cody and took off running down the street as fat raindrops came splatting down. Now Bluto was on the telephone. He exited, slamming the door and shooing away the few onlookers who had come to see the sign and the water. Oddly enough, the water hit the sign so that the shiny red horse seemed to shake in a frenzied dance, albeit upside down on his back.

But Donna Cody saw Bluto coming. She jumped into the Rambler right after Rockandy. She turned the key. Click. Again. Click. Nothing. Bluto watched her, laughing, and then drove off in a pickup truck.

Chapter 5: Donna Cody Returns Home with the Rescued.

Possum sitting on a log
Soaking up the sun.
Hound dog coming down the road
Possum better run.

—"Sugar Hill," traditional

Donna Cody sat in the Rambler feeling shaky as ferocious rain drummed an elusive pattern of splats on the roof, windscreen, and hood. Rockandy lay curled up mournfully beside her. She had to leave the window cracked open because human and dog breathing got things pretty steamy, but this made them both shiver. She mopped the window with her sleeve until the sleeve was sopping. It was getting dark. She decided it was time to eat a piece of cornbread with some of the strawberry jam. She even opened Edna's canned meat and gave it to Rockandy. He practically inhaled it, and it smelled so good that Donna Cody thought about trying it. But now, what was she going to do? The rain had stopped. And so had the water bursting out of the pipe.

She was just beginning to think that she needed to go find some help when a tap on the window made her jump. It was the boy. He was in ordinary clothes now, dungarees and a T-shirt, all of which looked pretty wet. He was scrawny but wiry, and he held some keys in his hands.

"Are you OK, ma'am?"

"Oh, hello," said Donna Cody. She stepped out, uncurling from the Rambler and towering over him.

"I've got the keys to the truck," the boy said.

"What truck?" said Donna Cody. "What's your name? Are you OK?"

"I'm Marvin. I'm OK, but now I've lost my job, I guess. So we might as well take the truck. You can't stay here."

"Hello, then, Marvin. What truck?" Donna Cody was oblivious to the fact that she had probably cost Marvin his job.

"That tow truck over there. I don't know what Mr. Briggs did to your car, but I can tow you to your house and put things right for you. And he can just wonder where his truck went."

Marvin did not realize that Donna Cody lived about 75 miles away, but when he found out, he was happy. A road trip with his boss's truck full of his boss's gas sounded good to him. He wasn't much for thinking about the consequences, but neither was Donna Cody. After he had backed the truck and hooked it up to the Rambler, Donna Cody found herself with Rockandy squeezed into the truck cab. And off they went, Donna Cody directing. Marvin, it turned out, didn't say much but turned on the radio to some station playing "Mashed Potato Time." Donna Cody sat in silence for a while during song after song, but then a trio came on singing "Blowin' in the Wind." Donna Cody clicked the radio off.

"Hey!" Marvin said, turning it back on, just as the voices soared. "My friend...is blowin'." Click! Donna Cody turned the radio off again and began talking:

"You don't want to listen to this junk," she admonished. "This isn't the real music. This is prettied-up bubblegum-pretend folk garbage. At least those other songs don't try to be anything much. These people take something they call 'folk music' and they turn it into money-making mush."

Donna Cody went on for some time, even offering up her own lachrymose rendition of "Barb'ry Allen" as an example of something more authentic. Marvin realized that he was trapped in the truck with a nut, listening to a song about some Sweet William guy lying around and dying, Barb'ry Allen not caring, then dying too and both of them becoming flowers. Marvin stared straight ahead and kept on driving. Donna Cody commented upon the speed with which he was driving. Silence. Then she said, "Marvin, what you need to do is find out what your family used to sing."

"My dad likes to sing 'Sweet Violets,'" said Marvin carefully, but then, carried away, he warbled, "Sweeeet, violets. Sweeter than all the roses. Covered all over from head to foot, covered all over with shhhhnow."

"Hmmm," said Donna Cody. "What does your mother sing?"

Marvin's mother, it turned out, sang Patti Page songs like "With My Eyes Wide Open, I'm Dreaming" and "Doggie in the Window." Luckily, Marvin did not attempt to sing them. Donna Cody sighed. Marvin switched the radio back on.

After a stop for dinner at an orange-roofed Howard Johnson's (Donna Cody treated) and some more driving, they pulled up in the dark at Donna Cody's house. It had been a long and weary ride. But what was the front door doing open? Why were so many house lights on?

Chapter 6: Donna Cody's Betters Decide to Interfere.

Throw out the life line! Throw out the life line!
Someone is drifting away;
Throw out the life line! Throw out the life line!
Someone is sinking today.

—"Throw Out the Lifeline," by Rev. Edward [Edwin?] S. Ufford

While Donna Cody had been out adventuring, her absence had not been unnoticed. In fact, it was vehemently noticed by a coterie from Aunt Jane's church who had promised to look after Donna Cody, even though Jane Porter had never asked anyone to look after her niece. However, as Aunt Jane had lain dying, she'd had no resistance to offer them. They needed to do good works, and this was one of them, a promise that was surely a comfort to a dying woman.

Jane Porter had tended to club around with some of the ferocious older dames that often embody the best of churches, cranky women who have finally learned to say "yes" to few and "no" to many. Mostly, only the children liked them, though that was often due to justified expectations of a piece of candy. Sometimes the children only got the candy after a little thwacking on their heads.

The deacon's wife kept an eye on Donna Cody's house and noticed any changes. She had come out of sorties with Aunt Jane and her gang badly scorched, and unconsciously carried on the feud with her niece, all in the name of Christian love. Like so many of us, she *meant well.* Fenélon said it in French, but here's his drift: "Nothing has been more common in every age, and still more so today, than meeting souls who are perfect and saintly in speculation." At any rate, the deacon's wife noticed the missing car. The coast was clear.

"Darlene," said the deacon's wife to her friend, "it has certainly been a baptism by fire for poor Jane's little niece."

"Who?" asked Darlene, timidly. A group of them in a sea of white yarn were knitting beautiful tightly stitched bandages for lepers.

"Donna. Donna Cody," the deacon's wife snapped.

Another cohort chimed in before the deacon's wife could say more: "She's going to seed there in that house, which is falling apart. Dear Jane would be so upset."

"Amen," everyone agreed.

"I thought that colored boy was working on it," said Darlene, faltering.

"Prayer," intoned the deacon's wife with a withering look at Darlene. "We can all start with prayer. That's the most important thing. But we need to pray in earnest, ladies. And we need to act."

Various degrees of assent were murmured, and the upshot of it all was that a few days later, a delegation of ladies drove over and bullied Mabel into opening up Donna Cody's house that afternoon. While Mabel stood there, her face like stone, the ladies looked around at the mess. Things were spotless (thanks to Mabel), but getting through the rooms was like walking through a maze. The LPs, the books, instruments all in their piles were tricky to navigate—booby traps! While Donna Cody was not exactly what we now call a *hoarder*, it's hard not to see a certain tendency in that direction. No dead bodies buried under stacks of newspaper or rotting food or anything like that, though. More of a scholarly hoarder, continuing in the line of Aunt Jane and so many before and since.

Mabel could navigate through it all just fine, but somehow a few of the ladies, and especially the deacon's wife (who was also a good-sized woman) found themselves knocking things over. A guitar fell from its precarious perch on a couple of stacks of books. A violin bow was stepped on. As is customary in such situations, it was much easier to blame the guitar and books and the fiddle bow rather than oneself. Mabel's face took on a thundercloud aspect. She crossed her arms, and this was an aggressive act.

"Now this is a mess," said the deacon's wife nervously. "We need to stack up some of this stuff and get Donna to go through it and get rid of at least half of it." The other ladies assented somewhat listlessly. As long as they didn't have to do much but toddle after the deacon's wife like a flock of geese they were fine, but stacking up books? Taking things? They hadn't signed on for that.

Mabel gathered herself up in protest, but then Duncan burst in from the back door. The ladies drew back. Duncan was definitely taller than Donna Cody by now. His hair was getting longer, and his skin, such a beautiful light brown, made them all nervous. He had a scowl that obviously meant dreadful menace. The deacon's wife looked for a phone to call the police.

"What do you think you're doing?" he said softly, warily. He looked down on them like a judge. The deacon's wife looked up at him and took a breath.

"We've come to help," she asserted and stepped forward, eyeing her flock to make sure they were all behind her.

"Help?" asked Duncan. "What do you mean, *help*?" He didn't budge. Mabel was right next to him.

"This mess," said the deacon's wife, waving her right hand around. "This can't go on. Jane wanted me to look after Donna, you know, keep an eye on her, and—"

"She did *not*," Duncan interrupted most firmly. He didn't yell. He just said it. There were some shocked gasps. But before the deacon's wife or anyone else could reply, suddenly the front door banged open and in strode a tall, thin woman in spike heels and a leopard-skin coat with a matching cloque on her carefully coiffed hair. She carried a matching suitcase and bag. Her lips were scarlet. Everyone stepped back from *her*, even Duncan and Mabel.

"What in God's green earth is going on here?" she demanded. "Who are you?" she snapped at the deacon's wife. "And you? And you?" she went on, fixing her eyes on various persons as she scanned the room. "What are you doing in my daughter's house?"

"Your daughter?" gasped Mabel, Duncan, the deacon's wife, Darlene, and a few of the other goslings.

At that point, many voices broke out at once, some shrill, some squawking; things were hashed out and then worked out. The upshot was that everyone was kicked out except Donna Cody's mother (who did the kicking, if only metaphorically) and the deacon's wife, with Mabel and Duncan hovering in the other room, muttering to each other. While Donna Cody's mother was a stick and the deacon's wife a pear, they both got along as they looked through the piles and began making yet one more pile: a giveaway pile.

"Look at all these scraps of paper all over the place," said the deacon's wife.

"Let's throw them here in the trash," said Donna Cody's mother. At this, even the deacon's wife wondered if they should be so drastic.

"Look," said Donna Cody's mother, taking out a cigarette and lighting it. "I'm here to get Donna back to college where she belongs. She's a talented if awkward girl, but she's not getting any younger. All this foolishness (a grand arm sweep that knocked over a little harmonica) is keeping her from her real music and her studies. She needs to drop all this crazy folk music stuff. She needs some true *help*." Setting an ashtray precariously on top of one of the stacks (you could see how Donna Cody and her mother were related), she continued tossing books onto a growing pile. Mabel and Duncan fumed helplessly in the other room.

It was an hour or so into this purge, and Donna Cody's mother and the deacon's wife were rooting around for something to eat in the kitchen, exclaiming over the lack or oddity of the foodstuffs, when, with rumbling and jangling, Marvin and Donna Cody pulled up in Bluto's tow truck, and Donna Cody jumped out. Rockandy jumped out. Marvin stood outside and waited. Mabel and Duncan ran out and hugged Donna Cody and filled her in on events. Duncan put his arm around her because she wasn't quite steady, which was a good excuse. "Uh-uh, uh-uh," said Mabel warningly, but she was too preoccupied to follow it up.

Some hushed talk went on. Donna Cody straightened up and stalked into her house, Rockandy trotting right behind her. Mabel and Duncan followed but stood in the doorway and watched. Marvin stepped out of the truck and joined them.

Chapter 7: Donna Cody Reclaims Her House. Duncan Fixes Everything. Donna Cody and Rockandy Meet a Companion. Duncan Almost Despairs. Marvin Settles In.

Just break the news to Mother
She knows how dear I love her
And tell her not to wait for me,
For I'm not coming home.

—"Break the News to Mother," by Chas. K. Harris, "King of the Tear Jerkers"

It was unusual for Donna Cody to shout, but it was not unusual for her mother to do so. As Duncan and Mabel stood outside, however, they did hear some shouting from Donna Cody. Definitely something about a fiddle bow. A minute later, the deacon's wife came hustling out of the room, scurrying past them and out the door, taking off in her station wagon. Marvin had followed the deacon's wife. Now he sidled up to Duncan and introduced himself. It wasn't long before they were talking about the Rambler and some pangs of hunger that Marvin was experiencing, in spite of his great dinner at Howard Johnson's. Mabel and Duncan, distracted by a guest in need, invited Marvin over to their house, but looked over their shoulders a few times as they walked across the yard.

Donna Cody was having it out with her mother.

"Donna, honey, really, you can't go on living like this." (Her "honey" was not sweet.)

"Living like what?" Icily.

"For Christ's sake! You had so much promise! Mr. Stewart thought you could have played in the philharmonic if you would practice." Cigarette waving about and big dramatic gestures.

"I play all the time."

"You sit here in this mess and play this folk music, when you could be a real musician—"

"I do *not* play *folk* music! At least, not that stuff you think is folk music, misnamed. I *try* to play the music of the folk, the music that is at the heart of all music, classical and otherwise."

"Whatever you want to call it. What about finishing your BA? Do you want to take this family backwards?"

"Hmm, that's an interesting idea," mused Donna Cody.

Her mother leaned in to deliver a smack, Donna Cody leaned back, and her mother's hand landed resoundingly on a pile of books, which fell to the floor in disarray. An array of startling profanity poured forth from her mother, while Donna Cody, still ducking, moved the books back into a bookcase she could protect. She hunched warily in front of it, looking like an angry crane trying to do Tai Chi. Her mother glared at her and took a long slow drag on her cigarette.

"Fine! Live like this, dressed like some vagrant! Throw your life away!"

Haven't most of us heard this and don't we know where it ends up? Donna Cody was her mother's daughter and could hold her own just fine when she needed to. It took a long time, with many more tedious arguments, but eventually around four a.m. Donna Cody's mother stomped out the door and caught a cab that Donna Cody had called for her.

After she flew home, Donna Cody's mother continued the conversation about Donna Cody in the third person instead of the second to anyone who would listen. Her husband had long ago taken the famed Mr. Bennet's role[12] and moved himself into his office at home when he wasn't in his office at work. Mrs. Cody, at least, cared. She *meant well*, as most of us usually do. Donna Cody's siblings were far too busy with their own lives to worry about her at all.

---

[12] See *Pride and Prejudice*.

When Donna Cody woke up later that morning, it was almost lunch time. Even she was hungry. She could hear Duncan and Marvin talking outside, along with occasional closings of car doors and hoods. Birds and particularly obnoxious crows were cawing and twittering and carrying on. She groggily shook off last night's dramatics, stretched, and luxuriated in her comfy old bed for a minute, then sprang up and enjoyed a shower before throwing on some jeans and one of her Peter Pan-collared white shirts. She ambled down to the kitchen to find something to eat. To her delight, she found that Duncan had surpassed himself, having baked a loaf of raisin bread with a halo of cinnamon hanging around it. There were eggs set out and butter and a frying pan. (Those were the days when you could eat a breakfast like that and not worry or feel guilty about it at all.) Soon, Donna Cody was frying eggs, drinking coffee, and munching on buttery raisin toast. Duncan came in the back door, and Donna Cody thanked him profusely. Marvin waved at her from the Rambler, where he was fooling around under the hood. Rockandy ran up to her from behind Duncan.

"You missed the bacon," said Duncan. "And the orange juice. It's in the fridge."

"Duncan!" said Donna Cody, her mouth full of toast, "I have missed you!" She dove into the refrigerator, pulled out the bacon, and popped some into the pan. She poured herself some juice. Duncan was ecstatic. Donna Cody was eating!

"Now, Duncan, can you sit with me a minute and tell me what was going on with all those ladies?" Duncan could. He told Donna Cody all about it (leaving out his heroic interruption of the ladies' progress through the rooms and his unheroic retreat from Donna Cody's mother, who had bested far greater foes). He could see that Donna Cody was getting mad all over again, but not at him, thank goodness, so he mentioned that he had replaced the Rambler's core wire to the distributor cap. He might as well have said he had placed the mandibles in the perambulator as far as Donna Cody was concerned. Now, he told her, he was going to work on the truck with Marvin as it apparently needed a bit of a tune-up after its long drive.

Slowly, with the crackle and heavenly smell of bacon, lots of buttery raisin toast, fried eggs, the spicy smell of the orange juice, the streaming sun, the lilacs nodding at the window, Duncan going on about car parts and such, the world stretched itself out, sighed, and purred. Rockandy leaned up against Donna Cody's leg. (He had also found a fine breakfast involving steak scraps waiting for him earlier that morning.) Duncan leaned over the table toward her, and Donna Cody noticed how big his wrists were now and felt a little something jump in her stomach. She smiled and ate, and that made both Duncan and Rockandy happy.

However, golden moments can only be golden by contrast. Marvin came clomping up the stairs. Behind him stood a short, curvy young woman with long straight dark hair and bangs that came right down to her thick, dark eyebrows. She had dark eyes with lots of eyeliner around them and thick red-lipsticked lips. She was carrying a worn black banjo case with a bump on it. She had a pack on her back. In her non-banjo-carrying hand she tapped a thick, vile-smelling cigar. Amazingly, Rockandy went right over and licked the hand holding the banjo. His eyes looked up at her adoringly. He was in love, though, thankfully, it was Platonic.

"Miss Cody," Marvin panted, "this girl wanted to find you." Marvin had obviously tried to outrace "this girl," but had barely done so. He looked back nervously at her.

"Hey. My name's Sandy Panther. You Donna Cody?" she said in a curiously husky voice. Rockandy was now licking her pant leg.

"I am," said Donna Cody, "and I would appreciate your extinguishing that cigar."

Sandy Panther flicked an ash onto the floor and looked around. She finally found an innocent little mustard yellow ceramic bowl and stubbed out the cigar in it. The smell was even more terrible. Duncan grabbed the bowl and made a hasty exit outside. Rockandy moved on to licking Sandy Panther's sneakers, which were pretty dusty.

"Hey, don't throw that out!" called Sandy Panther. "I'll save it for later. Waste not, want not." Duncan shook his head and put the bowl down by a lilac bush in the vain hope that the perfume would vanquish the stink, a hope unrealized. He waited outside the door with Marvin.

Donna Cody looked at her food and pushed the plate away.

Sandy Panther and Donna Cody stared each other down. If they had been dogs, there would have been prefatory growling and stiff-legged circling. Sandy Panther finally stepped forward.

"You'll be wondering why I'm here," she said as Donna Cody nodded her head and peered through her glasses at her. "It's C. C. He told me where to find you. Seek and I did find."

"C. C.," said Donna Cody, her face breaking out in an astonished grin. "You know C. C.?"

"Sure do," said Sandy Panther. "I was playing tunes with him day before yesterday. He told me you had learned a few and that you had some of your own and that you know 'Chickalielee Daisy-O.' I crave that tune."

Sandy Panther was clutching her banjo case, leaning it up against her voluptuous curves. Her fingers drummed on it. Her other hand was massaging Rockandy around the ears, with Rockandy leaning back into a new world of bliss and looking as foolish as a dog can look. Marvin tried to look over Duncan's shoulder again at this ravishing sight.

Before you knew it, they had their instruments out. They politely admired each other's: the dark rich wood of the fiddle,[13] the scuffed but beautiful old banjo with a wood resonator and worn but delicate inlay. The banjo's pot was large and rimmed with bristling brackets.[14] Then they looked at each other, suddenly shy. They tuned and hemmed and hawed, and then Sandy Panther played a D chord, her right hand bum-dittying and crackling and popping. Donna Cody found herself drawn in and sucked into "Chickalielee Daisy-O" as she never had before. The insistent rhythm, the crackle and pop was far more compelling than the pump organ. She rolled along, at first making sure to play the tune clearly, using the bow the way C. C. had showed her, self-conscious.

"Why do I care what she thinks?" she thought, but then realized she did care, that she wanted to do this as much as she could, that this was bliss. She lost herself in the music.

Sandy Panther upped the pace a bit as she got more and more excited. She would let out a little whoop here and there, stomp her left foot with her knee going up and down, the banjo pot resting on her right leg. She began improvising, sliding into notes, pulling off strings, walking up the bass string. She followed Donna Cody's every bow stroke and shoved the right notes in at the right time. Nothing too extra or show-offy except once in a while when she got too excited.

After what felt like an hour or two, Donna Cody looked up and realized that Duncan, Marvin, and Mabel were all standing there in the

---

[13]Donna Cody's violin was from her classical playing days, something her long-suffering parents had bought for her. It was a serviceable pre–World War II German factory instrument, with slightly antiqued red-brown varnish, beautiful "flame" on the back and sides, ebony pegs, and a fine tuner on the E string.

[14]Sandy Panther had a Bacon and Day Silver Bell Number 1, a rare instrument with the original Bacon stamped maple bridge. The friction tuners were stubborn, but Sandy Panther knew how to make them work. It was even in its original blue velvet–lined case.

kitchen listening.

"Oh, Miss Donna, that sounds good," said Mabel, beaming, her low voice purring. "That's even better than how I remember it."

"Not bad," said Duncan, keeping his eyes off Sandy Panther and firmly on Donna Cody.

"Kinda weird," said Marvin. "Is that hillbilly music like on that TV show where those guys find oil and move to Hollywood? I love that show." He said this to Sandy Panther, who pursed her lips and blew him a little kiss. At this, he turned as red as her lips and grinned like an idiot.

Much later, Donna Cody would think about Mabel saying she remembered the music, but right now, she was distracted. There were more tunes to play. After a while, everyone cleared out, but the two young women were still at it, figuring out who knew which tune and working them out. Donna Cody had learned things from books and records, standards like "Arkansas Traveler" and "Golden Slippers," but a few other odd things from the tapes she'd accumulated, tunes like "Grub Springs" or "Callahan's Reel."[15] Sandy Panther noted that the tunes Donna Cody had learned from books didn't sound as good. Donna Cody bristled at this for a minute but then realized that Sandy Panther was right. While Sandy Panther knew a lot of tunes, it was hard for Donna Cody to make sense of them. Many consisted of funny little songs like "Granny Will Your Dog Bite" or gory murder ballads like "Pretty Polly." Donna Cody wasn't sure what to do with those on the fiddle, but then they got excited when they found they could sing things together and that they sounded good, at least to themselves.

---

[15]She had learned "Grub Springs" from an old Library of Congress recording and "Callahan's Reel" from an old recording of Dykes' Magic City Trio.

In the next few days, Marvin found work at a gas station and settled into a shed in the back yard at Mabel and Duncan's house. Oddly, Bluto did not show up for his truck, and Marvin was tight lipped if anyone asked him about it. Sandy Panther settled herself, after a lengthy discussion, in the downstairs bedroom, which had been Aunt Jane's. Donna Cody took most of her aunt's things (pictures in pewter frames, more books, mostly mysteries, a string of pearls, and lots of clothes) and put them in her own room. Aunt Jane's clothes would never have fit Donna Cody, but it was hard to part with them. They included everything from boxy wool suits that would cover Aunt Jane's round little ball of a body, to tattered checkered shirts and dungarees. A few versions of the basic black dress. Lots of interesting socks that Aunt Jane had knit herself.

Sandy Panther agreed to smoke her cigars outside only. She built a little ring of rocks behind the back porch, where she would light a fire, sit on an old lawn chair, and, on nice nights, slowly smoke a cigar, and then stare up at the stars and whale away on her banjo at the same time. No neighbors had come by to complain as yet.

Donna Cody would often come and join her once the cigar was finished. They would drink cocoa (or at least Donna Cody would; Sandy Panther liked Jack Daniels, which she had managed to find tucked up in a cupboard), and they would play and talk about the music. Donna Cody told Sandy Panther about her dream of finding the real musicians, but especially about Dulcie Tobey.

"I don't know what you're talking about with *real*," drawled Sandy Panther. "Heck, they're all *real*. But like they say, each bird likes her own nest."

"You might not understand this," Donna Cody replied patiently. "I'm talking about oral tradition uncontaminated by pop music and trashy TV jingles."

"I don't know," said Sandy Panther. "I like Flatt and Scruggs good as anyone. Wish I could play like that, but I learned the old way from folks."

"But that's it, Sandy Panther!" exclaimed Donna Cody, springing up and coming close to upending her own fiddle. "That's the music we want. The music of the people. Before it all disappears. Let's get out there and find it. Let's hit the road. Let's find Dulcie Tobey."[16]

"Oh heck, why not? I'm up for a little travel," said Sandy Panther. "Folks as travels a long ways knows the most, they say. We can practice up and try winning some contests. They give cash prizes and then you get other offers. I know about that," she smirked. She took Donna Cody's vague nod as agreement.

---

[16] As Johann Gottfried Herder has said: ". . .One must go into the age, into the region, into the whole history, and feel one's way into everything."

Chapter 8: Song Butchering. Peace, Love, and the Folk Song. The Story Disappears.

Going round this world baby mine,
Going around this world baby mine,
I'm going round this world,
Be a banjo picking girl.
I'm going round this world baby mine.

—"Banjo Picking Girl," as sung by Lily May Ledford and The Coon Creek Girls

Duncan was not happy. He watched as Donna Cody and Sandy Panther packed up the Rambler, Rockandy skipping around them and yapping with excitement. Sandy Panther had named the Rambler—"Rambler."

"Fixing up ol' Rambler, are ya?" she'd sing, or "Rambler, let's go!" or "Here, Rambler, here," and then she'd howl like a dog and laugh. Duncan found this annoying. He and Marvin had gone over the Rambler with the proverbial comb of fine teeth, and Duncan had piled up a mountain of food for them. This time, he had made sourdough bread. More oatmeal cookies than anyone could eat in a year. Jars of applesauce. Jam. Peanut butter. Chocolate. Tins of sardines. Boxes of crackers. Cheez Spread (another favorite of Sandy Panther's). Pickles. Cans of pineapple. Vienna sausages. Tang. What was left of the Jack Daniels. (Duncan had not put that in.

Most of the nastier ones were suggested by Sandy Panther, whose taste buds had no doubt been crushed into submission by all the cigars she had smoked. Donna Cody seldom even thought about bringing food. Duncan tried to get her to buy some more, but she called him a good kid and drifted off to whatever she had decided to do next. Duncan would storm out and go kick a tree or something, but Donna Cody never noticed. She was busy figuring out money matters, which she was not good at. The bank that administered her trust luckily was, and set her up with a wad of traveler's checks and instructions. She could not be profligate, but it all seemed like endless cash to her. In other words, she had no idea. If she ran out of money for her monthly allowance, she just stopped buying anything until she had more money.

Sandy Panther had winked at Duncan more than once, but he would frown and turn or walk away. After a while, she left him alone and began visiting Marvin frequently, especially at night after she had smoked her cigar and played some tunes and Donna Cody hadn't come out. Duncan tried to ignore the sounds coming out of the cabin in the back.

But now the car was loaded up. Rockandy was not entirely happy. He had been moved to the back seat, where piles of food, bedding, ponchos, and the instruments were his only companions.

"Hold on," sighed Sandy Panther, taking a look at him. "Dog with money is called 'Mr. Dog.'" She let Rockandy out and squeezed him into the front.

"Not too near the shift," said Donna Cody, but she was happy because Rockandy was happy. They looked at each other with adoration and then he curled up.

"We'll be changing this situation, buster," Sandy Panther said to Rockandy.

Everyone was ready. Duncan and Mabel stood beside Donna Cody's door.

"You be careful, Miss Donna," said Mabel.

"I will, Mabel," she said.

Duncan didn't say anything. Donna Cody looked at him. "Goodbye, Duncan," she said, and smiled. But Duncan muttered something and then, uncharacteristically, turned around and left. Donna Cody felt a slight twinge, but Mabel apologized for her son. "He has hit his time, Miss Donna," she shrugged. "I never know what is with that boy these days. Now you don't pay any mind and go out and find your music or whatever it is you're doin'."

Marvin leaned on the passenger side car window, dejected. "Aw gee, Sandy Panther, do ya hafta go?" he whined. Sandy Panther winked and blew him a kiss with her freshly lipsticked lips. She was grinning as the Rambler fired up. She could be pretty heartless.

Heading down the road at her usual snail's pace, Donna Cody hummed to herself through the small gales and sudden sun breaks of late spring. The splatters of rain on the windshield would dry out and fall and dry out, so the air was fresh with scents of lilac and magnolia. After a brief argument about smoking cigars in the Rambler, one in which Donna Cody laid down the law, Sandy Panther had gone to sleep in the warm sun. She was snoring and leaning up against the door, and Rockandy was dozing as well. It felt great to be heading south and into more warmth. Wrathful drivers passed them whenever they could, honking and yelling. But for Donna Cody, all was serene. She tapped her fingers on the steering wheel.

A few hours later, as they were passing through a small town, she saw a sign for "Rotmensen's Coffee House and Restaurant." Over the sign was a replica of an old Dutch windmill, the sails spinning round. The sign advertised a special Dutch lamb stew. Donna Cody felt her stomach rumbling. She wanted a good bowl of hot stew. So even though she was driving along with a bunker's worth of food, she pulled the Rambler into the parking lot and saw that there were a lot of people inside, some of them with guitars.

Sandy Panther snorted and jerked awake.

"Mmm, lunchtime?" she said. "I have to pee. Good call, D.C."

Donna Cody winced and reminded Sandy Panther that she preferred to be called by her full name. "I like my full name, Sandy Panther," she said. "I will call you by yours, as strange as it is, and you must call me by mine."

"Fine, fine, names break no bones," said Sandy Panther, as she took Rockandy out, let him pee at the curb, and then put him back in, leaving the windows opened and his water and food out. A young man came outside to check them out. Thick blond hair hung over his ears. His blue work shirt was barely tucked into jeans topped with a wide leather belt. He wore brown suede boots with fringes on them. A big clunky metal peace sign hung around his neck.

"Hello, ladies," he grinned. "And who is this?" he asked, nodding at Rockandy. Donna Cody stiffened, but Sandy Panther introduced all of them and walked in with the man, whose name was Bob.

Inside, it was warm and steamy, full of dark little tables and a dark wood counter behind which a black-haired and trimly bearded older man in a striped French sailor's shirt was serving customers who sat there. Donna Cody smelled something delicious, along with some strong coffee. Her stomach rumbled again. She ordered the specialty lamb straightaway, with Sandy Panther seconding. They went to sit down at a table, while Bob wandered over to the small stage, where musicians were milling about. One of them began bawling out a version of "Shady Grove." Donna Cody grimaced as another woman attempted to come in with a harmony part that didn't fly high enough to reach its destination. Sandy Panther started bellowing out a lower harmony and got some appreciative grins until Donna Cody jabbed her in the side.

"Clean your finger before you point it at my spot!" Sandy Panther snapped. But before Donna Cody could respond, they were blasted by an electric guitar. Bob came out on stage, flinging out huge throbbing chords that went bum buh bum bum in the background. Someone else started in on bongo drums. Donna Cody put her fingers in her ears. Sandy Panther stared. The lamb stew showed up. Sandy Panther dug in, but Donna Cody stood up and strode up to the stage.

"Excuse me!" she shouted. "Excuse me! I am trying to eat!" Bob put down his guitar and the music faltered. "How could you massacre such a wonderful old song?" Donna Cody continued, waving a roll around that was clutched in her left hand. "And it comes from the even older and beautiful ballad 'Matty Groves.' It deserves some respect."

"Who do you think you are?" whined the girl who had been singing the high harmony part. "You can't insult our music and tell us what to do!"

"*Your* music!" spat Donna Cody. "You shouldn't be allowed to touch it. You're murdering it. Hundreds of years of tradition, and you're clubbing it to death. You can't sing your way out of a swamp. And electric guitar." She shuddered.

"Babe, c'mon, don't listen to this bitch," Bob said, grabbing the woman by her elbow and escorting her to the back of the stage. Once he got there, he turned around and gave Donna Cody the finger. The bongo player laughed and clapped his hands. Sandy Panther happened to look up from her stew at that point. She leapt forward, jumped on the stage and gave Bob a shove. Outside, Rockandy began to howl.

An hour or so later, they staggered out of Rotmensen's. The man behind the counter in the sailor shirt had turned out to be good at breaking up fights, but even he had an evil green bruise developing on his left cheekbone. Donna Cody had somehow been knocked on her tailbone. Since she had no fat to cushion it, she was lurching pretty painfully like a stick figure Frankenstein. Her fist was sore from some solid if ineffective contact. Her hair stood up in all directions like a hallucinogenic halo. Sandy Panther had bruises all over, but she was grinning and looked ready for more. She had certainly dealt out more than she had received. Rockandy also looked ready for more. He had figured that all these people were varmints that he needed to tree. His baying had drawn some interested stares and raised blinds from a bank across the street.

They only got to leave because Donna Cody paid Mr. Rotmensen far too much money from her first traveler's check, which she cashed at the restaurant. She hadn't meant to start a fight. She had been carried away, and it could be argued that it was Sandy Panther who actually caused the physical fracas. Whoever was most to blame, they both left to a chorus of curses from the musicians, who were all sitting around moaning and drinking coffee. A grim Mr. Rotmensen escorted them to the door. To the humming of the little windmill's sails going around, they were carefully easing themselves into the Rambler when Bob ran out.

"You goddamn whores!" he screamed, pounding on the driver's side window. "You broke my goddamn guitar! You'd better pay for it, bitches!" His hair was awry, and his peace sign necklace swung dangerously; it could have knocked out a tooth.

"Watch our smoke and excuse our dust, jerk. Gun it!" screamed Sandy Panther, pushing her foot on top of Donna Cody's, slamming down the accelerator pedal.

"Stop that!" yelled Donna Cody as they squealed backwards, then, with grinding gears, leapt forward, turned the corner on two wheels (at least, this is what Sandy Panther claimed later), and raced out of the parking lot and on down the road.

Neither young woman said anything for a while. Donna Cody was sore and pretty shaken up, especially by the sensation of the Rambler's sudden acceleration. Sandy Panther was mad and beginning to wonder if she wanted to stay with Donna Cody. However, she was often intrigued by people who started fights.

"Donna Cody, what do we care what other musicians want to do?"

"Musicians," sniffed Donna Cody.

"Look, they had the place before us. They can play what they want.

My Aunty says if you mind your own business, you'll be busy all the time."

"Now, Sandy Panther, that's where you're wrong," said Donna Cody. Sandy Panther noticed a weird and dangerous gleam in Donna Cody's eyes. She soon learned to associate this with harangues like the following:

"Sandy Panther," Donna Cody began, "traditional music is sacred. It passes down the joys, sorrows, and beautiful tunes of our ancestors. Just think: A tune might travel through ten or more generations of people, lovingly carried on, respected, carefully learned, and reproduced."

"But—"

"Folk music, by definition, is the music of the folk. But this new stuff, this so-called 'folk music' and now this electrified stuff, takes the player away from the wood, the tree that made the instrument, takes folk and makes it something to sell. These so-called 'folk singers'—I don't care if it's singing ballads in some high-voiced lah-dee-dah way or hardly even singing, pretending you wrote them, it's all bad. Folk music is *for* the folk and *by* the folk, and don't you forget it."

"But how are those people not the folk? How are they—"?

"No, no, Sandy Panther. They are not the folk because they are only in it to impress and make money. The real old-time folk music was never recorded. Oh, sure, we have the old records and some tapes and stuff. But you have to go back before all that, when the music was played for the sheer joy of it, the hymns were sung to God, the fiddle played for the dances, and back in a holler, a banjo player learned a tune from a slave."

And here she actually cited the *Definition of Folk Music* from the International Folk Music Council of 1954. She knew it by heart.[17] Sandy

---

[17]"Folk music is the product of a musical tradition that has been evolved through the process of oral transmission. The factors that shape the tradition are: (i) continuity which links the present to the past; (ii) variation which springs from the creative impulse of the individual or group; and (iii)

Panther missed most of it, but she was thinking.

"What about tunes on the radio? Heard a lot of good ones that way."

"That's different, Sandy Panther. You told me about how you learned from your grandma when you were little. And how she learned the old-style banjo from way back, the clawhammer, the up-pick, all that."

"Sure, but she'd learn anything, long as she liked it. Oh, OK, fine. Donna Cody, you aren't gonna listen, so there's no point to talking. They say someone with a fixed idea is like a goose trying to hatch a rock, and you sure have your ideas. But my granny, she loved Earl Scruggs. And that Don Reno. And Jerry Lee Lewis. Loved 'em." And here, Sandy Panther commenced a long ramble about her dead granny's listening proclivities, lapsing into sentimental bathos. Then she put on some mascara.

At times, Donna Cody would jump in and tell Sandy Panther why a certain artist was good or not so good. Neither of them listened to the other, as is so often the case—two monologues weaving around a spindly topic of converse. Finally, the sun getting low, they needed to pull off somewhere and camp for the night. They found a little field down a dirt road and set up some ponchos to make shelters, dug small troughs around them to keep out the rain (as Donna Cody had been taught at camp), and laid out their sleeping bags.

"That's ridiculous," said Sandy Panther, referring to the ditches. "There's no rain to be seen anywhere or coming, and these little things" (gesturing at the ditches) "wouldn't do nothin' to help anyway. But boy, it's still pretty cold."

Donna Cody looked up at her from where she was kneeling down and tearing up turf.

---

selection by the community, which determines the form or forms in which the music survives." (IFMC in Lloyd, 1967:15)

"All right, then," said Sandy Panther.

On Donna Cody's tiny Primus 210 camp stove they cooked themselves some soup from a can, ate some of the bread with sardines on top, and more than a few of the cookies. Donna Cody even helped Sandy Panther dispose of some of the Jack Daniels. Sandy Panther was shortly out and snoring. Rockandy and Donna Cody lay down together, and soon the dog was snoring along with Sandy Panther. But Donna Cody squirmed on the hard ground, trying to give her tailbone some ease.

It is at this point that we lose the story. It was impossible to get an interview with Donna Cody, who now sees few people. And Sandy Panther no doubt fabricated much of her past. Your author (or, I should say, editor) talked to musicians, librarians, professors, authors, friends and relations, enemies and detractors, folklorists, historians, and outright liars, but found nothing. Alas, the story of Donna Cody had ended with our three adventurers permanently trapped in the Stygian oblivion of poncho shelters and sleeping bags.

Chapter 9: The Story Is Found. Ups and Downs. Sandy Panther Defends True Christianity.

Do you call that religion, oh nooooo,
Do you call that religion, no child no,
Do you call that religion, oh nooooo,
I declare ain't that a shame.

—"Do You Call That Religion" as performed by Bill Monroe and the
Bluegrass Boys, traditional

Being easily discouraged, your author almost bailed on this whole enterprise. She tried Googling. The same stories came up on multiple sites. But nothing about what happened next. But with great hope, she consulted her college librarians, the true saints of the academic world (except maybe for English instructors who grade interminable numbers of essays, but the English instructors tend to get bitter, whereas, somehow, the librarians don't). These eager librarians combed the databases, searched mysterious places on the Web that no one knows about. They interlibrary loaned and kept the post office from going out of business. These people could find a black cat in a coal cellar. They came up with nothing.

But an archivist friend asked around. He had recorded tunes in Kentucky, organized folklore collections in Arizona, and now, happily, he writes a wonderful series about fiddle tunes: who played them, where they came from, when they first showed up in sheet music, where you can hear them in all their different versions, how they are structured. He obviously knew all about Donna Cody, since he has written an extensive history of "Chickalielee Daisy-O," which Donna Cody (along with Sandy Panther) made famous, so that it is played by musicians all over the world and is even the basis of a modern symphony.

While no corroborated information on Donna Cody and Sandy Panther's encounter with Dulcie Tobey has been found, Cody and Panther's recording of "Chickalielee Daisy-O" that became so popular in the early seventies and was copied from cassette to cassette seems to indicate a missing source. Having jumped the gun at a truly opportune time, Cody and Panther were seen by one music critic as "liberators of the music of the people" or "Pied Pipers who led us to our past and brought us the long-forgotten music." One might ask, *Forgotten by whom?*

The archivist looked in the National Folklore Archives from more than one state, tantalized by the hope of finding something new about Donna Cody. This was a challenge, what with each state's different musical formats, archiving systems, catalogs, and databases. My friend, in the midst of a project that dreams of standardizing all this (the great dream of archivists), was mortified by his inability to turn up anything your author hadn't already found.

Instead, it was my favorite of all librarians, who happens to manage digital content for an advertising agency, who finally found the shoe box with yellowing handwritten notebooks and dusty old tapes that yielded up more of Donna Cody's story. How this favorite librarian came up with this information is not clear, but she does have a plethora of friends, many of whom owe her various favors. Rather than inquiring too closely, I thanked her profusely.

One news article in the box chronicles an unfortunate incident that happened shortly after the altercation at Mr. Rotmensen's. Apparently, Donna Cody, Sandy Panther, and Rockandy were attending a small concert in West Virginia. From some other supplementary sources, your author has, to the best of her ability, pieced the story together.

Donna Cody had decided she wanted to go to the "Old-Time Hymns and Gospel" concert. Sandy Panther was not so keen on this. "Sounds like they'll be evangelizing, Donna Cody. I don't need none of that. Already been saved."

"But Sandy Panther, they say here in this flyer that they are singing traditional hymns," said Donna Cody. "It even says that someone is singing the old 'white spirituals' from George Pullen Jackson. Now *that* I want to hear."

Sandy Panther shook her head. She had no idea what Donna Cody was talking about, but this was often the case. "As long as they don't mess with me," she said. "I'm as much a Christian as the next person, but I don't take with that crazy-talkin', snake-handlin' stuff."[18] And she went back to applying her eyeliner.

The concert was at an old Free Will Baptist church, a humble white clapboard building with a small square suggestion of a steeple. Inside, it was all dark wood and old worn pews. At the door were some young people handing out tracts that looked like little comic books, with crude pictures.

"These are terrible." said Sandy Panther, turning on her heel and marching back to the earnest if somewhat quiet evangelists, startling a frail young woman in a frilly, firmly buttoned-up shirt.

"What is this junk?" Sandy Panther demanded, shaking the little booklet at the girl. "This is creepy! This ain't Christian! All the kids that drink and smoke die in a car wreck? What? You think Christian kids don't die in car wrecks? You think God kills kids 'cause they drink and smoke? That God is no God—"

"Don't you talk to her like that," a boy with a necktie and madras jacket said nervously. "You just back away—"

"HELL if I will!" bellowed Sandy Panther, louder than ever, thrusting her face right in front of the girl's face. The latter clutched her tracts with whitening fingers and backed slowly up against the wall. People were walking around them and trying to act as if they weren't there.

---

[18]Sandy Panther seems to have confused the poor Baptists with some of the more interesting strains of Pentecostalism.

Donna Cody had stepped inside, never having noticed that Sandy Panther wasn't with her. She was crammed into a dark pew, the wood warm and soft, as if all the bodies that had ever sat on it had kept it alive. The dark floor, walls, and ceiling added an ancient wooden solemnity. Families with small children, doddering oldsters, crying babies, and their parents, all of them were crammed in there with Donna Cody.

A man in a suit introduced the evening and then the first singer, Mrs. Anthus Clay. An old woman with glaring cat's-eye glasses and a dress that bulged all the way up, its buttoned front straining dangerously, walked up to the front. She began singing, and the audience was transfixed. All the squirming stopped. Even the babies stopped fussing.

How to describe the beauty of that cracked old voice? Each catch or voice break was like a jagged rock, an ancient and mysterious rift embedded in a pulsating, ringing tone that used the whole head as a glorious sound chamber. Notes stretched themselves beyond their boundaries: a C might have the ghost of an ascent up to C#, a G might fall suddenly in a swoop to the mysterious land between F and F#. The song's rhythm was something internal that danced around between the ideas of 4/4 and 2/4 or 5/4 and laughed softly as it slipped into something else. This was an old ballad hymn, and the singer had taken it, lived it, crawled inside it, yet made it her own as a mysterious communicant in that ballad's web of souls stretching into the past, a web of all who had heard it, loved it, sung it. Donna Cody felt mighty and ancient wings spreading under her and lifting her up, each shift in measure a swoop or dive through an endless blue sky.

But as the last note died out, noises from outside, unfortunate noises, prevailed. Donna Cody, even though transported, still managed to notice that Sandy Panther's voice was prominent in the mix. But Donna Cody was packed into the pew. No one seemed to be moving until a few men silently but determinedly marched outside, while a man who looked like he must have been a great-grandfather, sporting a glowing white bush of a beard, shuffled up with some sort of zither that he put on a table. Someone dragged a chair up. The patriarch seated himself.

"This here's a celestophone," he said, plucking a cloud of sweet chords. Donna Cody strained forward, trying to figure out how the little hammers were bouncing on the strings. It was as if he were playing a piano, but a miniature one with trembling, echoing notes. Then he began plucking the strings and singing. It was as ghostly and delicate as moth wings.[19] But, alas, the music came to an abrupt end as the doors in the back of the church burst open and in tumbled Sandy Panther with several men trying to hold her. She was hissing, spitting, and cursing a blue streak.

People jumped up and, in a remarkably short time, vacated the building, but not Sandy Panther, the men, nor Donna Cody, who was furious at this vile interruption. From the exaltation of heaven, she had been plunged into a raging cauldron from the nether regions. She leapt on top of one of the men who was ducking out of the way of Sandy Panther, who had somehow gotten her banjo case and was swinging it around her in a wide arc. The man had jumped back just in time, since a minute before a victim had gone down with a horrible thump. He now shook Donna Cody off easily. She fell to the floor.

When Donna Cody woke up again, it was to a huge pain in her ear, as if someone had kicked a hole in the side of her head. It was the most terrible thing she had ever felt, and she let out a great cry of anguish, only to choke with agony at how much it hurt to yell. It was dark, but she could hear some snoring and snorting. Then, something began to lick her hand.

---

[19]This instrument was probably a doceola.

"Oh, Rockandy." Donna Cody held out her fingers, and tears ran from her eyes. She realized she was lying on a bed. And then she fell back to sleep.

The next time she woke, it was day. Rockandy was sleeping on a hooked rug beside her bed. The light hurt her eyes, so she squinted. In another bed in the room, which looked to be a guest bedroom, lay a body tangled up in a sheet. From the strands of black hair going every which way, Donna Cody deduced that it was Sandy Panther. But she could not speak a word because her ear throbbed and the room was spinning. Someone came in the door, looked at Donna Cody and cried out, "Albert. She's awake." In walked a tall older man with a large blue bottle. He opened it, poured a little of its contents into a spoon, and thrust it in between Donna Cody's lips before she could begin to shut them. He then stood there watching for a while. But Donna Cody didn't know that. Donna Cody was asleep.

Chapter 10: Wondrous Balsam and Heavenly Hosts.

Oh! I love to travel far and near throughout my native land;
I love to sell as I go 'long, and take the cash in hand.
I love to cure all in distress that happen in my way,
And better b'lieve I feel quite fine when folks rush up and say:

I'll take another bottle of Wizard Oil,
I'll take another bottle or two;
I'll take another bottle of Wizard Oil,
I'll take another bottle or two.

—"Wizard Oil," Harry E. Randall

The next time Donna Cody woke up, it was daytime again, and she felt remarkably better. The bed beside her was empty, and Rockandy was gone. Panicking, she attempted to jump out of bed but found that she had to move her head slowly or she would get dizzy and nauseous. She also found her body had some new terribly tender spots. Getting her feet on the floor, she realized that she was wearing a long old-fashioned nightgown. She rose carefully and tottered through the doorway to find the facilities since her need was pressing. She entered a dark hallway with beautiful old wainscoting. Feeling her way along it, she came to a capacious bathroom with octagonal white tiles on the floor, a large tub, a toilet with a pull chain, built-in cupboards with crystal knobs and carving on their doors, and a beautiful old leaded beveled glass window that cast quivering rainbows. Donna Cody sat and stared, but hearing voices and the chime of dishes being set down, she finished her business and followed the sound down the dim hall, looking at the curious old pictures of landscapes, Jesus, and grim folks sitting in straight-backed chairs in front of cabins.

Around the kitchen table, from which the delectable odor of coffee was rising like a fog of joy, sat an elderly woman with barely any hair, only white wisps, the tall elderly man who even in overalls was regal, and Sandy Panther. A mass of platters covered the table, and these involved bacon, eggs, biscuits, and a custard with dried fruit on top. Sandy Panther looked up with her fork halfway to her mouth. The older man murmured hello, got up, and pulled up a chair. Rockandy came out from under the table and licked her hands. Donna Cody sat down uneasily (the chair was wood and hard), but she accepted a cup of coffee and began sipping.

Sandy Panther waved at Donna Cody and, with her mouth shockingly full, said, "Mith Vera, thith ith Donna Cody."

"It is truly a joy to meet you, Miss Cody," said Vera in a surprisingly rich alto voice with intriguing deep cracks in it. "I am so glad you are awake now. This is my husband, Mr. Albert. He is the one who rescued you." Albert ducked his head and murmured.

It turned out that Albert and Vera were religious people who had also been at the singing. They prayed before they ate, and they prayed afterwards. Albert didn't say much. Vera only spoke after pausing a bit, as if she were listening. She would cock her head, and often her eyes would crinkle at the edges in the beginning of a laugh, but she would say, "God bless you, honey."

Albert had dragged Donna Cody out, hauled her to their car, and scooped up Sandy Panther as well because she yelled and staggered after him with a trail of angry people after her. It was now three days later.

Donna Cody realized that she was starving. Vera passed a plate down, while Sandy Panther loaded some of everything on it for her. She ate sparingly, quickly, and then she began to wobble. "Catch her," said Sandy Panther. "She's going down again."

The next time Donna Cody woke up, she felt much better. It was pitch dark, but she sat up. The room did not move. "Sandy Panther?" she queried. Rockandy rose up, his collar jingling, and licked her hand with abandon.

"Donna Cody, are you awake now of all times? Must be three in the morning."

"Sandy Panther, where are we?"

"Up in some little mountain town with these folks. And I'll tell you what, Miz Vera and Mr. Albert Love is about the nicest people you could ever hope to meet, even if they pray all the time. They know how to keep you fed. I'll tell you, they walked in and it was like the sea shore parted."

"What? You mean the Red Sea parted?"

"Sure, whatever you want. No one was gonna cross them. But they're nice as pie, Donna Cody. They don't force nothin' on you."

Sandy Panther switched on her bed table light, and Donna Cody sat up. Eventually: "Donna Cody, you look better 'n cows in clover."

"Sandy Panther, what on earth are you talking about? You know, when I took care of C. C.'s cows—"

"You know what I mean," whined Sandy Panther. "Now that you're better, how 'bout we quit this wandering and fighting and head north to play some of these coffeehouse deals. Go to New York. Make us a record like the Old Town Rounders. Show a little leg. We could knock them out of the pond."

"Sandy Panther, you mean knock them out of the *water*," sighed Donna Cody. The room started spinning again, so she lay down, but she continued from a prone position: "Sandy Panther, I will make music with you, but we need to know the real music of the folk and bring that to the public. We can't be in this for the money. That is why we like the Old Town Rounders, because they have gone and found the real folk and the old tones. I mean, tunes. And that's what we need to do. And besides, I want to find Dulcie Tobey."

"Hold on," said Sandy Panther. "I don't see why we can't go get ourselves some money and take some little trips on the side. Then we're both happy. We need each other. But a bird never flew on one wing—I can't play fiddle and banjo together at the same time. Hell, I mean, heck, I can't even play the fiddle by itself." But Donna Cody was drifting off to sleep. Sandy Panther gave it up and was snoring again in a minute.

Donna Cody woke again in the early morning. The window shades glowed around the edges like a sign that something incredible was about to happen. And it was: the sun was rising. She felt the joy of possibilities rise up in her. Then she remembered dreaming a train was coming at her, but it was Sandy Panther snoring like one. Her ear was on fire. Gingerly she felt it and realized it was split in some horrible way, her earlobe all jagged. She started moaning and woke up Sandy Panther, who snorted, sat up, came over, and said, "Donna Cody, let me put some more of this balsam on it."

"What?" panted Donna Cody. And then she passed out.

The next time Donna Cody woke a man in a dark blue suit and skinny black tie was standing over her. Albert, with his beautifully carved face and dark hair shot with gray, stood next to the blue-suited man, watching his every move but bowing his head a bit. Vera in her old-fashioned flower-print dress stood at the foot of the bed, solemn but unbowed. She looked steadily at Donna Cody and summed her up but still liked her, if you could say she "liked" anyone. "Like" seemed too trivial an activity for her—she was deeply serious. Sandy Panther was squirming and standing beside her. The man in the suit was holding a strange little jar, and he promptly launched:

"Let me tell you about the most valuable remedy for man or beast. This balsam comes to you from the Far East, from the magical city of Bye Zan Teeum."

"Hmm, hmm," said Albert Love.

"What?" said Sandy Panther. "Where the heck is that?"

"Shhh," said Vera softly.

Donna Cody had drifted off and was softly snoring. The man regarded her solicitously for a minute and then turned to Sandy Panther.

"Ma'am, look at it—the stopper's still in place. Been there for hundreds of years. This miracle medicine cures colds, sore throats, blindness, deafness, asthma, stomach troubles, bowel problems. It'll heal cuts, wounds, rashes, any infection you've got. Do you have abdominal pain, intestine worm, hemorrhoids, headache, dizziness, ear or tooth pain? Ear trouble?" The man looked fixedly at Donna Cody's ear. Then he continued:

"The Lord Jesus himself was buried with balsam, and look how He came to life again." Vera bowed slightly, but the little man never noticed as he continued. "Why, I knew a man, his wife had the TB, you know, and he buried her and looked to be dying of the same thing. But a little Balsam of Byzantium and he was good as new, ended up burying his second wife 30 years later."

"Hmm, hmm," said Albert.

Sandy Panther tried to ask why the man hadn't used the balsam on the first wife, but the man went on. "Go on as long as you want," Sandy Panther muttered under her breath. Vera patted her arm.

"The Balsam of Byzantium was first made by an old monk, centuries ago, living in a cave. Folks from the city heard about these monks and how they lived such a long time and come to find out about it. That was the golden time!"

"But," he went on, "it's all herbs, all natural. Makes your body fight the sickness demons. No more skin problems. No more stomach problems. Not that it's likely, but if either of you young ladies feel tiredness, it'll fix that. It heals you inside and out. Put it on a cut. Swallow it. They used it in Europe and Asia. And now, only here, can you get the genuine article. It is our mission to bring this miracle to all who want it. It's good for whatever ails you, and if nothing ails you, it's good for that too."

"How do you make it, then?" asked Sandy Panther.

The man was suddenly quiet. It turned out, if you tried to get the formula for the balsam, he had nothing to say. He did talk a great deal about having to pray for years and live righteous. He suggested that perhaps Sandy Panther and Donna Cody needed more faith in their hearts for a healing to take place. If they were willing to pray with him, he might find a way to help. Sandy Panther brushed past all that, haggled with the man (his name was Vernon Lugner, and he was apparently well-regarded in the area), and finally used some of Donna Cody's remaining cash to buy some "at a special price."

Sandy Panther and Vera began putting the stuff on Donna Cody's ear, and a few days later the swelling receded and the terrible jagged tear on the earlobe began knitting itself back together. The stuff's smell was strong and piney mixed with something astringent. Sandy Panther kept needling Donna Cody about cutting a record, fame, and fortune. Vera would, thankfully, interrupt these harangues, usually because a glorious meal was about to unfold.

"I may not go for some of this religious stuff," Sandy Panther said to Donna Cody, "but your ear sure looks better. Maybe it is medicine from God. That Vernon Balsam fellow, Miz Vera says, is a true healer."

"I don't know about that," said Donna Cody.

"Well, Miz Vera's cooking could make a believer out of anyone," said Sandy Panther. And it was truly astounding to watch the way Donna Cody ate while she was there. Her skin took on a warm tone, her eyes began to sparkle, and her lips filled out, along with the rest of her, at least a little.

Vera smelled like pine, which she picked and dried and put in little pillows. Her hands were swollen and wrinkled and always moving—either making food or making things or washing up. She often sat in a favorite chair in the kitchen that had pillows at the back and on the seat, old and faded into gray, curved from her little body. Her dark eyes watched your face carefully (she was a little deaf), and her wisps of white hair in a tiny soft bun framed her face as if she were an old picture on the wall. She would lay her Bible on her lap and crochet or knit as she read. She smiled a lot, didn't speak much. When she did, it was usually about how God loved you and never to believe anything anybody told you that contradicted that idea.

Albert smelled musty, like the books in his study and the pipe he smoked when he read them. He was a lawyer, and usually you would expect a lawyer to talk a lot. Maybe he did in court, but at home he only spoke when he needed to, so you paid attention to what he said. The quiet and peace of the house finally made Sandy Panther restless, and she fretted to leave.

Before they went, however, Donna Cody recorded the Loves singing some hymns. (That was all they sang, music for the Lord. Vague hints suggested that this had not always been the case, but neither of them would talk about it.) Vera somehow managed to play an insistent alternating bass on a big old Martin OM guitar that would have players today drooling all over it. Her rich alto voice blended with Albert's light tenor perfectly—they took their breaths together—a tribute to harmony in all senses.[20]

Finally, Donna Cody and Sandy Panther were ready to move on.

"I don't think you should be going out there all by yourselves," said Vera, trying to reason with Donna Cody. "You need someone to protect you."

"Miss Vera," Donna Cody replied, "thank you. You and Mr. Albert are some of the most wonderful people I have ever met, and you have

---

[20] Two of Donna Cody's recordings of the Loves have survived: "We Must All Fade Away" and "Jericho Jubilee." They are, without doubt, the finest renditions we have of these rare gospel songs.

saved me from dying, I think. But you always say that prayer can fix anything, so please pray for us."

Vera smiled at her and then even laughed a little. "You have me there," she said. "Jesus bless you and protect you both."

"Amen to that," said Sandy Panther. Profusely thanking their benefactors, (who would not take any money), they left one morning when the last rains of spring were pounding into the mud. White mist rising up from the valleys in long horizontal puffs made it look as if the mountains were floating in the air with no bases.

"Look, Donna Cody. It's as if old Noah's flood was coming up to drown this sinful world. And all we have for an ark is Rambler." Donna Cody laughed, but with all the hairpin turns and mist it did seem as if they would be engulfed by a rising tide. Down the mountain they continued, along sinuous curves and past drop-offs on either side that they both tried to ignore, descending down to the plain. Sandy Panther was not pleased when they ended up camping out again under dripping ponchos. She ended up scrunched up in the Rambler, while Donna Cody raved on about being out under the stars, even if you couldn't see them at the moment. Rockandy looked longingly at the car but finally settled down in the stuffy poncho tent with Donna Cody.

Chapter 11: Where Small Change Can Lead You. Communal Hospitality.

I'll sing to you of the good old times
When people were honest and true,
Before their brains were rattled and crazed
By everything strange and new,
When every man was a workingman
And earned his livelihood,
And the women were smart and industrious
And lived for their families' good,
In the days of Andrew Jackson
And of old grand-daddy Grimes,
When a man wasn't judged by the clothes he wore
In old pod-auger times.

—"In Old Pod-Auger Times," possibly by "Comical Brown"

From all accounts, Donna Cody, Sandy Panther, and Rockandy followed the roads in front of them. When they came to a little town, Donna Cody would go into the market or the post office or some other public place and ask people about fiddle or banjo players around there. Sandy Panther would ask, too, often with better results and other offers. Donna Cody recorded a number of strange individuals, one of whom sat up with them in a barn all night and sang hymns while rain pattered on the roof, making for an interesting recording. Another banjo player showed Sandy Panther how to tune her banjo in lots of different ways. But we don't have much information to go on except the recordings, now firmly and thankfully lodged in the Smithsonian.

"Donna Cody," said Sandy Panther one morning, "while it's true that if you have no bacon, you gotta be content with cabbage, still, can't we get us some decent food?" She was rooting hungrily in a cold can of beans, swiping her finger along the inside of the can to get every last bit.

"What?" groaned Donna Cody. She was feeding Rockandy and, as usual, forgetting to eat her own breakfast. "I can't cash another check this soon. We'll run out. How could all that food be gone?"

"We ate it, is what," said Sandy Panther, morosely licking her fingers. "And some went bad. All that bread. Those cookies. Still got the Cheez Spread and crackers, thanks be. But we need to eat. Isn't that an emergency? What's gonna happen to Rockandy there?" she cunningly added. "You gonna starve him too?"

"I certainly am not, and I would prefer, Sandy Panther, to refrain from cashing another check so that we will not run out of money," said the ever-abstemious (except in the case of books and musical instruments) Donna Cody.

"Well," said Sandy Panther, "maybe you can chew on air, but I can't. I don't want to be a freeloader, so I'll help out. If you feel like you can't do it, then we've got to squeeze a nickel into a quarter. Let's play the streets. I bet we could at least get enough to buy a warm dinner tonight."

They bickered back and forth as they packed up and drove on. But finally, when they came into a good-sized town, they parked near a grocery store and put out their music cases and began to play. Donna Cody's case was made of light tan leather with darker brown edging threatening to come off as the threads holding it began to look like fringe. Sandy Panther's solemn black case had tattered and faded blue velvet lining it. Mostly, people walked carefully around the cases and their owners or even crossed to the other side of the street. But some of the younger kids threw quarters in, giggling at their own bravery. It was slow going, but they had close to two dollars when an official-looking man stormed out of the store and told them they needed to leave—NOW.

"I'm sure as heck not buying anything to eat at your store!" roared Sandy Panther at the back of the man as he walked back into the store. Donna Cody sighed, scooped up the coins, and was packing up her fiddle when a group of the weirdest people they had ever seen engulfed them. They were all young, and there were about ten of them. The men had hair down to their collars and weird wire-rim glasses. Some had strange felted green hats that looked vaguely German. They wore tight jeans or chinos or shorts, along with leather sandals. Some had wooden walking sticks. The women mostly had long straight hair and peasant blouses and very short shorts or denim skirts, and they wore sandals as well.

"Hey," one of them said. "You two sound wonderful."

"Do you need help?" asked one of the boys.

"Whoa," muttered Sandy Panther. Donna Cody couldn't even speak. Her mouth hung open.

"You girls have a place to stay? You need some bread?" asked a tall, skinny man whose ribs showed, especially since he wasn't wearing a shirt, just lederhosen and sandals. He was even taller and skinnier than Donna Cody.

"We could use some bread," said Donna Cody. "We're pretty hungry, but—"

They laughed. "No, you two musical chicks: money!" shouted the skinny man through a thick dark mustache that hung over his lip. "Hey, everyone, let's see what we've got." People dug into pockets and purses and came up with 14 cents.

"Hmm," said the skinny man. "We've got food back at the farm. You'd be welcome there."

Donna Cody and Sandy Panther looked at each other and agreed. "No need to buy a cow when you can get your milk through the fence for free," said Sandy Panther, winking.

"How does that even pertain to this situation, Sandy Panther?" demanded Donna Cody, who often notoriously missed the point, when there was a point. But they climbed into the Rambler and followed a school bus painted with pictures of trees and naked people who had no embarrassing bodily parts. Sandy Panther was silent for a whole minute. Then she said, "Whaddaya think, Donna Cody?"

"Think about what?" said Donna Cody, who was trying to keep up with the bus (even though the bus was probably going about 30 mph).

"These folks, are they beatniks or something?"

"Sandy Panther, I am not sure what to think," said Donna Cody.

"Maybe they're in a circus?"

"I have no idea. While this visit is taking us off the path of our quest, it is perhaps necessary for a bit of nourishment. Did you notice—Rockandy liked them?"

Both of them looked down at him and found comfort, though Donna Cody had to quickly look up again. They were now on a dirt road, climbing a steep hill. The bus was struggling up like the ancient behemoth it was, groaning, halting, and sliding back. Even Donna Cody realized adequate distance from the bus might be a good idea after the back end came much too close to their windshield, with Sandy Panther screaming, "Oh Lord, oh Lord!"

Finally, the bus crested the top of the hill and abruptly disappeared over it. As they inched up to the top, they saw that the bus was roaring down the other side at a truly terrifying speed. It careened into a left turn down another dirt road.

"Holy catfish!" said Sandy Panther. Her prayers evolved into stranger and more fervent idioms in direct ratio to an increase in the amount of danger threatening. "Why on earth are they going so fast? They gotta be doin' 70. C'mon, Donna Cody, we gotta catch up or we'll be lost."

Donna Cody said nothing as with clenched teeth and gripping hands she pushed the Rambler up to 45 mph. They made it in time to see the bus swerve into another left up a little hill. Finally, they pulled over to a flat field. People poured out of the bus: crying, laughing, screaming. Some of the men opened the hood and started looking inside, talking about the brakes going out again.

Other people were running out of a dilapidated old house. At one time it had been a dignified old dogtrot farmhouse[21], but now half its windows were missing. The front porch sagged under about six slumping couches in various states of raggedtry. More couches and chairs sprawled in the breezeway between the two sections of the house. People were draped all over them or sprawled on the floor: playing guitars, reading books, hugging and kissing, staring up at the porch ceiling. Cats stalked about but stayed close to the couches and people. Dogs lay in the dust.

Beside the driveway old cars of many different makes and models looked more like archaeological digs than cars. An ancient rusted truck rose right from a giant hole in the ground as if heading out of the grave for the heavenly resurrection, though, like so many of us, its back half was still buried in dirt. A bulldozer sat to the side with a grinning face and a banner that proclaimed, "I belong to Mike Mulligan." An ingenious ragged scarecrow with a tie-dyed scarf floating from its neck sat inside on the operator's seat.

Full clotheslines blossomed forth from one side of the house. Besides brightly colored items, strange little blobs hung heavily; on closer inspection, they turned out to be chickens, headless, hung by their feet to drain out the necks. Some women were tending fires and huge pots of boiling water. Their well-developed arm muscles flexed as they hauled pots, pulled chickens off the clotheslines, and stirred huge steamy pots that looked like bubble, bubble, toil and trouble. Behind them, someone was leaning crazily out of a tree house. There was too much to see, but Donna Cody and Sandy Panther valiantly tried.

Some dogs came running out the front door, the other dogs in the dust shook themselves and stood up, and Rockandy yipped and quivered.

---

[21]In this case, the original two cabins had been rebuilt into two substantial if run-down houses, but still with the tell-tale breezeway ("dog trot") between them.

Donna Cody promptly let him out of the car so he could go sort things out for himself.

They stepped out of the car as the skinny young man came up with another man behind him. That man stood out: he was also over six feet tall, but more muscular, with steely gray eyes and thick blond hair that fell down his back. He wore jeans and a linen tunic.

"Welcome to our house," he said in a rich, deep voice, holding out his hand to Donna Cody, who was floored, and grasped his hand weakly. "I'm Peter," he said, holding her hand a little longer than you were supposed to.

"Howdy," said Sandy Panther, shooting out her own hand. Peter looked at her for a minute and then shook her hand, but with no pause. He turned back to Donna Cody, while Sandy Panther fumed.

"Jimmy tells me you're hurt," he said, staring earnestly at her.

"Who told you that?" she said, turning to Jimmy.

"I could see it," Jimmy said, shrugging. "You kept pulling at your ear."

Donna Cody curtly noted that she was still having some problems with her ear. She was annoyed with the way Peter had held her hand.

"Come in with me," said Peter. "I can help." He took her by the hand and led her into the house. She pulled her hand loose, but she kept walking with him.

"Stay," she commanded Rockandy, who had come bounding over. He hung his head and sat, but then trotted over to Sandy Panther.

"What the heck?" said Sandy Panther.

"Don't worry about it." Jimmy grinned, punching her lightly on the arm. "Peter is a healer. He can tell where you're at. Come on, and we'll get you chicks set up with some beds. And you can have a good, natural meal."

Snorting with umbrage at being called a *chick*, Sandy Panther replied, "Healer? Humph! But I wouldn't mind spending a night indoors. I guess." She grabbed the instruments and followed Jimmy, Rockandy trailing after her.

"Where do you all come from?" asked Sandy Panther. "Don't think you're from around these parts."

Jimmy said, vaguely, that they came from out west. First off, he showed her the facilities, which turned out to be a spigot, an outdoor shower, and a circle of outhouses all facing center, all without doors.

"Are you kidding me?" said Sandy Panther, screeching to a halt.

"Peter says we should all be in the open, that nothing needs to be hidden, you know?" said Jimmy. "It's all part of our nature, who we are."

"Ain't nothing natural but nature," said Sandy Panther, shaking her head.

"What?" said Jimmy.

"Nothin' *natural* about going in front of everyone. Think I'll use the bushes when I need to go," said Sandy Panther.

They headed inside. People swarmed all over the place. Things were clean if threadbare. The rooms were large, yet cozy with low ceilings, old fireplaces, and a number of oddly beautiful pieces of furniture. They passed a dark-wood vanity next to a torn-up overstuffed Barcalounger, a tall oak bookcase across from a telephone wire spool table. Sandy Panther stashed the instruments in a corner.

Jimmy then led Sandy Panther up a wide staircase and down a hall to a room that had three sets of homemade double-wide bunk beds, each three bunks high, built up right to the ceiling. People had hung scarves and beads and things over some of the bunks so that they were like little rooms. The top bunk to the right, though, had nothing on it. Jimmy followed Sandy Panther's gaze and told her, "You two can have that one." Then he turned around and bounded out the door, calling after someone.

Sandy Panther eyed the bunk dubiously but saw she could climb up on a ladder of boards nailed to the posts holding up the beds. She wasn't much of a climber, but she managed to get up there and throw her stuff on the bed. She might have stayed there and slept, but her stomach was growling, and she wanted to know what had happened to Donna Cody. Going down the ladder was worse than going up, but she finally managed, and trotted down the stairs to see what was going on. In the kitchen, the women were getting a meal together, and it was smelling and looking much better. On a huge plank table in the dining room (with no chairs), they were piling giant loaves of bread and wheeling in a pot of soup half as tall as Sandy Panther. One of the women saw her staring and laughed.

"That's Big Mama," she said. "Lucky we have some wheels for it." The wheels were part of a retooled lawn mower, but the contraption worked.

"We'll be eating soon," she said, grinning and friendly.

"Thanks," said Sandy Panther, whose stomach was rumbling helplessly. "You all need some help? Know where my friend would be? She went off with this guy, Peter..."

"Oh, she's with Peter," the girl said, looking at her knowingly, which bothered Sandy Panther. "They should be down soon. Peter always blesses the meals."

This made Sandy Panther even more curious, but she followed the other girl into the kitchen and was soon busy chopping vegetables that had a lot of brown spots. She was told these had been "liberated" from grocery store dumpsters but that everything had been wrapped, so it was OK. And all the produce was fine once you cut the rot out.

When the table looked like it was about to collapse, one of the women stepped out on the back porch and banged a triangle. Mostly men came filing in since it was all women in the kitchen, and then Peter came in with Donna Cody in tow. She looked dreamy and dozy. Sandy Panther stepped forward, but Peter raised his hand. The room became silent, and even Sandy Panther stopped where she was.

"Peace," sang Peter, in a surprisingly rich baritone, elongating it to "peeeeeesssss."

"Peace," everyone sang back in the same elongated manner.

"Love," he intoned.

"Luh-uh-uh-uhvvvvv uh-uh-uh," they all sang back. Sandy Panther even found herself singing. It caught you up.

"Food," Peter finally sang. This time the response was even longer and more drawn out, with harmonies, improvisations. Sandy Panther's ears rang, but she teared up because it was so beautiful. And then it was over, and people lined up, grabbed bowls, and held them up for a generous ladle of soup and hunk of bread. Finding any space they could, they sat down and slurped, many of them cross-legged on the floor. Sandy Panther and Donna Cody grabbed bowls and loaded up while Peter went over to eat and talk with some people. Sandy Panther noticed that people's eyes followed Peter wherever he went, but then they pretended they weren't looking.

The two of them found a little corner and sat, with Rockandy curled next to them, all three of them chewing blissfully on thick slices of bread, sipping a thick chicken soup laced with chunks of onion, potato, broccoli, cauliflower, and cabbage. (Rockandy didn't go much for the soup.) Sandy Panther found wine and poured herself a large glass full. She was eating and drinking as if she had never eaten or drunk before and had to make up for lost time.

"Careful, Sandy Panther," Donna Cody said. "You'll become intoxicated."

"I'm fine," retorted Sandy Panther. "What I want to know is what you were up to with that Peter fella. Were you two doing something I should know about?" She smirked. Donna Cody was so virtuous and standoffish that it sometimes got on her nerves. Any chance to rib her was one she was going to take.

"No, Sandy Panther," Donna Cody said primly, "nothing salacious occurred. It does turn out, however, that Peter knows a surprising amount about the mysterious healing arts. He held his hands over my ears while I lay on a bed, and then he pressed my cut with a warm poultice and then he put some oil on it. I apparently fell asleep, but he came and woke me up for dinner."

Now, as she was saying this in a dreamy but knowledgeable way, it was obvious to Sandy Panther that something else had gone on. And it had. What Donna Cody *didn't* say was that Peter had massaged her all over, that he had intoned a weird chant over her, and that he had woken her up by kissing her deeply and tongue-probingly. Donna Cody was puzzled. Normally, she would never have allowed this.

"So, doth it feel better?" asked Sandy Panther, with her mouth shockingly full. "It lookth bedder," she said, the bread blocking a few consonants.

"You know, it does," said Donna Cody, still dreamy.

"Then that's good, anyway," said Sandy Panther, guzzling more red wine.

Later, tummies full, hazily comfortable (for different reasons), with Rockandy snoring beside them, Sandy Panther brought their instruments out, and they quietly played some tunes. Soon, a crowd had inched over before them. Sandy Panther, a natural ham and at least one or two sheets to the wind, began mugging and then singing a number of singalong songs like "Buffalo Gals" and "Banjo Picking Girl" and "Tom Dula." However, when they played "Sail Away, Ladies," Donna Cody cleared her throat.

"This is an interesting tune," said Donna Cody to her audience, who was willing to agree to a lot as long as it didn't stop the music for too long. Wrongly encouraged, Donna Cody continued:

"While many think of 'Sail Away Ladies' as an Uncle Dave Macon tune, it's Uncle Bunt Stephen's performance in 1926 that brought this to the larger world. He played it for Henry Ford's contest and became World Champion Fiddler. There are many verses, but we will only sing you a few."

"Well, sing 'em!" yelled someone in the back. They obviously did not know that this was not a good way to deal with Donna Cody. She began to open her mouth to explain the tune's relation to "Sally Ann" and sundry other items.

"In fact," said Donna Cody, "it is an interesting irony that an industrial tyrant like Henry Ford helped a song get out to the people, and indeed, by having a fiddle contest, elevated the fiddle. The fact that the verses may have come originally from Negro rhymes shows an interesting mix of dance music from the Civil War or even earlier merging with Negro traditions."[22]

At this point Sandy Panther jumped up, slamming out the tune on her banjo, shouting out verses, and clogging, her voluptuous figure jiggling away to shouts, hoots, and wolf whistles.

"I think I'm lit for sure!" she yelled, laughing. Pretty soon, people were scrambling up and dancing around, hair flying, beads of sweat rolling down, arms waving, feet stomping. Even Donna Cody ended up fiddling a bit like Uncle Bunt, her fiddle ringing as she shouted out verses along with Sandy Panther. The song had plenty of verses already, but people started making up their own, to the great annoyance of Donna Cody:

> *All I wanna do is dance!*
> *Sail away, ladies, sail away,*

---

[22]What Donna Cody didn't know until much later was that it was all much worse: that Henry Ford encouraged square dances and fiddle contests to combat the creeping influence of jazz and couple dancing that he blamed on African Americans, immigrants, and what he called "international Jews." It's enough to put you off square dancing except that we can't let Henry Ford ruin a good thing, now, can we?

Smoke some jane and find romance!
Sail away ladies, sail away.

Come and rock me, baby-o
Come and rock me, baby-o
Come lip lock me, daddy-o
Sail away ladies, sail away.

They weren't great verses, but they were original.

As things were winding down, however, Peter came walking in and, beside him, a well-formed man with a guitar. People (especially women) let out yells of pleasure. Donna Cody and Sandy Panther found themselves displaced. Sandy Panther yelled, "Hey, we was playing here!" The man nodded to them, stretching his handsome, pouting mouth into an ingratiating smile and deliberately turned his swooningly shapely back to them. Someone brought him a chair, he sat down, tuned the guitar, which was a 12-string, and began to sing. Sandy Panther muttered but was emphatically told to shut up by various people, people who had just been dancing to *her* music.

The guitar rang an opening chord, and the singer stared with smoldering eyes at various comely women as he sang:

Ooooo, I'm so gone
I'm so gone on you, babe.
Ooooo, I'm so done in,
So done in by your love.

This was the chorus, and it was repeated several times. One of the verses went like this:

You move through the trees, with your own special breeze
And the wind lifts your hair, and your scent is everywhere,
Like a song from the earth, that gave you birth,
Oh, I'm so done in by your love.

There was a lot more, but it is best to spare intelligent readers such as yourselves. Donna Cody and Sandy Panther, alas, were not spared.

Chapter 12: What Makes a Good Folk Song. A Precipitous Descent. A Narrowly Avoided Brawl. An Exciting Invitation.

You may be high, you may be low,
You may be rich, child, you may be poor,
But when the Lord gets ready, you got to move.

—"You Got to Move," traditional, as sung by Fred McDowell

Sandy Panther watched uneasily as Donna Cody fidgeted through the song. She knew the signs, and they didn't look good. As Donna Cody began to stand up and open her mouth, Sandy Panther pulled her down and whispered, "C'mon, let's go hit the sack. Look at Rockandy there. He's all done in." Donna Cody, distracted by the dear dog curled up next to them, agreed, and so Sandy Panther led them upstairs. Rockandy was not at all happy about sleeping on the floor with his mistress and one of his favorite humans so far away from him up near the ceiling. They, meanwhile, had to be careful not to bump their heads if they tried to sit up. But soon, exhausted, all three of them settled down and slept.

However, they were awakened later and again throughout the night by grunts, creaking bed slats, nuzzling noises. It was all disturbing, everyone acting as if private behavior was public behavior.

Donna Cody was feeling something over her, something huge and heavy coming down to squash the life out of her. Nearer, nearer…and she rolled over a railing. As she fell, she woke up to the floor meeting her rear end with a bone bashing thump, right in the spot she'd hurt before at Rotmensen's. She sat there for a while, moaning in pain, while various heads peeked out from behind the blanket curtains. Rockandy had sprung out of her way just in time. He whined and came over to lick her and give her morning kisses.

It was still dark, and she could make out Sandy Panther's snore from the top bunk. Donna Cody figured she was awake anyway, so she carefully pulled on her jeans, buttoned up her Peter Pan collar shirt, gathered up her few belongings, and, with Rockandy prancing excitedly around her, lurched unsteadily out of the room. Down below, she could hear pots clanging and lots of talk. The women were getting breakfast ready; she could smell cinnamon and vanilla and the sour-sweet odor of government powdered milk. She eased herself down the stairs with grunts and moans and hobbled into the kitchen. Immediately a tall woman with long brown hair swept up in a carelessly beautiful bun turned and yelled over the noise, "No dogs in the kitchen!" Donna Cody turned around and took Rockandy outside, where he was glad to go do his business and meet and greet his fellow canines. The sun was just beginning to streak the sky with light that made her eyes ache and her rear end somehow hurt even more.

She returned to the kitchen to help and was soon put to work chopping up a mish-mosh of fruit to put in Big Mama, where a mass of powdered milk, chunks of bread, cinnamon, and sugar were all swirling around like a giant threatening storm system. Donna Cody chopped and pared and tried separate out all of the rotten bits.

The girl next to her, who was cubing bread, asked if she was going to the festival.

"What festival?" asked Donna Cody.

"The Sweet Potato Festival. There's all kinds of music, so you'll really like it," said the grinning girl. Donna Cody felt a great warmth. "Joe told us about it," she added. "Too bad you girls didn't stay last night to hear him. I love his voice," she sighed. Donna Cody felt another kind of warmth. "But your music was cool," added the girl, who could intuit from Donna Cody's flushed face that she'd said something offensive to this strange character. "I wanted to dance my feet off," she added ingratiatingly.

Donna Cody smiled and thanked her. She was feeling a little better, and women were milling about in the dining room, grabbing bowls and spoons, which were piled all over the table.

Unfortunately, at that moment, Peter and Joe walked in the kitchen, sauntering right over to Donna Cody. "You two must connect," said Peter, in his otherworldly voice, a slowed-down pronouncement of revelatory truth. "You are both gifted."

Donna Cody still felt odd about and annoyed with Peter, but that was nothing compared to the singer. Joe held out his arms, a smile breaking across his handsome face, and moved in for a hug. Donna Cody held the knife out in front of her and stood there. An awkward moment ensued as Joe dropped his arms and his smile wavered.

"I heard you chicks made some cool sounds last night," he said.

"Thank you," said Donna Cody icily.

"I was hoping to jam with you and your little banjo player. She's cute."

"I don't think so," said Donna Cody, ice hardening further.

"Don't think she's cute?" laughed Joe. Peter watched it all impassively, his eyes boring through Donna Cody's skull.

"I don't think we'll be jamming with you," said Donna Cody haughtily.

"Oh, you don't, don't you?" snarled Joe. "Who do you think you are, Miss High and Mighty?"

"We don't play your kind of music," said Donna Cody in a dangerously even voice.

"All music is one," intoned Peter. Donna Cody and Joe ignored him and continued glaring at each other. The women in the kitchen bustled around, looking over curiously now and then.

"You'll have to miss out, won't you, then?" Joe said, breaking the deadlock with an awkward laugh. "I'll have to sing with that cute little banjo player." With that parting shot, he turned and walked out while Peter looked steadily at Donna Cody until she turned around to sort fruit. But apparently, her bread cubing partner had finished it up for her and swept it all into the fragrant, scary glop that was even now being scooped into people's waiting bowls.

They called this mess bread pudding, but it was like no other bread pudding Donna Cody had ever seen. They plopped some in her bowl, and she took a few bites and stirred it around disconsolately until Sandy Panther gave her a nudge. Donna Cody moaned.

"You were up kinda early," said Sandy Panther, bouncing over and depositing her things on the floor beside her. "Late to bed, early to rise, makes a woman healthy, wealthy, and wise. Early bird gets the worm. Rise and shine!"

"Please, Sandy Panther," said Donna Cody. "I am not in the mood for all your little sayings this morning."

"I can't help what I say," said Sandy Panther. "Sounds like you stepped out of bed on the wrong foot this morning, which I heard you most definitely did."

Donna Cody did not respond but looked down and continued to stir the soggy mess in her bowl. She mournfully picked out a few chunks of bread and chewed. Sandy Panther, seeing that she wasn't going to get much talk, got up and wandered around the room, chatting it up with different folks. Eventually she made it over to Joe, who asked her if she would like to play some music with him. Sandy Panther would play with most people, so she grabbed her banjo from the corner. Joe took up his guitar, and they began to play, to the delight of the folks in the room. But it was all Joe's songs.

"Every bird loves to hear himself sing," said Sandy Panther, at the end of the third song, which was about as many of Joe's songs as she could take. "Hey, Joe, I gotta go. Maybe we'll see you at the festival."

"Baby, I definitely want to see more of you," Joe smirked, stroking her flank.

"Oh, cusswords," said Sandy Panther. And then the Truly Regrettable Incident occurred, one that forced the quick exit of Donna Cody, Sandy

Panther, and Rockandy. The Incident involved using a banjo as a weapon, (swung from the peg head, where it made terrible contact with thighs, a move that is not advised for the sake of your instrument, let alone the people it contacts), a lot of shouting (from almost everyone including a scream from the victim of the banjo), a punch or two (mostly ineffectual but one, from a particularly tough and tall sister landing squarely on Sandy Panther's outthrust jaw, with another ineffectual one on the tough sister from Donna Cody), a little blood (a few people but mostly the victim), and, ultimately, some bad bruises (for more people than you might imagine).

They grabbed their instruments and belongings, ran outside, jumped in the Rambler, and drove off to raised fists, shouts, and yells. Peter watched them as they sped off.

Chapter 13: A Fellow Collector and Dog Lover. A Strange Gathering.

The day is past and gone,
The evening shades appear.
O may we all remember well
The hour of death is near.

We lay our garments by
Upon our beds to rest.
So time will soon disrobe us all
Of what we now possess.

—"The Day Is Past and Gone" by John Leland (1792), as sung by Jean Ritchie

Aunt Jane's Rambler hummed along at around 35 mph as the travelers pulled themselves together. Donna Cody had decided to head to The Sweet Potato Songfest even though they might run into members of the commune. "This event should yield some wonderful material," said Donna Cody, pausing from tapping her left-hand fingers underneath the steering wheel.

Sandy Panther wasn't so sure. "I don't think things would be too friendly for us there," she said.

"Maybe we can enter a contest," said Donna Cody slyly.

"That's true," said Sandy Panther, brightening up even while warily eyeing Donna Cody's attempts at steering. "Music makes friends everywhere. Maybe we could win the grand prize!"

"Hmm, maybe," said Donna Cody. "Meanwhile, a little look at that map would certainly be useful. And maybe it's time to go to a bank."

"Maybe a drugstore," said Sandy Panther, who had a big shiner on her left eye and some cuts on her left arm. When Sandy Panther moaned, Rockandy licked the cuts. Donna Cody also moaned when they hit a rough patch on the road. They passed through a tiny town here, a gas station there and got themselves set up. They bought and ate some crackers and

Cheez Spread and some baloney from a small market next to a gas station, where they also found a poster for The Sweet Potato Festival and copied down the information on it. On they drove until they needed a rest. They pulled over at a little roadside park with a picnic table to enjoy some of the other good things they had splurged on at the market. Sandy Panther had insisted on some Hostess cupcakes and began devouring one with abandon.

Nearby, a tall, somewhat round person with a tape recorder was holding a mike up to an ash tree. Upon closer inspection, they saw it was an older woman with thick black square glasses, thick graying wiry hair flying around her head, a huge nose like a beak, and what people politely call a "generous" mouth. She hadn't even looked up when Donna Cody and Sandy Panther drove up, and she didn't turn around now. They deduced she must be recording the birds in the tree, but then she stooped down and held the microphone next to the grass. When Rockandy went over to pee on the tree, she finally turned around, shutting off her tape recorder and putting her microphone away in a briefcase. A duffel bag lay beside it.

"Hello, travelers," she said in a low, raspy voice as she waved. "Looks like you two have seen some trouble."

"Nothing we can't manage," said Sandy Panther.

"Hello," Donna Cody said. "Can I ask what you were recording?"

"You can ask," the woman replied, and then bent over, slapping her thighs and laughing, "The tree has things to say, and the grass has things to say back."

"Oh, brother," muttered Sandy Panther. But Donna Cody was intrigued. The woman introduced herself as Viv Smythe. She outlined her theories of things: of the cosmos speaking, of the alchemical secrets in dirt, how trees talked, and the sky sang. This took a while, and Sandy Panther laid her head on the picnic table. Basically, Viv loved to record anything interesting, which she proved by rewinding and then playing her tape. It included a lot of wind sounds, a rushing sound that turned out to be pebbles being dragged back into the ocean by lapping waves, *clockety clockety whoosh*. This rather long section segued into a chorus of people singing and cackling and whooping in a language Donna Cody didn't recognize. "Serbian," said Viv, noticing Donna Cody's confusion. Then some bird sounds, and then, suddenly, an edgy, sharp voice singing "The Butcher Boy." The background was full of hiss.

"Whoa!" said Donna Cody. "Stop there! What's that? Who's that? Where did you record her? Is that off a record? Which one?"

Viv looked at her with interest. "Yes, that is off a record. I do have a few records," and here she stopped with a guarded look and quickly shifted gears. "But what are you two winsome ladies doing here in the middle of nowhere?"

"We might ask you that, ma'am," jumped in Sandy Panther. "I don't see a car or anything."

Viv Smythe laughed.

"We're heading to The Sweet Potato Festival," jumped in Donna Cody, who was embarrassed by Sandy Panther's rudeness. "We are traveling the country to find the old music before it is destroyed by the commercial interests that trample it in their greed. We have heard sweet hymns, and I have found some beautiful fiddle tunes, but we have also heard prostituted and supposed 'folk' playing that has nothing to do with real folk. And not only that…"

In the midst of this harangue, with which Sandy Panther and you the reader are all too familiar, Viv had clicked on her tape recorder. Not much would stop Donna Cody when she was launched, but this trimmed her sails a bit and she came to a halt.

"Why are you recording what I say?"

"You never know."

"Should I continue?"

"Please do."

And so, Donna Cody continued. And continued. And continued. Finally, she ran out of steam. Sandy Panther had gone to the car, lit up a cigar, and was sitting at the picnic table smoking, As a friend of your author's has put it, she didn't like having someone lay their meaningfulness on her. Rockandy curled up on the ground next to her. Meanwhile, Viv was interviewing Donna Cody.

"So you believe that some music is better than other music?" Viv queried earnestly, looking intently through her thick black glasses.

"Certainly. Everything comes in better or worse, doesn't it?"

"That may be correct, but 'worse' seems to mean music that is meant to make money."

"I believe that very strongly. It's when it becomes formula, like romance novels or so-called convenience food—it's not real music, it's an advertisement so that people can make money. The thing has become false."

"Young woman, all things are for sale," said Viv. "The music you have learned came from books you have bought, records that recording companies made, medicine shows in which people sang and played for money, ballad collectors who had to be funded by somebody."

"Now that's what I keep saying," called out Sandy Panther, waving her cigar for emphasis. "There's nothing wrong with making a little cash. What do they say—he who pays the piper calls the tune."

"I'll give you a proverb, Sandy Panther: A closed mouth catches no flies," was Donna Cody's surprising reply.

"Ladies, ladies. The point is that all music is part of an exchange and that exchange is at the heart of all encounters. That's why Dante put counterfeiters so deep in Hell; they falsify exchange."[23]

"I don't understand a word she's saying," grumbled Sandy Panther. Donna Cody didn't either, but she didn't want to admit it. She had not read Dante, but that didn't stop her. It doesn't seem to stop most people.

"I am not sure, Viv, that this analogy is pertinent. I am talking about music that expresses the soul of the people vs. music that is cheap, shallow, only there to sell things. What about advertising jingles? What about pop music?"

"What about all the *Titanic* songs? They were the pop music of their day. What about Martha White flour and Jed Clampett? What about English street songs and 'Cockles and Mussels, Alive, Alive-O'? And who are these people, these *folk* you're talking about? Isn't this a modern invention, in fact, one that dates back to Sir Walter Scott and all those other 18th- and 19th-century, fairy-tale-collecting proto-folklorists?"

"I have to think about that," said Donna Cody. That was usually as far as anyone got with her. The suggestion that Sir Walter might have been a modern inventor of the concept of "folk" disturbed her.

They moved over to the picnic table. Sandy Panther had thankfully finished her cigar and now had some bread and jam out. They all ate some, and Rockandy came up and made friends with Viv.

"This animal," said Viv, "is a credit to his race, with a fine occiput and lovely flews. He needs some rubbing on his acnestis."[24] And she proceeded to scratch him between the shoulders.

"What?" demanded Sandy Panther.

---

[23] Counterfeiters, falsifiers of exchange, show up in Circle 8, Maleboge 10, in Canto 30. (There's only one deeper circle: the traitors.)

[24] Rockandy's *occiput* is the back of his skull. His *flews* are his thick lips hanging down. The *acnestis* is between the shoulder blades where most of us can't reach to scratch those itches. Rockandy's *croup,* or the top line of his hindquarters, shows Viv Smythe that he is a nobly bred animal.

"His croup, his lovely high tail set, his rump," said Viv. "Not all dogs have such a lovely tail set." Rockandy leaned up against her and almost purred. Sandy Panther looked jealously on.

"You know a lot about dogs, don't you?" said Donna Cody admiringly, even if she didn't follow half of the praise. Anyone who saw Rockandy's good points was on the right side of things.

It never became clear how Viv had ended up in a rest stop in the middle of nowhere, but they were happy to offer her a ride to the festival, which was where she wanted to go. And she knew the way. They crammed her in the back, but she didn't seem to mind once she'd made sure the hole in the floor was covered. She told them a funeral was planned for a singer who had lately passed after a terrible fight with his girlfriend. Some people blamed the girlfriend.

"Too bad it's not that Joe fella," said Sandy Panther. "I wouldn't have minded sending him on to the next world."

Viv told them that they needed to meet the girlfriend, whose name was Marcy Mellow. "You may find her interesting," said Viv, who then rolled her eyes up and began humming something melismatic and indecipherable and nasal while staring up at the car's ceiling (if you can say that cars have ceilings). But every now and then she would stop and give them surprisingly cogent directions.

A few hours later they saw some funky, hand-lettered signs out in the middle of fields and more fields. They turned and found themselves in a city of cars. People were sitting in circles playing music or setting up tents or eating or making out. Dogs were running around. They passed the commune's bus and kept going, bumping slowly through the field, finally pulling over and claiming a spot. They set up camp and got out the Primus 210. Viv said that she already had someone to stay with. "But the funeral will be tonight, before the show," she told them. "See that little grove of cottonwoods over there? That's the place. Come over when it gets dark." She picked up her stuff and walked off whistling.

And so, after a hasty supper of canned beans and the rest of the baloney cut into them, carrying their instruments and bundled up for the cold, with Rockandy gamboling beside them, they set off across the field to the grove. As the sky deepened and receded into evening, they saw flickering lights. These turned out to be homemade luminaria: candles in jars of sand with paper bags around them. Focusing on the lights, they felt the darkness more as they slid into the crowd to listen. Six young men in leather jackets and jeans came forward with a blanketed form lying on what looked like an old door. People were shining flashlights on them.

Sandy Panther whispered: "Don't tell me that's the dead man."

"Couldn't be," Donna Cody whispered back.

"Not sure," said Viv, who had somehow found them and snuck up from behind.

After a moment of terror when the blanket was pulled back they were relieved to see an effigy with a loopy grin on its cloth face. It reminded Donna Cody of the scarecrow back at the dogtrot farmhouse. Someone came and propped it up against a tree and put a guitar in its lap, arranging the arms around it realistically and tying it all together. Someone else brought up a mason jar with some flowers in it. Finally, up stepped a short, dark-haired man with a five o'clock shadow and sideburns but in a suit, which felt very strange there in the middle of trees, grass, jeans, guitars, and luminaria. He proceeded to speechify at some length. The basic text was that the good die young, but the dead man's songs would ring on forever.

"No, they won't," muttered Sandy Panther.

"Shhh," said Donna Cody in her ear.

"Well, they won't," said Sandy Panther, rubbing her ear. "No one remembers most dead people for long, far as I can tell for all the talk."

"Shhh," someone standing beside them hissed reprovingly.

"Since Christopher wanted it this way, we're going to burn all his songs," the speaker said, finally. "But we'll sing them in our hearts," he added.

"What'd I tell you?" hissed Sandy Panther.

"Shhh," said Donna Cody.

Someone brought an empty coffee can, and someone else brought a stack of papers and tried to stuff them all in.

"They probably wouldn't get sung anyway," whispered Sandy Panther. "Like I was telling you—" But Viv jumped up at this point.

"Don't burn those!" she yelled, commandingly, striding up to the front. The preparations ceased. After a few minutes of wrangling, the speaker announced that Viv was going to sing one of the songs.

Chapter 14: A Strong-Willed Girlfriend Interrupts.

I never will marry, I'll be no man's wife.
I expect to live single all the days of my life.

—"I Never Will Marry," traditional

This was the song that Viv sang, *a capella*, in a hard, raspy voice with a surprisingly clear and bell-like pitch:

The first time I saw my dear Marcella
She was dressed in blue
The next time I saw her
She kissed me and swore to be true.

The next time I saw dear Marcella
She was all dressed in brown
She was standing on the side of the highway
Staring everybody down.

"Oh Marcella, Marcella, I love you
You know that I'd give you all I own."
"I don't care," she said, and wished me dead
And she cut me right down to the bone.

And now that I'm gone, Marcella,
Think on what you've done,
Your cruel heart has murdered this body
And taken me before my life was done.

The audience tried to clap, but the few who did found themselves on the losing side. Through murmurs, some scuffling and protests, a striking woman pushed her way up to the front. She was close to Donna Cody's height, in tight jeans, a brown leather jacket, and black leather motorcycle boots. Her dark hair sprang out in a curly mass all the way to her bottom. Her face was noble, her eyes large, her mouth set. And she was black.

"Marcy!" a few people yelled.

"Yeah, Marcy," she yelled back, in a hoarse but tuneful way. As she came up front, Viv handed her the guitar.

"No way! That bitch is not welcome here!" yelled one of the coffin bearers. Assenting grumbles from the crowd.

"I am not to blame for his death," Marcy shouted at them, quelling the lot. "I didn't ask for this, I can't help being a better musician than he was, and I'm free to be one. I'm sorry he died, but I don't have to follow that path and drink and be suicidal and f___ed up!" (The use of profanity elicited gasps. Those were different times, but as someone kept insisting, they were changing.)

"Liar!" shouted someone.

"Not if you say so!" she yelled, never missing a beat. Some laughter from the crowd. "Listen, I didn't ask for this guy to fall in love with me. I didn't want it and didn't lead him on. I am a free woman, and I plan to stay that way."

Marcy began picking and talking and other noises all over the field died down as an ocean of sound poured out with an insistent alternating bass. It was the blues she played and the blues she spoke and then sang, her voice husky, low, and huge. Everyone was mesmerized. The guitar moaned back with bent strings, ringing, marching. And then, even as the last chord was dying away, she thrust the guitar back to Viv and ran off. The spell holding the audience evaporated, and over Viv's protests, Chris's songs were burned. They were getting ready to burn the "corpse" when Donna Cody and Sandy Panther looked at each other and knew it was time to leave, abandoning Viv, who was locked in heated argument with several different men.

"Looks like what they say: There was many a dry eye at the funeral," muttered Sandy Panther.

Chapter 15: Further Adventures at The Sweet Potato Festival. A Much More Terrible Canine Encounter. The Folk and the Not-So-Folk.

If I'd a listened to what mama said,
I'd be sleeping in a feather bed.

—"Hand Me Down My Walkin' Cane," possibly by James Bland

Marcy had been a revelation for Donna Cody and Sandy Panther. Donna Cody was not sure what to make of her. They wandered around the field, restlessly hoping they were going to hear her play somewhere else. At times they thought they could catch her voice in the distance or a guitar sounded a little like her, but it proved to be some circles of people around their fires, playing away, mostly singing boring modern songs and badly. Finally, the flashlight flickered halfheartedly, and they found their way back to the Rambler and their poncho shelters and called it a night.

In the morning, after a quick breakfast, they decided to explore. Music was starting up all over. They found that there were two festivals. At one end of the park, near where they were camping, a swirling mob of young people in jeans were strumming folk tunes.

But at the other end of the park were fiddlers and banjo players, most of them playing a bluegrass style, but Sandy Panther noticed some excellent two-finger styles and an occasional frailer. They were all getting ready for the contest and hoping for cash prizes. Cloggers were lining up, the ladies with shiny white shoes, industrial strength nylons, very short skirts and stiff petticoats, the gentlemen with elaborate matching suits and shiny white shoes as well.

"Lord, it's hotter than a popcorn fart in a whirlwind," said Sandy Panther. How can they wear all that getup?"

"Shhh," said Donna Cody.

Three men, two with identical thick-framed black glasses, sat at a table on the back left of the stage. They had a pitcher of water and paper cups, ready for the long day ahead. A banner over the stage proudly announced: "The Sweet Potato Festival: A Place for Pickin', Playin', and Visitin' courtesy of the Sweet Potato Elks since 19 and 37." Below it, a smaller sign on the side of the stage announced: "Cash Prizes! $50 first place winners, $30 second place winners, $15 third place winners. Categories: Traditional Fiddle. Contest Fiddle. Traditional Banjo. Bluegrass Banjo. String Band. Ballad Singing. Clogging."

An audience had already set up camping chairs and were sitting in them. Mostly it was middle aged and older folks—the men in overalls, the women in print dresses and sweaters, some in stretch pants with sneakers. Kids ran around in packs laughing, taunting, yelling, crying. Lots of people knew each other, and they looked at Donna Cody and Sandy Panther with some suspicion, but also some curiosity. Sandy Panther stared back and they dropped their eyes and went back to their talk.

A tall, thin man in a suit tapped a microphone on the stage. There was only one. A big cord ran back to a little house way over at the edge of the field. Next thing, a grinning man with black, slicked-back hair bounded onto the stage. He wore a suit with a bolo tie and a cowboy hat. He grabbed the mike and yelled, "Welcome, everybody, to the 25th annual Sweet Potato Festival!" He continued during the scattered applause: "Keeping alive the music of days gone by and the almost lost art of visiting. And now, let's hear them fiddlers and banjer pickers!"

Time pretty much stopped for Donna Cody and Sandy Panther except that Donna Cody remembered to whip out her trusty tape recorder, thankful that she still had enough working batteries left. They stood and watched for a long time. Then they sat down and watched and listened. There were old fiddlers playing in strange tunings that Donna Cody had never heard of; young, hotshot fiddlers blazing through standards like "Turkey in the Straw" (and taking the music out of it, as Sandy Panther said); there were child fiddlers, some prodigies, some rank beginners. There were even a few female fiddlers. A shy woman hunched over her instrument. She played some tunes in C that had Donna Cody moaning in sheer pleasure. Another woman who was younger and comelier and also dressed like a cowgirl played some standards like "Ragtime Annie" and "Soldier's Joy." Banjo players came up and played: two finger, three finger, up picking, frailing. One of the frailers had a banjo with no frets and a neck apparently topped with white aluminum siding, the sound a jumpy, slidy, shivery blues that reminded Donna Cody of the way Marcy played.

The cloggers came out all dressed up, young, ready to take the world by storm, which they did as they stomped about the stage, the young women's petticoats bouncing like waves of cumulus clouds, their white shoes flashing. The band behind them played like fire. The rhythms had the crowd clapping and shouting before long. People threw down boards and clogged and buck danced on the edges of the audience. It didn't seem possible that some of these folks could dance—withered old men and ladies, children, housewives and fathers, the thin, the heavyset, all sorts and conditions. Each dancer had his or her own style, with some twirling around, others barely moving their upper body, while their feet shuffled and stomped.

People sang ballads or silly songs or reworkings of Tin Pan Alley songs: "Granny Get Your Hair Cut" and "A Distant Land to Roam" and the old ballads like "Fair and Tender Ladies" and "Young Edward." Some of the men performers wore top hats and ribbon ties and suits. Some of the women performers wore long calico dresses and bonnets. People played dulcimers, autoharps, jaw harps, harmonicas. But mostly they played fiddles or banjos. At one point, a group of people from the Horseshoe Creek Baptist Church of God in Christ Jesus (at least, that's how Donna Cody scrawled it in her notes) came on and for the first time they heard "Amazing Grace," lined out. A thin man in a black suit stood like a melancholy crow on one side of the stage, with a crowd of about twenty people on the other, facing him. He chanted out the first line in a booming bass. The "congregation" sang it back, slowly, in swooping waves of notes that felt like a roller coaster climbing slowly up in pitch on "amazing" and then shooting back down on "how." Donna Cody had never heard anything like this, but Sandy Panther said she had heard it before when her granny had dragged her to church.

Off to the side, occasionally, they noticed some earnest young men in serious black rimmed glasses, some with mustaches and beards (which you did not see so much on the players or the rest of the audience). They had hair past their ears. They were circled around various complicated pieces of recording equipment that they had managed to plug in near the stage. Some of them had instruments. Eventually, during a break in which a large group of cloggers was assembling on stage, one of them came over to Donna Cody and Sandy Panther and asked if they were going to play.

Sandy Panther couldn't wait. "You betcha! You all play?"

"We do," he said, in a pronounced New York accent. "You ladies know any old-time tunes?"

Donna Cody eyed him narrowly. She was not a fan of Bob Dylan-loving interlopers, but Sandy Panther jumped in and suggested things like "Banjo Pickin' Girl" and "Stoney Point." The young man looked at them with more interest.

"Great." He waved them over. Donna Cody quickly fell into conversation with a young man whose name was Guthrie. "Like Woody," he said, " 'cept it's my first name." He was operating the fancy recorder and explained that they were down from the Library of Congress, recording all this. Donna Cody was thrilled and quickly got into a discussion about Library of Congress recordings she'd taped from the college library.

Sandy Panther had taken out her banjo and wandered away from the stage with a group of three young men attached to Guthrie. They were huddled together playing. After a while, Donna Cody excused herself and got out her fiddle. Guthrie grabbed a guitar. The six of them all played tune after tune. Other fiddlers looked over at Donna Cody from time to time, amazed that a girl was playing such fast, hard-driving music. Finally, the man who had first talked to them told them they were going up on stage after the next set. "What should we call ourselves?" the bass player asked.

"Let's be the Okey Dokey Boys," the banjo player suggested.

"Ahem," said Sandy Panther.

"Oh, right. How about the Hokey Okey Dokeys?" chimed in someone else.

Everyone except Donna Cody agreed, especially since by now they needed to go on stage. "Number 73!" someone yelled through the mike. Donna Cody was nervous. These men were good, and she hoped she could keep up and not be paralyzed by stage fright. Sandy Panther, on the other hand, would have bit back if stage fright ever tried to bite her. She couldn't feel scared on a stage if she tried. When the announcer gave the name of their band, the silence was deafening. "Oh-oh," whispered Donna Cody. But she pulled out her bow and got ready. One of the boys played four strong bow strokes to give the tempo, and they were off on a wild gallop.

After a few measures, someone in the audience whooped like a fire engine. People clapped, hooted, hollered, and stomped. When different folks in the band took breaks, each break received more applause, and when Sandy Panther belted out "Banjo Pickin' Girl" and played and clogged at the same time, the crowd went bananas. Donna Cody's fiddle, on the other hand, was listened to in dead silence until the crowd erupted with clapping, yells, and whistles. Other musicians were staring at her. She was, at last, after all that playing with Sandy Panther and all that practicing, turning into a fiddler's fiddler.

They were led off the stage, finally, to a changed audience, one that grinned at them, while other players came over and slapped them on the back and shook hands. At least, most of them did. One muttered, "If I had to be beat by a woman, at least it was her." Sandy Panther knew even more what she wanted to do with her life, while Donna Cody felt intense relief but also the exaltation of being part of a new and huge family, one much more interesting and welcoming than her own.

It was then that the trouble began. The folks from the far end of the festival had wandered over, and a group with guitars and some bongo drums was pushing its way up on the stage as the next act (a woman autoharpist and a young boy with a ukulele) were trying to go up. The judges were conferring with each other and eyeing the intruders with outrage. Planting themselves on the stage, they sang a terrible version of "Bye Bye Love," and somewhere the Everly Brothers shivered and fought off nausea. The guitarists banged away, while the bongo player was on one beat and the tambourine player on another. One of the guitarists and the woman tambourine player sang harmonies that fought atonal duels to the death. More young people came over applauding as the band launched into "We Shall Overcome."

The men in the audience jumped up, and the fists began to fly. The guitarists were dragged off the stage by the outraged festival producers, one of whom ran down the stairs and over to the astonished Hokey Okey Dokeys, gasping, "C'mon back, please! We gotta get these folks dancing. Can you play behind me if I call some squares?"

They were up there in a flash, chunking out "Cotton-Eyed Joe." The caller bellowed into the mike, and some of the dancers who had performed (and obviously been asked to help) grabbed audience members and scruffy youngsters alike and made squares. It was hardly a minute before people were dancing, the old folks clapping on the sidelines (having hastily moved their chairs), and the scruffy young men and the women who hadn't been caught up in the dancing were slinking away. The Hokey Okey Dokies had saved the day, and as a result they won first prize for the old-time band competition.

Interestingly enough, when one of the men from the band wrote up this story years later, Donna Cody and Sandy Panther did not appear in it. There were some acerbic words over this between Donna Cody, the man (who shall remain nameless but is now a folklorist of some repute at an Ivy League college), and various know-it-alls who wanted to contradict both of them.

It was only a small festival, missing from most of the stories of those times. Now it's the site of LeHigh Estates. Brick and wood houses, bright green lawns, labyrinthine roads, and cul-de-sacs have obliterated any trace of the rowdy, the unkempt, the old traditions and the wild notes that danced there. Under someone's barbecue grill or driveway or living room lies the pretend corpse of a musician who supposedly died for love.

Donna Cody and Sandy Panther never did find Viv again, and after a gratifying and exhausting evening playing tunes and singing with many newfound young and old friends, they slept the sleep of the valiant. In the morning, they climbed into the Rambler and puttered off down the road, waving goodbye to their new friends. Someone had told them about a family they needed to visit, the Jankeys. They had some sketchy directions that seemed sufficient until they tried to follow them.

The curves on the dirt roads were getting steeper and bumpier with potholes. Donna Cody and Sandy Panther sang out tunes and songs together and argued about the words and how the notes went. Finally, Sandy Panther called lunchtime. They had made it to the top of the latest incline, and the lugging Rambler needed a rest.

A field stretched out like a green blanket, inviting them to recline and Rockandy to frolic. Below, the mountains were watercolored strips of a collage. A falling-down barn in the distance completed the picture. They had traveled back 100 years. "Like they say," said Sandy Panther, "From here on, the hills don't get higher, but the valleys get deeper." They stretched out in the grass, dozing in the sun.

But as a wise person has also said, "Chance and the devil are seldom asleep." They woke to a chaos of barking and baying. A hound dog, as pretty a bitch as ever you saw, with long silky black ears, soft brown patches over her gentle eyes, black and white speckles with some big black spots on her ribs, and her tail arced proudly in the air, was cavorting with the usually sober Rockandy, who had apparently been pierced by Love's swift arrow. A scene of utter canine depravity was humpingly unfolding itself. Donna Cody was shocked and jumped up after them, while Sandy Panther jokingly fanned herself, laughed, and said, "Ain't that the berries?"

"What?" queried Donna Cody, casting her an annoyed, brief look. She ran off to chase the two energetic and enraptured animals.

And then, about six men burst out of the bushes, calling, "Callie! Git over here, goddammit, right now!" and "What the hell you doing, bitch? Oh Lord, there goes her breedin'."

Donna Cody stopped abruptly, thinking they were talking to her, but they ran past and began kicking Rockandy, who howled heartbreakingly. Donna Cody turned into a tigress, and Sandy Panther ran up, swinging her fists. Donna Cody jumped on the back of one of the men and bit his shoulder. Sandy Panther punched one in the side of the head. They quickly turned, and six men against two women meant that pretty soon the latter were covered with blood and bruises. They and Rockandy were all lying on the ground. Rockandy was whimpering.

"Lookit this, Davis," said one of the men, prodding at Sandy Panther

with this foot. "Maybe them dogs ain't the only ones to have some fun."
Grunts and snickers from the other men.

"T'other's just sticks 'n' bones," another one complained. "She's so
tall if she fell down she'd be halfway home."

And then Donna Cody raised herself on one elbow and pulled out a
snub-nose pistol. The men all backed away. Sandy Panther gasped.

"Aw, shit. All right now, let's be calm," one of them said, backing away.

"I'll show you some calm," said Donna Cody evenly, between her
teeth. "Keep walking away." She pointed her pistol at Davis's genitals even
while she lay sprawled there. Then she shot at the ground.

"Jesus H. Christ!" someone yelled, and they scattered back down the
way they'd come. Their beautiful hound dog, chastened, her tail drooping,
probably knocked up, ran with them.

The two of them and Rockandy lay there. They could not move.
Sandy Panther was shaking. "You have a gun! You! And you never told
me! What else you got that I need to know about?"

"Of course I have a gun," Donna Cody said. "This is Old Bessie. Two
females on the road, who knows what could happen?"

"You can even aim it."

"Of course. Aunt Jane had some firm ideas about that."

"You can't go carrying a gun around. I've seen lots of folks get in
trouble that way. And dang it anyway, Donna Cody, I am sick and tired of
being dragged into these fights that you and now that dog starts. This is
plain dangerous. Better keep peace than make peace. I swear, it's time I
struck out on my own."

"Oh," Donna Cody groaned. "Oh no, please," and here she heaved
the beginning of a sob, something she hated to do. Then Sandy Panther
started to sob, and they both moaned and slowly dragged themselves over
to Rockandy, who could barely lick their hands. All the while, Donna Cody
was making promises:

"Sandy Panther, I swear if we get out of this that we will sit down and make a record together, and I'll play music with you wherever you want to play it. I will do my best not to start any fights. You know Rockandy would never hurt a fly…" and on and on.

"Yeah, as my mama used to say, Blessed are they who expect nothing, for they shall not be disappointed. Right now we need a vet and maybe a doc, not empty promises. Let's help Rockandy even if he don't deserve it."

Donna Cody was now annoyed, and this probably helped her more than anything. She snapped out of it and even tried to stand, while muttering a few out-of-character curses about their attackers and men in general. Crawling and slowly rising to her feet, she swayed and stood over Rockandy and Sandy Panther, who were still lying there, and intoned, "You do not have to lecture me, Sandy Panther. Time will put an end to all these memories, and death will wipe out our pains, as Vera might say. We have to pluck strength out of weakness."

"Vera might say," mimicked Sandy Panther. "She'd say you was no Christian! You had a gun."

"And you should be grateful that I did," continued Donna Cody.

"What if that thing had gone off in the car? And where is it, anyway?"

"That is for me to know."

"And me to find out. You got it in your pocket there?"

"Never mind that, Sandy Panther. Those evil men may come back. Let's get out of here and find some help." Limping, howling, cursing— each according to their proclivities—the three of them made it back to the Rambler, and somehow Donna Cody drove them up into the mountains. Donna Cody thought of Duncan and Mabel and her house, and wanted to cry. Sandy Panther kept up a non-stop stream of complaints that went from the stupidity of dogs to the music of the people when the people are jerks. She was finally silenced by pure astonishment as they came upon a tall, bushy-haired figure with a pack that had a banjo neck sticking out of it. He had just turned around and stuck out his thumb.

"It's Guthrie!" exclaimed Donna Cody. They screeched to a stop and in he got. It turned out he was going to the Jankeys.

"That's a godsend," said Sandy Panther.

"It looks like you two, I mean three," glancing at Rockandy, "got in trouble." They told him about the terrible incident, leaving out the gun.

"That's good they gave it up," he said. It was obvious that some of the story was not being told, but he was a polite and well-educated young man in spite of his scruffy looks. "I'll bet Old Eph will have something for your cuts and things."

"Who?" they asked simultaneously.

"Only one of the best fiddle and banjo players you will ever hear. You wouldn't have a bottle of whiskey in there?" he asked presently.

"No, I do *not*," said Donna Cody crisply.

"No, she does not," said Sandy Panther sadly. "We could use some about now."

"Luckily, I do have one," said Guthrie. "But it's for Old Eph. You always bring a bottle, though, being girls you might get by. I'll say it's from all of us."

Chapter 16: Cures and Amorousness Gone Astray, Again. A Fruity Debate. Sandy Panther Has a Vision.

I woke up this morning
Th[e] blues all around my bed
Woke up this morning
Blues all 'round my bed
I went to eat my breakfast
Had blues all in my head.

Th[e] blues jump like a rabbit
They run a solid mile
Th[e] blues jump like a rabbit
They run a solid mile
An' when the blues overtakes you
You'll holler like a newborn child.

—"Morning Blues," traditional, as sung by Ollie Gilbert, Mountain View, AR, in the Max F. Hunter collection

The women were snoring by the time Guthrie got them to the Jankey place. Dark was falling, but lights shone down the valley. They realized they must have come through a pass and down the other side of a hollow. Cars were parked all over, which surprised them, but Guthrie said that lots of people came to see the Jankey family, that it was quite a party here. He leapt out and grabbed the bottle of whiskey.

Sandy Panther groaned. The last thing she wanted was a party. She wanted to go to bed, and that meant she felt pretty bad. Meanwhile, Donna Cody had carefully eased herself outside and was talking to a woman who turned out to be Emma Jankey, Eph's wife. She had a pretty flowered apron on over a grubby dress that looked like sackcloth. Donna Cody awkwardly explained that they had had a little accident, with Mrs. Jankey looking more and more annoyed, but when Rockandy limped out, she cooed over him and went to fetch some of her special liniment. (Donna Cody became interested in this later: It turned out to have goldenseal, myrrh, and cayenne in alcohol, along with some things Emma didn't want to talk about, though she in turn was interested in The Wondrous Balsam.)

Emma called her son Zeke out and then went back in the house. He was a short and unfortunately shy young man with a harelip. He stuttered as he helped Donna Cody and Sandy Panther with the liniment. Sandy Panther grew impatient with him, but Donna Cody was grateful for his kindness and didn't mind that he was slow and clumsy at getting the liniment out and onto the dog as well as giving them some for their own bruises. The main thing was that Mrs. Jankey's liniment worked. They could feel their bruises sigh with relief.

Meanwhile, Guthrie was eagerly greeting about ten people who had strolled over, all young and bushy, mostly men. They seemed to be old friends.

"Hey, ladies," he called, "I'll bring your stuff over to the barn. We'll make you up pallets on the floor" (several people laughed at the reference). Within a few minutes, people had piled up straw with blankets spread over it and surrounded it all with two by fours. Donna Cody excused herself and staggered over, Rockandy right beside her. Several people helped Donna Cody down and put some of her clothes under her head and her sleeping bag over her since she couldn't get into it. She was asleep before they finished, Rockandy curled up beside.

Zeke had headed back to the house, so Sandy Panther went over and put out a bowl of food for Rockandy beside his mistress. She looked at the two of them and set up her sleeping bag on the other pallet, but then she heard a bell ring, and then someone bellowed, "C'mon, y'all! Let's go rattle the dishes and fool the cats!"

It was the famous Ephraim Jankey or "Old Eph." Sandy Panther limped toward the house. She never could resist the fray.

"Bell means it's time for dinner," Guthrie muttered unnecessarily to Sandy Panther as she came up to the door. "And get ready to do some chores afterwards."

Inside, people were swarming all over the place, mostly young men. Women were cooking as usual, Sandy Panther noted crankily. But in a corner a few hairy young gentlemen with scraggly beards stirred up a mess that looked like wilted spinach and potatoes with some possibly redeeming cheese melting all over it. Mrs. Jankey took out some pans while a young woman with sleek dark hair parted in the middle over her face stirred a huge pot of something that smelled good. Guthrie handed the overwhelmed and exhausted Sandy Panther a bowl and plate and silverware and she soon found herself sitting in a corner eating some fried greens, cornbread, and bean soup. She avoided the potatoes from the stringy young men.

But it turned out that dinner was a delicious prelude to the true highlight, a glorious sonker of all kinds of mysterious fruits. There were raspberries, but that was all that Sandy Panther recognized in the steaming soupy mix, like a cobbler but juicier and deeper, with a fine biscuit topping.

Everyone sat back and sighed except for a tight-knit group of women discussing the family tree of the sonker.

"Y'know, we call these *slumps* at home," said a thin little blonde.

"Where you from?" asked a more solidly built blonde.

"Connecticut," said the first blonde.

"In Boston, we call 'em *grunts*," said the second blonde. "But they're different. You cook the biscuits up on top on the stove."

"You mean like dumplings?" asked a brunette with huge glasses.

"No, it's more like a compote—" someone else interrupted, and soon a lively debate was going on about the differences between batter cobblers, the necessity of peaches, the cuppa, cuppa, cuppa measurements[25] for a pie crust or biscuits or even cake, though most of them pooh-pooed the latter. Someone mentioned sweet potatoes, another mentioned a dip (which turned out to be thickened, sweetened milk).

Finally, Old Eph chimed in. "Now lookit. You have the violin and you have the fiddle," he said. "They're the same thing but different. The sonker is the fiddle, then, ain't that right? And them other fancy things, they're the violin," and he leaned back and laughed so that all his gold teeth showed. (Unfortunately, some other frightening examples of dental decay showed as well, but the grin managed to mitigate them.) "How about a tune?" he asked. "Anyone got a little June Apple for that sonker?"

Old Eph had a face like one of those apple-headed dolls, with shiny red cheeks, white stubble, and a grim mouth until he smiled—though this is the case with many of us who have felt the effect of gravity for some time. He was tall and solid, with fingers that looked permanently swollen, but that moved nimbly enough. His booming voice lit up a room.

Out came banjos, fiddles, guitars, autoharps, even a cello. Guthrie nudged Sandy Panther. "Go get your banjo," he encouraged her. He had his fiddle out. People sat around Eph like disciples around a master, which was, basically, what they all were. Sandy Panther scurried out to the barn.

She was brought up short by a striking tableau. A lantern glowed softly. Donna Cody was awake, and Zeke Jankey was tenderly spooning some liquid into Donna Cody's mouth while he held her up awkwardly with his short arm. The rest of the barn was deserted, rolled out sleeping bags and small piles of belongings all waiting. Zeke saw Sandy Panther, almost dropped Donna Cody, and spilled his spoon of broth on her chest, causing her to sit bolt upright and open her eyes, knocking Zeke back on

---

[25]A cup of this and a cup of that. A handful of this and a pinch of that.

his haunches. Rockandy jumped up and bayed. Sandy Panther heartlessly began laughing. Zeke scurried to his feet, shot Sandy Panther a furious look, and stalked out without a word.

"Whew," said Sandy Panther. "Now what was going on here?"

"For Pete's sake," said Donna Cody wearily, "he was being kind."

"Looked like he was enjoying it," said Sandy Panther. But Donna Cody sank down again and lay there with her eyes closed. Sandy Panther, with no contrition whatsoever, grabbed her banjo and left. Rockandy settled down and, along with Donna Cody, was soon breathing heavily, no doubt dreaming of his lost lady love.

As Sandy Panther approached in the clear, starlit night, the sound of the fiddles, banjos, guitars, autoharps, bass—all spun like a cyclone about to pull the house up in the air and whirl it through the starry skies. Strings twanged, basses thumped, fiddles screeched, and voices bawled out indecipherable lyrics. She hesitated and then, with a sigh, entered the fracas and the bliss.

Much later, as people were crawling into their sleeping bags, Eph, carrying a lantern, hobbled out. "Now, fellas," he said, "watch for them snakes. They'll crawl right in your sleeping bags with you 'cause they can sense the heat." People groaned, and Sandy Panther clutched her bag around her.

"And don't forget," he continued, suddenly holding up a pistol. "I sleep with this under my pillow." Then he laughed and everyone else laughed uneasily and he tottered out.

Sandy Panther was exhausted, but she couldn't sleep. She was too worked up by all the music and fellowship. Drinking good (and bad) whiskey did not have a soporific effect on her, as with others. She had played some of the best music so far in her life, and she had won some respect. She lay listening to Donna Cody, Rockandy, and all the other snorers. She could hear people who were obviously having amorous adventures, and then, as the time ticked by, she heard the night rustlings of creatures (no snakes, she hoped) and the calls of a pair of barred owls echoing "Who cooks for you?" in a courtship of predators. Although she didn't know it, she fell asleep to their music.

An alert and wakeful person, however, would have noted that an hour or so later, someone crept out the back door of the house and into the barn. It was Zeke's older brother, Braxton, whom nobody had seen all evening. He and a young woman had planned a tryst. This young woman shall remain nameless, but she is actually a cousin of the now famous folklorist who told me much of this story. This folklorist is known for his meticulous research and accuracy, and he insisted on the details. We can only speculate on his role in the events that followed.

Braxton, unlike Zeke, was a good-looking fellow except for a disfiguring eye condition (probably thyroid eye disease) which caused one eye to look as if it were about to pop out. In all other respects, however, he was muscular, tall, lantern-jawed, the whole bit, and he was interested in getting to know some of the women who came around. He had worked something out with the sturdy blonde woman who had discoursed at some length on grunts and their possible relationship to sonkers. However, she was traveling with a boyfriend, and while he was much more interested in Eph and his music than in her, he was still possessive. So the tryst was to take place by a pallet in the back.

Braxton stumbled in, found the pallet, pulled up the blanket, and slid in next to Donna Cody. Donna Cody murmured, "Duncan?" and started to wake up. Braxton, realizing his mistake, slid out again, only to encounter the sturdy blonde with a stick in her right hand. She swung it with vigor and connected it to the lantern jaw with a terrible twang and thunk. She then connected it to Donna Cody's head. Donna Cody sank back on her bed like a stone. Pandemonium broke loose. Braxton ducked, rolled, and tried to hide by climbing in next to Sandy Panther, who kicked him in the shins. The blonde swung again and connected with Sandy Panther's shins as she tried to go for Braxton. The boyfriend was now up and wrestling with the blonde. Rockandy was baying, and everyone was yelling for everyone else to stop.

BANG! Old Eph, carrying a lantern, was at the entrance, and he had shot his pistol into the air. The whole crowd froze.

"Hey," he said, looking down at Donna Cody, "she looks poorly."

Chapter 17: Miraculous Cures—or Not. Sandy Panther Struggles to Maintain Trust.

Let us cheer the weary traveler,
Cheer the weary traveler,
Let us cheer the weary traveler
Along the Heavenly road.

—"Let Us Cheer the Weary Traveler," traditional

Three days later, Donna Cody finally talked again.

Most of the would-be musicians and folklorists had cleared out, Braxton and the blonde having disappeared first. ("And good riddance!" yelled Old Eph, who had grown tired of his son's amorous adventures and resulting progeny.) Even Guthrie was gone. Apparently, the fracas had put a damper on the festivities, and several relationships had been tested, if not fractured. Eph stalked around muttering while Mrs. Jankey and Zeke snuck into the barn and brought Donna Cody and Sandy Panther soup. They regarded Donna Cody as a perfect test subject. They brought tobacco and rubbed it on Donna Cody's forehead. They brought Emma's liniment. They brought various poultices of spider webs, kerosene, and spices. Emma even put a spider web on Donna Cody's forehead, "read" it, and then blew on it. Sandy Panther tried to get her to explain how she read the web, but all she would say was that it looked like Donna Cody would be fine. Mrs. Jankey's suggestion to eat some webs on moldy bread, however, was firmly rejected.

Zeke spooned something called "sweet shine," which was a mix of licorice and moonshine, between Donna Cody's lips. Sandy Panther tried some and spat it out quickly. "You probably want that marigold cider," said Emma later, explaining it as a concoction of marigolds steeped in apple cider vinegar. Sandy Panther shook her head, and lay there groaning. No one worried too much about her, but they did watch over her as well because she was obviously from not so far away and she could play that banjo. But she was feeling the effects of their terrible encounters.

Rockandy would come and lick their faces every now and then. Emma and Zeke made sure Rockandy was fed.

When no one was around but Rockandy, on Day 3, Donna Cody sat up, and she began talking. First off, she began yelling about men in general and mountain men in particular. Old Eph stalked in, waving a bottle in a threatening manner. Donna Cody admonished him about his no-good son Braxton. While Eph had had plenty of epithet-laden things to say about Braxton himself, he was not pleased that some girl was insulting his offspring. Things grew a bit tense, but certain laws of hospitality, ancient and ingrained, eventually brought the conversation around to fiddle tunes.

"I have heard," said Donna Cody, "that you play some of Dulcie Tobey's tunes. I play one of them, but I wish I knew more."

"Not sure where you heard that," said Old Eph, still a bit gruff. But his eyes sparkled and he leaned forward. "Let's hear it, then," he challenged her. Donna Cody reached for her fiddle and after a little warm-up, launched into "Chickalielee Daisy-O." Everything changed.

"C'mon inside, Donna," he said when she laid her fiddle down. "I'm not sure you've got that all the way right, but you've got it good enough." He helped escort her into the house and hollered back at Sandy Panther, "Bring that banjo along there." Sandy Panther ran after them, grinning.

They played together for a long time. Old Eph had a story for each tune. Donna Cody had to try to write it all down because Ephraim Jankey was not a fan of the tape recorder.

"They take our music and our ways from us like they take our coal," he said. "They're looking for money, like most." Donna Cody put her pencil and paper away guiltily. She stopped asking him for Dulcie Tobey tunes and let him play whatever he wanted. He wasn't going to play much else anyway. And she tried to remember the tunes, how he moved his bow, the rhythms. She hoped she'd gotten a few things down.

Old Eph lavished praise on Sandy Panther, and she beamed. "You know how to play that banjar," he said a few times with increasing emphasis. He whooped at the end of some of the tunes when Sandy Panther, never a subtle player, came crashing down on a note.

The next morning, they hobbled over to the Rambler and headed down the road after saying goodbye. Donna Cody gave Zeke a big hug, and he lit up. Sandy Panther kissed him on the cheek and he blushed. "Go on, now!" Mrs. Jankey said. And they went.

"Donna Cody," Sandy Panther grumbled as they headed down the road, "let's stay at a motel with flush toilets and a sink and some decent beds. How about you cash one of those checks? I'm about worn out with all the trouble you keep getting us into."

"Now that's hardly fair," said Donna Cody, hunched over the steering wheel. "That Braxton…"

"Oh, sure, that Braxton," said Sandy Panther. "But why were we even in this mess except to go find the music and find the people and all that? I will say, though, boy, that was the best music ever, that first night. And you never even heard it, Donna Cody," she added mournfully. "That was the best music ever, though I guess it was especially when most of 'em packed up and left, with just us, mostly. At least you got a few off of him."

Donna Cody sighed and agreed. She consoled herself by tapping out a few of the new tunes and, when Sandy Panther dozed off, she began humming them, too. As they drove down from the notch, Donna Cody saw a halfway decent-sized town down below that soon proclaimed itself as Muleboro. She cashed yet one more traveler's check at the town's bank.

The only place to stay was called The Dew Drop Inn a bit past town. (Hundreds, if not thousands of motels apparently feel this witticism is too good to pass up.) The place consisted of a neon sign, an "office" of sorts, and some 20x20 cabins with peeling white paint on their outsides.

A goat was tied to a stake up behind the cabins. Shifty looking folks lounged at some of the cabin doors.

They went into the office, where they met the proprietor: a scowling, obese man named Frank, with thin oiled hair. He grabbed their money with pudgy, dead white hands. When they entered their assigned cabin, Rockandy immediately became interested in something on the floor that appeared to be a bloodstain. There were no towels. They stripped the beds of the scary-looking sheets and blankets and brought in their sleeping bags. Something scuttled in the corner. The one chair was tied together with rope. The bathtub had about an inch of greenish water in the bottom, and while the toilet flushed, it was stained frightening colors in frightening places. A puddled-up cake of soap measured about 1" by 2". The mud-green walls gave the place the air of a swamp, and the smell of mold only accentuated this impression.

Donna Cody felt queasy. She decided to mix up some of The Wondrous Balsam with some sweet shine of Mrs. Jankey's.

"Donna Cody," Sandy Panther said warily, "I don't think mixing these is a good idea."

"Sandy Panther, I have found both remedies here extremely helpful. Combining them should be felicitous."

"Your funeral," said Sandy Panther. She and Rockandy watched with apprehension. Donna Cody downed the potion, which looked like something an Evil Stepmother would have cooked up. She stood there for a minute, triumphant, and then she began gagging. She tore into the bathroom and violently threw up in the sink. Rockandy followed her as she staggered back and threw herself on the bed, where she passed out. Sandy Panther watched the whole thing stoically. While she cared a great deal for Donna Cody, at this point she was fed up.

Seeing that Donna Cody was still breathing and sleeping and that Rockandy was guarding her and that the stench of the sink was pretty terrible, she decided she needed to take a walk and ponder her next move. She also did not feel so well and hoped some fresh air would do her some good. After opening a window, which took some doing, she walked out and past the other cabins. Some ne'er-do-wells sitting outside the doors hooted at her and called out various names that women in our benighted culture have, all too often, learned to ignore. At least most women. Sandy Panther was not most women.

"Shut your creepy faces, you morons," she called, after she had strolled to what she thought was a safe distance.

Their responses will not be repeated here, but at least two of the loungers jumped to their feet to give chase. They were dissuaded, however, when Frank waddled out and told them all to settle down before he called the law. He could bellow like an ox, and his arms looked like they could punch through a millstone. Sandy Panther continued on her way, strolling down the forlorn streets to town. Beautiful old brick buildings were now boarded up, and a sad little store offered sagging and tired groceries. A tavern slouched on the corner. No one bothered her, and she finally wandered back to the Dew Drop. Luckily, the men had disappeared. She still felt queasy and ached all over.

When she stepped in their cabin, she saw that Donna Cody was up and about, organizing their belongings. The sink was clean. Apparently, she now felt much better.

"Sandy Panther, you should try some of this. I think I've created a new medicine here." she crowed excitedly.

Sandy Panther, still feeling queasy, made a terrible mistake. She drank the potion.

The next morning, Sandy Panther was still groaning in bed. She couldn't throw up even though she wanted to, and she was a horrible green color. Donna Cody was worried about her and wanted to go buy some chicken soup. She wasn't sure how she was going to cook it as the pump on her wonderful little stove had broken. She went in the office to ask Frank about some kitchen facilities. Mine Host was not disposed to offer any.

"You gals need to pay for today before we talk about anything else," he said, narrowing his eyes. Donna Cody did not want to pay for another day.

"Sir, my friend is deathly sick, and I'm trying to help her get better so that we can leave," she said firmly.

"This is a motel, not a hospital, ma'am. You better pay before I throw you out." He could easily throw them all into next week as far as Donna Cody could tell, eyeing him carefully. But her dander was up.

"Sir," she said, "I am not paying if I'm not staying. Some things come first. I will return from town shortly," and she ran out and jumped in the Rambler, Frank huffing and puffing after her and yelling.

"You'd better come back soon. I'll kick that friend of yours out and sell that dog…"

But Donna Cody kept on driving, muttering comebacks all the while. She could have used Sandy Panther's help in the last endeavor.

Frank was not amused. He hauled himself up, stormed over, barged into the cabin, dragged Sandy Panther off the bed, and threw her outside. Rockandy bayed, bit, and yelped and got a kick in the ribs. He slunk off. Frank heaved more of their belongings out on the dirt and stumped back to his office. Sandy Panther raised herself up, staggered, looked wildly around for the Rambler, concluded that Donna Cody had abandoned her, and began using language that beat anything the ne'er-do-wells could conjure up. The scene had drawn them all out, and they laughed raucously. One of them said, "Hey, boys, let's give her some fun!" Sandy Panther balled up her fists, expecting the worst. But she was too sick.

They grabbed her and threw her to the ground in the middle of two thick blankets. Sandy Panther was outraged, terrified, and mystified until suddenly—whoosh! She was up in the air, scrambling around like a cat, landing in the blankets, then tossed up again, curled in fetal position, up again. This went on for some time, the men laughing so hard that finally they couldn't toss her up anymore. They dumped her on the ground and strolled back to their perches outside the cabins, spitting tobacco, laughing, and ignoring the crumpled-up heap that was Sandy Panther.

Donna Cody returned to this scene of mayhem as the last throw occurred. She actually laughed at the comical sight of Sandy Panther twisting in the air. But when her companion lay stunned on the ground, Rockandy running back and licking every exposed part of her, Donna Cody sprang into action. She loaded up all the strewn belongings and shoved Sandy Panther (who groaned horribly) and Rockandy into the car. Frank waddled out, quickly figured out what was going on and lumbered toward them. Donna Cody, who was getting more used to quick escapes, ran around throwing their belongings in the car, and then jumped in and gunned the Rambler, doing at least 25 mph as she sped off. Sandy Panther had enough strength to lean out the window, give the whole crowd the finger, and yell some extremely derogatory things. The last sound in her ears was laughter and a hawk and splat of tobacco juice from one of the men standing there, watching.

Chapter 18: A Disgusting Chapter.

Great green gobs of greasy, grimy gopher guts
Mutilated monkey meat, bitsy baby birdy's feet
One quart can of all-purpose porpoise pus
Floating in pink lemonade—think of me without a spoon!

— "Greasy Grimy Gopher Guts," public domain children's song, as sung
by your author

Donna Cody and Sandy Panther and Rockandy found themselves
driving between dry fields of stubble on a dusty dirt road. It was hot, and
the Rambler had no AC. They had to use what some folks called "4/60
air conditioning," except Donna Cody would never have considered going
60 mph.[26] That was back in the day when you used power steering by
Armstrong and power brakes by Legstrong. Those were the days when
you put up or shut up. But even while choking from the dust and guzzling
one of the colas that Donna Cody had thoughtfully purchased to settle
their stomachs, Sandy Panther was making her fury known.

"I'll tell you what, Donna Cody," said Sandy Panther. "I have just
about had enough of this. Those ruffians almost killed me, and you were
laughing. Oh, yeah, you can laugh, but flying through the air is no joke.
My back is paining me. I feel like I'm going to puke any minute. I've been
washed up and hung out to dry. I'm shivering like a dog pooping a peach
pit, and I'm chugged full with all these shenanigans."

Donna Cody pulled the Rambler over to the side of the road and
looked directly at Sandy Panther.

"Do you want to leave?" she said. Then she began choking and
spewing out cola.

"Hmm," grumbled Sandy Panther, ignoring Donna Cody's distressed

---

[26] 4/60 Air conditioning means rolling down your four windows and going 60
mph.

noises, "OK, well, I guess I'd like to make our record and show everybody some licks. We've seen and heard plenty enough."

"Look," choked out Donna Cody, who was gazing in the side mirror.

"Lord," said Sandy Panther as she stuck her head out the window and looked to her left. A huge cloud of dust was barreling or rather, lumbering toward them from the field. As it got closer, Donna Cody tried to start the car, but either the Rambler was playing tricks or (more likely) Donna Cody was too scared and nervous and shaky from her recent illness to start it.

"What's the matter with you?" said Sandy Panther. "Whatever it is, it'll be by us in a minute."

"No it won't," said Donna Cody, writhing around with the shift and flooding the engine. "It's that Frank and those men! They're coming after us. That's it!" She jumped out and pulled out Old Bessie.

"Wait, wait!" screamed Sandy Panther over the din. "Listen! Get back in here!"

"Listen to what?"

"It's cows, Donna Cody. They're runnin', and I'll bet you that means a bull. Get in here!"

"I don't see any—yikes!" And scrambled into the Rambler just as a huge bull came charging at her. He bumped at the Rambler instead, getting a horn caught in the grill and lifting it a little off the ground.

"Get away from my car!" screamed Donna Cody, starting to open the door again.

"Are you completely crazy?" yelled Sandy Panther, holding on to her. "Just wait and let it all calm down—Hell and high water!" she added as the bull gave them a shake.

The bull stayed stuck. He thrashed and crashed. "What a way to die," thought Donna Cody morosely. Every thump hurt her to the core. Aunt Jane's beautiful Rambler had come to this. Sandy Panther was yelling expletives and Rockandy was barking. But the dust was settling, the cows were past, and then, suddenly, the bull was free and loping heavily after them.

They shakily got out of the car and surveyed the damage. One part of the grill was twisted up, but otherwise, it wasn't that bad. Donna Cody shuddered with relief, but she was shaking.

"Sandy Panther, please get me that Balsam-and-shine."

"That stuff is nasty. Oh, OK." Donna Cody looked like she was about to fall over. Sandy Panther put the bottle in her hand, and Donna Cody took a huge swig, her hand shaking all the while. She slid down to the ground and sat there, moaning, leaning against the Rambler. Rockandy came over and sniffed her. Her lips were an odd shade, a light green. As Sandy Panther solicitously bent over to investigate, Donna Cody projectile vomited directly into her face.

"Guh! Argh!" bubbled Sandy Panther, who forthwith vomited back on Donna Cody. Rockandy barked and backed off. Donna Cody passed out. Sandy Panther reached around her into the Rambler's back seat and tried to find something to clean up with. As Sandy Panther grabbed a shirt and mopped her face (gagging all the while), she screamed, "That's it! That's it! I can't put up with this! It's been fire in the frying pan right into Hell 'n' gone!"

This stirred Donna Cody to consciousness. She motioned for the shirt and wiped her face with a clean part of it. The smell was horrible. She threw the shirt away into the field.

"Sandy Panther," she gasped, stumbling to her feet, "we need to find a better motel and sleep in some good beds."

"MOTEL!" screamed Sandy Panther. "BEDS! Look where that got us the last time! I'm not getting thrown around like some dog—no offense, Rockandy—and will that car even start?"

"It's going to have to start. At least we have to push it off the road," said Donna Cody. "Who knows what will come through here next?" She scrambled up unsteadily.

Sandy Panther looked wildly around. "Let's get in there and try it," she said. "How 'bout I give it a whirl?"

It was a measure of just how bad Donna Cody felt that she acquiesced. Sandy Panther climbed in.

" 'Bout time you let me drive this thing," she muttered. "Whew, I smell gas. Bet she flooded it. Let's see, Mr. Bull, if you made it worse or better."

The Rambler started up without a hitch.

"See now? You pump that accelerator like a woodpecker on a tree and wonder why it don't work. Let's get in and let me drive."

Donna Cody sullenly shooed Rockandy into the back and eased herself into the unfamiliar passenger seat.

"Just for a little way till we get out of here," she said. In a minute, she was asleep.

"Whew," said Sandy Panther to herself and Rockandy. "I got me some bad breath, but that's better than no breath, I guess. Now, let's see what this old beauty can do!" They shot down the road.

Chapter 19: Lost Again. On the Hunt. A New Companion. An Uncomfortable Tavern. Scary Noises.

Oh where, oh where has my little dog gone?
Oh where, oh where can he be?
With his ears cut short, and his tail cut long,
Oh where, oh where is he?

—"Der Deitcher's Dog" or "Oh Where, Oh Where Ish Mine Little Dog Gone," by Septimus Winner

In the next few days they explored some back roads that wandered all over through towns so tiny that they didn't have banks or, sometimes, even much in the way of a store, though they could always find gas stations. They also found a fiddler or two, but mostly they were met with suspicion and laconic responses. Donna Cody, as usual, managed to offend people left and right, and even Sandy Panther batting her eyelashes didn't have much effect. Luckily, the nights were warm, and no one came around where they camped. A few days later, they woke up to a fierce morning heat that felt like a racehorse about to burst out of the stable and trample them into the ground. They quickly fed and watered Rockandy and took off down the road.

"Donna Cody," Sandy Panther said, "none of this is getting us anywhere. You might have recorded a few things, but mostly you're just getting everyone mad at us. We were supposed to be finding the folks with the old music, not fighting with each Tom, Dick, and Harry that comes along spoiling for a rumpus."

"Sandy Panther, you are right. And I forgive you your own part in this."

"Wait, what?"

"Hitting people with banjos. Fooling around with blankets and men, that's the problem, Sandy Panther."

Sandy Panther squawked in outrage. The squabble continued for some time, with Donna Cody remaining maddeningly calm and Sandy

Panther yelling and thumping her fist on the side door. Eventually, she gave it up and went to sleep in the thick heat. She woke to find Donna Cody turning off on a side road to follow the call of nature. Everyone else went out to do likewise.

"So we haven't passed a store or anything? I am starving, Donna Cody," said Sandy Panther. "And Rockandy's going to run out of food soon. And we need some more water."

"Well, we'll keep driving. We're bound to find something," said Donna Cody.

"I still want to find a good motel."

"What we need is a bank. But a motel might be a good idea. I could probably cash a check there."

"Yeah. One of those fancy ones with neon signs and those vibrating beds and maybe even a pool," said Sandy Panther, also finishing up. Rockandy sauntered back from the woods.

"Let's try exploring up this way," said Donna Cody as they loaded up.

"I don't know," said Sandy Panther. "You're getting off the main road now."

"But it's not a main road if there's nothing on it," remonstrated Donna Cody.

"Fine, why not," said Sandy Panther. "We've still got some gas, looks like," she said, peering over.

The Rambler was jouncing through potholes so that Donna Cody had to drive even more slowly. There were no other cars. They noticed dense forest on either side. The dark descended and the road became a path in the tunnel of the Rambler's lights.

"Hmm," mused Donna Cody. "Perhaps I took a wrong turn."

"Not this again. So much for a motel," said Sandy Panther. "I guess—" but then they saw a bunch of lights coming at them. They were tiny little lights and barely twinkled, but they flashed around jumpily.

"Ah, here we go," said Donna Cody. "You see, Sandy Panther? It *is* a road. There are the headlights. I think we'll find something down there."

"Road? That ain't no road. Look at them lights!" said Sandy Panther. "Oh, Lord. They ain't natural. It's ghosts, Donna Cody, I just know it!"

The lights continued to bob around mysteriously and soon came closer and got a little bigger.

Donna Cody stopped the car and pulled over. Lightning bugs were flashing in the woods, and as the other lights came slowly down the road, it was if some strange and menacing fairy world were rising up to meet them. She thought of the fairies you didn't want to meet—the human-sized ones who took you underground for a hundred years or made you sick with longing and despair.

"Lord, Donna Cody, you think it's flying saucers?" chattered Sandy Panther.

And then, they both let out a yell as Rockandy bayed at the top of his lungs.

The lights began moving toward them at a faster pace. They could hear running and baying and shouts.

"Oh for the love of," said Sandy Panther, exasperated with herself and her fears. "It's a hunt. Probably 'coons."

"A hunt," Donna Cody said, eagerly. "Just think, Sandy Panther. The music of the hunt. 'The Keeper Did a-Hunting Go' and 'Old Blue' and 'The Tennessee Mountain Foxchase.' Old Bangum. Billy Barlowe. Reynard. Away, away, bound for the mountain."

Sandy Panther shook her head, while Donna Cody threw open the car door and scrambled out, with Rockandy bounding out over her lap and into the oncoming bobbing lights, baying like a demon.

"Rockandy!" Donna Cody shouted. But she shouted in vain. And then she saw the lights were flashlights and strange lanterns that refracted the light in odd ways. She was surrounded by a group of men and dogs, some of the latter yipping and growling dangerously, the former encircling her in a frightening manner. Sandy Panther was crouched down in the Rambler.

"This your dog?" one of the men asked gruffly, holding Rockandy authoritatively by the collar. "You need to get him under control." Then, warming a bit, "He's a fine specimen—nice ears," he said as he stroked them. "He a Bluetick?"

"Partly, we think," said Donna Cody, putting Rockandy in a sit-stay.

" 'Course, those legs are a little different," another man chimed in. "You know much about his sire or dam?" They were soon in the midst of an involved dog discussion. Finally, Sandy Panther, who had crept out once she heard voices, grew impatient.

"What are you fellows hunting?" she asked.

" 'Coon, naturally," the first man replied. "But this girl got herself in trouble—" and they now saw that the others were carrying a dog on an improvised litter of tree branches.

"And you need to put her down, George," said one of the men carrying the litter. "She's too bit up."

"She's your dog," another man said gruffly. "You gotta be responsible for her."

"What?" said Donna Cody. "You can't kill her!" She leaned down and looked: bite marks were on the small dog's face, neck, and chest. Her shoulder under her shiny black coat looked horribly out of place. She had brown "gloves" up her small legs, brown ribbons up side of face, and a short stumpy tail. She was a German hunting terrier.

"She lost her gameness," someone else said.[27]

---

[27] "Gameness" describes a dog's willingness to sacrifice all and keep on going no matter what, whether it's a fight or a hunt. Sometimes it's about being

"Damn Nazi dog anyway," said another. "Best thing to get rid of 'em. No good hunting to ground."

"Shut up," said George, the first man. "Just keep carrying her. I've bred three generations of her line. She's a good girl."

"Maybe you can get a ride with these young *ladies,*" said the man who had made the Nazi comment. (He said "ladies" the way you might say *idiots.*)

"Certainly, we'll give you a ride," said Donna Cody, while Sandy Panther, who had edged over, was drawing her finger across her throat. Donna Cody didn't look at her, but even if she had, she would have ignored her as usual. But one of the hunters looked over. Sandy Panther abruptly stopped gesturing and looked at the ground.

"Yeah, get a ride with the little ladies!" the hunter jeered. "Look at that one there! What's your name, honeybunch?"

George was a tall man, built like a mountain. He knocked the jeering man down. Someone else tried to restrain George. Men and dogs swarmed chaotically. Remarkably, Donna Cody, Sandy Panther, and Rockandy jumped back in the Rambler rather than joining in the fray. Apparently, they had learned a few things.

"Turn her around, Donna Cody, and let's get outta here," muttered Sandy Panther. Rockandy was whining plaintively, though. Donna Cody looked at him.

"You know, Sandy Panther," she said, "I think Rockandy wants us to rescue that poor dog."

"For crying out loud," spluttered Sandy Panther, slapping herself upside of her head. "Can't you ever stay out of trouble?"

---

vicious, but the great game dogs have loving hearts combined with bravery, focus, and tenacity.

But her remonstrances were useless. Donna Cody slipped out and through the brawl, and with adrenaline-charged strength, grabbed the litter, pulled it to the door and lifted the dog up into the back seat. The bitch was a bloody mess but so close to death's door that she hardly even whimpered. Rockandy did, though, and he began licking her wounds.

"Hey!" said George, rising from the ground on one elbow.

"What the hell?" said another man, staggering around. The rest of the dogs set up a howl, and it was to this music and a rain of curses and shouts that the Rambler spun around and took off down the road, men and dogs pursuing it. "Look out for Donna Cody! She is the Queen of Crazy!" called Sandy Panther out the window. For once, Donna Cody drove at a good clip, trying to miss the worst potholes. Finally, the men and dogs and the lights faded out.

"We'll name her Blue," said Donna Cody, as they pulled back onto the main road.

"Sure we will. Let's go find a hot dinner," said Sandy Panther. "I've picked me up a little change." And indeed, she had managed to filch a wallet before running from the fight.

"Sandy Panther! That's stealing. We need to go back."

"Excuse me, but what's that poor misbegotten dog if not stolen property?"

"Sandy Panther, you have me there," said Donna Cody. "But it still isn't right."

"Fine." Sandy Panther threw the wallet out the window. "They'll find it."

Donna Cody let out an exasperated sigh, but she kept driving, and after a while began humming "Blue, You Good Dog, You" after noting its probable origins in the Mississippi Valley, and its unfortunate recent popularity with the folk revivalists.

As they drove onto the main road, Sandy Panther looked back at Blue and Rockandy lying together and murmured, "You know, Donna Cody, you really are the Queen of Crazy."

Donna Cody shrugged. "While I find that title offensive, Sandy Panther, I will say that if 'crazy' means sticking to one's principles, then so be it. You can call me all the names you want, but I am who I am, and I do the best I can." She went on to say that her real calling, if Sandy Panther could remember it, was hunting for songs and tunes, not critters or even dogs, though, Blue had needed someone who knew how to care for dogs, and Rockandy had needed a companion. She kept this up until they finally saw a neon sign flickering. Sure enough, the sign proclaimed that this was The Dew Drop Inn. Sandy Panther shuddered, but they convinced themselves that there probably wasn't much else anywhere near and that one Dew Drop Inn wasn't necessarily another Dew Drop Inn and that they needed a meal and that the Rambler needed some gas. A sullen man gassed up the car and took a lot of Sandy Panther's newly acquired cash. They parked.

The tiny yellow light over this Dew Drop Inn's front door didn't begin to contend against the dark of the moonless night, and when they opened the door, it creaked and squeaked. Inside was a bar with a loud group of men sitting at it. The air was hazy with smoke, and the lights were low. Donna Cody was quickly dismissed as ineligible, but Sandy Panther, even in her current disheveled state, got a few appreciative stares. The archetype of all slatternly waitresses came out to wave them to a rickety table and take their order. With the rest of their newfound loot, they managed a fine meal of steak and potatoes. They actually ordered three so that Rockandy would have something good, and Blue would have something tempting that would induce her to eat. Donna Cody took it out to the car and put it on the back seat.

"It's creepy out there," she said when she came back. "Windy as the dickens. And there's something crashing around off in the distance. What could that be at this time of night here in the middle of nowhere?"

And as they sat chewing, they continued a conversation to be described in the next chapter.

Chapter 20: Storytelling Interruptus. The Scary Noise Is Found Out.

Well, if frogs had wings and snakes had hair
And automobiles went flying through the air
And if watermelons grew on a huckleberry vine,
We'd have winter in the sunny summertime.

—"Turkey in the Straw," traditional

"Whatever that noise is," said Donna Cody, "it doesn't concern us. And remember, Sandy Panther [sententiously], we're always somewhere."

Sandy Panther was mopping up the last bit of gravy on her plate with some concentration and eyeing Donna Cody's half-eaten plate with interest. Donna Cody passed it over to her.

"You know," said Donna Cody dreamily, "we are always somewhere, all of us, but we don't even think about it or know it. It's somewhere to the people who live there, maybe their whole lives. It's somewhere to the animals, to the trees, to the rocks."

"I do not know what you are talking about," said Sandy Panther. She flagged the waitress down by violently waving her arms and then asked for a whole berry pie. "We can eat most of it later," she said defensively.

Donna Cody ordered coffee. They asked about a room and were flabbergasted when told there weren't any.

"Now, come on—you don't have that many folks even parked here," said Sandy Panther.

The waitress gave them a cold eye, her eyeliner emphasizing a certain feral quality. "I don't have to make no excuses to you. Boss says we ain't got no rooms, we ain't got 'em."

"Fine," said Sandy Panther, carefully placing a penny in her glass of water. The waitress hissed and swished away.

"What are you doing there?" asked Donna Cody. Sandy Panther had grabbed the menu, put it over the top of the glass, and then flipped the whole thing over. She whipped the sodden menu out.

"Let her try to clean that up," said Sandy Panther.

"Oh, that's terrible," said Donna Cody. "You shouldn't do that." She reached for the glass, but Sandy Panther batted her hand away.

"You touch it, and you're making a mess. Let Miss Smartypants get it."

"Sometimes, you are impossible, Sandy Panther. You got your good meal, but nothing's enough. Though it does look like we'll be camping again."

The clientele did not make either of them feel like camping nearby. When they stepped outside, the wind was up, and the crashing, banging noises were louder.

"Whoa, what *is* that?" asked Sandy Panther.

"That's the noises I told you about. We should ask the bartender," said Donna Cody.

"Probably better than getting anything out of ol' Barbie, that's for sure," said Sandy Panther. "You first." Neither of them went in.

The dogs had finished their meals, and Blue was perking up a bit. But she whimpered as they started up the car, panting with each little jolt.

The banging noises were louder as they pulled into a little turnoff in the darkest part of the forest. Both of them were thinking of the hunters and the creepy folks in the latest Dew Drop Inn. And they were thinking of some of the other scary people they had met. As they set up their little camp, Donna Cody took out Bessie and put it beside her makeshift pillow of old clothes. Sandy Panther eyed it with trepidation.

"Donna Cody, I can't sleep yet. Let's build a little fire."

"All right. It's a little dangerous, but it will warm up the dogs."

Neither of them said anything about the banging, which seemed to have quieted down along with the wind.

"Sandy Panther?"

"Hmmm?"

"If anything happens to me, will you make sure to go back and tell Mabel … and Duncan?" Her voice broke a little at the end.

"Donna Cody, nothing is going to happen to you," said Sandy Panther, entirely unconvincingly. "But you know, this whole Duncan business…"

"There's no 'Duncan business,' Sandy Panther."

"Sure there isn't." (Smugly.)

Changing the subject: "What *is* that banging? I think I should go see." Reaching for the gun.

"No, no, no, no, no, no! And besides, Donna Cody, look at those poor dogs. Look at Blue. She don't need no more adventure tonight. Let's sit here and I'll tell you an old story I heard when I was a squirt."

Donna Cody relaxed, put the pistol down (but still in easy reach). The fire was crackling and the warmth, at least on her front, was mellowing her. The wind had died down, along with the banging noises. She beckoned to Sandy Panther to proceed.

Sandy Panther, sated, warm, commenced.

"OK, then. This is called 'The Sister's Dream.' Though I've also heard it called 'The Old Four Corner.' "

"Hmm, these are not titles I know. What is your source for this tale?"

"If you mean where'd I get it, I believe it was Auntie Rufe's sister's boy told it to me. He's a talker, I will tell you. Can talk anyone into anything. . ."

"What about his source, then? Was it your aunt's sister?"

"I don't know; that boy had tales from all over."

"I guess you should tell it."

"That's what I was doing, Donna Cody, when you interrupted."

"All I did was ask you where it was from."

"And interrupted. Now listen. Once there were three sisters. One, two, three. They—"

"Sandy Panther, we already know there are three of them. You don't need to count them out again. *Three*, you know, is a common number in Western European folk and fairy tales—"

"Are you gonna let me finish? This is the way you tell it. If you don't like it—"

"No, go ahead," said Donna Cody, slightly chastened.

"OK, then. Once there were three sisters. One, two, three. They—"

"Sandy Panther, you already told that part."

Dead silence.

"OK. Just tell it."

A long, drawn-out breath. "I'll tell it to you the way I heard it. These three sisters all loved each other, but then the first one up and died. Then the second one died. Both sisters died." Donna Cody began to say something and caught herself in time.

"The third sister's name was Maisie. Hmmm," Sandy Panther paused, scratching her head. "I think the first sister's name was Daisy, but then what was the second's? Crazy? Like you? Lazy? Like me?" Laughter. And at this point, she began trying out all the rhymes: "Baisie?" Brasie? Blaisie? Caisie?"

"You have got to be kidding me!" burst out Donna Cody. "Get on with it! What do we care what her name is? How about you go with 'Crazy'?"

A long, tense silence.

Finally: "Maisie was sleeping and she had a dream in which her two sisters appeared, and Maisie, while she was still asleep, cried out. Her poor old father ran in and heard Maisie say in a creepy voice—" (and here, Sandy Panther dropped her voice down low), " 'You must find the old four corner and ground crumble it open.'"

"What? Sandy Panther, that's not even English."

"Donna Cody. That is the way people talk in their sleep sometimes."

"It is unlikely. I have certainly never heard anything like that."

"Who have you heard talk in their sleep?"

"My mother told me that I used to do it. One night I came into their bedroom dragging a sheet around me. My head had poked through a rip, and I was moaning and tugging at it and telling them to get the rope off from around my neck. But I spoke English." Another long silence. "OK, then. Keep going."

A little snarl. But Sandy Panther dropped back to her sing-songy voice: " 'You must find the old four corner and ground crumble it open,' she said, and then Maisie was wailing and weeping, the wind whistling and wandering. And Daisy and—what is that other sister's name? If I could only remember it…"

"It doesn't matter," Donna Cody burst in with exasperation. "What is the four corner thing? Do you mean she has to dig it up? Is it a box? Is it treasure? The idea of the dead revealing hidden treasure, is, of course, a well-known motif…"

Sandy Panther jumped up in a fury. "That's it! Forget it! I'm not telling you any more! You are the worst story spoiler ever!" And even with begging and pleading that was it. Sandy Panther pulled out her sleeping bag and crawled in and at least pretended to go to sleep.

It wasn't a good night. The wind grew wilder again, along with the banging, off and on all night. Both women woke often. Blue whimpered in the car, and Donna Cody had to let her out in the middle of the night and then get her back in. Blue was pitiable. Donna Cody stubbed her toe on the way back to her sleeping bag. The bushes rustled as winged things whirred over them. There were roots under them they hadn't seen when they laid out their ponchos, but they were too tired to get up and do anything about it, as one usually is when camping.

The morning finally came, gray and wet, but the winds, at least, had died down again along with the banging. They made a quick breakfast of the rest of the pie. Blue was looking better, but she was still limp and had to be carried in and out of the back seat of the Rambler. Rockandy lay close by her side. Sandy Panther was brusque and slamming things around more than they needed to be. The banging started up after they had been driving a while, but there was no way out but through.

"You're a good companion, Sandy Panther," said Donna Cody. "You've put up with a lot." At this, Sandy Panther was somewhat mollified. The banging was getting louder again, and they were both getting more nervous but trying not to show it.

Suddenly, as they drove out to a cleared bluff, they saw a precipitous drop and a river below, looking like part of a tiny, other world. The road ahead wound down in graceful curves. And the banging was revealed as a whole group of shantyboats with their bows sheathed in metal and trains of little boats all bumped into each other in the wild waters of a high-running river. Sandy Panther began to laugh with relief. Donna Cody, however, shook all over for a minute with a pent-up release and actually punched Sandy Panther on the arm.

"Yow!" said Sandy Panther. "So much for all those fine words about my friendship and companionship! I'm gone, I'm going, I went! Watch me!" And started to open her door.

Donna Cody said her apologies, once more promised that they were going to find the motherlode of tunes and songs and that she and Sandy Panther would make records and be famous. Sandy Panther shook her head but shut the door again, and they putted down the road toward the shantyboats, where they saw a little ferry that could take them across the river.

Chapter 21: Boats. A Magic Fiddle. Another Storyteller Insulted and Offended.

I've always been cheerful and easy,
And scarce have I needed a foe.
While some after money run crazy,
I merrily Rosin'd the Beau.

—"Old Rosin the Beau," traditional

By the time they arrived at the river, the ferry was sitting tied up on the other side. No one was at the dock, but under a long line of willow trees that overhung the bank, they found a secret world of squatter shacks, a small, makeshift town. Children were playing, their hair streaming out in the wind, people were walking up and down makeshift gangplanks, and dogs barked and ran along the shore. The boats continued to bang into each other in a calamitous riot. They were mostly scows, with flat-roofed cabins pieced together out of every imaginable and unimaginable piece of flotsam and jetsam of the world: driftwood, old boards, chunks of sheet metal, hoods of cars, old windows, and doors. On top of the roofs, crates of chickens clucked, and crates of shoats oinked. Blue smoke drifted out of some of the crooked blackened stovepipes. Piles of nets and lines lay all over the decks, along with long sweep oars. There were canvas boat cabins, lots of lard cans (which they later found out were great for storing food), rope mooring lines, spars. Some of the nicer boats had round porthole windows, shutters, or even chimneys. And many of the boats were more like miniature trains, with lines attached to flat-bottomed aluminum or wooden jon boats about fourteen feet long, flat bottomed, square at both ends, oars shelved and often lying on top of all manner of junk.

An older woman sat in an armless rocking chair on the deck of one of the nicer boats. She was playing a fiddle that even from a distance, and with all the other racket, sounded as rich and dark and full as anything they had ever heard. Donna Cody immediately went nuts, forgot all about the ferry, parked the Rambler beside the ferry ramp, and jumped out of the car, striding toward the boat.

After their night in the woods and other adventures, she was a scruffy figure, as was Sandy Panther strolling behind, taking her time and smoking a morning cigar now that they were outside the car. Rockandy galloped out ahead to frolic with the dogs, while Blue whined from the back seat of the car. All in all, they fit in pretty well with the rest of the inhabitants.

The fiddler's boat proclaimed its name, *The Drifter*, on the bow in gold script against a vivid green. Geraniums and marigolds in pots lined the deck. A cat curled up on a little hooked rug. (It darted inside when it saw Rockandy.) Unlike many of the other boats, everything was neat and tidy, the ropes coiled, the fish boxes lined up.

"Hello," said Donna Cody, once the tune ended.

"Hello," said the woman. "What can I do for you?" She was old to them, and round as a butterball but strangely graceful as she sat there looking at them, her fiddle dangling from one hand, her bow from the other.

"I'm a fiddler, ma'am, and I find your fiddling singular."

"Ah, a fiddler. Come right aboard. You can come too," she waved to Sandy Panther and Rockandy, who had run up as he saw his mistress walking up the gangplank. Almost immediately, Donna Cody and the woman, whose name turned out to be Mandy Monroe, began talking fiddles and violins. Sandy Panther settled herself on an overturned box and smoked and listened.

Mandy Monroe was a talker. Her violin was a real Stradivarius, according to her dad, bless his departed soul. He had had it from his dad, and you could still see the label inside that told you so.[28] She showed them

---

[28] Reader, be advised that every violin shop has people coming in with "real" Stradivari.

a rattlesnake rattle inside, and they peeked through the f-hole curiously and shook the fiddle.

"Sucks up the moisture from the river. Keeps the mice and bugs out—they don't like the smell. You'll have to get yourself one. But this one is special, put in by my dad long ago. From a 30-foot hoop snake."[29]

"Hmm," said Donna Cody dubiously.

"What the heck, Donna Cody," said Sandy Panther.

"Maybe," said Donna Cody. Mandy went on. The way the rattle moved around meant that all the dust inside would spread out and make the tone sweeter. Donna Cody countered that she had heard that the best old fiddles had toneballs, a clump of dust that gave them their own special sound. Mandy countered back with the old lost varnish recipe story, the one that Stradivarius had, and that it was the varnish that made a fiddle ring out.

They got onto bows and Mandy allowed as how stallion hair was better than mare hair since stallions piss forward, while Donna Cody argued that it was entirely the opposite case and that horse piss supposedly made the hair pull out a sweeter sound.

"Excuse me, ladies," said Sandy Panther, who was getting bored, "but I need to get back to our other dog. She's bad hurt."

"Oh, but I would like to record you if you don't mind, Miss Monroe."

"Let me think 'bout that. But why don't you and your dogs come on back this evening when the fish are biting. They love the sound of the fiddle. Bring that poor dog, too, and I'll look at her. I have some dog doctoring in my past. Meanwhile, I've got my work to do." And she opened her old black case and took out a silk scarf, wrapping the fiddle up carefully. "Putting it to bed," she said. "Keeps the evil away."

---

[29] A hoop snake can grab its tail in its mouth and roll along, so they say. Whether it has rattles is another matter altogether.

"The evil away?" asked Sandy Panther. But Mandy only grunted and didn't say more.

"So," asked Sandy Panther, "where are you going on this boat?"

"Wherever I want, whenever I want," said Mandy. "Sometimes I sit on the deck and think. Other times, I just sit." They realized that they were being dismissed and began to climb down to the shore, but then Mandy called out, "See you for dinner in a few hours." and they assured her they would and that they would bring their instruments. Back at the Rambler, Blue greeted them with frantic tail wagging and whimpers. They immediately began tending to her, wiping out her wounds, taking her off to pee, feeding her. She whined and licked their hands and thumped her tail, her eyes brimming, trying to smile. The wind had died down, so they spread blankets out on the bank and sat with the dogs and their instruments.

"Sandy Panther, I want that fiddle," said Donna Cody as she looked over her own. "You think she would be interested in trading it?"

"Don't seem likely," said Sandy Panther. "Besides, it ain't any better 'n yours. Maybe it's that rattlesnake rattle that makes it good." She snorted.

"Do you think," said Donna Cody icily, "that I don't know anything about violins? You don't realize its value."

"And you do? You think it's a Stradivaripuss or whatever? How much is it worth? And that Mandy, she's OK, but she's full of baloney; anyone can tell."

This bickering went on for a while until Sandy Panther picked up her banjo and began playing some dark mountain minor tunes and ghastly murder ballads. Donna Cody stared off across the river, but after a while she couldn't resist and joined in with the fiddle. Soon a small crowd of children had gathered around them. From the kids, they learned that most folks had been moored here for a while, thanks to something called Urban Development upstream, where they were putting in a huge modern bridge and didn't want any shantyboaters "messing up" the banks.

Sandy Panther hastily tuned and played some more appropriate songs for children like "Jenny Jenkins" and such, which everyone enjoyed. But the kids eventually got bored and wandered off to play on the bank and run with the dogs. The sun finally began to hit the tips of the trees, and so they packed things up, found a few tins of beans for a contribution to the dinner, gathered up the dogs (with Sandy Panther carrying Blue and Donna Cody carrying the banjo and everything else), and they made a slow progress down to *The Drifter*.

First of all, Mandy tended to Blue. She put her on a pile of blankets, cleaned up the wounds, sniffing them, and queried them about what they were putting on them (some Wondrous Balsam), shook her head, and put her own salve on them. Blue stretched out and sighed.

They had a wonderful meal. Mandy Monroe happily accepted the beans, put some bacon and other tasty things in them and served up biscuits, collards fried in bacon grease, and great slabs of ham. She served Chianti to drink, eliciting sighs of content from Sandy Panther. The dogs got some of the ham. Rockandy wolfed his down, while Blue delicately inhaled pieces of hers that Sandy Panther cut up and then fed her. Dessert was a sticky pineapple upside-down cake. Sandy Panther gorged herself. Donna Cody thought wistfully of Duncan and the Leggetts and other luxurious repasts.

Throughout, Mandy Monroe talked. She explained the shantyboat life.

"I was born in the jon boat with the catfish. I learned to help others and they would help me, 'cause you don't go do things only for yourself."

They learned that *The Drifter* could run up a bank, that it was great to fish from, that the river was your bathtub as long as it was clean and you had a deep-watered shore.

"Not that it's so clean anymore," Mandy said. "You see it from the river here, pipes of terrible black stuff a-pourin' in, lot more than ever before."

A glum silence and then she was off again. "The river, she rises, she falls. You always have to be on the watch, you look for anything good floating by, something you can use. But you look out for that driftwood and some of the big stuff—that can take out your boat real fast. One time a car came floating down the river. Yup, you can believe it. That's the shantyboat life, the price of independence. You never know what's going to happen. And then you got to watch the supposed boat pilots who think they own the water and will crash right into you, when the river is God's gift to all of us."

Having washed up, they all went out to the deck, took out their instruments, and played tune after tune and sang song after song. Mandy had the huge rich alto (close to a tenor) so often found in women of a certain age. All around them, people came out to listen and clapped at the end, and a few harmonicas and rhythmic spoons joined in. A lady dragged out a piece of a dock and began stomping along. "My music's in my feet," she cackled. Donna Cody recorded a few things, but soon she was caught up in playing. Time melted away until suddenly the stars were all out, and everyone had gone back home to bed.

Mandy said, "You girls play some interesting tunes. I like your playing a lot, Donna Cody, and I am going to give you something to make it even better." With that, she rummaged in her fiddle case and pulled out something that looked, at first in the dark, like a caterpillar, but then she shook it. It was a rattlesnake rattle. Donna Cody felt ashamed of her greedy thoughts and coveting of Mandy's violin

"Here, give me your fiddle," Mandy said, and she popped the rattle right in the F hole. Donna Cody thanked her profusely, and even played her C. C.'s special tune, "Chickalielee Daisy-O."

"Now that is a crackerjack tune," said Mandy.

"Ain't it, though?" said Sandy Panther.

"I'll reckon there's some history there," said Mandy.

"I'd like to find it out," said Donna Cody.

"I believe that was Dulcie Tobey's tune, now, wasn't it?"

"You know about Dulcie Tobey?" said Donna Cody. "Do you know if she's still alive? Have you ever seen her? Did you ever hear her play?"

"Hmm, no," said Mandy, "but everyone who fiddles, just about, knows *her* name. She whupped all the men at the fiddle contests, made 'em so mad. She could fiddle through a whole night and never blink an eye. She had more tunes 'n you could count, but she had her special ones, her old ones she wouldn't always play for anyone."

"Where was she from?" asked Donna Cody.

"Hmm, Kentucky, maybe up around Hazard. Though some folks say more like West Virginia, some say North Carolina."

"Someone's got to know."

"I reckon that's true. So many mysterious things in the world."

And then the stories began. Even Donna Cody couldn't drag the talk back to Dulcie Tobey. Mandy was a true teller of tales and she was not to be stopped. I will try to tell you one of them, but you have to imagine yourself on a gently rocking deck, the air warm and balmy, the stars so thick that in spots they blotted out the dark sky, only the sounds of slapping water and tiny breezes, little boat nudges instead of bangs and crashes. A little coal fire in a small old bucket contraption created the magical center of light and warmth needed for the best storytelling. Everyone plumped pillows and blankets around themselves on the deck. The dogs slept in the cabin. And Mandy began:

"Ladies, I learned my fiddlin' and my boatin' from my dad and granddad, and Granddad was a river man, piloting flatboats down to Arkansas. He would bring animals, fruit and vegetables, cattle, you name it, all down the river, or maybe families with all their earthly belongings: their stock, their car or wagon, everything. He'd take 'em down the river through the Skillet, the Narrows, the Boiling Pot. That last was the worst, but that's what they paid him for.

"He was taking a family downriver—the Coals, they were named. Lots of kids, an old cow, some odds and ends. Poor as poor could be. The father was a shy, scared man who looked like he never knew where he was. He did what Granddad told him to do to keep afloat. It was a foggy night, fog you could cut with a knife. Granddad was a bit of a drinker, and he'd had a few that night while manning the steering oar, the raft going downstream slick as goose grease. He was feeling pretty good when he came on a bunch of lights you could barely see over the fog. He could make out people dancing to a sprightly tune that Granddad had never heard, and he'd heard a lot. So he hummed it; he liked that tune all right and wanted to learn it there and then and get out his fiddle, but Mr. Coal, he surmised, wasn't up to steering in the strong currents at night.

" 'It's a jolly crowd there,' says Mr. Coal.

" 'Yes indeed, and some fine playing of a fine tune,' says Granddad. 'We can drink to that.'

"They continued on a ways, Granddad humming away, and both of them enjoying the bottle. And after a while, what did they see? Another bunch of lights, people dancing, and someone fiddling the same tune.

" 'Now, if that ain't a coincidence, I don't know what is,' says Granddad.

" 'Sure is a lot of dancing on this river,' says Mr. Coal.

" 'Success to 'em,' says Granddad, raising the bottle. He takes another drink and keeps humming. And then, you guessed it, they go on for a ways, and bingo. Another bunch of lights and dancing and that same tune again.

" 'That's more than coincidence!' said Granddad. 'I know I'm not *that* drunk! Stars say one a.m., and we've been going since sundown. Must be a dance up every creek of this river, and they're all playing the same tune. Grab that rope and we'll tie up at the landing.'

"And so they did that and turns out they had gotten to the Boiling Pot a good bit earlier than Granddad had calculated. They had been going round and round in circles. Granddad talked with that fiddler and they all laughed and he learned that tune, but he named it 'Coal's Pot's a-Boil.' And he passed that tune down to me."

Here, Mandy picked up her fiddle and played a haunting tune with a hitch in it so that it didn't come out even but rather, fell into the first measure, and then did it again. Donna Cody picked up her fiddle and Sandy Panther her banjo. They had to go round the Boiling Pot of the tune many times before Mandy was satisfied that they had it just right.

Mandy told more stories about her granddad. "He used to stretch himself out and say that he was busier than he appeared to be. He'd play a dance all night, go off to hog butchering that morning, get paid with some of the meat, pack it all up on his horse, and the wolves would chase him through the forest, but when they caught up, he'd pull out his fiddle and they'd all back off, especially when he hit the high notes.

At this point, Donna Cody said something about a similar story found in one of her collections, and things got a little tense.

"Are you calling me a liar?" asked Mandy.

"Darn," muttered Sandy Panther.

"The nature of the folktale," Donna Cody began, "is to travel and be adopted by various people, borrowing events and giving them a local color—"

Mandy jumped up and the dogs roused themselves. The night had become deep and dark and silent, that time when so many of us who have tossed and turned for hours finally slither into sleep. Sandy Panther moaned. She knew what was coming. And indeed, before they knew it, they had been kicked off the warm and cozy boat and were straggling back to the car.

"You can't keep your mouth shut, Donna Cody! I have had it! As soon as we make a good friend, you have to go after her, don'tcha? Interrupt her, just like you did me. And then throwing up on me. Laughing while those sons of bitches threw me up in the air!" Sandy Panther was tired and ready to stack up grievances. Before she got further, Donna Cody jumped in and attempted to rationally discuss the situation.

"Sandy Panther, I merely brought up an interesting folkloric fact. And you weren't hurt anyway. You looked funny tossing and turning like that. If you had been in serious trouble, you know I would have come to your defense."

Sandy Panther lengthened her stride to pull out ahead, snorting and muttering. They trudged along in silence.

"Now let's at least get a little shut-eye," she said, grabbing her sleeping bag and falling on top of it in sheer exhaustion. Everyone else followed suit.

Chapter 22: An Unfortunate Encounter with the Justice System.

The next time I seen darlin' Cory,
She was standin' by the banks of the sea.
She had a .44 strapped around her body
And a banjo on her knee.

—"Darling Cory," traditional

The sun was high by the time they woke up.

"What do you want to do about breakfast?" asked Donna Cody.

"Mostly eat it," snarled Sandy Panther.

After a sulky and silent repast of Crown Pilot crackers, sardines, and Cheez Spread, they packed up. Donna Cody drove them carefully onto the tiny ferry, with men at the dock yelling, "Move it up there, then." Once across the river, they crawled up the road to the top of the bluffs and on to new horizons.

At one point, with Donna Cody nodding over the steering wheel and Sandy Panther snoring and waking up with a start when the Rambler lurched, both of them realized they needed more sleep. Donna Cody found a little turnout by a meadow, and after taking the dogs out to do their business, everyone settled down for a nap. Sandy Panther dreamed she was playing a banjo that had a piece of crispy bacon for a neck and a biscuit for a pot. She kept trying to play it but ended up breaking off pieces of the bacon, which she popped into her mouth. Donna Cody dreamed she was whirling round and round in a boiling pot of soup. She knew she had to get out. She kept swimming to the side, trying to pull herself out. Then the whole thing tipped over, and with a roar, the soup poured out.

"Help!" screeched Donna Cody.

"Hot damn, what?" spluttered Sandy Panther, sitting bolt upright.

Blue gave a bark, and Rockandy a snort. They had been having their own dreams.

A school bus painted white roared by with a thrashing racket.

"Holy hogwash," said Sandy Panther. "They look like the devil's chasing them."

"We need to get a move on ourselves," said Donna Cody, jumping up. "It's getting late."

But when they had driven about an hour, they came upon the startling sight of the bus sitting sideways across the road. Around it swarmed a group of young women, mostly black, in stiff shirtwaist dresses the gray-blue of institutional clothes and high school gym suits. They were sitting by the side of the road and singing in beautiful harmonies, snapping their fingers or clapping on the back beat.

An older woman and man dressed in harshly ironed clothes stood off to the side talking. One of the tires of the bus was shattered, and it was obvious that there was no spare. Donna Cody reached for the tape recorder, stashed down behind Sandy Panther's seat.

"Whoa," said Sandy Panther, "you see that?" She pointed to the side of the bus, which bore the title "Nob County Correctional Institute."

Donna Cody was oblivious, listening to the singing. "I most certainly have to record this," she said, digging out her tape recorder and fresh batteries. She stepped out of the car, Rockandy slipping out right behind her. "This is beautiful! And these women probably have some interesting tales to tell," she said, turning back to Sandy Panther.

"Donna Cody. These women have broke the law, and you better not mess with the law down here."

"*Broken* the law," Donna Cody replied, automatically. "And don't be ridiculous. These are modern times. They can't do anything illegal to hurt us. Look at them. I'll bet these young women are wrongfully imprisoned. Look how many of them are colored."

"That's all well and good," said Sandy Panther, looking uneasily at

Donna Cody, "but most of those gals probably deserve to be there. Not that these jails ain't criminal in themselves. I saw this movie once where this lady was chained to a post, and those guards were standing over her like to kill her, and her clothes were all torn so you could see—"

"For Pete's sake," said Donna Cody. "Those prison movies are disgusting."

"Sounds like you know about 'em," said Sandy Panther.

The prisoners had noticed them and so had the guard, who strolled up in a patronizing manner, taking his time and looking down at Donna Cody as if she were a future prisoner herself while giving Sandy Panther a thorough once-over. He was tall, with a buzz cut and glittering eyes. He had a gun in his belt. The woman hung behind him, twisting her hands. She was old and tired, with stringy gray hair.

"Best put that dog on a leash, ma'am," said the man.

"What you doing, way out here?" asked the woman, querulously.

"We think that's our business," said Donna Cody. Sandy Panther cautiously emerged from the car.

"We haven't done nothing wrong," she said, eyeing Donna Cody in a way that would make anyone think they were bank robbers or at least runaways.

"I'm *sure* you haven't," said the man, mockingly, "but these gals have, so you'd best stay back. Keep singing, ladies," he shouted. Everyone stopped singing.

"Fer Christ's sake," said the guard, spinning around and heading toward them. "You smart assin' bitches—"

"Now, Mr. John," said the lady.

But he stopped and just glared, his hand on his hip and thumb hooked in his belt loop in that way some men stand that says, "Look on my works, ye Mighty, and despair!" He was actually a handsome man, with a large angular jaw.

"You've got them in chains!" yelped Donna Cody, just noticing. Sandy Panther kicked her leg in warning.

"These gals broke the law, ma'am, and they have to pay. What we need to do is have Miss Evans here go along with you so that we can get some help with this bus."

"What'd they do?" asked Donna Cody.

"That's not to the goddamn point," snapped Mr. John. "What's to the point is that I am telling you that you need to help the law here before you get in trouble your own selves."

"Oh, we do, do we?" said Donna Cody. "I don't think that's true. And what about their civil rights? Why are there so many Negro girls?"

Mr. John and Miss Evans froze at the mention of "civil rights." Mr. John's face hardened even more, and he stepped toward them a little while Miss Evans's eyes widened and she stepped back a little.

"Oh Lord, Donna Cody, you are so dumb sometimes," moaned Sandy Panther. " 'Course, they done something wrong. They have to pay and get rehabilitated."

Rockandy had stiffened, though Donna Cody had her hand firmly on his collar. Blue whined softly from the Rambler.

The prisoners had stood up and now shuffled a bit nearer, and one of them, a woman with a beehive hairdo, called out, "We ain't hardly done nothing! Don't listen to them! I shot a man who was trying to force himself on me!"

"I passed some bad checks!" said another. "Only for four dollars and seventy-five cents total."

"I don't even get to see my little boy!" called out an older woman.

"What we did is we f___ed with the patriarchy!" shouted a tall black woman with bleached blonde hair. In her rage, she was beautiful, a chiseled face and figure. She could have been a runner. She couldn't have been more than twenty-five.

The guard turned furiously, unstrapping his club. "You shut your filthy mouth, Gina, or I'll shut it so you don't say nothin' for a long time!" He took a step toward her, but Miss Evans grabbed his elbow.

"Mr. John, don't you want to be careful?" she quavered. "You know those government people been givin' us a lot of trouble, and here we are out in the open and all."

Mr. John shook off her hand, let out a string of unfortunate language, and snarled, "Those n_____-lovin' sons of bitches in Washington. Excuse me, ma'am—" (here he nodded to Miss Evans), "but first you got the n_____, now you got these women, and they're turning it all upside down."

"You bet we are, you poor piece of white trash!" shouted Gina. Shrieks of laughter from the prisoners. "I'm writing a whole book about you and your kind. Some of us have been to college, some of us have read *The Feminine Mystique,* you dumb cracker."

Mr. John erupted into action, tore loose from Miss Evans's restraining hand, ran over and began beating Gina with his truncheon. It was a terrible sound. Gina threw her arms around her head and fell to the ground. The other prisoners kicked at Mr. John, who waved his club around and reached for his gun.

"Oh, no, girls, no!" cried Miss Evans. "Mr. John, Mr. John! You don't want to be doing that!" She stumbled in and tried to pull him back, but she was flung to the ground.

BAM! A shot went off and everyone stopped dead. Donna Cody was standing there with Old Bessie.

"Lord God. You have done it now," said Sandy Panther.

"That's enough of all this!" said Donna Cody, her voice a bit wobbly. "Now you, Mr. John, whatever your name is, stay right there. You, Miss Evans, you get his gun and that club. You can say we made you do it. There, now, don't be afraid—grab it—no, hey, don't you move, sir. Don't think I can't shoot you where it hurts to be a man. Now, put that gun over here by us." Miss Evans dropped the gun at Donna Cody's feet.

Everyone suddenly burst out talking, whooping, crying, Gina sobbing and rocking, Mr. John snarling but then, surprising everyone, collapsing on the ground and crying with rage.

"Yeah, cry, you piece of shit," cackled Gina. "You know you gonna get in trouble, don't you?" More vituperation burst from the other prisoners, but Miss Evans walked over to look at Gina's rapidly developing bruises. She was crying and trying to find something to do to help.

"Miss Evans, you're a good one," said someone.

"Mmm-hmm," others asserted. "Oh yeah."

They got Mr. John put in the bus and tied him to a seat, with some rope that Duncan had thoughtfully put in the Rambler's trunk. Donna Cody got water and some old clothes and offered them to the prisoners for washing up. Rockandy ran around barking, whining, and licking people. Even Blue managed to crawl out and stand looking at the scene. Everything felt dangerously wonderful. Finally, the prisoners, upon being entreated, all sat down, while Donna Cody brought out a few bottles of fruit juice and passed them around.

"Y'all have to realize," gulped Miss Evans, "things don't have to be this way. When I worked up in Ohio, you know, they rehabilitated the gals, and we all got along. We had these nice little cabins. Down here, they're so mean to them, but now the Federals are checking up on us, and no one knows what to do next."

"I'll tell you what," said Gina. "There's more change coming, and these folks can't make us the mules of the world anymore. We're rising up."

"It seems you didn't do much to end up in prison," said Donna Cody. "Passing bad checks? You can go to prison for that?"

"You can if you're a Negro and you're a woman," said Gina. "Am I right?" Again, assenting nods, mmm-hmms, and amens. "Now you look here—I shot a man, it's true, but it was self-defense. Doreen here passed those bad checks because her man left her with three kids, and Julia was accused of stealing, which she never did do. No, the ones in jail should be the white men who rule this system, that's who."

"Whew," said Sandy Panther to Donna Cody. "I think she could burn down the whole world."

"You know," said Donna Cody meditatively, "while shooting a man is pretty bad—but you didn't kill him, right?—I don't think you women should be in jail. How about we let you go?"

"Donna Cody, you are completely loco!" shouted Sandy Panther.

"No, you don't want to do that, ma'am," said Miss Evans. "You would end up in jail yourselves. And they're not telling it all, now, are you, Gina?" Some of the prisoners hung their heads, but Gina spat on the ground. As they sat there, Donna Cody got up and went off to attend to nature's call, completely forgetting that it was only her gun that was keeping everyone in place. Sandy Panther was not attending.

As soon as Donna Cody was out of sight, terrible things immediately happened.

The prisoners put a chain around Miss Evans' and Sandy Panther's necks, apologetically but firmly, and then indicated that they needed the key to their chains. Miss Evans was shaking as she handed it over. Then someone knocked her on the head with the club and she fell in the dirt. Gina grabbed Mr. John's gun. Mr. John was yelling from inside the bus. The prisoners went to pillage Donna Cody's Rambler. However, Rockandy and Blue barked and growled with a wonderful ferocity, bringing Donna Cody back, hobbling with her pants only half up, waving Ol' Bessie futilely. By the time she was back on the road, all the prisoners had run off into the surrounding woods.

Donna Cody and Sandy Panther poured some water on Miss Evans' face and brought her around. All of them were shocked and dazed. "What will we do?" wailed Miss Evans.

"You bitches better untie me right now," said Mr. John, but the three women looked at him and thought not.

"We'd best cut out of here," said Sandy Panther.

"Hold on. Miss Evans," said Donna Cody. "Let me leave you with some food." She found what was left of the Cheez Spread and the crackers and some juice and handed them over. "I know someone else will be along to help you out," she said, giving Miss Evans a hug. And guiltily, they drove off to find more populated roads and places. Sandy Panther fervently hoped they weren't going to be arrested and thrown in jail. Donna Cody didn't even consider this.

"I wish I'd recorded them when they were singing," she said.

Chapter 23: Losing and Finding.

Little girl, little girl, now don't you lie to me
Where did you sleep last night?
In the pines, in the pines,
Where the sun never shines,
And we shivered the whole night through.

—"In the Pines," traditional

Instead of finding more populated roads, however, an hour later they found that the dirt road forked, forked again, and then forked a few more times and headed up until they found themselves in some heavily wooded foothills.

"We'll come out somewhere to a main road," said Donna Cody, not believing it herself.

"Guess we can't turn around," said Sandy Panther. "You get lost more often than it should be possible."

And at that point, the Rambler came to a slow halt, the needle of the gas gauge firmly on **E**. No one could say anything, not even Sandy Panther.

They stepped out into the woods. It was about seven p.m. by Donna Cody's watch. They had meant to buy more food, especially for the dogs. They walked a little ahead to see if they could flag anyone down. If anything, the road was turning into a path, maybe leading them to an old abandoned house or one with hostile folks and mean dogs. In dejected silence, they laid out blankets for Blue and gathered wood for a fire.

While they were out in the woods picking up sticks, tinder, whatever old branches they could find, they heard a "putt-putt" sound, furious barking, a yell. Each girl ran back in time to see a little motorbike zooming off, with the angry Gina on it. Rockandy and Blue were in frenzies, barking. They shouted after her. On a hunch, Sandy Panther looked in the Rambler's glove compartment. Sure enough, all the cash was gone.

It was a dismal dinner of mostly Campbell's vegetable soup, peas, Ry-

King Crisp Breads, and a small tin of deviled ham for the dogs, who also got most of the water. They sat around the feeble fire, then took out their sleeping bags and crawled in.

The next morning dawned sunny and bright, but mostly all they had for breakfast was water, and not much of that.

"Sandy Panther," Donna Cody said briskly, "take these jugs and see if you can find us some water. I'm going to take Rockandy and head down the road to see if I can find anyone that can get us some gas."

"Good luck with that," said Sandy Panther, "and what about Blue?"

"Here's the keys. Let's put everything in the Rambler and lock it."

And so they left Blue lying on a blanket and tied up. Donna Cody headed left down the road, while Sandy Panther walked through the woods, listening for water sounds. She eventually found some, filled the bottles, came back, untied Blue, gave her some water, drank some herself, and played her banjo to distract herself from her rumbling stomach and the loneliness of the place, as well as to scare off any bears or other animals.

Donna Cody hiked briskly down the dirt road, Rockandy trotting at her side. The sun shone, the birds twittered, her stomach growled. When she came to a fork, she decided to take a right. After a few hours, about noon time, she was feeling pretty woozy, but the road had broadened out encouragingly and then suddenly, she was out of the woods and confronted with a beautiful expanse of young green corn and a farmhouse off in the distance. And then she found a small leather rucksack lying right there on the side of the road.

"Helloooo," she called out hoarsely. "Anyone here? You leave a pack here?" Her cries echoed emptily across the fields. She figured she would look inside for food. And yes, there were some peanut butter and jelly sandwiches, neatly wrapped up. There were also some clothes, a bandana, a thick notebook, and, amazingly, a wad of 100-dollar bills.

Donna Cody struggled with her conscience, her stomach, and the pitiful look on Rockandy's face. Conscience lost some of the battle, and the two of them wolfed down the three sandwiches. In a way this made it worse because they were even thirstier afterwards. And they wanted more. But first, Donna Cody took a peek in the notebook.

The first pages had some pencil drawings of strange and creepy creatures—one with three eyes, another like a giant manta ray but with a woman's face. There were flying saucers, but all this right next to a beautifully and carefully rendered picture of a man playing a banjo, then on the other page drawings of the woods full of eyes. It was a jumble but all delicately if chaotically rendered. Past the drawings were stories with titles like "Prester John and the Dragon at the Three Forks of Mossytown" and "The Bodysnatchers of Garrett Fork" and "Prester John and the Snakehandlers." There were vivid descriptions of various characters with names like Ezra, Jarvis, Felicity, Plutina, Quillar, and Shade. She squealed with delight when she saw songs and even some tunes notated, some of which she recognized. There were pictures of banjos and dulcimers, with each part carefully labeled, there were some old-fashioned poems about Mountain People and Granddad and Moonshine. In the flyleaf of the book was the name "Carden Wade Goodman."

It was only when Donna Cody gagged on the last of the peanut butter still stuck in her throat that she tore herself away, realizing that she needed to find water and get back on track. She hitched the pack on her back and they set off for the farmhouse.

The walk took longer than she thought it would, but their arrival was trumpeted by a pack of farm dogs who all ran out snarling and barking. Donna Cody and Rockandy had the sense to stand perfectly still until a gaunt woman in a faded flowery dress with an apron over it stormed out and yelled at the whole lot. They all slunk away to the side of the house and growled with their confrères. The woman's face was lined, grim, and closed.

"What you want?" she said in a monotone, staring at Rockandy.

"Ma'am, I found this rucksack," said Donna Cody, who had learned a little about how to address people in this part of the world. "Says it belongs to someone named Carden Wade Goodman. If I could trouble you for some water, please, well, our car is broken down back there." Waving hands in an indeterminate direction. "We got lost. We. . ." and here, embarrassingly, she began to cry, which she later attributed to her weakened state.

The woman frowned but pointed over to a water pump and a bucket. Donna Cody and Rockandy went over and partook. The woman and the dogs watched their every move. But Donna Cody must have looked pitiful because the woman gave a sigh and went inside. She came back in a minute with some Wonder Bread and gave them each a few slices, and it tasted like a wonder, which shows how bad off they were. Donna Cody thanked her profusely as soon as she'd finished, and the woman nodded.

"My man's out there with the tractor," she croaked out. "You go get him, and he'll take you back with some gas."

Donna Cody offered to pay her later and the woman drew herself up, clearly insulted.

"Sorry. Thank you, ma'am," said Donna Cody, slinking away and leaving her standing on her porch and watching them until they faded from view.

The grim-faced lady's husband proved to be a different sort, as is so often the case with couples. His name was Enoch. He turned off the tractor and gave Donna Cody full and open-faced attention. Once he understood, he nodded his head, slowly got down, disengaged a piece of machinery that involved dragging logs around, and he had Donna hop up on the tractor, where she sat on a fender over the right rear wheel. He knew who the rucksack belonged to, he told her as they chugged back to the house, with Rockandy running and barking behind them.

"He's from up north, like you, maybe?" he asked. Donna Cody allowed as how she did come from the north but was looking for good music along with her friend who grew up not too far away from here. That did the trick.

"That feller what the sack belongs to, he's always writing stuff down—songs, fiddle tunes, stories, you name it," he said. "Tried to take our pictures, too, but we didn't want that. Erma don't like that kind of thing and shooed him off pretty quick."

"I'd like to return this to him and meet him!" exclaimed Donna Cody.

"I reckon I can show you how to do that very thing," said Enoch. They stopped, and Donna Cody jumped off. Erma came out, but she didn't say anything. Enoch told her his plans and she turned and went back inside.

"She don't like strangers," said Enoch somewhat apologetically. "I'll be only a minute."

He came out with baloney sandwiches, some cornbread, and more water in a jug. He swung a big gas can and funnel into the back of a faded red old Ford truck and ordered Rockandy back there as well, and then they got in, while the truck sputtered to life with some coughing and belching.

It's always a wonder to travel back by car where you just took a long walk. To Donna Cody everything was whirring by, even though they were creeping along even more slowly than she usually drove. She bemusedly ate a piece of cornbread while she watched and listened to Enoch, who was continuing on about that crazy Mr. Goodman and his city friends and how he wrote books and tried to play the guitar but wasn't any good.

"Now that neighbor of his, name's Othar Roman, now he is a banjo player and singer. Plays with that Bayard Roy up the next holler, and they been on the radio and what-not." Donna Cody made a mental note of this for Sandy Panther and grew more and more excited about finding Mr. Goodman.

They soon pulled up to the scene of desolation, and Sandy Panther came running over. After brief introductions, gas was poured into the starving Rambler, and Enoch sat and waited while they packed up. Donna Cody got his mailing address and promised to send him a check for the food and gas as Sandy Panther shook her head, telling her "No." Enoch drew himself up and absolutely refused, becoming a bit more like his wife for a minute.

"We thank you kindly" said Sandy Panther. "But you know, they say money is like manure; it's only good when it's spread around."

Enoch grinned and gave them his full name (Jenkins), PO number and town, Sullivan's Hollow. "Don't know who this Sullivan was," he said, "but this Goodman fellow, he might. You follow me," he told them, "and I'll take you up to his road."

Donna Cody explained it all to Sandy Panther as they drove behind Enoch's truck, which belched out some foul black exhalations that made them roll the windows up.

"Donna Cody, how much money are you talking?" whispered Sandy Panther. She wasn't so interested in the rest of the story except the pack, the money in it, and whether more food might be involved.

Chapter 24: Stories and Stackcake.

I like my ground hog stewed and fried,
An' a little piece of cornbread by the side.

Well, the meat's in the pot, and the hide's in the churn,
If that ain't ground hog, I'll be durned.

—"Groundhog," traditional

Enoch waved them over to a road that was two dirt tracks with a lot of grass growing up in the middle. "He's down there a ways, and he'll probably be glad to get his things back," he shouted over the truck's grumblings. "Reckon I'd better get back to work. Bye now," and he was off. They both thanked him, sat there a minute, rolled down the windows, breathed some fresh air, and looked at each other.

"I wish we could go get us a real dinner," said Sandy Panther. "Who knows what this oddball might do or whether he has anything good to eat. And I wouldn't mind picking up a few more cigars. At least he's got some cash. That's a good sign."

They headed down Carden Wade Goodman's driveway, which was fringed with trees that made a green tunnel over them. Eventually, a mile or so in, they came across a fairly substantial cabin, with old-fashioned chinking, but newly cut logs, a wide porch with beautiful handmade rocking and ladderback chairs with woven seats, a spinning wheel, and a broad bench made from a half of a single log. Some hides were hung up on the wall, along with various ancient axes and other strange implements. Buck horns were nailed up over the door. Ceramic jugs and crocks lined the porch where it met the walls. Blue smoke dribbled out a large stone chimney. In front of the porch sat a giant wooden trough and an old wagon beside it that said, "Doc Arthur's Medicine Show." A butter churn, an old iron, lanterns, an oxen yoke. A giant kettle that could have cooked up our heroines and their dogs. A bell hanging on a tall post. Dark wooden barrels held together with rope and as tall as Donna Cody lined the path up to the door. Giant millstones and wagon wheels lay all over the place. It was like a museum.

An older man came out and almost posed against the backdrop. He was wearing elegant creased flannels, a string tie, and a jauntily perched felt hat on his salt-and-pepper, slicked-back hair. His thick black eyebrows crowned large black square glasses. He was Carden Wade Goodman and a professional Southerner. He wasn't the least fazed to see them.

"We've got your rucksack," said Donna Cody, leaning out the window. "And sorry, I ate your sandwiches because we were starving."

"Thank goodness," he said, in a plummy, vaguely British manner, waving them out of the car. "You have truly worked a felicitous miracle, ladies."

"What sorta talk is that? He kinda sounds like you," muttered Sandy Panther to Donna Cody, but she got out and let the dogs out as well.

"Ah, two noble animals," he added, while he snatched the rucksack from Donna Cody, checking, she supposed, for the journal and the cash. Donna Cody apologized again for eating the sandwiches, but he waved that aside.

"Ladies, I am in your debt and offer you the hospitality of Wandering Creek. The fare is simple, but I believe we can accommodate you." He was in and out of the house in a flash with two bowls of water and two bowls of meat scraps that he put down on the porch. The dogs lost no time even though they had been fed previously. Blue's walking seemed to improve minute by minute. Then their host was inside for a while. Donna Cody and Sandy Panther stood awkwardly on the porch until he returned with plates of tuna sandwiches (with spicy green ramps cut up in them, which added a great kick), olives, glasses of milk, some dense and sweet cornbread, and apples and set them on a table. Our heroines also lost no time. Carden Wade Goodman sat down with them with what appeared to be a shot glass of whiskey. He lit up his pipe and informed Sandy Panther, when she asked, that indeed, this tobacco was a special mild Cavendish blend that he had especially sent to him from a shop up in Virginia.

"I'm more partial to the occasional cigar myself," she said, and they got talking about various brands and preferences. At last, when everyone was satiated, he said, "I notice a violin in your exquisite automobile. Perchance, does one of you play?"

"We play fiddle and banjo together," Donna Cody began, "and I noticed you have a lot of interesting tunes in your journal—excuse me," and she turned red, realizing she shouldn't have been reading it in the first place. But Carden Wade Goodman once more waved away her embarrassment and with interest asked her if she enjoyed the old folk tunes. The two of them quickly dove into talk of tunes, tunings, and lore. Carden Wade Goodman was so interesting that even Sandy Panther paid attention and chimed in from time to time. Eventually they went out to the Rambler to get their instruments. The dogs lay on the porch in great contentment.

As they played, Carden Wade Goodman rocked, smoked a pipe, sketched, and wrote. The cozy atmosphere of Wandering Creek (you could hear the creek, faintly, out back), the warm welcome, the beautiful glow of wood, the smell of Carden Wade Goodman's pipe, mild but rich with a hint of vanilla in it—all put them at an ease neither had felt in a long time. Donna Cody twisted her fiddle pegs to go into a mysterious sounding tuning that Sandy Panther loved.[30] Tunes she played in this tuning were slower and meandered like a river, with twists and turns. Sandy Panther could follow almost every one. Some of them were tunes Donna Cody had learned from Old Eph and she had practiced them.

---

[30] It was AEAE. While common now among the old-time playing aficionados, back in Donna Cody's day this tuning was not as well known.

Sandy Panther was appreciative. Donna Cody beamed and noted that Sandy Panther's ability to follow and embellish was extraordinary.

Between tunes, Carden Wade Goodman told them how he had grown up in Africa and had learned British English before his missionary parents came back to the States. He had, he believed and hoped, Cherokee blood in his veins. He had worked as a stevedore, a waiter, a bartender and bouncer, a farm worker. He had written for newspapers, especially the crime beat. He had reviewed films, he had even written textbooks on the Civil War. He had been a minor football star at his college. He had been an English professor. He had worked for the WPA. He knew poets, folklorists (Donna Cody perked up at this), and lots of science fiction writers his listeners had never heard of.

Apparently, his parents, teachers, and colleagues had not understood his wish to write.

"Snobs!" he said, slamming his whiskey down. "But they meant well," he added.

"What stories do you write?" asked Sandy Panther.

"Ladies," he said with more than a hint of satisfaction, "I write them all."

He told them about the trickster African rabbit tales as they had been told to him when he was little, about the trickster Cherokee rabbit and how the two had mixed and become Br'er Rabbit. "And now, we have Bugs Bunny," he laughed. "You can't kill off that wabbit."

He told them about invaders from Mars, from Jupiter, from Pellucidar. About Jefferson Davis and his secret mystical powers, about a New York detective who could scent evil and would do battle with it, about charms and amulets and monsters and cowboys and savants. About a Cherokee detective and magician who fought the Thunder Giants whom only he could see. He told them about Prester John and his magical banjo with the skin of Beaver and the silver cross on the headstock, how he fought the Raven Men, who tried to steal souls from the dying and eat their hearts.

"But it's getting toward evening, and indeed, one of the best banjo players you've ever heard is coming over tonight. Let's get you ladies set up in the back room and get some supper on the table," he said, jumping up. Donna Cody and Sandy Panther shook themselves out of a trance and bustled.

Inside, it was dim, the wood furniture simple yet with elegant curves, thick cushions covered with weaving and vivid patterns that spoke of expensive upholstery and more modern tastes. Thick hooked rugs lay like islands around the larger continents of braided rag ones. A little sea-green and white enamel wood stove sat in a corner, beside it a neatly stacked bin of wood. A sturdy wooden dinner table and chairs. Plenty of ashtrays, noticed and approved of by Sandy Panther. Strings of dried peppers and garlic hung from the ceiling, along with gourd dippers, shiny copper pots, and cast-iron pans hanging from nails. Plaques that were obviously awards hung in several places. There were framed photos, some of a younger Carden Wade Goodman as a dark-haired, mustachioed, nattily dressed young Lothario with an elegant, long-legged lady. Many more of distinguished-looking folks who looked familiar or famous, and even more of the beautiful woman with the long legs and curly dark hair and quirky grin.

But most of all, there were books, bookcases full, stacks on the floor, everything from Shakespeare to Captain America comics to H.P. Lovecraft to Vance Randolph and Carl Sandburg. Donna Cody let out a little sigh because she felt she was home and didn't realize how much she had missed it.

They were put to work chopping ramps and shelling corn for a big stew. Apparently, along with all his other talents, Carden Wade Goodman could cook. They added tomatoes and some dangerous-looking dried chilies. Carden Wade Goodman seared a little meat that turned out to be goat.

Then they heard the noise of a truck, and then another. Doors slammed, and in came a crowd of people carrying food and instruments. All of them were interested in Donna Cody and Sandy Panther, but everyone was careful not to act nosy. Things began speeding up: plates were laid, dishes put out, the stew ladled into bowls. Soon they were all sitting down at the big dining table. Carden Wade Goodman offered up a picturesque prayer: "Lord of the four corners of the earth, light of the world, enliven our food and protect us from the evil."

"Amen," said everyone, though one of the women rolled her eyes and said firmly, "In Jesus' name."

"That's right, Annie," laughed Carden Wade Goodman.

Everybody served themselves a bowl of stew at the stove and then sat down with it and piled their plates high with sweet potato biscuits, chow chow, pinto beans with little bits of bacon, and, cornbread or "co-orn-bray-ed," as someone said. Things got a little quiet for a while, but under the influence of good food and some of the whiskey that Carden Wade Goodman passed around, people began talking, especially when they found out that Donna Cody and Sandy Panther played.

"Well I never," said a tall, thin man. "You play the banjo, do you?" he asked Sandy Panther.

"Yes, sir," she said. "Learned it from my auntie up over in Kentucky."

"And you the fiddle?" he asked Donna Cody.

"Yes, I do my best," she said in a dignified way that pleased everyone. They took to the dogs as well. When a lady named Louella brought out something called a "stack cake," layers of sponge cake with tangy apple preserve between them. Everyone ate and ate, even though it didn't seem possible to eat any more.

A fire was lit, chairs were pulled up in a circle, and instrument cases were unbuckled. The tall, thin man was named Othar Roman. He pulled out a banjo and began singing "Pretty Polly" in a high tenor that raised the hairs on Donna Cody's neck. Sandy Panther stared. A tiny old man took out his fiddle and Carden Wade Goodman pulled out a small old guitar. A woman had a dulcimer, and out came another guitar, and a mandolin. The other women were back in the kitchen or sitting on the couches watching, knitting, talking softly.

"Ladies, get out your instruments," commanded Carden Wade Goodman, as Othar finished his song. Donna Cody and Sandy Panther did so and everyone asked them for a tune. Donna Cody retuned her fiddle while Sandy Panther retuned her banjo, and off they went. The room quieted as people grew attentive and then joined in one by one. They picked up the tune right away, and Donna Cody and Sandy Panther and all of them got excited. Carden Wade Goodman stomped his foot and smiled broadly. Finally, at the end, everyone laughed and clapped and patted them on the back.

"I believe that's a Dulcie Tobey tune," said Othar.

"Yes, sir," said Donna Cody. "It's called 'Chickalielee Daisy-O'. It's my favorite."

"Ah, Dulcie Tobey! That is someone I have tried to track down with no success," said Carden Wade Goodman.

"So have I," said Donna Cody. "I have to find her."

"Not sure she's still with us," said Othar, "but if she is, she'll be up in the hills somewhere. She's not one for mixing with folk, so I've heard. Been many a year since she played out."

"You don't know where she'd be?"

"Sorry, I can't help you there," said Othar. "Now, Miss Panther, that is some banjo you have there, and you sure can play it."

Sandy Panther basked.

From then on it was tunes and songs and whiskey all night. The women listening behind them began to doze and occasionally snort. Some of the players seemed to fall asleep but managed to play even so. Sandy Panther smoked a cigar and no one minded. At one point Othar wanted to prove that he could take a banjo apart and put it together again before they would even know what had happened, and he did it.

A little before sunup, people left. Carden Wade Goodman became melancholy. He talked about a folklorist he'd known named Louis Baker Brown and how he missed him, even if he had made mountain folks organize fake cornshuckings and then promised them liquor and pay if only they would square dance in outfits he'd picked out. He would film these events. They gathered that Mr. Goodman regretted these events and his part in them, even if he missed Louis.

Then he began talking about his wife, Frances, who was a writer of tales as well as a screenwriter and had been doing well in Hollywood. Donna Cody and Sandy Panther wondered if they could ever go to bed. Finally, they just did. As the sun came up, they could hear Carden Wade Goodman bumping around, still talking, but then they were out, along with the dogs, who had wisely slept through most of the party.

Donna Cody woke up to gray light and saw through the little high-up window that it was as if they were inside a cloud, a bright fog. Sandy Panther lay beside her, snoring as if she were boring through a tunnel, which maybe she was, a dark sleep tunnel with walls of stack cake and whiskey bottles and cigars.

All was quiet otherwise. Donna Cody gave Sandy Panther a nudge. This had no effect except for a brief snort and then more tunnel boring. Donna Cody sat and worried. Her travelers' checks were getting low. Perhaps she could work. Carden Wade Goodman might have some ideas; he had tackled every job you could think of. She thought a bit about getting some farm job since she now had experience, and then she dreamed about discovering a whole musical family who had never been discovered and working for them. She would record them and play their music and they would all be good friends. People would listen to records of her and of them and she would be famous—oh, now she was turning into a fame mongerer like Sandy Panther. She snapped out of it with some self-disgust. Meanwhile, though, she needed to obtain some cash, and playing out in front of some store in a small town wasn't the way to get it.

Rousing herself, she got up and dressed and opened the door. A scene of utter abandon presented itself: chairs overturned, full ashtrays (and two cigar stubs), plates with leavings on them, glasses overturned or half full, and the rank smells of whiskey, ramps, and apples, along with cigar and tobacco. Carden Wade Goodman was nowhere to be seen. Donna Cody started picking things up and felt oddly better. She dumped the ashtrays. She found a broom and swept. The green and cream-colored wood stove still had barely glowing embers, so she fed it some wood and got some water boiling. Once she found some soap, she washed up. In the middle of all this, Sandy Panther staggered out holding her head and moaning. She stopped and stared.

"You are cleaning up? The world's coming to an end," she said, only to then press her hand against her temple.

"Sandy Panther, I am not blind to the fact that Mr. Goodman may need a little help, especially when we are sleeping in his house and eating his food."

"And his friends' food—" but here, Sandy Panther gagged a bit, thinking about food.

In came Carden Wade Goodman. He was carrying a dead rabbit and a shotgun. Sandy Panther ran back into the bedroom.

"Good morning, or, actually, good afternoon. I thought I'd hunt us some supper. Now this is a fine job you have done, Miss Cody." He beamed. "I wish I had a housekeeper like you. However, I have this nice plump rabbit to skin and cook. Would you want to help with that?"

Donna Cody hesitated and then finally confessed that she didn't know how to skin or cook a rabbit, but she would try if he would show her how.

"Certainly, certainly. Everyone should know how to skin and cook a rabbit," he boomed as Sandy Panther came back out.

"I see the evening's celebration was not entirely salubrious," he laughed, looking at her. "A dip in the creek in back of the house might aid in a postprandial recovery." And out he went, rabbit in hand.

"Sandy Panther," said Donna Cody, "we don't have that many checks left. Do you think Mr. Goodman here would hire us for a while to clean and cook?"

"Clean and cook?" squawked Sandy Panther. "Clean and cook? What? I am not aiming to clean and cook, Donna Cody. I am aiming to play some music, make our record, and get famous."

Donna Cody calmly reminded her of the facts again and suggested she pay for their trip and recording. Sandy Panther changed her mind.

Over a soothing stew of rabbit, Carden Wade Goodman agreed to some housekeeping, offering them 20 dollars each for a week of cleaning, which was such a large amount that it seemed suspiciously like he was just helping them out, Sandy Panther thought. But she kept her mouth shut for once and in the following week worked on sweeping out the barn, weeding the garden, and doing most of the outdoor tasks. Donna Cody worked inside and out, but she quickly reverted to her usual abstracted state, so that one shelf would be clean and another dirty, a flowerbed half weeded, or some of the flowers pulled out. Sandy Panther tried to cover for her but finally got angry and said, "You aren't any kind of help at all, and this was your idea. I didn't come with you so that I could be household help, I'll tell you that for dang sure."

Donna Cody had to admit that she was not up to snuff. "However, Sandy Panther, our week is up soon, and then we can get on the road and back to finding the music. I want to visit those folks who came over."

"Yeah, that Othar fella for starts." said Sandy Panther.

Carden Wade Goodman pressed all kinds of food on them and restocked the Rambler with jars and boxes of things that would keep. However, on their last night, as they all sat around the stove and talked, Donna Cody actually managed to wrest the conversation away from a Carden Wade Goodman monologue. Things had been a bit too centered on his problems with his wife, who wanted to stay in Hollywood rather than hide up in the mountains. She didn't appreciate the richness of the place, said Carden Wade Goodman, the magic and folklore, the people, the quiet.

"This is a rich repository for authentic and untainted music," agreed Donna Cody. "These are people who play from the heart and carry the tradition. They haven't been bought by record companies. They are the last bearers of the old oral traditions, and they play the real folk music."

Sandy Panther groaned.

"Miss Cody, while in some ways this is true, many of the players from here as well as their fathers and even grandfathers have landed record contracts that have fed their families. I would hardly say—"

"Then they are *professional* musicians, not *folk* musicians," said Donna Cody. "People who actually live here, who eat and breathe the music, like all those folks last night, who don't go after it for personal gain or try to pretend they're all folky and down-home and all."

Carden Wade Goodman shifted nervously and then got up and began walking around the room. Donna Cody just kept talking. The dogs and Sandy Panther watched both of them nervously. Finally, Carden Wade Goodman stood right in front of Donna Cody, looming over her.

"This is an ignorant, bigoted, and dangerous view of things," he said, looking down at her upturned face. "Everyone here came from somewhere else. And I can tell you a lot more about the actual folklore of the region than most of the folks that live here can. Does that mean, Donna Cody, that no one can play anything unless they learn it from their Great-Aunt Jenny or something? Are you suggesting that because I write about my neighbors and their beliefs that I'm insulting them or using them in some way? They are happy to be recorded, as you well know. You yourself plunder to your heart's content, don't you?"

Donna Cody struggled to frame a reply. Carden Wade Goodman, his thick eyebrows knitted together alarmingly, started walking around the room again.

"If you think I was referring to you," said Donna Cody, "I certainly wasn't. I mean, I guess. . ." and she trailed off, suddenly realizing for once that she had walked herself right into a swamp.

Carden Wade Goodman, meanwhile, grabbed his rucksack. "I need to walk for a while," he said politely but firmly. He slammed the front door on his way out.

"But it's nighttime," said Sandy Panther. "Pretty excitable, ain't he? High strung. Seemed kind of upset. No wonder, with all that weird stuff he writes and draws."

They went to bed, silent and uneasy. In the morning, Carden Wade Goodman was nowhere to be found. Donna Cody said nothing, but she arose, stalked grimly into their room, and began carrying things out to the Rambler. She whistled up the dogs.

"What?" cried Sandy Panther. "What now? Is everybody crazy? Shouldn't we wait for Mr. Goodman?"

"Remember, Sandy Panther, that we found that rucksack last time. I think Mr. Goodman may take these walks of his all the time. I am not going to wait around for him, but I will leave a thank-you note."

This is what they left:

Dear Mr. Goodman:

Thank you for all your hospitality. I regret that we had some disagreement.

Sincerely, Donna Cody.

Thank you for the cigars and the good food. I ain't got no quarrel with you.

Signed, Sandy Panther.

Chapter 25: More Contention, Resulting in a Parting of Ways.

Going down the road feeling bad,
I ain't gonna be treated this a way.

Going where the weather suits my clothes,
And I ain't gonna be treated this away.

—"Going Down the Road," traditional

They jounced along the road, Donna Cody's mouth clamped shut. The dogs curled up in the back with their heads tucked down. Sandy Panther finally broke it up.

"OK, now, Donna Cody, for once you're not talking, but I don't like it as much as I thought I would. I swear, you could argue with an empty house. I hope you recollect that we're s'posed to be musical partners here, but you're not even talking to me and going all high-falutin' and crazy. It's plain stupid to get all heated up over where the music comes from and who said what and to be against money. We could use us some of that stuff. You realize you forgot to feed the dogs this morning? Forget about them like you forget your promises?"

"That is a baseless accusation. Baseless! I would never forget the dogs."

"Well, maybe not," said Sandy Panther, a bit cowed, "but then I fed 'em. Why do you have to be so contentious and prickly about every little thing? Mr. Goodman took us in and fed us and here you treat him bad. You know what they say about the fish: He wouldn't get hooked if he kept his mouth shut."[31]

---

[31] Sandy Panther was, perhaps, trying to tell Donna Cody to quit being hooked by everything she disagreed with, but the meaning is unclear. See Penhall, D., "The Aphorisms of Sandy Panther," in *Folk Linguistics* no. 56 (June 2009): 208-25).

"What are you talking about?"

Sandy Panther continued at some length, with Donna Cody interrupting whenever she could. But for once, Sandy Panther had the floor, and she continued dancing on it for miles. But even she eventually and reluctantly ran out of steam.

"I am sad," Donna Cody began, "sad, Sandy Panther, that in spite of my attempts to show you a more excellent way, so to speak, that you persist in a money-grubbing and selfish vision. We are not traveling to make money or take advantage. We are bringing back songs and stories and tunes that might be lost if we don't record and learn them. We need to find Dulcie Tobey if she's to be found. We have a responsibility to the music, and future generations will thank us. However, you are correct that I should have thanked Mr. Goodman for his hospitality, if not for his slipshod approach to folk tradition and the music, which he uses to promote himself and his writings. Now we do not have a chance.

"It's the last harvest, Sandy Panther. Radio, TV, these folks will be gone, and no one will care about who they were and the music they made. *Plundering!* Now, if I were selling the tapes I've made—"

"Who'd buy 'em?" asked Sandy Panther.

"If I were *selling* these tapes," continued Donna Cody, "or if I was using people in some self-aggrandizing manner, or if—"

"That Carden Wade Goodman just got under your skin, didn't he? Why are you making all those tapes?"

"So something will be left," said Donna Cody, almost crying. "Because it's so beautiful, because I love it, because it's already going away."

"Now, don't get all worked up," said Sandy Panther. "You are a huckleberry beyond my persimmon."

"What?"

"Just plain strange—something Auntie Rufe says. But look, the big fish eat the little fish, the little fish eat shrimps, and the shrimps eat mud. This is the way it is in this world. Folks mostly mean well, but everyone kinda lives off everyone else, don't they? So, maybe we're the shrimps, maybe the little fish if we get lucky. And you know what they say, better born lucky than rich. Speaking of which, don't you need to get us some more money?"

"I am tired of money," sighed Donna Cody.

"Well, I ain't," said Sandy Panther. "No matter how thick or thin you slice it, it's still baloney to think you can't get on without money. That's how the world goes 'round, even if it is the root of all evil, like the preachers say."

They drove on for a while. Their windows were rolled down and through them came a spicy, intoxicating smell of pine. Deciduous leaves shone golden green.

"Sandy Panther, I think I need some time alone, in the woods here, settling back in this camping place that's coming up." She had just seen a sign for it.

"What?" said Sandy Panther. "What camping place? Wait, what about our music and finding folks and learning tunes? What about all that stuff you just said about recording? And what am I supposed to do?"

"I don't know exactly," said Donna Cody, dreamily. "I want some time to play and think, some quiet. Wouldn't you enjoy that, Sandy Panther? Just a little chance to experience the wilderness? To feel what it was like to live here in the old days?"

"What? No, I got to enjoy the wilderness my whole growing-up."

"Oh, Sandy Panther, I haven't! I need some time to think."

"Donna Cody, you can think while you drive."

"Not when I'm constantly assaulted with those sayings of yours—"

"Insulted?" roared Sandy Panther. "I'll tell you who's insulted! Pull the darn car over!"

Donna Cody was so surprised that she did so.

"Now, I'll tell you what. I've put up with fights and lectures and being tossed around in a blanket and vomit and everything else. I won't say some of it hasn't been fun, but that's it for me. You can just finish this up yourself! And I'm taking Blue with me!"

She grabbed her banjo and her backpack and the startled Blue. Rockandy looked at her mournfully.

"Goodbye, ol' fella," she said, stroking him. "Goodbye, Donna Cody. I hope you come to your senses someday."

Donna Cody hardened herself, though she wanted to cry. "Goodbye, Sandy Panther," she said, and then drove on.

Chapter 26: Penance.

In the bright sunny south in peace and content,
The days of my boyhood I scarcely have spent,
From the deep flowing springs to the broad flowing stream
Ever dear to my memory, and sweet is my dream.

—"Sweet Sunny South," traditional, as sung by Dock Boggs

Donna Cody chewed her lip and felt herself between tears and a green reverie. She had headed a bit south after the departure of Sandy Panther, turned off on the National Forest road, and was now following signs to Yunwiya River Gorge, where signs promised camping places and waterfalls. She could hear birds, trickles of water, and rustlings as she crawled along the dirt road. Rockandy sniffed and sniffed out the window. Luckily, she wasn't heading for one of the Valley Authority lakes, where everyone went to go swim and water ski and drink and preen.

The Rambler climbed up slowly, and finally a sign pointed to the Yunwiya Gorge turn-off. The campground was what we now call "primitive," with some dark and grooved old picnic tables, some rotting away, and a few elegantly fitted stone walls from the time of the WPA and the New Deal, built by all those hardworking young men that President Roosevelt sent out to create the parks we love.

Donna Cody brought the grumbling Rambler to a halt. No one else was there, and this suited her perfectly. The campground was free, a sign announced, which suited her perfectly. She and Rockandy got out and stretched their legs. All around them were tall hardwoods: beeches, an occasional ash, hemlocks, and Donna Cody for once felt uncertain, insignificant, and even a little fearful. A whippoorwill call made her jump.

A creek nearby gurgled and gossiped about woodland matters, but it was private talk and she felt as if she were being left out of things. A path to the left proved to lead down to the water. Both Donna Cody and Rockandy took a long drink, saw that the path continued on the other side. They followed it after crossing the creek on a series of flat rocks. Scrambling down the path after that, they turned a corner and were confronted with an immense gray boulder covered with green and grey and white lichens. A rushing noise signified a good-sized waterfall, and when they came upon it, a rainbow shimmered above the water, entrancing Donna Cody even more. Finally, as Rockandy wandered back and farther into the woods, she snapped out of her fuddle and called him, her voice echoing eerily. They scrambled back up to the Rambler, which was packed with all kinds of food from Carden Wade Goodman. While Sandy Panther had judiciously snatched some staples before jumping out, Donna Cody found apples, nuts, the inevitable cornbread, jars of fruit, a huge ham, and pickles. She sighed to see such generosity and felt even worse about her behavior toward him. She nibbled enough to sustain herself and gave Rockandy a sizable chunk of the ham since it wouldn't keep very long. Why had she left in such an abrupt and unthankful way? Some of Sandy Panther's words about her quarrelsomeness had hit home, at least a bit. Donna Cody felt something reaching in to change her. She thought about what Vera might have had to say.

Finally, she roused herself again, cleaned up, took the wood someone had left by the old picnic table, put it in the fire pit, and got a little blaze going. As the dark fell and the world narrowed to her tiny blaze, she saw the fireflies again, like quivering lace in the bushes. She took her fiddle out and played some old and mournful tunes in an odd, ringy tuning, Rockandy curled up beside her. The fiddle rang out in the woods, the fire died to embers, and Donna Cody's head began to nod over her chest, the fiddle slipping down. Soon, she was slumped up against a log, asleep.

She dreamed things that she could barely tell of afterwards, but in one dream she found herself walking down again to the waterfall, Rockandy at her side. On the side was a little bridge and a hidey hole big enough to walk into. And surprise, the hole turned into a room—a giant room that was squared off, not a cave. It was full of cross-shaped crystals that reflected the light in fiery flashes. But where did the light come from? Behind her, Donna Cody could hear strange songs and booming drums and stamping feet. The songs were in a different language than any she had heard, with buzzy and "sh" sounds. She found she had her fiddle, and she began playing along. The other sounds hushed, and then she was surrounded by a crowd of short, handsome people who were chattering eagerly and smiling. They sang with her, until Donna Cody felt herself going to sleep (which is an odd thing to feel when you're already asleep).

And then she awoke for real, covered in dew. Her fiddle was lying on her stomach, her bow in a bad way thanks to the dew, and she felt some uncomfortable rock under her. She moved and saw it looked like a little cross, which spooked her. Was this Jesus or something? She wasn't quite ready to say, but she popped the rock in her pocket.

Meanwhile, Sandy Panther was experiencing a far less bucolic world. She had decided she was going back to get Mabel and Duncan. Donna Cody had obviously lost her mind. So, still furious, partly at herself for even caring, she stuck out her thumb and right off was picked up by a kind old trucker who liked to knit and steer with his knees. He told her the joke about the cop pulling up to a speeding trucker who was knitting.

"Pull over!" yelled the cop.

"No, cardigan!" yelled back the trucker.

Sandy Panther laughed nervously and kept her eyes on the road, but he got her many miles north. It made her a little nervous to watch him steer mostly with his knees while he knitted away, grabbing the wheel every now and then. He fed her peanut butter and jelly sandwiches and coffee and told her jokes. She had a few other nondescript rides with silent men and then with a menacing guy in a business suit that she had to talk tough with and who finally pulled over and let her out in the middle of nowhere and squealed away, in the middle of the afternoon. She had to hoof it until she got to a gas station with a pay phone. She called Donna Cody's house and Mabel picked up.

"What?" Mabel said more than once during Sandy Panther's long-winded and somewhat murky description of the current state of affairs.

"Sounds like her wits have departed," said Mabel. "I reckon we'll have to come down there and get her. Why did you leave her alone?"

"Leave her?" spluttered Sandy Panther. "*She* left *me*. Just ditched me on the side of the road, like she was bewitched. Ma'am, you know how Donna Cody is. She wasn't gonna listen to a word I had to say, and I wasn't about to go tootling around the woods. We're s'posed to be looking for songs and finding stuff to make us famous."

"Never mind that foolishness," said Mabel. "Tell me where you are. Out on the road hitchhikin'? Well, I never."

"I know how to take care of myself, but I admit I wouldn't mind some help. I'm somewhere near a little town called Goggle Gap. I'm not kidding, Bible swear. No ma'am, no disrespect. Yup, I'll keep working my way north up the highway. You can look for me on the road." And then her minutes ran out. She looked in her little coin purse. She had $18.73 left from Carden Wade Goodman's money. She went in the ladies' room, brushed her hair, put on some more mascara and lipstick, and headed back out to catch a ride.

Mabel, Duncan, and Marvin took out the big atlas in the living room. They looked and found Goggle Gap. Duncan's car, which he said was someday going to run on chicken manure, was up on blocks at the moment, an unsightly annoyance that Mabel did not appreciate. Marvin suggested they take the truck. There was some contention about this with Mabel since it was, technically, a stolen vehicle. However, his dad, he said, had worked something out with his former employer.[32]

Mabel did not want to go south. She wouldn't talk much about it, but she put together a large hamper for Marvin and Duncan, who were, truth be told, excited at the idea of such a trip. It didn't hurt, for Duncan, that he was going off to rescue Donna Cody. Marvin, while excited, had a lot to say about driving the big truck down south with someone who had suspiciously "tan" skin. Duncan glared at him.

"OK, OK, what have I got to lose?" cried Marvin in the face of Duncan's silence and Mabel's crossed arms and commands to get going. "Just my life, right? Just a little party with the KKK! Just 20 years in jail! Sure, fine! Boy, I don't know what Dad's gonna think about this."

"You boys just get down there and find that Sandy Panther," Mabel said. "And then Miss Donna. Call me when you do."

---

[32] It turned out that this something involved blocking a complicated lawsuit based on past unsavory behaviors of J. Q. Briggs, including the treatment of Marvin. Marvin's father was a lawyer. All he had told Marvin, who gave him a headache at best, was: "Keep it for now. But don't use it more than you have to. It's better you keep away from home for a while. Your mother's upset."

Chapter 27: To the Rescue. Sandy Panther Makes an Important Contact. The Story Dries Up Again.

*So we bundled up our clothing, resolved at least to try
And tempt old Madam Fortune, root, hog, or die.*

—"Root, Hog, or Die," by O.A. McGrew

Two days later, they found Sandy Panther by dumb luck, if the Lady Fortuna can be said to be the dumb one in her dealings with humanity. A big black Cadillac was pulled up on the other side of the road, right before a turnoff, and there was Sandy Panther, leaning into the back passenger's window with Blue at her side.

"Sandy Panther!" Marvin bellowed out the window as they pulled up on the other side of the road.

"Hey!" said Duncan.

Sandy Panther looked up and jumped up and down with astonishment, all the while holding Blue's leash in one hand and her banjo in the other. She put the banjo down, made unintelligible hand signs, leaned her head into the window, and took something that was handed to her. Then the Cadillac whooshed off. Sandy Panther ran across the road, squealing with delight. Duncan and Marvin jumped out, and even Duncan had a hug for her. Marvin went for as big a hug as he could get away with.

"Who was *that?*" asked Marvin.

"Some actor and director guy from Hollywood. Do you believe it? He gave me his card."

She did not show it to them.

"And this is Blue. C'mon, I'll tell you all about it." She squeezed herself and Blue into the truck after putting her banjo and belongings in the back, and everybody talked at once. Sandy Panther finally convinced them that the best way to get to Donna Cody was to go back to Carden Wade Goodman's house to get help. She reasoned that he had money and manners. She also missed the comforts of Wandering Creek and even

Carden Wade Goodman. "He's kinda funny," she said to them. "He uses lots of big words and has some strange ideas."

"Sounds like Donna Cody," said Marvin.

"It does not," said Duncan.

"Never mind that. They did have a little fight, but I think he can help us as much as anyone."

"A little fight?" said Duncan. "Tell us about that."

Sandy Panther told them as they drove. She wolfed down Mabel's cheese and bologna sandwiches and then told them some more about Donna Cody's adventures and her decision to go camping.

"She sounds nuts!" said Marvin.

"That's what I thought, not that she isn't regularly crazy," said Sandy Panther. "But this camping thing seems a little more crazy."

"Why don't we go where she's camped out?" said Duncan, reasonably but with an edge in his voice.

"We could," said Sandy Panther in that patient tone of voice that everyone dreads. "But you know, I think, even though they fought, that Carden Wade Goodman understands her as much as anybody, and I think he'd be some good help for us. He loves the things she does. And he can help us find her. He knows the country all around there, or so he told us. One of his books is about it. Hmm, I'll bet that's where she got this crazy idea to go live in the woods and all," she mused.

"I understand her," said Duncan. But Sandy Panther, with Marvin's help, overruled him, and after a night of driving, with everyone taking turns and then dozing while the other person drove, they found the old road and turned up it to Wandering Creek a little after sunrise. No one was feeling too great, though Marvin had enjoyed Sandy Panther sleeping on his shoulder.

If Carden Wade Goodman was surprised, he didn't show it. He met them at the door with his usual elegant manners and welcomed them to his home and all that he had. He seemed to have forgotten about his last altercation with Donna Cody. Sandy Panther eyed him warily, but he wasn't acting crazy at all right now. He brought them inside, clasped Sandy Panther's hand, shook hands with Duncan and Marvin, and promptly offered them some coffee and eggs. While he was scrambling up a dozen or so and frying up bacon and frying up bread in the bacon grease, they all caught up. Carden Wade Goodman did not say anything about his sudden flight or the fight that caused it, so she didn't say anything about it either.

Duncan could sense that some information was missing. He was restless and worried about Donna Cody and ready to take off and look for her.

"Son," said Carden Wade Goodman, "pardon me for saying this, but you are the wrong color to be taking off looking for a white woman."

"Sir," said Duncan, "I don't care."

"Son," said Goodman, "it will not do Donna Cody much good if you're at the end of a rope necktie."

"He's right, Duncan," said Marvin. He mopped up some egg with his toast and looked at Sandy Panther with longing, but she wasn't interested.

Duncan frowned but nodded his head in acknowledgment. After racing down here, now they weren't sure what to do.

"Based on the conversation you describe," said Carden Wade Goodman, after Sandy Panther had been fed a venison sandwich and drunk two tall glasses of milk, "I believe I know where she may have gone. There are several camping spots in that area. We must go track her down. Perhaps, Miss Panther, you could take the truck."

Marvin jumped in. "Now you may forget that this truck is not exactly mine," he said. "If Sandy Panther gets caught driving it, she'll be in jail. If anyone should go, it should be me and her."

"She and *I*," groaned Carden Wade Goodman. Everyone ignored him.

"You just want to be with me, you little love bunny," said Sandy Panther. "But, well, he has a point." She winked at Marvin. He brightened.

"Wouldn't you be an accomplice if they caught you with that truck?" asked Duncan.

"More like an unwilling captive," and she smiled as sweetly as it was possible for her to smile. Marvin smiled back. He couldn't help himself. Carden Wade Goodman and Duncan would follow a bit behind them as backup. Although, Carden Wade Goodman added, there was the little matter of his Jeep not working at the moment.

"Duncan can fix it," said Marvin and Sandy Panther at the same time. And before five minutes were up, Duncan and Carden Wade Goodman were out back in the barn, where an old World War II Willys Jeep was sitting with hay bale seats in its back.

When Duncan and Carden Wade Goodman came in some hours later, Marvin and Sandy Panther were sitting on the couch at either end, their heads tipped back, and snoring away. Carden waved Duncan into the guest room and let him go do the same.

It wasn't until after breakfast the next day that Carden Wade Goodman sent Sandy Panther and Marvin off, having given them directions and stopping points for meet-ups. Duncan fumed impatiently while Carden Wade Goodman closed up the house. At last, they were off in the newly revived Willys. The two of them proved to be a great combination. Duncan was a good listener. He heard more about Carden Wade Goodman's life than any of the others had, especially about his wife.

"She was enticed into a circle I know all too well and have abandoned for something better," said Goodman. "She writes better than ninety percent of those fellows, and they try to cozy up and steal her ideas. I know how those lunches are: there's booze flowing and loose tongues waggling, and before you know it, someone's got something in *Worlds of*

Tomorrow or over to Marvel, or on TV or in some collection and it was your idea and they stole it. I've begged her to be careful, but she's convinced I'm trying to squelch her career. She doesn't want to leave Hollywood, but I can't stand the place.

"She used to love it down here. We went on collecting trips with the greats. Vance Randolph, Carl Sandburg"—these names were lost on Duncan —"and all of us were inspired. Art poured forth from both of us. She wrote archetypal horror masterpieces published everywhere: *Incredible Stories, Unbelievable Stories, Creepy Stories*; she penned stories for comic books, she even worked in television for a while. We had a houseful of mountain people, artists, singers, in and out. But then, along came that Marcela. And off they went together; she was lured, positively *lured* back to California. Marcela actually said I was holding Frances back."

Carden Wade Goodman chewed angrily on his pipe, took it out, and continued. "I suppose I went a little crazy after that," he mused. "It's a good thing your friends found me when they did. They found the notes for my latest novel. It's about—" But you, Dear Reader, shall be spared.

Chapter 28: Contrasting Females. A Wise Man Keeps Silent.

All the good times are past and gone
All the good times are o'er
All the good times are past and gone
Little darling, don't you weep no more.

—"All the Good Times Are Past and Gone," traditional

What would have happened if no one cared, if no one loved all things old and intricate? What if everyone had decided to work for oil companies and advertising agencies, let alone the posturing young computer moguls of the future? What if Pete Seeger and Woody Guthrie and the great Folk Scare hadn't come along to throw at least a tiny wrench into the industrial juggernaut? What if people hadn't collected those records sitting in barns, interviewed people who learned from their mothers and their fathers or the fieldworkers or the maids or the factory workers? What if they hadn't risked poverty, disdain, shootings, lynchings, being run over as they slept on the side of the road?

What if Donna Cody and Carden Wade Goodman and all their ilk had not loved the mysterious old tunes, whose roots stretch all over the world in a fibrous mat of folk knowledge that goes back to who knows where? To the animals? The trees? The lonely clouds blowing across a savanna or a skin kayak pushing through slapping waves pulsing in their own rhythmic language? The haunting intervals of a cuckoo's call or the huff and chuff of the wind?

But some folks cared, and the world is surely a bit better for it. Things could be worse, even if they don't look so good right now.

The ride in the Willys Jeep was not smooth, and since it was even slower than Aunt Jane's Rambler, they took twisty and small back roads trying to catch up with Marvin and Sandy Panther. As they crawled and bumped along, the Jeep belching blue smoke, they saw a slender young man in overalls and a felt slouch hat, his thumb sticking out. He looked like a caricature of a hillbilly and was even chewing a piece of straw. Duncan, who was now driving, pulled over at Carden Wade Goodman's insistence.

And they stared. The young man was a girl with huge green eyes, rich auburn braids tucked up into her hat, and a wide, smiling mouth that revealed perfect little pearls of teeth. Her skin gleamed, white and clear as moonlight. Luckily, both men were already obsessed with other difficult women, but they did find their attention diverted.

"Please join us," said Carden Wade Goodman, holding out his hand. "I will decamp to the back."

"No, don't bother," she said, in a husky and spine-tingling voice. "I'm younger and don't mind sitting on hay. My name is Dora." And she jumped in, Carden Wade Goodman barely noticing the sting of her words. They introduced themselves and asked her where she was going.

"Same direction as you are, seems," she said.

With that, they took off down the road. Conversation was difficult in the Jeep, even at such a slow speed, but they got the idea that Dora was from Kentucky, that she had been brought up nicely, that she was a singer who had sung all over since she was fourteen. She played the dulcimer and the guitar, she said, which she had learned from her older brother and a sister, who had learned from their father. She had thirteen siblings. She had recorded a number of albums, had seen Nashville destroy her music with 1001 strings, had been forced to wear big hair, polyester, itchy petticoats, and white shoes. After that, she had managed to make a big hit by singing a folksong written by a coffeehouse player up in New York City. Then she had sung pop, but she hated it. And then her manager had forced himself on her. Smiling sweetly, she told them that she planned to hunt him down and kill him.

Of greatest interest, however, was her mention of a singer named

Marcy, whom she admired deeply. "Marcy doesn't let anyone tell her what to do. She sings what she wants and with whoever she wants. It may be a bit different from what I sing, but she is a fine example of strength and courage."

Carden Wade Goodman controlled himself with difficulty for a while. Finally, he exploded, "Marcy! That woman is a menace, as much as she may have helped you. She has taken my wife and led her away and destroyed our marriage."

Duncan glanced at him with some worry. He seemed to be turning into someone else—the crazy person Sandy Panther had described.

"There is that little problem about Marcy," said Dora. "While she helped me out in the music business, she'd up and leave in the middle of a job. They even say she killed a young man by breaking his heart. She broke a lot of contracts, and I reckon it's cost her. I'm sorry to hear about your wife."

Carden Wade Goodman, whose eyes had been rolling back like those of a startled horse, slowly calmed down. With far more conviviality, he and Dora shouted back and forth over the noise of the Jeep and got into a long musical discussion about songs, sources, exploitation, and villainy. It turned out that Dora's large family was well known for its rare old tunes and ballads, passed down from the 1700s, if not earlier. Cecil Sharp had recorded some of them in his search for olde English ballads, and various eccentric collectors had been showing up regularly ever since. At this point, Carden Wade Goodman knew who was sitting in his Jeep even though Dora hadn't mentioned her last name.

On another subject, Dora and Carden Wade Goodman made an informal pact that he would help her get revenge on Fred (her manager), while she would entreat Marcy to urge Frances's return to her husband. Killing was vetoed by Carden Wade Goodman, but their schemes did not sound particularly nice. Recited in Dora's young, sweet voice and Carden

Wade Goodman's plummy, cultured voice, they sounded creepy.

Duncan nervously kept his eyes on the road and his thoughts to himself.

Chapter 29: Song as Bait.

Shady Grove, my true love, Shady Grove I know,
Shady Grove, my true love, going to Shady Grove.

—"Shady Grove," traditional

As the pensive crew barreled down the road, who should come flying by from the other direction but Marvin and Sandy Panther. Both cars screeched to a halt, pulled over to the side of the road, and everyone jumped out to confer.

"Have you found Donna Cody?" said Duncan. Marvin shook his head. Sandy Panther was looking at Dora.

"Who's this?" said Sandy Panther suspiciously. She worried about competition.

"I'm Dora," said Dora. "I'm from over the notch at Calhoun." She had astutely figured out from Sandy Panther's talk that they might be neighbors.

"I'll be!" said Sandy Panther, too excited to notice that Dora didn't give her last name. "It's about time someone from our neck of the woods showed up. I grew up a bit north of you, the Panthers, you know our family?"

"Why, indeed I do," said Dora. They proceeded to name various persons they both knew, various places they'd both been, etc., etc. Carden Wade Goodman joined in, talking about spots in Kentucky where he had collected material with a famous folklorist and poet back in the forties.

"Sandy Panther," Duncan commanded. "What about Donna Cody? How is she? Why aren't you with her?"

"I'll tell you why she isn't. Doesn't want to come. She's crazy as a loon. We finally found her up at this Yummy Haha place, camping up there and saying she won't come back till she has created the perfect fiddle tune. I thought she wanted to collect 'em, not write 'em. There's plenty of 'em already. I don't know why you'd want to write any more of 'em."

"Does she have enough to eat?" Duncan plowed on methodically.

"She lives on air," snorted Sandy Panther. "Practically. No, she's got some stuff, thanks to Mr. Goodman here, and plenty of water. But she won't see anyone till she's written this tune. She sits there and saws away, lonesome tunes, and that 'Chickalielee Daisy-O.' "

" 'Chickalielee Daisy-O'!" said Dora, perking up.

"Ah! 'Chickalielee Daisy-O'." said Carden Wade Goodman.

"The words for that have been in my family for 100 years at least," said Dora. "But no tune. We used to have it."

"And now you have the tune," said Carden Wade Goodman. "Now, this is exciting. I heard about it from Alan Lomax, and he looked for it, but couldn't dig it up anywhere." (Carden Wade Goodman could be a terrible name dropper.)

Sandy Panther and Duncan both watched with some impatience as the talk moved from versions to variants, verse structure to origins. C. C. Leggett's name came up. Sandy Panther chimed in. Dora remembered some Leggetts up in a holler north of Bixby.

"There was a Clarence Leggett we found up that way in 1947," said Carden Wade Goodman. I wonder how this C. C. is related. Or if that's him? Did Donna Cody go to Kentucky to see him?"

"No, sir, she went over to Indiana because that's where he lives," said Sandy Panther.

"Indiana?" said Dora and Carden Wade Goodman.

"Yes, sir, ma'am. I know because I visited him there and he sent me over to find Donna Cody in the first place." More interest.

"Enough!" said Duncan. "Donna Cody has had a breakdown and probably isn't eating or drinking and all you can talk about is some tune? We need to go get her right now!"

Sandy Panther, slightly cowed, responded. "You can say you want her to come back, but she runs off and hides or gets herself down by this waterfall and stands on a ledge like she's gonna jump. She won't listen to a thing you say. You're right, she's having a crazy spell, and I don't know who can get her back."

A tense silence. And then: "Let me try to get her back," said Dora. "You get me up there. I'll talk 'Chickalielee Daisy-O' verses to her."

"That's not a bad idea," said Sandy Panther.

"It could work," said Carden Wade Goodman. "I would be happy to talk to her, but we didn't part under the best of circumstances."

"I'll say," said Sandy Panther. "But you have been good to us all, Mr. Goodman. I was thinking you could get her to come back with all your talk."

"I think you're all as nuts as she is," said Marvin.

"I'm the one that can talk to her," said Duncan. "Who here has known her longer than I have?"

They argued about it and finally agreed that Marvin and Sandy Panther would take Dora up, while Duncan and Carden Wade Goodman would follow in the Jeep. "That way," said Sandy Panther to Duncan, "you won't be driving with a white girl either."

"Who's going to see me up there? You said no one was around. This is ridiculous!" said Duncan.

Carden Wade Goodman patted his shoulder to steady him. He had to reach up a bit to do it. "Duncan, you just never know. Things have been pretty touchy down here what with the marchers, God bless them, and all the rest. And I'm not sure that you are the one to talk to Donna Cody right now, from what I infer of your friendship with her."

Duncan bristled a bit, but he was a listener and a thinker. He agreed that they would wait down the road.

They drove through the cool woods in Marvin's big truck, except that it wasn't Marvin's big truck. Sandy Panther tried to give Dora advice:

"Now, don't come at her too sudden. Like my auntie says, 'Patience is the wisest recipe for success,' " she added sententiously. "A crazy person thinks everyone is crazy but herself."

Marvin groaned but quickly shut up when Sandy Panther shot him a look. Dora smiled sweetly and nodded. After all, advice is something the wise don't need and fools won't take. Luckily, Dora was of the first order.

Finally, they got near Donna Cody's mysterious campground. Sandy Panther suggested that they stop there and let Dora walk up further. Dora walked and in her husky but bell-toned voice chanted an odd little verse that went like this:

The froggy went chime, a-chime, a-chime oh!
As he hopped up and down in the swamp-ie-oh.

Chickalielee-o, Chickalielee-o,
Chime, chime, chickie, chickalielee-o!

They lost the thread of the song as Dora rounded a corner, barely hearing the "chickalielee" from time to time, then a low murmur of two voices, then some fiddling. This went on for a few hours.

"Sandy Panther," said Marvin, "when we get out of this, why don't you and me go off together? I can get another job and. . ."

"Hush up," said Sandy Panther. "I think I hear the Rambler." And sure enough, it crawled creakily toward them from around the bend. Donna Cody leaned out the window. "Hello, Sandy Panther! Hello, Marvin! How are you? Isn't this Dora wonderful?"

Rockandy bayed out the open car window and Blue bayed back from the truck. Dora was driving, and she nodded at them to jump in the truck and follow, which they did. Near the entrance to the park, they came close to running over Duncan and Carden Wade Goodman, who were standing by the Jeep. It was tipped on its side in a ditch. Dora and Donna Cody came to a stop, Marvin and Sandy Panther close on their tail. Everyone jumped out.

"Donna Cody!" Duncan said as if it were a song, running over and hugging her. Everyone watched as Donna Cody twitched and then settled. But then she broke free.

"What are you all doing here?" she asked. "Are you all right? Is Mabel all right?"

"Mama is fine," said Duncan. "We came down for you."

"Oh, now that is sweet of you all," Donna Cody beamed. "Mr. Goodman! My, what are you doing here? What is your Jeep doing in a ditch?"

"We were set upon," said Carden Wade Goodman glumly. "They jumped into the Jeep, took everything we had, drove it into the ditch and ran off. Duncan tried to stop them."

"There were too many," Duncan said. "They were wild women, and they had this leader they called Gina. She was the one that gave me this cut." He pointed at his head, and they noticed the blood crusted on his forehead. Donna Cody turned back to him and exclaimed, touching the edge of it carefully.

"And me this bruise," said Carden Wade Goodman, touching his cheekbone with care.

"Oh," said Sandy Panther mournfully. "I think we know them gals."

Chapter 30: Some Creative Folklore.

You want to get your eye knocked out
You want to get your fill
You want to get your eye knocked out
Go to Sugar Hill.

—"Sugar Hill," traditional

It was now that a somewhat abridged story of the prison bus liberation emerged.

Something needed to be done," asserted Donna Cody at the end. "The unfortunate results of freedom on some of these people is the risk we take for doing the right thing."

"I am not sure, Donna Cody, that you did the right thing," said Duncan, firmly.

"What?" she asked incredulously.

" 'Bout time," said Sandy Panther. "You can talk about the right thing and all that, but I always heard that you should be good, and if you can't be good, be careful. You don't *think*, Donna Cody."

Carden Wade Goodman bravely stepped in. "Whatever Miss Cody may have felt necessary at the time, the fact is that these ladies seem prone to continuing their criminal behavior, and they are dangerous. And we need to report them to the police."

"It's mostly that Gina," said Sandy Panther. "She's got hooks in the others' noses and drags 'em along. But it's true; you can't unscramble eggs."

"What?" said everybody.

"Meanwhile, we need to do something about the Jeep," noted Carden Wade Goodman airily, as if he were talking about a misplaced pencil. Donna Cody, who was still gaping at Duncan, who was reprovingly staring back, marched over to the ditch. The others followed. Shortly, with a great deal of sweat, some regrettable language, particularly from one person, and a lot of discussion, the Jeep was finally pushed out of the ditch. Marvin remarked as how it was too bad the winch wasn't working on the truck. Everyone glared at him, even Dora. But along with Duncan he hooked it up to the truck when they found it wouldn't drive. Donna Cody and Dora climbed into the Rambler with Rockandy. Carden Wade Goodman and Duncan awkwardly climbed back into the Jeep.

As Marvin and Sandy Panther and Blue drove along, the conversation in the cab of the truck was one-sided. Marvin grimly watched the road while Sandy Panther told him all sorts of tales. In the Jeep, Carden Wade Goodman speechified about ballads, folktales, mining disasters, and especially his wife. In the Rambler, following behind, Donna Cody and Dora discussed ballads.

After a few hours, Sandy Panther announced that she had to piss so bad her eyeballs were turning yellow. The truck pulled over in a field and everyone else followed. People jumped out to relieve themselves, stretch, etc. Dora and Donna Cody continued their earlier discussion of "Chickalielee Daisy-O." They discussed possible origins of the lyrics that Dora's family had had for so long in the family.

"My family was German, way back, immigrating over to these parts around the early 1700s, but the lyrics are in English. And supposedly, they were copied down by my great-aunt's mother, Lotte. But I don't know if she sang them," said Dora. "We never found any old copies, but we wrote them down."

"But she must have, or heard someone sing them," said Donna Cody. "Look how well they fit this little bit—" and here she hummed and sang the refrain.

"Don't you think," suggested Dora, "that it might be better to study this at your home, where you have access, it sounds like, to books and materials that would help you put all this together?"

Donna Cody thought about this for a minute but then responded that she would actually like to meet Dora's family and talk about their tunes and songs.

"You and a hundred other people," sighed Dora. "I do miss them, though. Maybe we should head up that way."

Sandy Panther jumped over, took Donna Cody by the arm, and steered her off to the side. "So," she said, "let me revisit the wheel of my conversation round the axle of your understanding. Are you joining up with that woman and leaving me in the lurch?"

Donna Cody looked at Dora. Duncan had wandered over, and he and Dora were arguing. It made her a little uncomfortable, but she didn't know why.

Carden Wade Goodman was stretched out on the ground.

Marvin was relieving himself in the woods, but he came running back shouting. "C'mon, let's go get her! Some woman grabbed my wallet, right out of my back pocket! They're on motor bikes!" He and Duncan tore into the woods.

Dora sat down beside Carden Wade Goodman.

"I'll tell you what," she said. "I think you folks are even more tangled up than I am."

"I have written many tales," said Carden Wade Goodman, "but no one could make up anything as strange as the adventures of Donna Cody and her cohorts, of which, apparently, I am now one."

Chapter 31: The Long Arm of the Law.

This world is not my home, I'm only passing through,
My treasures and my hopes, are all beyond the sky,
I've many friends and kindreds, that's gone, along before,
And I can't feel at home in this world, any more.

—"This World Is Not My Home," traditional as quoted in James Agee's
Let Us Now Praise Famous Men

The quiet deepened around the group as everyone got more and more nervous and ran out of words. There was no sign of Duncan or Marvin, no sound of motorcycles. So everyone jumped a little when Donna Cody turned to Sandy Panther and blandly asked, "How did your traveling go, Sandy Panther? And why are Duncan and Marvin here?"

Sandy Panther, her attention previously fixed on the theft, now swung it over like the boom of a sailboat in a strong wind. "So glad to see you're back with us on Earth, Donna Cody. My trip northward was fine, great, not that you cared to notice till now. I had to ride with some pretty strange folks. Couple of men tried some stuff. But what do you care? You were busy daydreaming and gallivanting around in the woods, writing some fiddle tune, and now you're talking wild stuff about little people and all that craziness. Well, you oughta know that all these people, myself included, came to get you back to civilization."

"I assume, Sandy Panther, that you speak of my visions," Donna Cody said haughtily. "I can only say—"

"You wouldn't see the truth if it looked you in the face. 'Course, there are plenty weird things in the woods, I'll give you that. Why, my Auntie Rufe said that one time she saw this critter, half-human they say, the Wolfman, tall as a Georgia pine. Auntie Rufe said she was so scared she—"

"You are talking about a *werewolf*, Sandy Panther, an entirely legendary creature."

"Now, you didn't see it, did you?" said Sandy Panther. "Got your nose so high in the air, you could drown in a rainstorm. T'ain't no legend but the goldang truth. But listen, Donna Cody—" (switching gears again) "I've got a card from this guy who says he'd like to record us. Actually, me, but I told him about you. We could get out to Hollywood and stuff. He wants me to take a test or something. I think it's about time we did something *I* want here. You've been promising, but it's been a 'coon's age and nothing but trouble."

"I prefer you not use that expression, Sandy Panther. And Hollywood? Not too likely. Next, you'll be talking Trashville. If you want to prostitute your beautiful playing—"

"Don't you call me no hooker!" said Sandy Panther. "You know, you have promised me that we would make a record of us together. A promise made is a debt unpaid."

But as she and Donna Cody were winding up yet one more iteration of their quarrel, Marvin and Duncan and Rockandy burst out of the woods, Blue hobbling behind. The humans were looking wildly around but then put their hands on their thighs and doubled over, panting for breath. The dogs flopped down.

Marvin and Duncan described a tall, startlingly blonde-haired woman who had run off with Marvin's wallet. She had jumped on a motorbike and headed down a trail.

"Gina," said Donna Cody and Sandy Panther simultaneously.

"We almost had her," groaned Duncan.

"What do I do now?" moaned Marvin.

"There is nothing much we can do except contact the police and head back to Wandering Creek," said Carden Wade Goodman. "You can all rest up and we'll wait until they catch that woman."

"Let's not contact the police, sir, if that's OK. I'll figure out how to get a new copy of my license," said Marvin. "Boy," he added, "I don't feel so good." He sat down. His face was pale and he was sweating.

"Are you going to be able to drive?" asked Duncan.

"I, I don't think so," said Marvin.

"Let me do it," said Duncan.

"What about me?" said Sandy Panther.

"You don't even have a license, Sandy Panther," said Donna Cody. "I know I've let you drive a little, but it wasn't a good idea. Besides, have you ever towed a car?"

"Wouldn't you know," said Marvin wearily. "You just wait. I had a bad feeling coming down here, don't you forget."

"I am not sure," said Dora, "that having a Negro driving a truck and towing white people in a Jeep is actually much better than having Sandy Panther drive."

"This thought also occurred to me," said Carden Wade Goodman. But in the end, Duncan was driving the Jeep with Marvin slumped over in the passenger seat. Sandy Panther made it clear that it was time for her and Blue to take their rightful places in the Rambler. So Dora ended up in the Jeep with Carden Wade Goodman.

Sure enough. As they jounced along, they came to the small town of Bumble Creek. People looked up at them as they drove past, the heat shimmering on the road. As they were heading out of town, a sheriff's car came racing up right behind the Jeep, gave them a short siren beep, and pulled them over. Everyone in their respective vehicles groaned. Donna Cody and Sandy Panther pulled over behind the sheriff and came walking up. The sheriff was looking with some concentration at Duncan.

"Step out of the truck, boy," said the officer. He had the requisite aviator mirror shades and large stomach.

"I don't think this is exactly Andy Griffith," said Sandy Panther to Donna Cody.

"Sir," called out Donna Cody, "You shouldn't call him 'boy.'" Her voice shook, and her eyes teared up a bit. Duncan swung his downcast gaze over to her in amazement.

"Quiet, there. Who're y'all?" the officer demanded of the girls. "Move along. Get back in your car and keep going." He looked at them again and then said, "Hold on, are you part of this little parade?" And before they could answer, he commanded, "Stay right there and be quiet. Now, *boy*, do you have yourself a license to be driving this truck?"

Duncan clenched his mouth shut and took out his license. The officer took it and then walked back to his car to check in. He returned with his walkie-talkie. A sharp squawk, several more squawks, the officer reading off the plate numbers again. Marvin began to crack.

"I knew it! I *knew* it! Why did I take that truck? Why did I ever get involved with you, Donna Cody? Why—"

"Shut the heck up, Marvin," said Sandy Panther. "Do you want to tell the whole world and land in the slammer?"

"Looks like this is a stolen car, folks, belonging to one J. Q. Briggs," the policeman said. "C'mon, boy," thrusting Duncan's arm behind his back.

"Wasn't him, sir," said Marvin.

"Explain," said the officer, holding Duncan firmly. Duncan was a powder keg about to go off even if he was looking at the ground.

"I'm borrowing this truck from Mr. Briggs," gasped Marvin.

"Let's see your license," said the officer. Marvin began explaining.

Meanwhile, the others were conferring frantically among themselves. "Quick," said Sandy Panther to Donna Cody. "Let's jump in and go!"

"I don't leave my friends," said Donna Cody, forgetting she had done exactly that not too long ago.

"I don't think that is a wise idea," said Dora.

"Certainly not," said Carden Wade Goodman. "I believe I can talk with this minion of the law."

"I'll talk to him," said Donna Cody, striding toward the car.

"No!" shouted everyone, grabbing her and pulling her back.

The officer now came ambling back, but there was a new tenseness about his shoulders, and one hand rested lightly on his gun. Everything was quiet.

"Seems we have some car thieves here. You, boy, let's get in the back of the car right now." And he snapped handcuffs on Duncan quick as a snake might strike, dragged him over to the patrol car, thrust him in and locked the door. "And you," he pointed at Marvin. "Let's go."

Donna Cody struggled and was held firmly in check.

"I told you, sir, my license was stolen, my wallet!" wailed Marvin. He went on to describe Gina and added, "Officer, Duncan shouldn't be in there. It was me that stole the truck. You might as well take me in."

Everyone gasped, some shouted, "NO!" (Sandy Panther). Others charged forward (Donna Cody).

"My good man," said Carden Wade Goodman to the policeman while grabbing Donna Cody's arm. "This is a misunderstanding. Marvin was merely borrowing the truck for a rescue excursion to help these ladies, who were stranded."

"And who are *you*?" said the officer. "You," he said to Marvin, "you get back in there with that boy." He escorted Marvin to the police car and locked him in with a second pair of handcuffs. "I need some help out here," he said into his walkie-talkie. "Bring a tow truck." He strode back to the truck. The amble was gone out of him. "OK, folks, I think you'd better start talking. You first," he pointed at Carden Wade Goodman.

It took some time. A wiry little man arrived with a tow truck named "Truck Beast." Donna Cody almost got herself arrested when she made a few wild charges. Finally, though, Duncan was released, with some strict and degrading warnings. He stared down at the ground but never flinched, leaving the sheriff angry and unsure. The tow truck man worked a bit on the Jeep and got it running again. They thanked him, and Carden Wade Goodman paid him. Then he drove off with the tow truck now in tow itself. They all begged, but to no avail. Marvin was doomed. He hung his head. He was crying and didn't want anyone to see. He was young.

"Marvin," called Donna Cody again, "we will deliver you!" The officer ignored her as he got into his car.

"Leave me alone, Donna Cody! I wish I'd never met you!" shouted Marvin with a sob as he was driven away.

Chapter 32: Dropping In.

Tell me have you ever heard this melody
Da, ya, ya, ya, ya, ya, ya

. . .

Here lingers in my brain
I've really gone insane
Oh, how I love that strain
Of melody
Da, ya, ya, ya, ya, ya, ya
Where have I heard that melody
It seems so familiar to me
It goes Da, ya, ya, ya, ya, ya, ya

—"That Haunting Melody" by George M. Cohan

It was many hours later when a chastened group pulled up to The Dew Drop Inn, apparently the only place to stay in this neck of the woods. The neon sign still glowed, and Sandy Panther shuddered as they turned in behind the Jeep. Donna Cody and Sandy Panther agreed (for once) that it was wise to wait outside while Carden Wade Goodman and Dora walked into the office. They noticed that Duncan lowered himself in the Jeep so that he was barely visible. There was also a pay phone. Donna Cody found a dime and called up the police to find out about Marvin.

"I'll fix this miscarriage of justice if it's the last thing I do!" said Donna Cody.

"*Click*," replied the phone.

"We're going over there in the morning," vowed Donna Cody.

"He said he didn't want to see you, Donna Cody," said Sandy Panther. "If I were me, I'd get his dad on the phone—didn't he get him out of trouble before with that whole truck thing?" She looked nervously around, but the louts from before didn't seem to be there anymore.

"That is a good idea," said Donna Cody. She decided to talk to Duncan about it.

"My daughter and some fine young friends and I would like to rent two cabins for the night, sir," said Carden Wade Goodman, planting some cash down on the desk. Frank looked at them and then looked at the cash. His eyes were tiny in his huge pasty-white face.

"Well," Frank drawled, looking appreciatively at Dora, "I guess that's OK."

"We have two women and their dogs as well," said Carden Wade Goodman. "They will stay with my daughter."

"Two women and dogs? Hold on," said Frank, rising from his chair in a mountainous, quivering mass. He lumbered over and peeked out the window, but Donna Cody, Sandy Panther, Rockandy, and Blue were nowhere in sight, having wisely driven the Rambler around the back. Carden Wade Goodman put some more money on the desk. Frank snatched it.

"You keep an eye on those two," he grumbled. "My maid almost quit after trying to clean up the mess they left. They took off without paying, and I don't put up with that no ways."

Carden Wade Goodman apologized for them and put another twenty down. "They are still young, sir, and we will certainly make sure they behave."

Frank apparently decided getting paid was the best policy. He explained in his pinched, suffocated voice how he had been through hard times and how these so-called guests who run out on him was not what he needed, no, sir.

"Mmmm-hmm," said Carden Wade Goodman.

"That is a shame," added Dora.

Finally Frank's monologue of complaint (and don't we all have one?) dried up. He asked where they were headed.

"We're headed back home," Dora offered. "Pa here took me to

Nashville to make a little record." Carden Wade Goodman looked at her admiringly and vaguely assented.

"Recording, eh?" said Frank. "I have a whole passel of records. One of the folks as stayed here, couldn't pay, gave me all these silly old things."

"You don't say," said Carden Wade Goodman, breathing more quickly. "Could we see them?" Dora leaned toward the desk and smiled.

"I s'pose so, why the hell not," said Frank. "They're out back there." He lumbered out the door and led them to a falling-down little wood shed, unlocked the door, and held out his arm to wave them in. They entered hesitantly: there was a fog of dust and a terrible musty smell. Spiders scurried into darker corners. But stacked everywhere were piles of 78s.

It was bedazzling, even if a few of the cardboard and paper sleeves (where there were sleeves) were moldering and stuck to each other. The labels, even faded, were beautiful: a Creamsickle orange "Parlorphone," a lavender "Harmonairs," a green-and-yellow "Zone-o-phone," a bright green "A440," many "Victor" records with the iconic Nipper inquisitively listening to the old record player cone, Paramount records with names that Dora didn't know, like Robert Johnson, Skip James, Ma Rainey, Geeshie and Evie.

Carden Wade Goodman was practically jumping up and down. "This is some of the most amazing shellac I've ever encountered," he gasped asthmatically.

"My folks had some of these," said Dora. "But look at all these old tunes. I never heard of half of them."

"Good Lord, man, uh, Frank, what are you going to do with these records?" huffed Carden Wade Goodman.

"I dunno. I guess sell 'em if I can. They're junk now—who wants stuff like this?"

"Sir, I will give you ten dollars for every hundred."

"You got yourself a deal." They shook hands on it.

"Really?" said Dora quietly to Carden Wade Goodman. "I mean, what are you going to do with these things? Don't you want to listen to them first? Only take the ones you like? How would you even play them? Where are you going to put them?" (Carden Wade Goodman had heard this last question before, mostly from his wife.)

Frank caught the last part and, anxious lest he lose a sale that was clearly a steal from a gullible if high-toned fool, jumped right in. "I've got an old Victrola we can listen to them on," he offered.

"That's all right, sir; I'll take 'em all," wheezed Carden Wade Goodman. "But—" (looking longingly with bugged-out eyes at a Black Patti label) "—perhaps we could listen to some, too?" He picked out two dozen or so and carried them carefully out.

Once they had snuck Duncan into Carden Wade Goodman's cabin and the girls into their own cabin, Dora and Carden Wade Goodman found themselves, later that evening, back in Frank's living room / bedroom / kitchen listening to the mysterious music of another, almost disappeared world. (Donna Cody had wanted to come, but for once, Carden Wade Goodman was very firm.)

Frank's Victrola was a beauty, a dark mahogany bureau with an elegant old needle and small doors at the top that regulated the volume. (The farther you opened them, the louder it got.) There was even a small brown-paper envelope with extra needles in it. Frank had apparently acquired it from the owner of the records.

"I don't know who has time for these things. There's plenty of good music on the radio, I figure," said Frank. "You and your daughter here, you must have heard some good stuff in Nashville."

"I sure did," said Dora, a bit too brightly. "There was Porter Waggoner, Dolly Parton, Molly Bee—all kinds of folks."

"Your voice sounds kinda familiar," said Frank.

Dora shifted uncomfortably. Carden Wade Goodman had brought his beloved silver flask of excellent whiskey. He deemed it a good time to share it. Frank nodded and took a swig. Dora rolled her eyes at Carden Wade Goodman, who ignored her and said, "Let's listen a little to some of these records, Frank."

Frank waved that idea away, but he gestured to the Victrola. Carden Wade Goodman was up in a flash, waving a 78.

"This is called 'She Just Couldn't Let It Alone,' and I must say, I have never heard of this song, or the singers, The Pinewood Sisters. And that is strange because I know most of the songs and singers out there," said Carden Wade Goodman, a bit arrogantly. He carefully lowered the needle.

Chapter 33: A Sad Testing.

God bless the dove that mourns for love
And flies from pine to pine.
It mourns for the loss of its own true love.
O why not me for mine?

—"Giles Collins," Version B, in Cecil Sharpe's *English Songs from the Southern Appalachians*, Vol. 1. Sung by Mrs. Hester House at Hot Springs, N.C., September 16, 1916

Sound erupted from the Victrola. Dora leaned forward and closed the doors a little to damp it down. In spite of some whoosh and swish, an authoritative guitar clearly picked out the tune, doubling the melody played in tremolo on a sweet mandolin; then both instruments dropped back to chords and little runs, as a rich alto and tenor from long ago sang the following in a tight harmony:

Pretty Annie and Lottie, they was the best of pals
But Annie married Cameron, and that split up the gals,
Annie was afraid that he was a cheatin' man,
So she pestered Lottie to help her, for she had a wicked plan.

Chorus

She just couldn't let it alone, she just couldn't let it alone,
The women how they make each other weep and sob and moan,
'Cause they just can't let it, just can't let it, just can't let it alone.

Chorus

"Go to my husband, my best friend, and do all that you can
To see if he'll betray me and be a faithless man,
To see if he will hug and kiss and meet you with a smile,
I want you to be a true friend, Lottie, and so my man beguile."

Chorus

"Oh no, oh no, dear Annie,
Don't ask me for to sin."
But Lottie pleaded and wept in vain
And finally gave in.

Chorus

Lottie with some sighing began to smile and wink.
Good Cameron was troubled and didn't know what to think.
Annie watched and waited and thought it all high jinks
Till Cameron and Lottie, they into vice did sink.

Chorus

Cameron said, "Oh Lottie, look at the trouble I'm in,
I loved my pretty Annie, but now I'm full of sin."
And Lottie cried, "I've betrayed my dearest friend, and lost my honor too,
While trying to be a faithful friend, I've fallen in love with you."

Chorus

They finally up and run away, and Annie learned too late:
Don't test your man or your best friend, or love will turn to hate.
Cameron he run off to the war, and Lottie she died of grief,
Pretty Annie died right after her, it was a sad relief.

Chapter 34: In Which *De Gustibus non Est Disputandum* Is Sorely Tested.

Such dreams, such dreams as these
I know they mean no good
For I dreamed that my bower was full of red swine
And my bride's bed full of blood.

—"Lady Margaret," traditional

"Whew," exhaled Carden Wade Goodman. "I have certainly never heard anything like that. Who were these Pinewoods Sisters? While I've heard of German influence in the Appalachians, nevertheless, the name 'Lottie' is peculiar."

Meanwhile, Dora had jumped up and was doing a little dance around the room. "I know that song, I know that song." she said. "Or at least, I know that story. But my mama sang it different, one of her ballads. Something like this:

Fair Annie and sweet Lottie were dearest friends, the best that ever could
be
But Annie she teased the gentlemen sore, though Lottie did not agree
And that handsome man, Lord Camson, a knight of high degree,
He fancied pretty Annie, and with pomp they did marry.

Now Annie she had rings and things but soon began to moan
For missing her dear Lottie and all her friends at home,
Lord Camson bade her invite them all, but Lottie came alone
And in joy the two dear friends did walk and sweetly did they roam.

While walking in the gay green fields, the friends strolled arm in arm
"My fortune is so fine," said fair Annie, "with Lord Camson to keep me
warm"
But I am sorely troubled and it does to me some harm.
"Tell me, then, my dearest friend," said Lottie in alarm.

Said Annie, "I'm still lonely, without my sweetest friend,
I never would have married if I'd known this was the end."
"Oh do not say so!" Lottie cried, "for you married one so fine."
And so they laughed and wended their way, and the sun did brightly
shine."

Carden Wade Goodman had stopped talking, and even Frank gaped at that beautiful voice ringing like a bell, but with that same rich nasal haunting sound as those on the record. Dora's voice was heavy with centuries of women lamenting the murders, the lost loves, the cruel wars, and the terrors of passion.

"That's all I remember," she said.

"Wow, you sing real good," said Frank. "Real-old style, though."

Carden Wade Goodman covertly shuddered. Dora said thank you.

"And I swear I've heard you sing before, but different. But that song, you know, that's the dumbest thing I ever heard. What man would ever put up with that? Two women carrying on like that?" He took another swig from the flask.

Carden Wade Goodman said, "Frank, I guess folks have different tastes. I believe these different versions of the song hearken back to Boccaccio, and in fact. . ." Dora cleared her throat and looked at him with her eyes wide and signaling.

"OK, well, here's your money," said Carden Wade Goodman, handing over the cash. "I'll load all these up in the morning."

Frank clutched the money and grunted a dismissal.

Chapter 35: Feelings and Felines: A Late-Night Stroll.

I got an old Tom Cat, when he steps out
All the pussy cats in the neighborhood, they begin to shout
Here comes the Ring-Tail Tom, he's boss around the town
And if you got your heat turned up
You better turn your damper down.

—"Tom Cat Blues," probably by Cliff Carlisle

But before they could leave, the door suddenly burst open and in rushed Sandy Panther, gasping, her thick dark hair standing up every which way. Frank rose up like a looming mountain, moving faster than one would think possible, and grabbed her by the arm.

"Get away from me, you pile of blubber!" shouted Sandy Panther, trying to rip her arm out of his grasp and batting at him with her other hand, Frank grunting and immovable. "Mr. Goodman, come quick! Donna Cody has gotten herself all scratched up and Duncan's trying to help, but she's a bloody mess. Let GO of me, damn you!"

"You shut your mouth right now," said Frank, shaking her. "You and that friend of yours, you're nothing but trouble." He looked with suspicion at Dora and Carden Wade Goodman. "Who's this Duncan?"

"Now, now," Dora soothed, "slow down, Sandy Panther. Mr. Frank, how 'bout you let her go? She's not causing trouble, and she's very sorry she called you names, aren't you, Sandy Panther?" Her sweet voice had just the slightest edge to it at the end. Both recipients of this speech capitulated; Frank let go and Sandy Panther muttered an apology of sorts. Carden Wade Goodman looked at Dora with even more respect as he hovered protectively over the stacks of 78s, but he sighed, "Right, let's go see what our hapless friend has gotten into now. Sandy Panther, you can fill us in on the way. Don't worry, sir—I'll take care of it. Good night," he nodded. "I'll collect the records in the morning." He eyed the stack of disks mournfully, obviously wanting to play all the rest of them. He wheezed, coughed, turned, and left, Sandy Panther still tugging on his sleeve.

"I better not see any kind of mess up there in the morning," said Frank. He slammed the door shut after them.

Earlier that evening, Duncan and Donna Cody had decided to take a little walk together when it became obvious that Sandy Panther was not going to shut up and let them talk to each other. Donna Cody wanted advice about Marvin and a phone number. Duncan had some other things in mind. Rockandy and Blue sprang up to go with them, but they both decided they'd be better off without the dogs. Sandy Panther huffily took out her banjo and played, fixing her gaze in the middle of the air and ignoring them both.

They snuck around the cabin and back into the woods. Duncan, who had the wit to be carrying a flashlight, shone the way, though there was enough moon in the clear sky to help. They stopped at a low split-rail fence bordering a field.

"Duncan, we've got to do something for Marvin," she began.

"Stop right there," he said. "Mr. Goodman already has it all arranged. Marvin's dad is coming down and will fix things up, it seems. But he's pretty mad. Marvin was pretty mad too. Mr. Goodman had to calm him down."

"You two did this without talking to me?"

"Yes, we did. I know he's your friend, but he's mine too, and we thought it might be better if you weren't involved. Remember when we stopped for gas and Mr. Goodman was in that phone booth?"

"I thought he was calling his wife."

"Nope, he called Marvin and Marvin's dad. We figured we can check on him later. But he doesn't want to talk to you. I'm sorry, Donna Cody."

Donna Cody sighed. "I guess I am too," she finally admitted. She looked up at Duncan, and he looked back at her and then put his arm carefully around her shoulders. Donna Cody stiffened and then, to Duncan's amazement and delight, leaned into him.

"Donna Cody," he whispered. "You know I love you, in spite of everything."

Donna Cody stiffened and drew back. Duncan's arm fell forlornly.

"What do you mean, *in spite of everything?*"

"You know," he said, "Mama working for you and all."

"What do you mean? You know I love you, and Mabel too," she said. "You are a good young man."

"But Donna Cody, I don't love you that way. Donna Cody?" But he had lost her attention and she was now staring past him.

"Look over there," she whispered. The moonlight, so romantic a minute ago, now revealed hundreds of gleaming eyes. When Duncan trained his flashlight on them, they could see that the eyes belonged to a swarm of cats in a pen. Donna Cody asserted later that there were at least fifty. Now she ran over, Duncan shouting out to her to stop and be careful.

"Those poor cats!" said Donna Cody. She stuck her finger through the chicken wire pen, which ran around and over the animals. "YOW!" she screamed as a cat chomped down on it. They all began howling and caterwauling, hissing, screeching, growling, and snarling.

"Are you all right?" said Duncan, grabbing her finger. "I don't think these cats are pets, Donna Cody."

"They are most certainly not," said Donna Cody, gasping with pain, snatching her finger away sucking on it and then wiping it on her pants. "But they shouldn't be penned up like this, Duncan. This is cruelty to animals."

"Donna Cody, these cats belong to someone. They look feral. Listen to all that noise. Come on, let's go back and tend to that bite," Duncan remonstrated.

But Donna Cody pushed forward, looking for a way to let the cats out. Duncan leapt after her and tripped, falling on top of her, both of them crashing onto the chicken wire top, and the cats howled and yowled as the whole pen caved inward. Claws raked them as they scrambled to get up. Then there was a snapping sound as a door burst open and a rush of cats streamed out yowling and caterwauling and shrieking into the night. Duncan and Donna Cody finally struggled to their feet, snagging their hands, clothes, and hair in the chicken wire.

"I cannot believe you did that," said Duncan.

"If you hadn't knocked me over, everything would have been fine," said Donna Cody.

"You!" said Duncan, shaking all over for a minute. "Come on, let's get back. I must be crazy, and I *know* you're crazy, Donna Cody. But let's get out of here." They half-ran, half-limped back and staggered into the cabin. Sandy Panther looked up from playing her banjo and let out a yell at the horrible sight.

"My God, my God!" she said. "You two been fighting?"

Chapter 36: Reunions.

Out in this cold world alone,
Wand'ring about on the street,
Asking a penny for bread
Or begging for something to eat.

I'm nobody's darling on earth,
Heaven have mercy on me
For I'm nobody's darling;
Nobody cares for me.

—"Nobody's Darling on Earth," by Will S. Hays

The next morning, in spite of Carden Wade Goodman and Dora's ministrations (and Sandy Panther's running commentary), Duncan and Donna Cody lay in their respective cabins moaning in distress. They both had dangerously warm foreheads. Long, angry, red highways of cat scratches ran all over their arms and faces. Donna Cody's bitten thumb was swollen up like a little pink balloon.

Sandy Panther and Dora set them up with some coffee and a little toast from the restaurant down the road, but in both cabins it sat on the bureaus getting cold. They put Mercurochrome on the worst of the scratches, adding a ghastly pink glow to the lurid mess, and especially to Donna Cody's thumb.

"If that doesn't work," said Dora, "we'll go buy some iodine."

"I hate that stuff," shuddered Sandy Panther. "Stings."

"We've done what we can," said Dora. "Let's go help Mr. Goodman load those records. C'mon, Rockandy, c'mon, Blue." The dogs were glad to get out, though Rockandy cast a mournful look at his mistress as he left.

Over by the shed, they found Carden Wade Goodman huffing and puffing as he carried stacks of records over to the Jeep and piled them carefully into every nook available. Frank came out briefly to check on Sandy Panther, but seeing her busy and the dogs lying quietly nearby, he stumped back into his office.

"Say," said Carden Wade Goodman, sweating profusely under the hot July sun and leaning up against the car for a break. "Do you girls realize it's a big parade in town today? It's their celebration of the founding of Muleboro."

"Let's go, then," said Dora.

They knocked on the office door and inquired. Frank grunted and confirmed that there would be a parade downtown shortly and big dinner at the county fairgrounds, a few miles or so south-southeast. Wayne Carden Goodman reaffirmed with Frank that he would be loading the rest of the records later. Frank grunted a vague affirmative.

"Let's leave the dogs up at the cabin," said Sandy Panther. "You think Donna Cody and Duncan will be OK?"

"Donna Cody and Duncan will probably be fine," said Carden Wade Goodman curtly. He was annoyed with Donna Cody at the moment, though he felt sorry for Duncan.

The sun was shining, and even if it was too hot and muggy, a parade was a parade. Carden Wade Goodman parked the car carefully in the shade of a large oak so the 78s wouldn't warp. He had stacked them carefully on their sides, crammed them in so they couldn't budge and then craftily hidden them the best he could. As they came to town, they saw the usually drab main street was transformed. Bunting hung everywhere in the good old red, white, and blue, though some of it had Confederate flags hanging from it. Crowds of people lined the sidewalks. Children ran around, grownups fanned themselves and shouted at the kids, but they were almost as excited.

At the staging area, all sorts of people and vehicles were assembling themselves. Cars were crawling into order: a canary-yellow Mercury convertible, a white Buick Electra 227, a blue Ford Ranchero, a few tractors. A Packard was being draped with more of the red-white-and-blue bunting, some gentlemen sweating in antique suits in the front and two in the rumble seat. Two other cars were full of official-looking Grand Poohbahs with suits and funny hats. Behind the cars, a float with flowers and beauty queens toting parasols maneuvered itself into place. A ragged marching band, clowns, kids on bikes with red, white, and blue crepe paper in their wheels and streamers coming out of the handlebars and flags (both American and Confederate) grouped behind that.

Slowly, things got moving as the band began to play. The cars inched along, the girls on the float tossed candy amid hoots and whistles. Veterans from World Wars I and II, Korea, and even Vietnam hobbled and marched. Two clowns scampered around with more buckets of candy. A few Boy Scouts and Girl Scouts walked past. An old fire engine with ladders on the sides and gleaming white tire sidewalls around its shiny red hubcaps rolled proudly by. Probably the weirdest thing was a giant caterpillar. It had a box for a face, which was worn by someone covered with a sheet. Subsequent jointed sections of this animal were also covered with sheets and propelled forward (theoretically) by legs in black tights and shoes; however, some mobility problems had caused the caterpillar to curl up in a perilous position.

"Wow," said Sandy Panther, Dora, and Carden Wade Goodman.

"Let's run on ahead," suggested Dora, and so they plunged into the crowd on the sides of Main Street and tunneled through until the press thinned. Soon, the parade was going full tilt, the band running through the usual repertoire of "Star-Spangled Banner," "America the Beautiful," "Stars and Stripes Forever," and, of course, "Dixie." Marchers threw more candy, cars rolled by, bikes zoomed around upsetting everyone, and the caterpillar, looking a bit frighteningly like a KKK mascot with all those sheets, disjointedly brought up the rear. Everyone cheered and laughed and clapped. Sparklers and firecrackers went off in various parts of the crowd, and a policeman was kept busy running from incident to incident.

The crowd surged down the road to a big park with a gazebo in the middle and picnic tables laid out around it. Someone intoned through a megaphone about a barbecue and picnic for all. As the last people drifted out of the street or parked or threw their bikes down and thronged into the fairgrounds, a cherry-red Mustang with the top down came speeding down Main Street. Carden Wade Goodman, Dora, and Sandy Panther jumped off the street. Sandy Panther yelled, "What's the matter with you? Idiots!"

"Oh no," said Dora.

"Darling!" cried out Carden Wade Goodman. He ran to the car, which had screeched to a stop. An elegant woman with a huge red-lipsticked smile, dressed in a perfectly fitted light-blue summer suit with a faux white necktie and matching blue heels stepped gracefully out and hugged him. They laughed, cried, hugged, talked, laughed some more, held hands and looked at each other. You will have guessed, no doubt, that this was Carden Wade Goodman's wife, come to find him, but you may not have guessed that she was driving with none other than Nashville's own Fred Jones, that famous producer. He had tracked down Dora at last.

He stepped out on the sidewalk. Although short, he was lean and muscular, and with his black hair slicked back, spotless slacks, carefully pressed blue workshirt, and a pencil-thin madras tie, he was a natty figure. He sauntered over to Dora, grabbed her hand, and kissed it. Dora snatched her hand away and stood there like stone.

"What do you want, Fred?" she asked carefully. "What are you doing here?"

"Mr. Jones offered to drive me down," Carden Wade Goodman's wife said carefully, looking at them and realizing something was up. "We met at a party in Nashville."

"I see," said Dora, all ice.

"Now, Dora," said Fred, easily, "let's let bygones be bygones." He hugged her to his side, and she grimaced and pulled away.

"We had quite a time finding you," interrupted Carden Wade Goodman's wife, stepping adroitly between Dora and Fred. "Mr. Jones, I expect you'll want to get settled," she said, dismissing him. He glared at her and began to step forward. Carden Wade Goodman stepped in front of his wife, his chest inches from Mr. Jones's nose. Jones turned and walked back to his car. He threw a suitcase out on the ground, and it lay there in the dust while they all watched him drive off.

"How could you have found us?" demanded Carden Wade Goodman.

"Apparently, Mr. Jones has quite a network of, ah, friends," said Mrs. Goodman. She turned to Dora. "My ride was not at all agreeable. I am sorry to have distressed you."

"Thank you," said Dora. "There's bad business between us. He is no kind of gentleman."

"No, I think not," said Mrs. Goodman. "I did not realize until we had ridden for a while. Be careful about whom you meet at a party! He was charming at that time and eager to see you. But meanwhile, how about we all get ourselves some fried chicken or barbecued pig or whatever it is they eat down here." She steered Dora masterfully through the gates, Carden Wade Goodman following hurriedly beside them carrying his wife's suitcase.

Which left poor Sandy Panther standing there. No one was paying her any attention. No one even cared about her. She felt tears come into her eyes. There wasn't anybody for her. Marvin was in jail, not that she was all that attached to him. Donna Cody had gone over the edge. Sandy Panther was watching everyone else's lives unfold, while her own sat, an unbloomed bud. She was never going to get to perform and be a star. She would have said she felt like she'd been beat by a bag of nickels. No one even noticed. She didn't even want the stupid dinner. She trudged back gloomily to the motel, sinking deeper into a depressive trough.

Chapter 37: Commercialization, Capitalism, Corruption, Confrontation, and Convalescence.

Turn your back, sweet Willie, said she,
O turn your back unto me,
For you are too bad a rebel
For a naked woman to see.

She picked him up in her arms so strong
And she threw him into the sea,
Saying: If you have drowned six Kings' daughters here,
You may lay here in the room of me.

Stretch out your hand, O pretty Polly,
Stretch out your hand for me,
. . . .
And help me out of the sea.

She picked up a rock and threw on him, saying:
Lay there, lay there, you dirty, dirty dog,
Lay there in the room of me.
You're none too good nor too costly
To rot in the briny, briny sea.

—"Lady Isabel and the Elf Knight," Version B, in Cecil Sharpe's *English Songs from the Southern Appalachians*, Vol. 1. Sung by Mrs. Bishop, Clay Co., Ky., on July 16, 1909

Sandy Panther tugged on Donna Cody's hand.

"Wake up, Donna Cody," she whispered. Donna Cody stirred slightly. Sandy Panther jostled her again but more quietly.

"What? I need some water," moaned Donna Cody.

"Shhh. Here. Now listen to me. Here's some water."

"Is that you?"

"Yeah, it's me," said personified dejection.

"Sandy Panther, for Pete's sake, what is the matter?" Donna Cody slid up a notch into the beginning of a sitting position.

"Where am I going, Donna Cody? Nowhere, I figure. What's the point of all this? We could be big, Donna Cody, but you gotta face it that you need to talk to these people like Mr. Jones to get a real record out, not fool around with all these folks living out in the middle of nowhere. I've been there, and I'll tell you, it's no fun to live without a pot to piss in."

Donna Cody was now fully awake and struggled up another notch.

"Who? What?" she asked. "Who is Mr. Jones?"

Sandy Panther explained. Donna Cody scooted up another notch.

"That is fine if Dora wants to throw her past away and watch these people suck at it like vampires and use it for their own money-making, self-serving ends. The stuff they promote, that's taking the old music and destroying it."

"She can't stand him, you know that! She's left all that behind. And at least she was getting famous and getting paid into the bargain."

"Sandy Panther, you can't turn on your roots; you know that."

"I s'pose not, whatever that means in your brain. But my roots don't have to sit there buried where they can't be seen by anybody. They can grow a great big ol' tree, that's what."

At that moment, there was a soft knock on the door, and Sandy Panther went over to let Duncan in.

"You two OK?" he asked, wobbly. "I thought you were going with everyone else," he said to Sandy Panther.

"Too bad, I came back," said Sandy Panther nastily. "I'm fine, but you ain't. Here now, you sit there. I hope ol' Fat Frank didn't see you come in here."

"Duncan, are you feeling better?" asked Donna Cody, who, after her fervent converse, had slid back down onto her pillow again.

"Getting there," said Duncan. "What's all this talk going on in here?"

"No talk you ain't heard before, most likely," said Sandy Panther. "I was just saying that—" and she began a catalogue of woes, during which Donna Cody drifted off to sleep.

"Enough," Duncan said, rubbing his head and blinking. He said it loud enough, though, for Donna Cody to wake up again.

"I'll tell you when I've had enough," said Sandy Panther contentiously.

"This discussion is important, Duncan," said Donna Cody as if she had never dozed off. "The problem here is a complex one that demands attention. Sandy Panther is an example of why the commercialization of the arts is a destructive force that obliterates the true and beautiful music of the people. This music is disappearing or becoming nothing but supposed 'country' or 'folk' or rock and roll. A true folk musician is part of a tradition that respects the song or tune, and they're careful about making sure they get it right. You should have seen Calvin Cecil Leggett. He loves that 'Chickalielee Daisy-O,' and he made me get every piece of it just so. We serve that music, Sandy Panther, rather than having it serve us. We don't electrify it and sell it with slick arrangements and tricks for the stage so that modern people will like it. We carry on the tradition and learn from it. Someone said that tradition is the democracy of the dead, and we honor those dead when we continue in their paths."

"Donna Cody," said Duncan. "Lie down and forget all this for a little bit. And don't you start on her," he said to Sandy Panther.

Donna Cody and Sandy Panther were so surprised at this that Donna Cody actually lay back down to sleep, while Sandy Panther stormed outside. Fireworks blooming in the now-dark sky made her feel even worse. She watched a while and smoked a cigar. When she finally came in, she saw that Duncan was snoring in his chair. The dogs were both shivering from the fireworks. She petted them a while and calmed them down, then sighed, woke Duncan up, and sent him off to his cabin. She curled up on the other bed with her blanket. Sometime later that night, she vaguely heard people coming in and settling themselves. She pretended to be asleep, and pretty soon she was.

Sunlight was peeking in the window when there was a knock and Fred Jones entered the cabin. He looked around the room with some distaste, as if some of its grubbiness might stick to his carefully arranged hair, his tight chinos, his crisply ironed madras shirt, his shiny black shoes, or his even shinier sunglasses, which he finally took off. His hand on his hip showed off a chunky golden watch. As he worried a toothpick, he scanned the room and saw Dora's luxurious auburn hair spread across a blanket. He went over to her bed and shook her arm a little.

"Dora," he said. "Honey."

Dora rubbed her eyes, automatically tried to smooth her hair, and blinked. Her eyes turned to stone.

"Give me a chance to kill you right here," she said.

"What are you doing here?" said Sandy Panther, sitting right up. "That's Fred," she said *sotto voce* to Donna Cody, who was also struggling to sit up in the other bed. Everything was deadly still. Then Duncan came into the cabin. "I heard something," he said, and then stopped.

Fred Jones looked him over, and an even bigger thundercloud entered the room.

"What the *hell*, Dora," said Fred. "What, you turning into some free love, sleep-with-the-n_____s-kinda gal?"

A terrible silence.

"This is your manager?" said Duncan. Young as he was, recovering from his injuries, he was still an intimidating sight, towering over Fred Jones, who tightened into something more compact and threatening. Rockandy and Blue began to softly growl.

"Shut up, boy. Dogs, too? What a party we're having here," he said, evenly, between his teeth.

"Whoa," muttered Sandy Panther. "Let's not corner something meaner 'n us."

"You?" said Donna Cody. "You—you're the one taking all her money while she does all the work? You—forcing yourself on her, get out of our cabin!"

"You heard the young lady," said Dora, suddenly coming to life and jumping up. "Clear out! You're not getting no more of nothing from me, you son of a bitch!"

Donna Cody was rummaging around, looking for something.

"Don't you dare!" hissed Sandy Panther to her, jumping out of bed and grabbing her hand.

Fred Jones turned his attention to the two of them struggling and scanned Sandy Panther from top to bottom in a way that made her suck in her breath. Duncan took another step into the room, and Donna Cody opened her mouth to launch into another diatribe.

Fred Jones looked appraisingly at Sandy Panther for little longer, then at Dora, and then he took out a toothpick and picked his teeth. And then hawked a loogie right into the middle of the room.

"Ugh!" cried Donna Cody, Sandy Panther, and Dora.

Duncan stepped forward.

"Back, n_____!" said Fred Jones, raising his fists. Then to Dora: "You want to take up with these n_____-lovin', crazy folk, you bitch, fine. I give it up. You could be making millions, and you're throwing it away. God*damn*, woman!"

Dora put her hand on Duncan's arm, restraining him.

"Now you listen, Fred, and you listen good. You steal every cent I make and you know it. You stole more than money, you no-good polecat. Get away from here before I call the police, and don't you ever come near me again. I could kill you and never feel a thing 'cept relief."

"I know someone could help you do it," muttered Sandy Panther, who had not liked Fred Jones's look at her at all. But she still held on tightly to Donna Cody's arm.

Fred Jones eyed them carefully and backed toward the door. "Goodbye, then, Dora Richards," he snarled. "See if you can find someone else to f___ to get yourself some contracts!" and he slammed the door. They all sat and stood in silence till they heard his car roar off. Dora was shaking. They all wanted to wipe Fred Jones off, Sandy Panther doing so with a towel from the bathroom to clean the floor.

"Whew," she said, getting up and chucking the towel into the bathroom. "How'd you ever take up with him, Dora? He's one mean bastard. I hope all those producers ain't all like that."

"Quiet, Sandy Panther," said Duncan. He was holding Dora's arm carefully. "Are you all right?"

"Don't tell me to hush," said Sandy Panther automatically.

"Thank you, Duncan. Yes, I feel fine," said Dora shakily.

"Dora, you have been brave and true to yourself!" exclaimed Donna Cody. "You have a wonderful family, beautiful, ancient songs, and you know how to sing them. I would love to visit your home with you, Dora Richards!"

"Donna Cody—all of you—how can I begin to thank you? I would be honored to have you visit. I don't know how that devil got his claws into me, but I'm free of him now. My dad always said that good judgment comes from experience, and a lotta that comes from bad judgment. He's not getting any more of my royalties! And maybe I don't have to kill him."

"Mr. Carden will be sad to hear that," said Sandy Panther. "But then his wife is here now, that Frances. And where are they, anyway? But Dora, I'll tell you some advice from my Auntie Rufe: Keep your fences horse-high, pig-tight, and bull-strong. You get yourself a lawyer and go after that devil. And then you can go sing some more hits and show 'em all."

"No, no, no!" Donna Cody protested. "You don't want to sing that modern junk. Leave all that and get back to your old songs, to your family songs."

Dora smiled at Sandy Panther and Donna Cody. "Donna Cody, we each have our path to take. Mine, I think, is with you for a while, but I have a living to make, and it's gotta be with my voice. That's how I can best help my folks. Now, let's get up and out and get some breakfast for everyone."

Donna Cody, it turned out, was still not up to breakfast. She was shaken from the awful encounter with Fred Jones. It was discouraging to know that there's such meanness in the world and exhausting to try to keep people out of its clutches.

However, her lassitude probably had more to do with a red line that had moved up her arm. She sank back into bed and waved Dora and Sandy Panther out the door. Duncan left reluctantly. She quickly fell asleep but tossed and turned and sweated. She dreamed a shantyboat floated by, lined with screeching cats playing fiddles. The boat drifted into a barn that filled with light as it developed high windows and then turned into a church, but it still had straw on the floor, and the pews were full of instruments that could walk and talk: banjos like the broomsticks in *The Sorcerer's Apprentice*, fiddles who gestured with their bows, guitars thrumming and singing out of their big O's of mouths, basses thumping back, and up front a giant figure singing out a sermon.

"Get over here," the figure said, and all the instruments scurried over. Something like fire tore at her arm. A knife. Something wet and mushy plopped on her arm, one of the cats, she knew it, her eyes flew open. And she started to faint. Everyone was crowded round her bed, but in front of them all, winding plastic wrap containing something mushy around her arm—was Mabel!

"Listen to her breathin'. And her heart, goin' like crazy. And a fever. Don't any of you have any sense? She's got the blood poison is what. Cats? Filthy creatures and you be lucky, Duncan, you didn't get the same.

Look here where I cut open, running pus. You can't let it stay in there. Now this potato, this'll draw out that poison." She was now wrapping up the arm with a strip of cloth.

"Ma'am, don't you think we should immediately depart for the hospital?" inquired Carden Wade Goodman worriedly.

"What hospital?" said Frances. "God knows where the closest hospital is."

"They'd kill her there anyway," grumbled Mabel. "You all wait and see, and if she gets worse, maybe, but I know this works."

"Mama, are you sure?" said Duncan. He stroked Donna Cody's wild fluffy hair and Mabel looked sharply at him. He pulled his hand back. Donna Cody stared at them all with cloudy eyes.

" 'Course I'm sure. Used this on you more than once if you don't care to remember." Duncan remembered. And he was glad that he had called his mother.

"Donna Cody," said Sandy Panther, melodramatically grabbing her hand. "Don't you die on us!"

"Now that's enough talk about dying," said Mabel. "You hush that talk."

"Here's some water, ma'am," said Dora, bringing over a cup.

"Something useful at last," said Mabel, and she poured as much as she could into Donna Cody's mouth and then used part of a sheet to wipe her forehead with the rest.

"Something useful," mimicked Sandy Panther under her breath. She was still unhappy. Everyone loved Dora.

"Mabel, is that you? Mabel? Duncan? Sandy Panther?" Donna Cody struggled with her twisted sheets. They all began talking at once until Mabel gusted out a long "Shusssssh."

"Donna, honey, Mabel is here. Now, you sleep some, and we'll wait with you," said Mabel. Rockandy whined and gave a little yip. Blue dared to thump her tail a bit.

"What, and now you got yourself another one?" said Mabel. "Come over here, boy, and you too, honey dog," she said to Blue. They both leaned up against her.

"Ahhh," sighed Donna Cody. She reached up and grabbed Duncan's hand, and then she fell back into sleep.

The others slowly left the room, even Sandy Panther and Blue, while Mabel and Duncan caught up with each other. They hugged, once Donna Cody let go of Duncan's hand, but then Mabel asked her son if he had lost his mind and what had he been thinking and didn't he know you had to be careful down here and if he thought he was going to have a little romance with Miss Donna he better think again and it was a good thing his mother had found her way down here but a terrible thing to have to come back down south after all these years.

Duncan, wisely, hugged her again. She heaved a bit and then sat down on the edge of the bed, the one rickety chair in the room looking ill equipped for her. Even as nice looking as she was with her glossy black purse and shoes, her string of fat white fake pearls, her dark-blue print dress and raincoat, and her kerchief on her head, Duncan could see that she was exhausted. He made up a space on Sandy Panther's bed and moved her over.

"Mama," Duncan said, "you need to be careful, y'know—the man that runs this place is as bad a bigot as I've seen in a while."

"Duncan, you don't know nothin' about bigots. I can tell you stories about bigots, things you never heard about. And there weren't no people marchin' then nor any of that."

"I've always wondered, Mama, where did you come from? You've never told me anything, and it is surely about time you did."

Mabel sighed wearily. "Not now, Duncan, not now. It was a long train ride down, one I never thought to make, 'specially with taters in my pocket. Lord have mercy! I need to get me some sleep. That Sandy Panther can sleep on the floor, don't you think? And what are you doing in the ladies' cabin, anyway?"

"Mama, it's not like the old days. No one worries about all that now. Besides, that Frank, the one that owns this place, Dora told him I'm Italian. Otherwise, he'd probably call the Klan or something. They're big around here, I guess." (Carden Wade Goodman had passed on this bit of unsavory information to keep Duncan aware of his position. Whether it was true or not, it was true enough.)

"Eyetalian!" snorted Mabel. "I think you better worry." But finally, after some gentle persuasion, she took her shoes off, stretched out on Sandy Panther and Dora's bed, and slept the deep and blessed sleep of the useful. Duncan went back to the Goodmans' cabin and did the same.

Chapter 38: Healing. Another Discourse on the Nature of the Folk and Their Music. A Promised Story.

Thro' all the tumult and the strife
I hear the music ringing;
It finds an echo in my soul—
How can I keep from singing?

—"My Life Flows on in Endless Song," by Robert Lowry

The next day, Donna Cody was much better. Sandy Panther was cranky about being moved to the floor, but she kept uncharacteristically quiet in the presence of Mabel, who had freshened herself in various mysterious ways and was tending to Donna Cody. She unwound the cloth, then took off the potato poultice, and saw that the red streak had retreated to barely half an inch and that green pus was all over the potato. She threw that mess outside in the bushes, cut another potato in half and scraped out the middle, which was mushy in the right way. She slathered it on the bite, took out more plastic wrap, and used some medical tape put it all together. Donna Cody was sitting up and watching all this with great interest. The only hitch was when some of the potato juice got all over Mabel's dress. Apparently, the starchy stains were not easy to remove.

Pretty soon, there was a knock at the door, and in stepped Carden Wade Goodman, Frances Goodman, Dora Richards, Sandy Panther, and Duncan Watkins. In their arms were all sorts of fine-smelling bags and boxes, breakfast from the café and the sad store down the road. Hot coffee, boxes of cereal, milk, orange juice, biscuits in gravy, butter, jams, peach pie. Cornbread. There were even some sausage patties. And more potatoes. They piled everything on the chair and rickety little table. They all settled themselves in whatever spots they could find, and ate. Donna Cody, as usual, only ate a little bit and could not be coaxed into more. Since she finished first, she had a captive audience of munching, chewing, and gulping friends, so she held forth:

"I do not know how to begin thanking you, my dear friends. Mabel, you have probably saved my life. Duncan, you have always been the truest of friends. Really, you and Mabel are my family. Sandy Panther, you have stuck it all out through the thick and the thin. You are my musical partner and best companion. Mr. Goodman, you have protected us and shown us some wonderful music. Mrs. Goodman, I do not know you yet, but you appear to be as wonderful as your husband. And Dora, you have stood up against a creature who represents all the evil in the music world." (Sandy Panther said an "Amen" with her mouth full of corn muffin, her jealousy calmed for the moment.)

"You are all part of a beautiful and noble endeavor, whether you know it or not. We live in a time when the almighty dollar is king, where the very term *folk song* has been stolen by people interested in nothing except personal aggrandizement. Pop tunes have not made their way through the filter of tradition but are weeds crowding out the songs and tunes loved and cherished for so long. They mutilate them, running them over, and they cut people off from their past. Worse is calling these modern things *folk songs*, confusing everyone. If these pieces of trivia are *folk songs*, then what do you call the old ballads and fiddle tunes, the banjo pieces with their beautiful tunings?" (Sandy Panther perked up for a minute, but then slumped down as Donna Cody continued.)

"As in literature and art," Donna Cody intoned, "without time as an arbiter, people only see half-baked creations that haven't been winnowed out, that haven't had time to become classics. Time reveals what matters and unveils the mystery of excellence. You can't see, hear, or read everything in the world. Some things are truly more important than other things. These things must continue to be cherished and preserved."

Here, Carden Wade Goodman opened his mouth to speak, but he waited a second too long and lost his chance.

Furthermore," intoned Donna Cody, "it is the folk, the people who play their music for the love of it, who are the true artists. They support all the others who feed off them—the performers and the producers and all the rest. Antonin Dvořák said that all the great musicians have borrowed from the songs of the common people. It's that music that will save us all.

"You may say," she continued, though no one had said anything, "that everything changes, that we do not need to preserve the beautiful music of the folk because they will always make more. But we must preserve it because it's being killed, with no time to develop naturally as it used to. These people who copyright a song that's belonged to everyone for hundreds of years? They might as well stick a knife in and cut out its heart. No, as Cecil Sharp and many other people I have read noted, one person might make up a song, but it's the whole community that shapes it. Someone else might play a tune and play it differently, but the communities need time to develop. But today, we don't give anything or anybody enough time. Everything is going too fast."

Donna Cody was obviously feeling better.

The intelligent reader (who is surely you) may have noticed before this point that Donna Cody's folkloric fundamentalism had some major difficulties. Oddly, for someone who loved the old music so much and listened to and collected and played it, she used few actual examples to support her romantic view of things. Others might also note (along with Sandy Panther), that people haven't changed that much and that even performers need to eat. If crass modern folk singers wanted nothing but money, they could surely find an easier way to make it. Not only this, but the idea of some mysterious "folk process" that causes some old-time musicians to hunker around until they play it the way Earl or Bessie or Tommy played it can surely deaden and freeze the music into an artifact. Is there a "correct" version of things? Are there "classics"? Isn't this a snobby idea, a strange irony in light of the idea that the supposedly great music or stories or art come from the "folk"? Who are these folk? Aren't they just people like you and me? Are there some traditions that just need to go away?

Should the music of the people only be acoustic? Unpopular? Have a well-documented genealogy? Should it plagiarize or not? Can it be professional?

Or is there a secret, mystical, rushing, living stream running beneath the world, one that even money can never buy?

The last crumb had been eaten, the last bit of coffee drunk. No one was going to stand for much more of Donna Cody's high-falutin' talk except, perhaps, for Carden Wade Goodman, who mostly wanted to argue with it. Mabel stood up from the bed and said, "That's all well and good, Miss Cody, but it's time you be gettin' back home."

"And Mama, we need to get *you* home," said Duncan, eying Donna Cody, who was mustering up a counterproductive response.

"Never mind that," said Mabel, "I know all I need to know about getting home. It's getting Miss Donna and you home I'm here for."

"Mabel, I'm sorry to oppose you, but I plan to visit Dora Richards' family now that, thanks to you, I am healed. Sandy Panther will go with me."

"Oh, I s'pose," said Sandy Panther.

Mabel objected and did so for quite a while. When she was done, Duncan said, "She's right, Donna Cody."

Dora chimed in. "My family's house—no, it's closer to get there than to yours, Mr. Goodman, it really is, though you have to drive around some of the hollers. It would be a good stop on Donna Cody's return journey and then everyone would be happy. You would all be welcome."

"I would like to accompany you, then," said Carden Wade Goodman, looking sideways at his wife. "You have no objections, do you, Frances?"

"Only if I don't come along," she laughed.

"What about Marvin?" demanded Sandy Panther.

Carden Wade Goodman explained that Marvin's father seemed to have the situation in hand.

"Lord, Lord. I hope that child gets out of there soon. He doesn't want to be stuck in a jail down here," said Mabel.

"Now, how would you know about jails down here, Mama?"

"Know? Know? Child, I know more about jails down here than you ever better know!"

"What? How?" said Duncan and Donna Cody.

"That is a story for another time," Mabel said primly, as she began sorting out the remains of breakfast.

"No, really, Mama," said Duncan.

"You were in jail, Mabel?" asked Donna Cody in astonishment.

"Not me. Your daddy, Duncan. And it's Miss Porter, Miss Donna, who is to thank it wasn't worse."

"My aunt was involved?" asked Donna Cody with interest.

"You never told me any of this," muttered Duncan.

"Child, you never asked. But things happened before you was born, believe it or not."

"Mabel, how *did* you get to know my aunt?"

"Miss Donna, your aunt, bless her, rescued me from a mighty bad situation, but it's a long story that never has had the tellin'. And now is not the time."

Chapter 39: Mabel's Story.

Troublin' mind, troublin' mind,
Troublin' mind, Troublin' mind,
Troublin' mind, troublin' mind,
God's a-gonna ease my troublin' mind.

—"God's Gonna Ease My Troublin' Mind," traditional

It was not time for Mabel's story until several things happened. First of all, Donna Cody had to recover entirely, which she had by the next day. Then, Frances and Carden Wade Goodman went off to call Marvin's father to check in.

"She is one great lady," said Sandy Panther, talking about Frances. "She don't take no foolishness from Mr. Goodman. She writes science fiction and monster movies and all kinds of stuff, like he does. But she gets her stuff on TV shows!"

The following day, Frances Goodman took Donna Cody to a bank and then together they split the bill for everyone's stay. It was more than past time to leave. Mabel and Duncan were getting tired of hiding, though they were certainly having some interesting and lively talks, which would cease the minute anyone else walked into the cabin. Everyone had decided to go to Dora's. The Goodmans and Donna Cody were excited about seeing her legendary family. Sandy Panther, though still feeling that things were off track, didn't mind the idea of seeing some of her people nearby. Mabel and Duncan weren't happy about going to Dora's.

"But they will love to meet you," said Dora to them.

"You sure that—" asked Mabel with a frown.

"Absolutely," said Dora. "Do not even think about it, ma'am."

"Reckon I'll go drop in on Auntie Rufe if we're headin' up that way," said Sandy Panther. "Check in on the ol' cuss."

"You shouldn't talk about your auntie that way," said Donna Cody. "I wish my Aunt Jane were still alive. You should be glad she's there. And besides, it sounds as if she knows a lot of tunes. But let's go to Dora's first."

"I do not disrespect my family, Donna Cody. Anyway, not most of 'em. But Auntie Rufe, she'll give you a run for your money," said Sandy Panther. "Sure, I'll take in Dora's place first, but don't expect me to linger too long."

Everyone loaded up in the cars. By shoving the dogs over, Duncan could curl up in the back of the Rambler, though they leaned and squirmed and slithered back until they were almost on top of him. Mabel squeezed herself into Carden Wade Goodman's Jeep with Dora and Frances.

"Goodbye, Fat Frank!" Sandy Panther yelled out the car window. "You want to see just how much we're going to miss you, just stick your finger in a pond, pull it out, and look at the hole."

Frank lumbered out of his office, but they were pulling out and glad to leave him behind.

After a few hours, they pulled off at an inviting field and, as they all talked and the dogs ran, they realized that they faced an interesting dilemma: where to stay the night.

"We need the old Green Book," muttered Mabel.

"What is that?" asked Frances.

"Told us where we Negroes could stay. Couldn't stay just anywhere. Couldn't just go do your business anywhere. Couldn't get your gas for the automobile."

"Have you traveled much, Mrs. Watkins?" asked Carden Wade Goodman.

"Just up to school with my daddy. He had him a Packard car."

"Indeed," said Carden Wade Goodman. "It sounds as if you came from a well-off family."

"For Colored, you mean," said Mabel dryly. "That's OK. I know you all ain't prejudiced that way, but I grew up way down south of here, little town called Moreland. My daddy was a preacher; he loved any book he could find, loved the Good Book most of all. So he had learnin', but it didn't do him much good in the end."

"I'm sorry," said Frances.

"Thank you, ma'am; it was a sorry situation."

"Please, call me Frances."

"I don't feel comfortable doing that. How about I call you 'Mrs. Goodman'?"

"I would never wish to make you uncomfortable," said Frances. "That is fine."

"But Mrs. Watkins, how did you come to know Donna Cody?" persisted Carden Wade Goodman.

"Through her aunt, Professor Porter," she said. "I was her housekeeper." And she clamped her mouth determinedly shut.

But Mabel wasn't going to get off easily. Carden Wade Goodman or Frances would politely persist, and then later use the facts in some fanciful science fiction yarn set in a town a lot like Moreland. Duncan, meanwhile, was realizing that he came from somewhere.

Duncan, Donna Cody, Sandy Panther, and the dogs came over. They had been swarming around the Rambler, getting dogs set up with food, putting things in the trunk, getting things out of the trunk.

"Any ideas about where we can stay?" asked Duncan.

"I don't see why we can't camp out the way we have," said Donna Cody. "Our funds are limited, and we can't keep depleting yours, Mr. and Mrs. Goodman."

"Not at all, not at all," said Carden Wade Goodman, waving away such an idea like bad-smelling smoke. Frances looked sharply at him. It was a look that said there would be a private discussion about Carden Wade Goodman's funds later.

"Don't be dumb, Donna Cody," said Sandy Panther. "We still need a place. Mr. and Mrs. Goodman can't just sleep under some poncho. And Mabel and Duncan can't stay just anywhere."

"In this day and age? That is ridiculous. They should be able to stay wherever they want."

"You've missed a few things," said Duncan, looking at her steadily.

"Looks like we're coming to a bigger town in about 25 miles," said Dora, studying the state map they had picked up at the gas station. "I expect we can find something there. I can go in and say that we're traveling with our housekeeper and her boy, which is the case," she added. Everyone agreed with that, except for Duncan and Donna Cody. The latter had to be talked down from wanting to go in and "handle the situation." No one wanted her to try handling any situation.

"What about you, Duncan?" she asked him. "What do we say you're doing for us? But then why should we have to say anything at all? You let me in there. They can't—"

"I'll be fine, Donna Cody," Duncan said, but he was scowling. He did not like being called a boy, even by friends.

"You will not," said Donna Cody.

"Uh-uh," agreed Mabel.

"Not too likely," from Sandy Panther.

"Duncan will be my mechanic," said Frances Goodman, ending the discussion. Duncan grimaced. "We will stop at a motel and all chip in as we can. Dora, Donna Cody, you are far too young (she meant "scruffy looking," but only some people understood that) to be believed. You leave this to me."

They recognized a leader in Frances and so, for the moment, agreed. As they drove through a good-sized town, they bypassed some of the more dramatic motels with giant stars, arches, neon, large glass doors, free color TV, and pools, much to Sandy Panther's regret. Instead they found a plain brick place that looked a little run down and a lot older than the other motels. Frances Goodman swept in, requested rooms, and brooked no resistance. The cowed couple who ran the motel booked them into three rooms: the Goodmans in one, Mabel and Duncan in another at the end of a long, dingy hall, and Donna Cody, Sandy Panther, and Dora in the third, dogs included at extra cost.

"Thank you, Mrs. Goodman," said Mabel later, when they all met back at the Goodmans' room. It was the largest and nicest of the rooms. Donna Cody and Sandy Panther were assigned dinner duties, and they departed to see what they could find. Duncan had wanted to go with them.

"Now that would be nothing but trouble," said Mabel. "Colored man with two white girls. Could be a sundown town, too."

"What's a sundown town?" asked Duncan.

"I know that one," said Frances Goodman. "That's usually a small town where all Negroes have to be off the streets by sundown unless they have the misfortune to live there."

"We don't have any colored people up in our holler," said Dora. "I never even knew about that."

"I heard of it," said Sandy Panther.

Donna Cody seethed in the background.

Later, Donna Cody and Sandy Panther came back with sacks of hamburgers and fries, two boxes of Ding Dongs, a gallon of milk, a loaf of bread, some peanut butter and jelly, a jar of pickles, and two fancy cans of dog food. Rockandy and Blue were served immediately. The odor from the cans was pungent, but once the dogs inhaled their food and Donna

Cody washed out the cans, everyone's appetite returned, except for the Goodmans'.

"Interesting choices," muttered Frances to Carden Wade Goodman. They had gone out to dine earlier, where they had had steak and potatoes with a few strong whiskey sours. There, they had discussed things between themselves, especially Mabel, who fascinated them. They had filled their notebooks to the brim with jottings. Now, as everyone relaxed and ate, Frances pulled her notebook out and asked if Mabel wouldn't tell them a little about her growing-up.

"Please, Mabel," said Donna Cody.

Duncan was not so happy that others were prying into his mother's life, though he was realizing, like so many younger people, that he didn't know a lot about his mother as a person before he, Duncan, had come into the universe.

"That's all right, son. Miss Donna should know some things. And so should you. The rest of you, though, you been good to me, but you have to keep this to yourselves."

She looked at Sandy Panther, who snorted and said, "Don't you worry, ma'am. I can keep it shut when I need to, unlike some people I could name." Donna Cody leaned up against Mabel and hugged her.

"I believe I was born 'bout 1910, down in Moreland, Georgia, and it was hot, steamy, dusty—yes, we was poor. At least, we was poor compared to now. How poor? Cornhusk and Spanish moss mattresses. We ate soup turtles, baby 'gators, raccoon, possum, rabbits—propped 'em up with a stick. We kept some turkeys, had a swayback mule to plow the garden, and we'd plow up and down that field, even the little children. Had a hog for a while down on the bottomland, but it got stuck in the creek 'n' drowned. My mama, when she wasn't washing everyone else's clothes, made quilts and sold 'em. Our house dresses was decent. Mama always made sure our hair was plaited, but no one ever had shoes. We chopped the wood, killed the snakes, climbed trees and shook down skittle bumps."

"What's a skittle bump?" asked Donna Cody.

"I believe this is a term for the hickory nut," said Carden Wade Goodman. "Please continue, Mrs. Watkins."

"Uh-huh," Mabel continued patiently. "Most folks worked the cotton fields, but my daddy was one of the better off ones, so he could farm his own self. He was generous to all. He loved Jesus and was a deacon. He went out to fight in the Great War, and when he came back, we was all so happy. He would bring other colored soldiers home. He couldn't stand how they was all treated after having fought for their country that way, come back, and be treated like dirt. My mama was worn out all the time, cooking and cleaning for the white folks and then for us, but she told as how she'd been a Washing Amazon back before she met my daddy."

"What's that?" asked Duncan.

"They don't tell you 'bout that with all this civil rights talk? Now, I love Dr. King, but way back before him, when Mama was a girl down in Arkansas, they stood up for decent pay and treatment, like that Rosa Parks done."

"It sounds as if your mother was part of the strike of 1881," said Carden Wade Goodman.

"I don't know, sir. It was back when she was young, 12 or 13 maybe, just a girl and already taking the white folks' laundry and scrubbing from dawn to dusk. But my mama told us stories. Told us how she hardly knew her own mama cause her mama, my grandma, was a mammy for the white children. She grew up thinking her momma loved white babies them more than she loved her own.

"My mama, she sang to us, and how we loved her songs. Such sad songs, 'nough to break your heart. The old men sang with the guitars and the one string. I caught trouble on that—pulled a wire out of the screen door and nailed it right on the house over a medicine bottle. Got switched for that."

"What?" interjected Donna Cody. "Did you sing, Mabel? What was this thing with one string? Do you know some old songs?"

"SHHHH," said everyone else. Duncan, sitting beside Donna Cody on the floor, nudged her.

"A diddley bow," murmured Carden Wade Goodman.

"Honey, I did and I do. But my mama worked mostly. The white folks wouldn't even pay her lots of times, just give her old clothes or leftovers from their dinner. She cleaned and bleached and ironed and starched all the day and half the night.

"She could have made more, maybe, if she'd worked cleaning houses, but she said she would still rather do their laundry at home. She died soon after Daddy come home from the war. It was like she was waiting to see him and then she could go. Daddy, he was crazy for a while, but finally he called us children in and he said that he wasn't gonna let us live a life like Mama's had been and that we had to get out of the South. We knew about the lynchings. We saw how the white folks hated us even more, seemed like, every day. Daddy didn't figure it was gonna get better. He was gonna sell the farm, take all the money he had and split it four ways, one part for him and one for each of us girls.

"Now, that was something. Usually, they didn't let you go, those fathers—kept you to slave for them. But my daddy was a fine man. I had two sisters, Rosie and Lala, me the youngest. Rosie, she was 'bout 14 maybe, had boys courtin' her already; she was a beauty. They'd ride over on their horses, if they had 'em, talking sugar talk in the front room, us peeking 'round the corner and laughing, and she'd cut us a good one and tell us to hush, but then laugh with us later and make fun of 'em.

"Daddy picked the fellow he liked, though; he'd fought in the war. Said he trusted a fellow soldier and was gonna settle some money on them to go to New York and find his kin and get out of Georgia. I didn't like him, and he come and pinched me where he shouldn't have all the time. And I knew he was only in it for the money and that he would be a bad husband.

"But she was for sure heading for trouble where she was working. One of the white boys there calling her 'Jezebel,' figuring he could do anything he wanted. She was having to dodge him all the time, get her work done. So she figured it would be better to be married. And there was no sayin' anything to Daddy anyway. His mind was made up. Rosie and that man left, and I never heard from her since. None of us did and it broke our hearts. I just know something bad happened to her."

"Couldn't we find out?" asked Duncan.

"We could go to the library," Donna Cody suggested. "Go to the college library."

"We can and we should. Thank you, Miss Donna. But back then we couldn't go to no libraries. Barely had schools. Half the children 'round me couldn't read. My daddy, now, he could read; read the Bible and brought folks to the mourning bench.

"But let's see, my other sister. Lala, he wanted to marry her off too. She wasn't gonna do that. No, uh-uh, she was the wild one, and no one was gonna tell her nothin'. She aimed to go out West, but the Depression was on, and she couldn't stand the idea of marryin'. Told Daddy she wasn't gonna be a slave to no man, that they was worse than the white folks, beggin' your pardon. Daddy never beat her to get some sense into her the way most daddies would have in them days. She was strong. She worked the fields, chopped cotton, but it was gonna wear her down. And besides that, cotton wasn't doing so good then. And then one day she told him she and her best friend Matty, they was leavin'. 'I just want to get on a train and head out to the setting sun and feel free,' she said. That was a dangerous thing in those days. Wasn't till years later I heard from her, out in LA, workin' as a housekeeper, still not married.

"But I was the one Daddy wanted to send to school, to Greene Women's College up north. 'It's learning that will set you free,' Daddy used to say, 'and you're the smart one.' He wanted me to be a nurse, all dressed in white. Wonder what he'd say now. No, I'm happy. I've had a good life, but back then I was always pesterin' him about religion and this and that in the Bible. Pestered my mama about all her herb doctorin' and singing'.

" 'Bout that time, though, things kept gettin' worse. We had to go to town and we'd have to slink by, you know, keep out of the way. We didn't have much to eat, and Daddy said it was time for me to work and earn some money.

"It was a sufferin' life, and I'm blessed to be here now with you folks. A book was a miracle. A song was like a drink of cold water, like it says in the Bible. I saw my friends beaten, their daddies and mamas fired. They had a lynching next town over. Begging your pardons, we was the white people's dogs, 'cept they treated their dogs better."

Two tails thumped. No one else said a word, but Carden Wade Goodman's flask appeared along with some small paper cups from the bathroom. It was dark now, and Dora got up and turned on the bed stand lights. The whiskey went around.

Chapter 40: Mabel's Story Continues.

I'm going to the river, get me a tangled rocking chair.
If the blues overtake me, I'm gonna rock away from there.

—"Motherless Child Blues," first recorded by Robert "Barbecue Bob" Hicks

"That's as it all was," said Mabel at last as a new, whiskey-tinged ease suffused the room, "and you can guess I didn't make it to nursing school. I was scrawny, hard to believe now, I know. But I was black as I am now. You know: W*hite*, you're right; *brown*, stick around; *black*, stay back. I wasn't gonna get courted, my face was always in a book if I could get one, too scrawny for the fields if you can believe it, though I had me the big garden that Mama had worked, and I did OK with it.

"I ended up cleaning for this family wasn't all that much better off 'n' us, but she had to have her maid. They had a mess of kids, bratty and mean like their parents. The oldest boy was around my age, and he was always hanging around, smokin' his daddy's cigarettes when his mama wasn't around, flickin' butts at me when I was trying to clean, cook, change diapers, keep 'em all from killin' each other. Patched up their cuts, gave 'em herbs from our garden to make 'em healthy. They never thanked me. Threw stuff at me, books even, and I hid those books with my stuff and snuck 'em home. Not that they had many books.

"And her? She lay around, always sick or something. Married to that man, you could see why. I could feel sorry for her 'cept she was so mean. He was short and skinny with eyes like a snake waitin' to strike. You wanted to be sorry for her till she opened her mouth. But that boy, Lamar."

Here, for the first time, Mabel stopped and uncharacteristically tipped a substantial swallow of whiskey down her throat. There was a long pause. Duncan was sitting up straight and tense, still trying to register the idea of his mama drinking whiskey.

"You don't have to talk about this," said Carden Wade Goodman softly. Duncan reached behind Donna Cody and put a hand on his mother's shoulder. Mabel patted it and sighed.

"Thank you, sir. Actually, feels good to tell it to someone. Never have 'cept to Miss Porter. Duncan, honey, you're old enough to know, I think," said Mabel. "They try to shame us, as if it's our fault. But it's not, and Hell is waiting for these white men who take advantage. That's right," she said, her voice so low it was like an organ bass.

"One day, the missus went out with the children. They had to go to the store, something, I can't remember, but there I was, cleaning the stove, and that Lamar come in."

She paused.

"There was nothing I could do. He was strong and tall and he'd been drinkin'."

"Lord," sighed Dora.

"Oh, Mrs. Watkins," said Frances.

Duncan sat stiff as a stone. For once, it was Donna Cody who reached out a hand to him. But he hardly noticed.

"I got him back," Mabel finally said. "Yeah, I got him, and he can never forget. I grabbed a pan of water boiling on the stove, and I threw it at his face. That boy done screamed and screamed, runnin' around in circles. And I picked up my things and I got out of there."

Chapter 41: How Can We Bear It?

Mary had a little baby,
Born in Bethlehem.
Every time the little Baby cried,
She rock'd him in a weary land.

Ain't that rockin' all night?
Ain't that rockin' all night?
Ain't that rockin' all night,
All night long.

—"She Rock'd Him in a Weary Land," as sung by Sister Thea on a tape: 'Round the Glory Manger Christmas Spirituals.

"Daddy, he moved fast. He got some help from the church, God bless them, and he took me up to Chicago, and got us a place where we could stay with a preacher friend of his. Neither of our lives was worth anything if we stayed south. So all that hard work, our land, our house, we had to up and leave and catch that midnight train. And Preacher Thomas, it was good of him, but they had six kids themselves. We didn't feel like we could stay. But then, that Chicago winter, it was too much for Daddy, and he passed without ever seeing his grandson."

Duncan began to gag and heave. Donna Cody threw her arms around him, but he jumped up and headed for the bathroom. Donna Cody sobbed softly. Mabel stood up.

"Excuse me. I think that's about all tonight." She followed her son into the bathroom.

Intruders all, they left, even Carden Wade Goodman and Frances, forsaking their own room and, with arms around each other, walked out into the night. Donna Cody, Sandy Panther, and Dora walked slowly and silently back to their room, the dogs following.

"So, I guess that nasty ol' Lamar was Duncan's dad, don't you think, Donna Cody? I mean, he's pretty light and all."

"Please don't talk to me right now, Sandy Panther."

"Lord," said Dora. "I know who that Lamar was."

"What?" cried out Donna Cody and Sandy Panther. "Who?"

Chapter 42: People Go Where They Need to Go.

Ain't gonna let nobody turn me 'round
Turn me 'round, turn me 'round
Ain't gonna let nobody turn me 'round
I'm gonna wait until my change comes.

—"Ain't Gonna Let Nobody Turn Me 'Round," traditional African-
American spiritual

People didn't start looking for each other until midafternoon. They were blurry, overwhelmed with emotion and lack of sleep. Frances and Carden Wade Goodman had returned to their room after a long discussion at the all-night diner. Mabel and Duncan were awkward, worn out, and evasive. Sandy Panther moped. Donna Cody was quiet and sat around a lot. But you could almost hear the gears turning in her brain. At last, they gathered again in Frances and Carden Wade Goodman's room, with Dora sneaking Mabel and Duncan through the hall. They were reluctant, but Dora insisted.

When they arrived, the others were eating breakfast that Donna Cody and Sandy Panther had purchased from the all-night diner up the road. They passed biscuits and bacon on to Dora, Mabel, and Duncan. Dora put her food down, though, and said, "I have to tell you all something. I already told Donna Cody and Sandy Panther. That man Mabel described, I'll tell you, I know who that scoundrel is, and sure enough, he's related to that scoundrel you met. He's Fred's uncle. I have seen that face wearing that scar only once, but you never could forget it. Fred had me up at some family get-together at a big fancy Nashville house—the pillars and all in that Belle Meade section where people are so rich and snobby. I couldn't stand it, but there that man was, presiding over the whole thing. He was skinny and he had a cane, didn't look too good. Pinched me and laughed with Fred. I brushed it off, back then, too young to know better. Guess he did OK for himself. Makes me so mad."

Mabel stood dumbstruck. Duncan stared at Dora and clenched his fists. The Goodmans shook their heads and Sandy Panther said, "It's too small a world sometimes, ain't it?" For once, Donna Cody had to agree with her.

"You know where he lives?" asked Duncan.

Dora shook her head. "Duncan, you don't want to mess with Fred Jones or this fellow."

"I think, actually, that's just what I want to do," said Duncan.

"I'm coming with you!" said Donna Cody, jumping up.

"Absolutely not," added Carden Wade Goodman.

"Some things you shouldn't tangle with," said Sandy Panther.

Mabel then spoke. "Duncan, son, you can do what you think you need to do, whatever it is, as long as it doesn't involve anything the Lord would hate. You are my boy, not Lamar's. For my sake try thinking about the good people in your life. Professor Porter took us in and gave us a wonderful life. She put you in those good schools, and she saved you up a college fund—did you know that? You gotta be grateful for how life has treated you."

"But Mabel, it's got to be terrible to have a father you hate," interjected Donna Cody.

"He's not the first, Miss Donna, as has had that and isn't likely to be the last."

"You can all stop talking about me and about what I should and shouldn't do!" Duncan shouted suddenly. People jumped with surprise.

"How would you like it if it was your family life being talked about in front of people? I knew I had to be part white, my skin this color, my mama's her color. I knew something wasn't right, I know Miss Porter is one of the best women that ever lived, and Mama, you know I love you. I don't want to hear any more about it, and I believe I'll be getting out of here about now."

"NO!" shouted everybody. Donna Cody threw her arms around Duncan in yet one more astonishing display of affection that would usually have filled him with joy. As it was, he gently peeled her arms off and gave her a kiss on the top of her head, to an exclamation of dismay from his mother and to the astonishment of Donna Cody. He shook his head and strode out, with Carden Wade Goodman running out after him. Mabel started to follow, but Frances laid a hand on her arm. "Let them talk, Mrs. Watkins," she said. And she hugged her. Mabel was now in tears.

"I know I should've told him sooner and not in front of you all, but he never would let me tell it," she sobbed. "He knew it was something bad. And this puppy love with him and Miss Donna, this will not do."

"What?" said Donna Cody, turning around. "What?"

Sandy Panther snorted heartlessly.

"Things are changing, Mabel," said Frances. "It's a new day, I believe, with new laws, and we are going to win this fight for civil rights."

Mabel shook her head. "I hope so, ma'am, but I see the hate down here. Saw it in Chicago. Even see it at home. I don't think things have changed as much as you think, begging your pardon. Black and white together, that's still nothing but trouble, and don't I know it."

In a little while, Duncan and Carden Wade Goodman came in. They were both agitated.

"Duncan, tell them," Carden Wade Goodman said.

"I'm going to join up with Dr. King," said Duncan. "I can't stand it anymore."

Objections immediately poured forth. Donna Cody was worried that he wouldn't be safe. Sandy Panther thought he shouldn't be joining with Northerners who didn't know anything even if she sure believed it was time to change all the hateful things. Dora thought he should think it all through more and go later.

Surprisingly, though, Mabel not only agreed with her son, but said she was coming with him.

"Mama, I don't see how you can do that," protested Duncan. "There's danger, people getting shot, bitten by dogs, put in jail. This is something for the young people. And what about Donna Cody?"

Mabel reared up. "You don't think I can't stand up to that? If this world is gonna change for the better, we're the ones gotta change it." And she would not, she would not be moved. Her only regret was that she would not be there to get Donna Cody back home. Duncan was clearly agitated about this as well, but he was a young man of few words and always would be. He didn't say anything. Then Donna Cody decided she wanted to come too.

"Now hold on," Sandy Panther said. "You and me, we have some unfinished business here, Donna Cody. You promised. You can't desert me again."

"What do you mean, *desert?*" said Donna Cody, especially annoyed at being snapped back into this pettiness after imagining herself at the forefront of a march battling cruel sheriffs and snarling dogs.

"Like that little jaunt up in the woods, playing around with fairy people and who knows what all craziness—"

But we will leave them to their usual bickering and ignore them as other sensible people did. It took Frances to finally talk her down.

"I've got some money," said Mabel, "and we'll take the train out tomorrow."

Many protested, especially Donna Cody.

Dora was full of regrets. "I wanted you to meet my family, Mabel," she said softly. "But I understand, I guess, as much as I can."

The upshot was that the next morning they saw Duncan and Mabel off on the morning train. Mabel was regal and buttoned down. Duncan escorted her onto the train, then jumped down and hugged Donna Cody so hard that her ribs were sore for the rest of the day. They received evil stares from passengers and folk on the platform, but neither of them noticed. Then Duncan bounded up the stairs and onto the train. Donna Cody had tears on her cheeks, but most of them were tears of sheer frustration.

"That boy is truly sweet on you," said Sandy Panther.

"Be quiet," said Donna Cody.

With a sense of relief, they started another fight as the train pulled out.

As they headed down the road to Dora's family, everyone except Sandy Panther wondered in various ways about the triviality of their concerns compared to those of Duncan and Mabel. They wondered about themselves and their lives. These little seeds were the starts of all kinds of future books and essays for Frances and Carden Wade Goodman, while for Donna Cody they were added to the paving stones of a long path of well-meant but reckless and sometimes ineffectual good deeds. But she was on that path.

The main road they were on met up with a minor road; the minor road, after many twists and turns, led to a dirt road with a hand-painted sign that said, "Diamond Mine Road." As they headed back into a valley and followed the shallow river that had carved it, the world closed in. Twilight lit up the opposite ridge, edging the top with a ribbon of light, and then the valleys began to darken. The road narrowed and looped back. They bucked and crawled over ruts and bumps. They crawled down again into another holler, saw a few mysterious lights up in the distance, and then suddenly the glow of a house. They pulled in and sighed to a stop.

The house looked like three houses stuck together, all surrounded and united into one house by a flowing, generously wide porch with peeled trees acting as rails and ladderback chairs with woven splint seats, including a homely worn rocker. The softly lighted windows were steamed up. They could make out a wooden double oxen collar hanging by the front door. The small but central section of the house had huge square weathered beams chinked together. The right side was two stories with an upper porch. The left, also two-storied, had an oddly placed door at the far left corner and two lone windows, one above the other, on the right. There were many chimneys. Donna Cody was surprised at such a substantial, if somewhat quirky house way out in the middle of nowhere. And people were pouring out of it.

Dora leapt out yelling, "Mama! Papa! I'm back home for a while!" A storm of hugs ensued. Dora kissed each child, young woman, and young man as they came out; then she skipped back to her parents, grabbing their hands and pulling them off the porch and toward Carden Wade and Frances Goodman and the others. There were general introductions all around.

Dora's father was named Horace, her mother Elizabeth. Both had carved-in-stone faces of Abraham Lincoln, both of them were as tall and elongated as him, with deep-set eyes that judged and appraised, but Elizabeth's face was softened by an especially wide and what is often called a "generous" mouth. It was a mouth disposed to smile, but the lines around it showed that hard years had tempered the smiles.

"We are honored to meet any friends of Dora's, except one," said her father.

"Daddy," interjected Dora, "that one is no friend of mine. I am finished with him!" Her father looked at her steadily and a slow smile stretched his mouth a little, while Elizabeth's lit up her face as she hugged her daughter.

"Come in, come in," she crowed happily. "We were just setting supper."

"But there won't be enough," said Frances. "We have some food we can eat."

After a strained pause, Dora said, "Mama, Mrs. Goodman meant well by that. She doesn't know how we do things. Mrs. Goodman, once you're asked to supper, you can't say no. Come on, now." Elizabeth, mollified, walked quickly in, presumably to rustle up something for the crowd that had descended upon her.

As they walked toward the house, Dora introduced her brothers and sisters. There were thirteen of them. The girls, from oldest to youngest, were named Clara, Maritrue, Susie, Dory, Phoebe, Anna, and Sally. The boys were Likens, John, Paris, Vidam, Henry, and Philip.

"Reckon their parents been busy," whispered Sandy Panther to Donna Cody, who shook her head warningly. "OK, but you got all them names memorized yet?" she said. "Whew."

Meanwhile, the smaller children, after Dora's introduction, shyly stared at the guests and the dogs.

"Your critters friendly?" asked Sally, who looked to be about six.

"These dogs are loving and faithful," said Donna Cody.

"You bet," said Sandy Panther. "Y'all come over here and meet man's best friends." And the children did, except for Clara, Maritrue, and Susie, who had run in to help their mother with dinner. The boys slowly moved forward except for Likens, who stood watching Donna Cody. He was easily 6' 5" and had the easy grace of someone who worked hard and competently. His pale skin shone in contrast to dark black hair and dark, intense eyes.

"Hmm," Sandy Panther muttered to Donna Cody, "seems like that one's taken an interest in you. Now watch out: love can make anyone crazy, and you're crazy enough already."

"Hush, Sandy Panther," said Donna Cody. "What do I care about any of that? But I hope we can get Dora's mother to sing for us. Dora's been saying these children sing some as well. Dora said they have their own versions of ballads that have been in the family for centuries." Donna Cody seemed not to notice that a few of the "children" were older than she was.

"Dora says, Dora says," simpered Sandy Panther. "Don't be surprised, is all, Donna Cody, if that one comes your way looking for something. Watch yourself. Love is blind, but the neighbors ain't. But that other one's a good-looking man too, now, ain't he?" she said, pointing covertly at Paris. "But like they say: Man is straw, woman fire—and the devil blows."

Donna Cody, in exasperation, marched off, Likens staring after her. Sandy Panther lingered a minute, her eyes on Paris. He looked back shyly, quickly turned away, and went back in the house.

Things were bustling, with children dragging out mattresses, setting up an extra table, bringing in chairs, and laying plates. They all sang while they did so, Donna Cody chasing after them with her recorder and trying to write down the lyrics. While the children were polite, it soon became obvious that it was annoying for them to try doing their chores when they had to stop and repeat things while Donna Cody scrawled away. But their singing was worth listening to, full of mountain lilt and nasal resonance, even from the little ones. Donna Cody gave up and recorded them with all the thumps, bumps, and animal noises in the background.

Dishes of food came out: bread, beans, something called "short sweet'nin'" that turned out to be syrup of some kind. At some signal that remained elusive to the travelers, the family bowed their heads, and Horace said a short grace. The meal commenced.

As usual, Carden Wade Goodman and Donna Cody did most of the talking during dinner. Horace sat at one end of the long plank table and Elizabeth sat at the other. The younger children were well behaved, but Maritrue occasionally whispered in Clara's ear, and Clara would blush.

Dora cast them some stern looks and they would melt back into adoring sisters.

As a many-stranded narrative of adventures emerged, with some ends running out or running together or left out, Horace said, "Mmm-hmm," or Elizabeth said, "My goodness!" Her children, even the older ones, heeded every word. Dora sat next to her mother and kept grabbing her hand and holding it. Likens stared down the table at Donna Cody, who was waving her spoon around for emphasis. Sandy Panther, for once, was quiet and attending busily to the food at hand. She hadn't had cornbread or biscuits like these for a long time, let alone black-eyed peas with ham. She heaped on the syrup and preserves and only looked up to compliment her hostess. Most of the children were of a mind with Sandy Panther.

Finally, everyone was full. The children went off to wash dishes and do chores. Elizabeth went to check on beds in the large part of the house with the second-story porch. Some of the children, she said, could sleep in the barn. (This, perhaps, was what determined some of the later behavior of these children, but causes are open to conjecture.) Donna Cody and Sandy Panther and the dogs had one room downstairs. Carden Wade Goodman and Frances had another upstairs. Dora insisted on sleeping in the same room with Donna Cody and Sandy Panther, so she dragged a cornhusk mattress in. The travelers were given oil lamps, directions to the bathroom (there was only one, with a clawfoot tub and beautiful old sink, on the first floor), blankets and pillows. Everyone hustled off to bed.

Thousands of stars looked down from the sky, but Donna Cody, Sandy Panther, Dora, Rockandy, and Blue didn't see them. Instead, they all slept, snorting and shifting contentedly. The calls of owls, the creaking of the old house, the whine of insects, strange little swishes and barks— nothing interrupted them until there was a soft knock. The dogs sprang up, but they didn't bark since it was Carden Wade Goodman. Dora's mattress was nearest the door, so he bent down and tapped her on the shoulder. She immediately sat up.

"Listen," he said softly. "You might want to wake Donna Cody up so that she can hear this." Outside, a dulcimer strummed and a beautiful male tenor was singing the story of "Barb'ry Allen."

Chapter 43: Madness at Midnight. A Visit to a Strange Ancestral Dwelling Place.

Down stepped her old father dear,
He stepped over the floor.
It's how do you do, Lady Maisry, said he,
Since you became a whore?

O dear father, I am no whore,
Nor never expect to be;
But I have a child by an English lord,
And I hope he'll marry me.

—"Lady Maisry," Version B, sung by Mrs. Dan Bishop at Teges, Clay Col, August 21, 1917, from Cecil Sharp's *English Folk Songs from the Southern Appalachians*, Vol. I

Dora tried to wake Sandy Panther first since she was in the next bed. Sandy Panther opened her eyes and appeared to listen for a bit and then closed her eyes and began snoring. Donna Cody, on the other hand, jumped out of bed as soon as she figured out what she was hearing.

"Shhhh," said Dora, finger on her lip. Donna Cody nodded and then scrambled for her tape recorder, crashing into Sandy Panther's banjo. But soon the tunesucker whirred. Dora and Donna Cody sat on the edge of the bed, their bare feet resting on the warm bodies of two happy dogs. Carden Wade Goodman stood in the doorway. The moon shone, the dulcimer played, the man's voice flowed up and down with the turns of the ballads. He finished "Barb'ry Allen" and began "The Brown Girl," with its ghastly murder by penknife and kicking of heads against walls. He sang "Locks and Bolts," about a determined lover, he sang about milk-white steeds and dapple grays, beaver hats, rings, lords, ladies, bloodied shirts, swords, Fair Ellender, Sir Hugh. And then it was silent except for the soft night noises.

"That was Likens," whispered Dora. "Doesn't he have a beautiful voice?"

"Hold on," said Donna Cody, struggling with her tape recorder. "I think I got that. Now, wait, do you know these versions? I should have been recording you all along."

" 'I certainly do," whispered Dora, laughing softly. "Remember? All my family sings, even the little ones. You heard them. Mostly they play dulcimers and some banjers. I'm the one that learned guitar and went out to try to help back here. But now he's done—let's get some sleep."

"Yeah," grunted Sandy Panther from her pillow. "It's way too noisy around here."

"Sandy Panther!" said Donna Cody. "Wasn't it beautiful?"

"Cat's courting is noisy," muttered Sandy Panther cryptically as she rolled over and snored even more loudly than before. Donna Cody lay in her bed, trying to figure out if she'd been insulted, and then let it go. But she couldn't sleep. All the images from the beautiful, terrible ballads danced around her. Finally, though, they became wisps of dreams that wove her a gently rocking hammock of sleep.

Donna Cody was on the rampage the next morning. She woke at sunrise, threw on her clothes, and tracked down Likens before breakfast, following him out to the barn and around the yard, asking him about the songs he had sung last night. Likens grunted out replies, every now and then turning on her and staring at her silently. Anyone else would have realized that something was going on, but Donna Cody kept pestering him. Finally, at breakfast, she asked him if she could record him some more.

"Do you ever consider, ma'am, that maybe I'm someone besides a singer of songs that you want to take and talk about like they're your own? Like all those people coming down looking at us like we're bugs?"

"Likens!" his mother protested. Horace half rose in his seat. Dora put her face in her hands. The other children's mouths were O's, as were

Donna Cody's, Sandy Panther's, and Frances's. But then Carden Wade Goodman burst out laughing.

"He's got it exactly right," he said, pointing his fork a bit rudely at Likens, who stared at him with distaste.

"There is no excuse for such rude behavior," said Elizabeth, not referring to Carden Wade Goodman.

"Apologies," said Likens gravely and insincerely. He rose carefully and walked out.

"Apologies?" said Carden Wade Goodman. "Mr. Richards, your son should be exonerated. It is you, Donna Cody, who needs to apologize."

"Wait, what for?" chimed in Sandy Panther. "And why should he be exorated or whatever if you think he's right?"

"Because he *is* right," said Frances. "Donna Cody, my dear, you do need to realize that people are more than subjects for you to study." And she looked at Carden Wade Goodman, who looked back, both of them acknowledging mutual guilt.

Donna Cody was mystified. "All I did was ask him to sing," she said.

Elizabeth sighed. "Honey, you have to realize that we get asked this a lot by a lot of people, some of whom have put out records of us. We've never seen any money from them, except for a few folks like that Viv Smythe. Now, she was an interesting and gracious person."

"Viv Smythe!" shouted Sandy Panther. "We know her, ma'am, begging your pardon."

"Viv Smythe?" said Carden Wade Goodman. "You girls know Viv Smythe?"

The discussion developed. Likens was the other major singer in the family besides Dora, both of whom had been recorded by Viv, years before while Dora was still going to school.

"And that's it, Donna Cody," said Dora earnestly. "Likens is heading to college this fall, starting a little late, but then from there he wants to be an engineer and help get rid of the coal companies and all those who destroy this precious land."

"Aunt Molly Jackson!" said Donna Cody. "Sarah Ogun! Organize!"

"You may say so," interjected Horace. Everyone turned to face him. He didn't speak often, so when he did, people listened. "You may say so, but you say so here and nowhere else. I'm a lover of the union, but folks depend on that coal. Coal built this house, coal near destroyed this house."

"But the music saved it, Daddy," said Susie, looking adoringly at Dora.

"That's right, honey," said Elizabeth, "along with some education and determination."

"She's talking about the kids," explained Dora. "Each one of them in school, and each one of us away from the mines. Daddy, he was a coal miner's son, and he saw some bad times. But you came through it."

Horace nodded. He didn't smile.

"And he taught me the dulcimer, my first instrument," said Dora.

"You mean you taught yourself and then told your daddy you wanted to learn. She was a bad girl, this one, sneaking in to get that old dulcimer." Elizabeth laughed and Horace's face slowly relented into his thin hint of a smile.

"You thought I was naturally a musician and me only four," said Dora.

"Appears I was right," said Horace.

This resulted in Donna Cody talking about dulcimers, where they probably came from, how so-and-so in such-and-such a book made them, how John Jacob Niles sang with them, and more. The Richards were patient and polite, while Sandy Panther rolled her eyes and Carden Wade Goodman kept trying to interrupt. Frances Goodman was attentive. It would all be going in her notebook later.

After lunch, the Goodmans headed to their room for a nap, and Sandy Panther headed out with Paris and some of the other siblings to help with the garden up on the hill. "Dogs can come with me," she said. Donna Cody went off to look for Likens, but she ran into Maritrue, Anna, and Sally. Maritrue was coaching the littler girls through mucking out the donkey stall, and all of them were singing a song about a horse. Donna Cody pulled out her tape recorder. As soon as Maritrue saw this, she waved to the others to stop.

"Please, keep singing," said Donna Cody.

"We can sing for you later, ma'am, and it will be easier to catch," said Maritrue, the other girls watching her carefully. "We thought you might want to see Black Bird Rock and the cave where our Great-Great-Great-Great-Granddaddy Solly lived back before the Civil War; he's the one wrote that tune named after it that you liked so much."

"Solly's Cave?' Fantastic!" cried Donna Cody. "You bet I want to see it. And hear that song. Thank you, Maritrue. Can we go now?"

"Sure 'nough. Mam'll spare us for a bit, I believe, right, girls?" Anna and Sally gave scared little nods, putting down their shovels. "Follow us, then," said Maritrue. "We know a back way in. They say that Great-Great-Great-Great-Granddad Solly lived in that very spot and later guided people over to t'other side where they'd go to see all the old things."

"Old things?" queried Donna Cody.

"You'll see," said Maritrue airily, hardly stopping. "Great-Great-Great-Great-Granddad was born there."

They wound through a mosaic of green leaves, following what looked to be game trails, they were so narrow. Donna Cody was quivering with excitement. They turned a corner and almost collided with a massive rock pile, layers of gray rock flaky like phyllo dough, piled up at various angles. They scrambled around it, and Donna Cody saw a black hole at the edge of the pile, over which a large shelf of rock projected, looking ready to collapse at any moment.

Donna Cody stopped and stared. Sally put her hand in Donna Cody's and sucked the thumb of her other hand. Annie looked uneasily at her big sister, but Maritrue said, "Don't worry. It's safe. We've been in here many times, haven't we, girls?" The two sisters gave unconvincing nods and murmurs, but Donna Cody wasn't noticing anything except the dark black of the cave. Old oak leaves from last year lay all around and swished as the girls walked toward the entrance.

"I don't want to go in there," wailed Sally.

"Me neither," said Anna.

"Fine, then—you two sissies wait outside, and I'll take Miss Cody in. Or are you scared, too?" she insolently asked Donna Cody.

"Thank you for being so considerate, Maritrue," said Donna Cody, charmingly oblivious. "Now, show me where your Great-Great-Great-Great-Granddaddy lived in here. He surely wouldn't have gone back too far in here. Let's see the old things." And she plunged in, holding Sally's flashlight. Maritrue plunged in after her. The two younger girls held hands and watched them go.

After a while, Maritrue emerged. "All right, c'mon," she commanded her sisters. "She'll find her way out soon and serve her right, thinking she can up and steal our brother and our songs. Stop your fussin', Sally. Cut it out, Anna. We're showing her how it would have been in the old days, like she keeps talkin' about. Now she'll know what it was like for Great-Great-Great-Great-Granddad and what that song is about, being lost in a cave." And they headed home, Sally snuffling all the way.

Donna Cody crawled around in the dark, flicking her flashlight around eagerly. She wondered what the "old things" were and if Maritrue had gone off to get them. She knew she could get back, that Maritrue would come find her. Her flashlight held steady, but she thought about Tom Sawyer and Becky lost in their cave and about the outlaws who had lurked there. Maybe outlaws had come to this cave. Maybe they still did. No, now, look at that magnificent stalagmite. And those stalactites, and that river of white rock.

Donna Cody was pretty fearless. But she heard rustlings, and she tripped a few times, covering herself with clay and muck. In one corner, she found old candle stubs. Now she wished she had brought string for this labyrinth. Where was Maritrue? She hoped nothing bad had happened to the girls, and she thought about their Great-Great-Great-Great-Grandfather Solly Richards and his family, when Indians and animals but no white people lived here. She began to feel cold and tried singing a little, but her voice echoed eerily, and she stopped.

"I need to stay still in one place," she finally said to herself. "That way, they'll find me."

The flashlight seemed a little dimmer. She turned it off and sat and began singing again, humming Solly's song and other songs and fiddle tunes, her left hand curled upward around an imaginary fiddle neck. The darkness hung about her, but Donna Cody kept the music going as if her life depended on it, which, she figured, it did.

Uncharacteristic thoughts plagued her: voices whispered to her about the futility of her life, of her passions, of her loves. She pictured the faces of Aunt Jane, Mabel, Duncan, even Sandy Panther. She thought of old school chums she had breezed by and forgotten in her self-absorption. She thought of Vera and Albert. "Say a prayer for me," she whispered to them, astonished at herself for saying such a thing. She wondered if there were bones in this cave, human bones. She remembered all the songs about dead miners: "Dream of the Miner's Child," "Only a Miner," Sara Ogan's songs, especially "Come All Ye Coal Miners," and she thought, "I have to join the fight." She wondered what that would mean and how she would do it. And she felt a terrible sense of futility and despair as the silence deepened.

Later, she found she had slept. She felt shaky now, and she didn't have much voice, but she definitely heard something. Heavy breathing, running, animals, getting closer. Donna Cody's heart hammered as she flicked her flashlight on. She might as well see what was coming for her. She began singing "Battle Hymn of the Republic," which was a strange choice, but odd things come to us in moments of panic, and Donna Cody's mind was full of odd and old things. "Mine eyes have seen the gloreeee," she shouted, and then, wham! Rockandy was on top of her, barking, licking, and jumping all over her. Donna Cody sobbed with relief. "How did you get here, boy?" she asked lovingly.

"With me, that's how," said Sandy Panther, stepping around the corner, swinging a huge bright flashlight all around the walls of the cave, Blue at her side. "And I'll tell you, that Maritrue's gonna get a whippin' from me personally if her pa don't beat the molasses out of her. And you should see Likens—he's mad, and right behind us, I think."

Donna Cody sobbed a little more, hugged Sandy Panther, hugged Blue, and then hugged Likens as he came around the corner. He had some cornbread and water for her, and she swallowed it all down and thanked him. Likens said, "Miss Cody, I do not know how to apologize for my sisters. I cannot tell you how sorry I am about all this."

"Mistakes will happen," said Donna Cody agreeably, licking the crumbs off her lower lip. "I hope Maritrue is found too? Is she OK?"

Sandy Panther and Likens looked at each other. "She's fine," said Sandy Panther, "All's well as ends well. Now, let's get you back for a real meal. It's dark out, but Likens here can show us the way home and outta this cave. Right?"

"Yes, ma'am," he said. "Follow me."

The walk back was much longer than Donna Cody remembered, but finally they saw the soft glow of kerosene lanterns in the distance. Donna

Cody's heart lifted. The dogs bayed and received answering bays from the Richards' dogs. And then, again, bright white lights pierced the dark, and car headlights swung into the drive by the house. There were doors slammed, shouts of surprise, and familiar voices. As Donna Cody staggered into the light, she saw it was none other than the Hokey Okey Dokies.

Chapter 44: Cultural Collisions.

I'm troubled, I'm troubled,
I'm troubled in mind,
If trouble don't kill me,
I'll live a long time.

—"I'm Troubled," from Alan Lomax's *Folk Songs of North America*

The Okey Dokies stared at Donna Cody, Sandy Panther, Rockandy, Blue, and Likens, and especially at Donna Cody, who was covered with mud and unsteady in her gait.

"Donna Cody!" shouted Guthrie. "Sandy Panther! I'll be. So you found the Richards."

He gave them each a big hug, not minding the mud covering Donna Cody at all. "Hi, dogs," he added, rubbing the tops of their heads. "And how are you, Likens?" he grinned. The two shook hands warmly.

Dora rushed out to the open arms of Josh Coshinsky. Tom and Bob chatted amiably with Horace, while all the kids and dogs swarmed around, except for Maritrue, who had made herself scarce.

"We need to get this girl bathed and in bed," said Elizabeth. She and Francis steered Donna Cody into the house.

"Come in, everyone," said Horace. "We've waited on supper. Young 'uns, hop to it. But find me Maritrue," he said grimly. "I know you were with her, Annie. You get her here now."

"Me too, Daddy," wailed Sally. She began to cry. Horace picked her up and carried her into the house.

All the other children hightailed it into the house, Dora coming after them to supervise. The Okies and Likens followed, Sandy Panther trailing behind and muttering.

Dinner magically appeared once Elizabeth returned from helping Frances minister to Donna Cody. The whole crowd sat down to soup beans (pinto beans and pork), cornbread, fried okra and green tomatoes, and even beer, brought by the Okies, all of it a delicious background to some animated discussion. It turned out that a bigwig folklorist at the Library of Congress had given the boys grant funding to fetch Likens to perform and be recorded. And it turned out that these were none other than the Old Town Rounders *aka* The Hokey Okey Dokies. Donna Cody and Sandy Panther gasped in astonishment and suddenly felt nervous around them. "Wait till Donna Cody hears about this," she thought.

But Likens was not having any of it.

"I am honored that you want to record us and bring us to this nation's capital," he said, "but as I have told you before, I want to help folks down here and not just entertain some people with our old ways. But what about Dora? You know she's a performer. . ."

An awkward silence while Dora looked fixedly at Josh, who squirmed a bit, then squared his shoulders and said, "Why not? If we can't get you to come, Likens, I think Dora could do a great job with a more traditional approach."

"Second best better than nothing, huh," she said. "Little too much Nashville taint for you, Likens?"

"Now that's enough of such talk," said Horace.

"Nobody's saying anything like that," said Likens.

"Dora, hon, you know it's not that, but you haven't been interested in, ah, our approach," Josh said cautiously.

And at this moment, Annie came in with Maritrue, who was looking at her feet and trembling all over. Horace got up, told Annie to sit down and eat her victuals and Sally to hush her blubbering. He went out the door with Maritrue. A minute later, there was a terrible yell and what sounded like the whomp, whomp of branches. Elizabeth, white faced, got up and left. The thrashing went on for a while, and most of the adults at the table stopped eating. The smaller children tucked in as if nothing was going on. Likens frowned and Dora put her head in her hands. Elizabeth and then Horace returned after a few minutes. Maritrue did not show herself. They sat down, Elizabeth biting her lip, Horace not saying a word.

Slowly and awkwardly, the talk began again. Dora agreed to go with Josh.

"We'll have to call Stephen and see if it's OK," said Guthrie. "You know that, Josh."

"We'll make it OK," said Josh.

Tom and Bob looked dubiously at Guthrie, but didn't say anything. Dora was holding Sally's hand and whispering to her because now she was crying and afraid to look at her father.

"Get your thumb out of your mouth, Sally," said Horace.

"Now don't go after her," said Dora. "You know she's too little to have known better."

"Don't get to backtalking your dad," said Elizabeth.

"And this is one more reason you can see it's time for me to go," said Dora.

"We will see," said Horace, but he finally dipped his spoon into his beans and began eating. The tension in the room eased. He had given the expedition as much of his blessing as they were going to get.

Guthrie turned to Sandy Panther. "You know, Sandy Panther, we recorded Mandy Monroe on our way down. She says she's looking for you two, says you stole her rattlesnake rattle. I don't know what you all have been up to, but you better watch out. I'd give it back if I were you. You don't want to get on her bad side."

"*Stole* it?" said Sandy Panther, her voice rising. "She *gave* it to Donna Cody as I understood it. If someone was stealing, 'tweren't me."

"Do you think Donna Cody took it, then?" asked Frances.

"I saw her give it to Donna Cody," said Sandy Panther. "She popped it in herself. But I'll tell you that Mandy is something touchy. She *gave* that rattle to her. Donna Cody is the fiddlingest fiddler ever, but she got even better after she got that rattle."

"Just look out," said Guthrie.

Chapter 45: Donna Cody Eats and Argues. Rattlesnake Rattles. Old Disputes Resurface. The Law Returns.

I'm going where the weather suits my clothes. . .

—"Chilly Winds" and lots of other songs, traditional

It was at this moment that Donna Cody tottered in. She looked a good deal cleaner. Most of her hair was plastered to her head, except for a slight aureole of dry, rebellious fluff rising up in a wispy haze.

"You're supposed to be in bed," Frances scolded.

"I'm still hungry," she said. Someone slid a chair out for her, someone else dished up her food, and she began eating in a hypnotic trance.

"We was talking about that rattlesnake rattle, Donna Cody," said Sandy Panther. "Guthrie saw Mandy, and she thinks you stole it. But she gave it to you, didn't she?" Donna Cody shoveled some more beans into her mouth and drank a huge amount of water.

"She's gunning for you," said Guthrie.

Donna Cody swallowed and took a breath and haughtily said, "I cannot imagine, Guthrie, why Mandy Monroe is *gunning for me*. The object in question was a gift, and once a gift is given, it should not be taken back. If she is attempting to accuse me of stealing this item, you must doubt her veracity."

"I don't know what the big fuss over those rattles is anyway," said Josh. "I doubt they do a thing except bump into your soundpost and finally turn to dust."

"No," said Donna Cody. "That rattle has given my playing a whole new and better sound as Sandy Panther can attest. I cannot, of course, tell you the scientific reason for this, but I have no doubt that someone could, some luthier with an open mind."

"Mandy told us it keeps the bad spirits away," Sandy Panther interrupted.

"That's what I've heard," said Horace, unexpectedly. "Dries out the fiddle and sweetens the tone."

"Very interesting," said Josh, who had whipped out a pad of paper in the middle of all this and was taking notes. "Maybe I'll have to try one."

"You'll have to git one first," said Sandy Panther. "And it has to have the right blessing on it and all. That's what Mandy told us."

"And speaking of blessings," said Likens, turning to Dora, "who has blessed this new 'friendship' between you and Josh? Haven't you had about enough of men using you for your music?"

"Hey, hold on," said Josh.

"I cannot believe you just said that, Likens," said Dora furiously, blushing with anger.

"Likens, I am hurt that you would think I was in the same category as Fred Jones. Yes, I think Dora's singing should be heard, but on her own terms—" Josh began.

Dora jumped up. "That's enough!" she yelled. (Even her yell was beautiful, with a husky little catch in it that could break your heart.) "What I decide is what I decide. There is nothing romantic about my friendship with Josh Coshinsky." Josh looked pained. Dora continued.

"We are interested in bringing the old music, the at-home songs to the world. I know I was derailed for a time, but I am turning in a new direction—"

"Hear, hear!" shouted Donna Cody, pounding her fork and knife on the table and making everyone jump.

"Thank you, Donna Cody," said Dora, smiling. Then, seeing her father's frown, "Don't you even think about it, Daddy. You know I'm too old to switch now." Horace glared back at her.

" 'Deed she is. You hush, Likens, and tend to your own self," said Elizabeth.

"Mama, I don't want to see her used, even by friends, which, Josh, you know you and I are. I know you mean well, but as soon as money gets tangled up in it all, there's nothing but trouble."

Donna Cody looked at Likens with new admiration.

"What's wrong with Dora making a little spare change?" said Sandy Panther. "Money greases the axle, they say. I aim to work as a musician, don't want to work cleanin' bedpans or flippin' burgers or something."

"None of us wants to do these things, Sandy Panther, but someone has to do them," said Frances.

"Perhaps we need to share tasks," mused Carden Wade Goodman. "Everyone do a little of everything. We need a society in which everyone is respected. A William Morris approach."

"You better not be talking about Communism or something," said Horace.

"He's not, Dad. But who are 'these people,' Mr. Goodman?" said Likens. "You'll find they are folks who save to send their kids to college and not live the hard life they did. We can't go back and all be farmers, not in these times. Everything's changing. I love the old songs with all my heart, and I can't stand seeing them disappear or get turned into something for people to exploit. But they need to be saved."

"I'm with Likens," said Donna Cody. "The minute you commercialize art, you get trouble. You get hangers-on and folks that want to prostitute it—"

"No language in *this* house, Miss Cody," said Elizabeth, looking at the children.

"That's not quite what I said, Donna Cody," said Likens.

"Sorry, ma'am, Likens," said Donna Cody, hardly braking. "I can't tell anyone how to make a living. I don't have to do that, and I know I'm lucky. Recording for the Smithsonian, now that's a good thing. But what about after that? Dora, are they going to let you be part of the band?"

"We haven't talked about that, Donna Cody, and really, it's not your business," said Dora, still flushed with anger.

"But Josh, Guthrie, how do you feel, making money off of your collecting, so that you're famous, but not the folks who make it?" said Donna Cody.

"Donna Cody! How can you say such a thing?" said Josh. "First of all, as you yourself said, you don't have to make a living, so you really don't even have a voice in this discussion. Second, we've brought many musicians back to New York, and now they play all over and they get long-overdue recognition and some pay for their work. Third, our records get the music out there. When we collect songs and tunes, Donna Cody, what do you think we're doing? We're bringing them out to the public, that's what. Do you think this music should be hidden? Don't you think it can hold its own against all the fads out there? I think it can. In fact, I know it can. People will find it like you have, and spread it, like we do. I don't know if that makes the world a better place or stops segregation or solves poverty or gets rid of atom bombs. But it puts something fine and good and beautiful out in the world. Dostoyevsky said that beauty would save the world, and if this music of the people isn't beautiful, then what is?"

Likens began slowly clapping, and almost everyone else joined in, even the smaller children, who had no idea what the grownups were talking about.

"I admit you have some good points, Josh," said Donna Cody magnanimously, "but there's always someone who will destroy things for greed. You want to talk about this place, this beautiful holler? It can sit here and be beautiful till some strip mine operation comes in here and takes the top off the mountain. These songs Likens and Dora sing, and the rest of you? Some producer gets a hold of them, some supposed *folk singer*, and they put in their electric guitars, the ladies pile on the eye makeup and fake hair and all, and they destroy it. People hear it, and it's just more trash floating by."

"Donna Cody, think of the records I just found at the Dew Drop," said Carden Wade Goodman. "These were commercial ventures, yet they preserve something terribly important. And you yourself have told me about all the recordings you've used to learn the music."

"You have to take the risk, Donna Cody," said Frances softly.

"Look at God," said Elizabeth suddenly. People turned her way. Dora smiled. Horace grimaced, his face twisting so that it was hard to tell if he was moved or pained or both.

"God took the risk," Elizabeth said. "He made a beautiful world and gave us beautiful things. And He still loves us, even when we destroy them." There was a silence. There wasn't much arguing to be done against that, and even Donna Cody knew it.

"Amen to that," said Sandy Panther. "But I'll just say this. Money talks, and usually all it ever says is goodbye."

The next morning was sunny and humid, with locusts singing overhead. As people were washing up the breakfast things and off doing chores, a crunching rumble announced an approaching vehicle. It was shiny black with a white panel on the front door and a gold star of David in the middle of the panel. But it wasn't a Jewish car, and the driver wouldn't have felt too kindly toward you if you had mentioned that idea.

"What's the sheriff wanting with us?" said Horace. The Old Town Rounders huddled together and whispered. Slowly, the sheriff parked behind the OTRs' disreputable Chevrolet Nomad station wagon, Carden Wade Goodman's Jeep, Donna Cody's Rambler, and assorted vehicles in various states of viability that made up the Richards' driveway, if you could call it a driveway since it was more of a field with ruts.

"Oh-oh. Here comes trouble on the half-shell," said Sandy Panther.

The officer slowly emerged. "Good morning," he slurred, looking suspiciously at the strange assortment of folks lined up outside, cracking a smile at the children, then remembering himself and narrowing his eyes as he espied Donna Cody. "Mornin', Mr. Richards, Miz Richards. I believe I'd like to speak with those two young ladies you're harborin' here." He pointed at Donna Cody and Sandy Panther.

"Ricky," said Likens. "How's your folks? What's the problem?"

"Folks is fine and it's no problem for you all," said Ricky curtly, dismissing him. Then, apologetically, "Sheriff sent me out, told me to check these here guests of yours. Now, missies, why don't you come over here for a minute?"

"Remember, Ricky, these are our guests," warned Horace.

"Yes, sir," responded Ricky, "but—"

"Certainly, officer," Donna Cody jumped in. "We will be glad to help you in any way we can." She stumped over to the car. Donna Cody, even in her exhausted state, was excited to see a guardian of justice. She pumped the officer's hand enthusiastically.

"Damn, damn, damn, damn, damn," muttered Sandy Panther, looking over her shoulder and wondering if she could run into the woods. But the gun on his dark brown belt didn't reassure her on that count. "Damn, damn, damn, damn, damn," she muttered again as she remembered that Donna Cody might be carrying her gun.

"We're always happy to help solve any injustices," Donna Cody crowed. "And I must say, officer, that I have seen plenty in my travels. For example," she continued, cutting off Ricky's attempt to speak, "the prejudice is terrible. And the animal cruelty. I have been shocked, sir. Of course, we have met many good and kind souls, souls who appreciate traditional music."

Ricky's jaw hung a little open, his brows lowered. Donna Cody went on talking. Ricky kept trying to get a word in edgewise.

"Go inside," said Elizabeth to the children. No one budged. Carden Wade Goodman briefly whispered to Frances, who blanched and said, "They did *what?*"

Everyone watching could see Donna Cody smiling, and they were reassured. But then she drew herself up to her considerable height, which was about eye to eye with Ricky. She was still talking and waving her hands all the while. Sandy Panther sidled up, trying to get a word in, but Ricky wasn't paying much attention to her other than the typical once-over look that Sandy Panther was accustomed to. He did, however, pay attention when he saw Rockandy and Blue, along with the Richards dogs come sauntering over.

"Here there, you hounds," called Horace. "Git over here." The Richards hounds slunk back, but Rockandy and Blue, ever faithful, ignored him. Instead, they kept coming and began faintly growling. Blue was lowering herself to the ground as she slunk up. (It's always odd when dogs do this and think that they're magically invisible or something.)

"Quiet, Rockandy. Quiet, Blue," Donna Cody commanded.

"These your dogs?" queried Ricky in a higher-pitched voice. Donna Cody nodded and Sandy Panther shook her head. Donna Cody settled the dogs, who didn't go away but did lie down like two waiting sphinxes. Ricky continued looking nervously at them from time to time. There was more talk, but they could see that Donna Cody was doing most of it. Then she burst out, "We would never aid or abet criminals. Look, do we look like women who would do anything like that?" More talk. Snatches of:

"It's important for you to preserve the precious gift of song—"

And later:

"Tradition, sir, is rooted in the—"

Sandy Panther waving her arms, "You must be confusing us with—"

"I'm going over there," said Carden Wade Goodman.

"Be careful," pleaded Frances.

"I'm going too," said Josh.

Chapter 46: The Uses of Fame. The Root of All Evil Expounded. Donna Cody Actually Apologizes.

Well, they started out one morning on a dapple and roan
Through the tall shivering pines where the mockingbirds moan
Where it's dark as cabin windows and eyes never see
Across the Blue Mountains to the Alleghenies.

—"Across the Blue Mountains," traditional, from Jim Ketterman

But it was Frances who gently took over and planted herself in front of Donna Cody.

"I think I can help straighten this situation out, officer," she said pleasantly.

"And who are you, ma'am?" Ricky asked, but politely. Anyone with any wits was polite to Frances, especially if that someone were male.

Impeccably, as always, Frances explained. "Sir, I am the wife of that man, Mr. Goodman. I have traveled with these young ladies for some time and found them to be delightful girls, committing no illegal acts."

"You realize that there's a call out on some girls that aided and abetted prisoners next state over? That's jail time. They said it was two young women with a gun and dogs, though I don't see a gun. These two fit the description. I'm afraid they will have to come in for questioning."

"Do you have a warrant, sir?"

Ricky squinted at her. "Are you a lawyer, ma'am? Don't think I need a warrant."

"I am merely a citizen who is fairly well acquainted with the law, sir. All those scripts we wrote for *Dragnet* helped," she added as an afterthought.

"*Dragnet?*" Ricky said. "I love that show. He stared at her with admiration and awe.

"Thank you. I was chief writer for a number of episodes," purred Frances. "That Jack Webb, what a character. We parted ways, however, over *77 Sunset Strip.*"

"You wrote for that show too?"

"Only a little," said Frances demurely.

"Is the LAPD like the way they show it? I've thought about going out there to California," said Ricky. He was so young.

"Pretty much," said Frances. "We always used real files from true cases, changing names and a few facts, of course."

"Of course," said Ricky. "But, excuse me, ma'am, you can vouch for these girls, that they had nothing to do with this incident where a correctional officer was tied up and then these girls escaped?"

"Let me ask this," said Frances. "Did the suspects actually help the prisoners escape? Did witnesses name names? Do these young women look like people who could perform such a heinous deed?" She could tell that Ricky wasn't always following her, but he was impressed.

"There is some conflicting evidence, but they still need to come in for questioning," said Ricky. They both looked over at the suspects. Donna Cody was sitting on a bench, leaning back against the wall, eyes closed. She looked like a straw the wind could blow over. Once again, her adventures had caught up with her. Sandy Panther was standing in front of her, talking at her and waving her arms. She had lit a cigar and puffed it furiously from time to time. Donna Cody turned her head to avoid the smoke. Rockandy and Blue lay in front of the bench, Blue rolled over on her back and vaguely waved her paws in the air. Elizabeth had brought out some water and was working on getting Donna Cody to drink it. She was also staying out of the way of the cigar smoke.

"OK, I'll tell you what," said Ricky. "Make sure these girls don't go anywhere while I check in with my superiors. If you will be responsible for them—and you, Mr. Richards," he called out.

"Of course," said Frances.

"We'll do that, Ricky," said Horace.

"But ma'am—" said Ricky.

"Call me Frances," said Frances warmly.

"Miss Frances," said Ricky, "do you think you could give me your autograph?"

Ricky drove back out.

"Now Donna Cody, Sandy Panther, I have bought you a little time," said Frances sternly. "So hop to it. They can't force you to say anything, and apparently there's no warrant out for your arrest. But I suggest at this point that we trade cars and split you two up. Hmm, we'll put you, Donna Cody, in the Jeep—don't worry, Carden, it will be fine—and I can drive the Rambler with Sandy Panther. We should all head back to Donna Cody's house separately. Once you're back up north, I don't think they'll come looking for you."

Donna Cody did not like this at all, but Sandy Panther said, "For once, Donna Cody, have some sense. I'm not doin' jail time because of you. We're listening to Miss Frances and we're doing what she says."

"But what about the Richards?" asked Donna Cody. "Won't they get in trouble?"

"You two just ran off and we couldn't find you anywhere," said Likens. "Ricky knows you're going to run off. Everyone does. We're all used to it around here."

The Old Time Ramblers were huddled together. Dora ran out with a big suitcase. "I'm ready to go!" she said. Josh threw his arm around her, but there was more arguing among the group.

"She'll split us up," muttered Tom.

"Now give it a chance," said Josh. "People think they can only listen to this music if people like us play it, but Dora will connect the city with the country. And she is a wonderful singer."

"That's right," said Guthrie.

"Hold it now," said Donna Cody, butting in. "Are you using her?"

"Not this again," muttered Guthrie.

"Donna Cody, how can you say such things?" said Dora, her beautiful eyes tearing up, her voice huskier than ever.

"For crying out loud, Donna Cody, shake your tail and keep out of it. We've got to get moving," said Sandy Panther, tugging at her.

"Dora, honey," Elizabeth said, reaching out her arms, "you go find your life. Get yourself out of here."

Dora ran into her arms, sobbing.

"Fact is," continued Elizabeth, "we're giving the children as much schooling as we can, but that just means they'll go off for sure somewhere else. I just hope one of them comes back. Yes, Likens, I know you hope to stay, but you ain't cut out for farming. And Dora neither; she has a God-given talent, just like you, and you both need to use them."

"Not only that, Donna Cody, but folks pull themselves up by their own bootstraps 'round here," said Sandy Panther. "You don't like it when people make a little money off music, but good Lord. How'd you think my granny got her tunes down so good? She went travelin' around in the Dixie Creek Medicine show, that's how. What do you think all them folks in Bristol was up to when they recorded? They needed the dough."

"The *do re mi*," said Tom, but nobody recognized that line from Woody Guthrie except for the other Old Town Rounders.

"And all this time," continued Sandy Panther, who was now thoroughly worked up, "you've said and said we'd make a record and sell it and get famous, and instead, here we are running from the law and trying to keep someone from an honest living. I swear, Donna Cody, if you weren't such a great fiddler and we didn't play together so good, I'd be gone tomorrow. But they say: Never leave till you know where you're going."

Donna Cody looked as if she were about to fly into a million pieces, she was so upset. Her hair practically stood out from her head. "You, you, you!" she spluttered. "Who has bought our food and gas, Sandy Panther? Who has taken you to all these wondrous places? Didn't we go to find the tunes? Didn't I keep my promises? Sure, we'll make our record, and you can have all the money it makes. And Dora, if you think this is the only way you can survive, I guess that's what you have to do, but remember what happened to you before. Remember that nasty Fred Jones."

"I find that quite offensive—" began Josh.

"Hold up," said Dora. "Everyone makes mistakes in this life. Donna Cody, you need to apologize, especially to Sandy Panther, who has been a true friend to you in spite of everything. And to Josh, who has always been a gentleman."

"That's right," said Sandy Panther, waving her cigar dramatically for emphasis. "What about them boys as tossed me about and that DIS-GUS-TING balsam and getting lost a million times, Donna Cody? What about them times?"

"Dora is right, Donna Cody," said Frances.

"She certainly is," added Carden Wade Goodman.

"I apologize for offending any of you," said Donna Cody magnanimously.

"Yeah, thanks for nothin'," said Sandy Panther, kicking at a rock.

"Haste is advised." said Carden Wade Goodman. "I suggest we abscond."

Chapter 47: Rolling Along. A Surprise Meeting.

Now I wandered far away,
From my home I've gone astray,
I'm coming, coming home,
Never more for me to roam.

—"A Distant Land to Roam," Vance Randolph's *Ozark Folksongs,* Vol. 4

Donna Cody was packed up and bustled off to Carden Wade Goodman's Jeep, mostly by Elizabeth and Frances, who found her clothes, fiddle, and Rockandy's bowl. They steered her out, Rockandy mopey but following them. Finally, they left her splayed out in the Jeep's passenger seat, while Rockandy splayed out in the driver's seat, to the annoyance of Carden Wade Goodman, who shooed him into the back. Every now and then, Donna Cody would blurt out something about Dulcie Tobey; then she was talking directly to her. Then she seemed to be talking to her aunt, then berating Sandy Panther, then smiling and saying, "Yes, thank you, Duncan. That looks delicious."

"Good Lord. She's gone off again. I don't see why we need to go separate," Sandy Panther complained. "But I do say, let's stop at my Auntie Rufe's. She's just north of you all up past Dog Lick Holler, and we can lay low for a few days. No one wants to mess with her. Heck, they say, 'The worse the trip, the better the stay.' It's rough country up there, and I s'pose we'll be able to handle trouble at Auntie Rufe's."

"Dog Lick Holler?" Frances laughed and then stopped quickly when she saw the look on Sandy Panther's face. Instead, she conferred with Carden Wade Goodman.

Elizabeth intervened. "Horace," she called. "Didn't you go up by that Dog Lick Holler years back?" Horace came over.

"That place wasn't no good back 50 years ago, and I don't reckon it's much better now. Had some stills up there, and there was some bad fights with the families and then the government and later some miners hid there after that fight back in the twenties. I hear tell there's even a bunch of Communists up there."

"Dog Lick Holler," mused Carden Wade Goodman. "That name, I know I've heard that name. Which fights are you referring to, Mr. Richards?"

"Never mind about that right now, dear," said Frances gently.

"Don't you fret, Mr. Goodman," said Sandy Panther. "I'll steer you right and keep you low and out of trouble. Lots of folks hidin' up there for sure, but ain't that what we want? A place to hide? Hmmm, with the law on us maybe me and Donna Cody should change our recording names—"

"I hate to say it, but Sandy Panther may have the best solution for now," said Frances, stemming the tide.

"I reckon," said Horace. "But it's still not a good one."

"My records," said Carden Wade Goodman mournfully. "At least the weather is holding and they're out of the rain. And there should certainly be some interesting material up there." Frances grimaced, and Elizabeth looked at her and smiled.

Finally, everyone was ready. The Old Town Rounders drove off with Dora, and Elizabeth cried, standing next to Horace and all the children. Next, it was Frances and Sandy Panther and Blue, Frances handling the Rambler so well that Sandy Panther realized just how terrible a driver Donna Cody was. No grinding gears. No sudden stops. No bumps, or at least not as many. Close behind them came the Jeep. Before they left, Likens came over to the Jeep and kissed Donna Cody on the top of her mussed up hair. She was oblivious.

The two cars drove along down narrow roads, through tunnels of green. It was high summer. Tiny clusters of old houses made up the towns. Men in plaid shirts and overalls, women wearing curlers and sack-like dresses, sneakers with no socks lounged outside as children played and chased each other. Deserted houses sagged into the ground beside ash trees covered with white lichen, buckeye, birch, hickory. Towering rhododendrons looked frazzled, all their lower branches eaten away by deer. And in the distance a monstrous kudzu creature was devouring an old barn and turning trees into thick green snags that writhed under the oppression of its leaf and vine.

When they finally pulled off by a creek, the stillness of the place entered into them. Little patches of pink meadow rue had silently exploded like small fireworks, bluets glowed, flat liverworts nestled against a multitude of green mosses. Lacy ferns sighed in the heat. The creek swished over its gravelly bed in a friendly way. The water was cold and woke people up in the dozy heat: Frances patted it on her face, Sandy Panther sloshed it up her arms, while Donna Cody bent over it as if she were looking for a sign, her head right near the surface. Carden Wade Goodman stuck his face in it. The dogs drank it.

The cool air was full of spicy, earthy, fishy smells. They heard bird calls that Carden Wade Goodman told them were phoebes and Carolina wrens. They saw huge blue-eyed and green-eyed dragonflies coursing around the water, some brown butterflies that Carden Wade Goodman said were spicetails. Up the creek, brown boulders looked as if a giant had rolled them down in a bowling match much less polite than the one Rip Van Winkle had encountered. Carden Wade Goodman pointed out some lumps in the boulders and said they were concretions in ironstone.

"I'll be lathered," said Sandy Panther. "I never figured they was concrete. I've seen them things sliced open, real pretty with all these lines and stuff."

They dozed.

It was Sandy Panther who woke with a start and hustled them all back into the cars. As they drove on, the landscape changed to steep eroded ridges wiped out by farming and overgrazing. They drove past acres of stumps, young trees fighting their way out to grow and hide the carnage. A small river flowed by, but it was thick with silt. Beside the river was a moss-covered bit of railroad track that disappeared into a cave.

"Old mine, I'd bet," said Sandy Panther to Frances. "I guess my daddy worked in a mine like that, way back, when things was booming, before they closed it. They say he disappeared a little after that, after I was born."

"How did you-all survive, Sandy Panther?"

"Mama went back to her folks, and all of us were shipped out to the relatives." And here, uncharacteristically, Sandy Panther clammed up and looked stonily out the window. And Frances felt a chill of collaboration with all the extraction that had gone on, that was going on in this place. How many coal fires had she enjoyed? Her own love for this country, she thought, was a clutching, hoarding thing. Donna Cody, she worried, was getting to her.

In the Jeep, Donna Cody, still exhausted from her ordeals, slept uneasily and dreamed she was being chopped down, sawed into boards, and then nailed up as a house. She told Sandy Panther about it at their next stop—a tiny, dusty gas station.

"That's hardly a nightmare," said Sandy Panther. "Folks 'round here lived that."

The gas station was in a tiny town of tiny houses all stacked up on a steep hill overlooking a river, all built as a beehive for millworker drones. Since the time of the mill, people had worked to give the houses individuality: Some were different colors or had porches or a chimney. A group of grubby toddlers played and cried in a front yard, under a line of laundry, their own clothes filthy and torn. Dogs barked, porches sagged, paint peeled. Some of the houses were on stilts.

"We're getting close," said Sandy Panther excitedly. "This old town had a mill—see over there? Shut down about twenty years ago, I believe, before I was born. And see to the left there? We'll be following that road out."

And then, across the street, they heard, "Donna Cody! Sandy Panther!" Someone was running over, bouncing like a compact rubber ball with black glasses. It was Viv Smythe.

"Hello again, fellow travelers," she panted, pushing her round glasses back over her eyes, her voice even raspier from the effects of rare physical exertion. She carried her large briefcase and a duffel bag.

"Viv!" yelped Donna Cody. "We lost you back there at that Sweet Potato Festival, didn't we?"

"Hey, Viv," said Sandy Panther, less enthusiastically. She knew that the combination of Donna Cody and Viv Smythe could be tedious.

"Viv Smythe! My goodness, it has been many a year," said Frances, running up and giving her a great hug.

"Frances Augustinia Goodman. A woman of true depth and understanding. What are you doing with these two wanderers? Ah, Carden. How are the weird tales going? Are the mushroom people about to invade Riestown? What are you all doing here?"

Carden Wade Goodman lifted his head and began a detailed précis of his latest, if severely interrupted literary endeavor. Frances laughed, Donna Cody beamed, and Sandy Panther scowled, took out a cigar, lit it, and tried to work out whether she and Donna Cody had been insulted.

"Ugh, please, Sandy Panther, could you move off with that cigar?" said Donna Cody.

"Yes," chorused Viv Smythe, Frances, and Carden Wade Goodman.

She slunk off to a bench in front of the station, muttering, "Augustinia? Well, la de dah." Rockandy and Blue looked at the group reproachfully and loyally followed Sandy Panther, flopping themselves in the shade of the building.

Much converse ensued. Viv wanted to know about Blue and was impressed if somewhat dismayed by Donna Cody's belabored and sometimes cryptic summary of events. Frances and Carden Wade Goodman threw in their two cents plus. They wanted to know what Viv was up to. She explained that she was taping the river, which, she said, was one of the oldest in the world, so it had the best stories. "You know, they say it's old as the Nile, old as history and older, like these ancient mountains."

"Find any good records lately?" asked Carden Wade Goodman slyly. "I must say that I have done well in that department lately."

"Maybe I have, maybe I haven't," replied the other fanatic, but I think I have found some interesting variations on a ballad known as "Annie and Lord Camson." Perhaps you've heard of it?"

"What?" said Carden Wade Goodman and Donna Cody together. A long and lively discussion followed. Donna Cody demanded a copy of Viv's tape, and Carden Wade Goodman demanded the names of the people who had sung it for Viv since, it turned out, she had recorded them.

"Was it somebody here in Riestown?" asked Carden Wade Goodman. "Did you record here?"

But Viv Smythe smiled a smile, pushing some of her wiry graying black hair behind her right ear.

"I see," said Carden Wade Goodman.

"You have every right to keep your own counsel," said Frances, laughing at her husband. But Donna Cody wanted Viv to tell her about the Pinewood Girls' recording. She wanted to talk about Dora and Likens and Solly's Cave. She wanted to ask her about the song the prisoners had sung and about the Cherokee. If she were a cartoon, smoke would have been pouring out of her ears. She didn't notice that a quiet had descended and that Sandy Panther, reeking of cheap cigar and sporting fresh eyeliner and lipstick, had come back with Blue, and that Rockandy had come over and now worriedly leaned on Donna Cody's legs. Finally, Donna Cody ran out of steam.

"Donna Cody," said Viv in a stern voice. "You have, as people say, leapt over the edge, flipped your lid, blown a gasket, gone off the deep end, come apart at the seams, lost your marbles. Let me put a bug in your ear. That insect would be this: our love and devotion have curdled and crazed you. You need to calm down, go home, settle down, and reconnoiter before you once again pursue your noble calling."

However, trying to get someone to see another side of things is often like trying to get a turtle to roll over. Also, this advice, coming from this party, was a bit ludicrous. Soon each woman was launching diatribes against electric music (DC), the poison of country music (DC, VS), the Great Depression signaling the end of the "real" blues (VS, CWG), and the problems of what was "authentic" (everyone except SP). Near the end of it all, Sandy Panther, having heard something about capitalism's destruction of true folk music, threw a fit, stomped her foot, scared the dogs, and even drew the attention of Donna Cody.

"I want to make a record!" she said. "How hard is that? How terrible is that? What's so bad about getting a little piece of it all?"

Frances laughed and gave her a hug while Sandy Panther squirmed uneasily. "And there you have it," she said. "The people have spoken."

"So, Miss Smythe," said Carden Wade Goodman, ignoring all of it, "are you staying in town for a while?"

"As a matter of fact," said Viv, "I could be persuaded to share any accommodations you might have."

"We're headin' up the road to my Auntie Rufe's," said Sandy Panther after an awkward and sullen pause, "and I s'pose you could stay there with us. We do need to get a move on to get there before dark."

"Oh my, we certainly do!" said Frances.

"Excellent," said Viv. She climbed into the Jeep's front seat, while Donna Cody climbed into the back with Rockandy and was soon asleep.

Chapter 48: Large as Life and Twice as Natural.

Note: *This whole next section may be apocryphal. The existence of "Dulcie Tobey's Tune" on the now-missing Cody – Panther tape, while it doesn't prove anything, does lend credence to this story of the visit described as follows. In addition, other sources mention this visit, including a letter from a student to his friend, written on the back of 19 soup-can labels. Oral sources were recorded as well by the folklorist Lowell Allen, who heard his students telling the story.*

Viv Smythe and Carden Wade Goodman bickered affectionately as they followed the Rambler, crawling up an ever-narrowing road that snaked around increasingly impossible curves that followed a creek. It all made perfect sense if you were a creek.

"You may disparage my books, Miss Smythe, but I am trying to do something new," said Carden Wade Goodman as they inched around a particularly stomach-churning curve. "I want to bring the dreams, the nightmares, the mythologies of the nation together, consummating the marriage of folklore and science begun, perhaps, by Mary Shelley, perhaps by the Greeks.

"I am contextualizing. I'm giving the folk a new voice so that they will be heard. Someone may read about Jack, or some young girl may read about Pretty Polly, and they will find in those tales the spirit of the folk that we both love. Remember that the government of this country used to fund folklore research that wasn't just academic folderol. Folklorists were paid, when FDR sent out the photographers and writers to document the people and their beautiful, terrible lives. And what now? We have a government doing its damnedest to blow us off the face of the earth. Where's the funding for the things that matter? For the lifeblood of the nation?"

Viv laughed, not unkindly. "I hear, Carden, that science fiction sells, and it's fun to read."

"My wife and I have to live—"

"Yes, you do, but you're not even putting in the best and the weirdest. Look at that girl sleeping back there. Now that's a story worth telling."

"Donna Cody? I don't think anyone would believe it. And [*sotto voce*] she's not exactly a heroine most people would like. She is a good soul, as my wife would say, but—"

"Gurgle."

"Woof."

"What is going on back there?" asked Viv Smythe, craning her head around to look back.

"Nothing too good," said Donna Cody, white as a sheet, crossing her legs, clamping her mouth shut as soon as she'd spoken. Rockandy whined and laid his head on her lap. "I think I ate something I shouldn't have."

They arrived, finally, at a dead end. A rickety suspension bridge swung alarmingly over a deep valley. A path on the other side ran into some dark woods. They were in the shadows of a holler, and it was getting dark. Only the bridge convinced anyone that people might be nearby. Sandy Panther jumped out.

"Hello the house!" bellowed Sandy Panther at the edge of the bridge. Then turning, "C'mon! Donna Cody! Rockandy, Blue! Mr. Carden, Mrs. Carden, Viv, c'mon! Donna Cody, you don't look too good. Do you need to go do something?"

"Yes, I do," said Donna Cody, who skedaddled into the brush. Terrible noises blossomed forth. People valiantly ignored them, except Rockandy, who galloped over in alarm.

"A queasy type of person, isn't she?" said Viv Smythe.

Chapter 49: Queasy but Lively Enough. A Mysterious Hostess. A Hospitable Dinner and Some Disputation.

Coming home, coming home,
Never more to roam;
Open wide Thine arms of love,
Lord, I'm coming home.

—"Lord, I'm Coming Home," by William J. Kirkpatrick

"You see," Sandy Panther began explaining, "this is how it goes with Donna Cody. She won't eat anything, so that when she does, she doesn't know what to do with it."

"Sandy Panther," said Frances, "Donna Cody can't help it if she's sick."

A groan from the bushes.

And then, on the other side of the bridge, a figure emerged, tall, whippet thin, wearing a faded blue-flowered apron, a brown dress, men's lace-up boots, and an old felt hat that looked as if it lived underground when not on the figure's head. She walked calmly across the bridge. Her face was a mass of lines, and her gray hair hung down in a braid. Some hounds appeared on the other side but hesitated at the bridge. As she arrived on their side, she said to Sandy Panther, "I swear, girl, you could raise the dead with that smell. What you doin' back here anyhow? And who's all these folks?" But she held out her arms.

Sandy Panther gave a whoop of joy and wrapped her arms around Auntie Rufe, for, of course, it was she. "These here folks are all my friends what need a place to stay and lay low for a little while," she said once she had gotten her breath. "Sorry about the smell. My friend is sick back there."

"Now what have you gone and done, girl?" said Auntie Rufe, her voice so low and gravelly that it resonated like a drum.

"Gone and found my music partner," said Sandy Panther. She pointed to Donna Cody, staggering out of the brush. "This is Donna Cody, and she's whiz-bang on the fiddle. Wait till you hear her."

"Mmmmpf," mumbled Donna Cody.

"Hmmmpf," muttered Auntie Rufe. "Looks more like a big plucked chicken in gumbo mud. But if my niece vouches for you, you're OK with me."

At this point, Viv Smythe held out her hand. "Miz Rufinia Joan Blechard, I believe we have met."

"Well, I'll be," said Auntie Rufe, dropping her arms from around Sandy Panther and staring.

"You two know each other?" said Sandy Panther. "How's that, Auntie?"

"Now that's a story for later," said Auntie Rufe, but she grinned at Viv Smythe, and they shook hands warmly.

Viv quickly introduced everyone else and Auntie Rufe's shoulders relaxed. The situation was explained, with many false starts, interruptions, digressions, disagreements, and disputations. The upshot was that Auntie Rufe showed them where to park their cars behind some trees so that no one could easily see them. Then she led them, each clutching his or her belongings as well as some foodstuffs, over the swaying footbridge. (This dilemma encouraged some temporary eschewing of earthly possessions.) Donna Cody had a challenging, staggering time, as did Carden Wade Goodman (he had most of the bags). Rockandy and Blue brought up the rear. After the dogs agonized and edged their way across, they ran over and sniffed, licked, and peed with the other canines and quickly worked out who was who in the mysterious social order of doggery.

A short way in, the trees gave way to a clearing with a chinked cabin and lots of outbuildings in various working and non-working states. A beautifully carved sign said: The Camp. Things were neat and orderly:

Piles of things had discernible borders, and a fence ran around an enormous vegetable garden. Various men and women came out, some with rifles.

"They're checking on things." Auntie Rufe said. "It's OK, folks," she called out.

"What have we here?" Frances whispered to Carden Wade Goodman trailing in the back.

"I believe you can smell what we have here," he said. "I believe we have a still."

"That's not what I meant."

"Hush," said Viv Smythe. "You'll want to make sure you don't notice."

Sandy Panther greeted various folks, dancing around excitedly and introducing the listless Donna Cody. An old lady with missing teeth had her yellow-white hair in a tight bun, and her shirtwaist dress was spotless. A few men in overalls represented various ages and were somewhat grubby. A slender young man who shyly looked down and would speak to no one seemed to have walked right out of an Ivy League college in his white shirt, sport jacket, and neat chinos. Little cabins dotted the area.

"What have we here?" said Carden Wade Goodman in Frances' ear. "We have a social experiment, perhaps. A little kibbutz, collective, village."

"Hmmm," said Frances.

A few trestle tables were laid out in the yard with oil lamps on them. Chairs were pulled up and food was brought out. "Long sausage and a short grace. Thank you, Lord, Amen," intoned Auntie Rufe.

The talk flowed as they told Auntie Rufe about all the adventures already narrated, while she nodded her head, grunted, and occasionally said things like, "If you talk with a hog, don't expect much but a grunt" or "Takes all kinds" or "Sometimes you have to eat it up, wear it out, make it do, or do without." The rest of their audience was mostly attentive, though the old lady got up several times to lead various loose animals out of the dining area. These included some chickens, a dog, and a goat.

After wash-up, Sandy Panther lit a cigar with a contented sigh and said, "So, Auntie, how 'bout some of the good stuff?" When Auntie Rufe stiffened, she added, "You don't have to worry about none of these," and she gestured at Donna Cody, the Goodmans, and Viv Smythe.

"I suppose not," said Auntie Rufe, and out came the sweetest shine ever, not the harsh moonshine caricatured in bottles with XXX on them, but something more like applejack—fragrant and quite potent, as it turned out. Donna Cody, who hadn't eaten much, unfortunately could not resist it. After a few sips, she was wound up and ready to go.

"Oh no," muttered Sandy Panther, tapping her cigar in annoyance.

"Mrs. Rufe," I wish to thank you for such wonderful hospitality," Donna Cody began, as she rose to her feet and swayed a bit. People tried not to laugh.

"Call me Auntie Rufe, girl, and forget if you heard any other names," said Auntie Rufe, looking peevishly at Viv Smythe, who nodded as a vague apology.

"Auntie Rufe, then," said Donna Cody, unperturbed, "I thank you and would add that you have done a great job teaching your niece how to play the banjo. Her playing—"

"I didn't teach Sandy how to play," said Auntie Rufe. "She fell into it her own self, with her granny, though she did pick up a few tunes from folks passing through."

"Thanks, Donna Cody," said Sandy Panther. "You play the best fiddle ever. You all wait till you hear her."

"I believe," said Donna Cody, ignoring the interruptions, "that this music is more than something carried over from England and Scotland. I believe it is older than that, that the land itself sings through these ancient mountains and ancient rivers, the dark hollers, the mysterious haunted forests."

"She sounds a bit like you, honey," whispered Frances in Carden Wade Goodman's ear. He snorted.

"You need to get your feet on that ancient ground, Donna Cody," said Viv. "On this oh-so-mysterious ground. After all your adventures, you still think that Appalachia is a Disneyland of the past? Nostalgia can gum you up as badly as noble intentions."

But Donna Cody was not to be brooked.

Chapter 50: Yet Another Discourse, but Kept Brief. A Friend to Animals.

The time's been sweet I've spent with you,
The time's been rolling by,
But now we'll part to meet no more
Till we do arrive at home.

—"Hick's Farewell," Version A, sung by Mr. Silas Shelton at Spillcorn, N.C, September 6, 1916, in Cecil Sharp's *English Folksongs from the Southern Appalachians*, Vol. II

"When I was by myself, up at Yunwiya River Gorge," Donna Cody began, ignoring Viv Smythe completely.

"Where?" asked a thin little old man with a round black hat and thick shirt even in the heat.

"She's talkin' 'bout this Cherokee place," said Sandy Panther. This inaugurated a discussion about the Cherokee.

"Hold on!" yelled Donna Cody. Everyone looked up and shut up. (Donna Cody would find her ability to hold a crowd develop over the years until she finally wouldn't have to resort to drastic measures such as shouting. While she had a long way to go, her absolute confidence in the rightness of her beliefs and cause helped her audiences to believe as well. Your author certainly cannot recommend such an approach, but it has certain terrible advantages.)

"I had a dream and heard voices, and a waterfall talked, and that might sound strange, but I believe, as I've thought about it, that maybe all things have a voice, like Viv says."

Frances' notebook came out. Viv Smythe took out her tape recorder and a fresh pair of batteries. Auntie Rufe and her people sat still and waited.

"I found this little rock," and here she held up the cross-shaped rock. "It was as if someone put it in my hand.

"It's the Lord," said a lady in overalls. "The Lord visited you, honey."

Sandy Panther rolled her eyes, but Auntie Rufe gave her a look, so she went back to sucking on her cigar.

"I don't know that God intervened," said Donna Cody, "but I won't rule it out, either. All I know is that the music has led me ever since I first heard it, especially music from around these mountains."

Scattered agreement: Uh-huhs and amens and nods.

"I listened to it on the old records. I saw visions of people in dark valleys singing and playing the night away, people singing in churches, people playing on their porches. You sing the old songs, but you also sing and play the land itself. I can hear the dark hollers, the ancient mountains in all of it," she waxed on.

"And that's why we need to save it, the land, the music, and I am so grateful to you all for letting me be part of that, letting me play the music you all play, and collect it. I promise not to make money from it—" (Sandy Panther groaned) "—but to spread it in the world. I want people to hear what I have heard, the beauty and the voices of these mountains."

She finally took a breath, and a few people clapped. Some even suggested that she and Sandy Panther should play some and stop talking, but then a stout old woman with a rag around her head wandered through, following a goat and talking to it as she went. It was hard to understand her as she was missing more than a few teeth.

"Here now, sir, you just come on here with me." The goat bleated. "What you say? Sure, there's lots of people, now what did you 'spect?" They wandered off, arguing and bleating.[33]

"Auntie, now who's that?" asked Sandy Panther.

"That's Old Mother, that is. It's what she calls herself most times. Showed up a while after you left. She thinks she can talk to the

---

[33] She actually said: "Here now, thur, you jisht come on heah wif me..." etc.

animals, she says, like your friend here," she said, waving at Donna Cody.

"I can't talk to animals," said Donna Cody, "although Rockandy and I sometimes commune closely."

"She looks a little familiar," said Viv Smythe, musing. "Now I wonder."

"There's more to her than meets the eye, that's for sure," said Auntie Rufe. "Maybe she can talk to critters. Any rate, we let her stay and give her food and a bed. The goats love her. Sometimes she hums to them."

"I wonder if she knows some songs," said Donna Cody. "Does she sing the old ballads?"

"I don't believe so, just little tunes and such," said Auntie Rufe. "Now, how about we hear you and Sandy play for us."

They played, with Viv Smythe, Carden Wade Goodman, and other residents joining in. Some folks dragged some dancing boards over and began clogging and jigging around. By the very late end of that evening, Donna Cody and all the others had become beloved members of the strange little family high up and hidden away in Dog Lick Holler.

Chapter 51: Auntie Rufe's Tale.

I believe I'll go back home, I believe I'll go back home,
I believe I'll go back home, acknowledge I've done wrong.

—"Prodigal Son," traditional, from the singing of Dock Boggs

The next day Donna Cody and Old Mother got into a fight.

"I have never seen the like," said Auntie Rufe to Sandy Panther, who nodded sleepily. "Never have I seen Old Mother fight about anything unless she sees someone mistreating the animals. Your friend do anything like that?"

"No, ma'am, on the contrary," said Sandy Panther. "But I'll tell you, Donna Cody is the fightingest girl I ever seen, and you know I'm not always exactly Miss Priss in that department."

Auntie Rufe laughed and ruffled Sandy Panther's hair. "Well, no, now, you aren't. But they say a woman fights with her tongue, so I hope that's all it comes to, nothing but smoke."

"That's how it begins, Auntie, but sometimes, somehow, things get lively."

"Then we had better go put a stop to it," said Auntie Rufe, and they sauntered over.

Donna Cody was holding her fiddle in one hand and her bow in the other and gaping, while Old Mother was stomping around in circles and shouting. She had a pipe clenched between her teeth, making it even harder to understand her imprecations.

"Shorten it and make it go. Slide and move that big ol' bow," she said. Then she resumed walking back and forth and muttering, with the occasional shout of "Hoo!" or "Whoa!"

"What in the Sam Hill?" said Sandy Panther.

"She doesn't like it when I play the fiddle," said Donna Cody disconsolately. She was not used to this.

"What's the matter, Old Mother?" asked Auntie Rufe, wrinkling her brows. But Old Mother kept muttering, clenching her pipe, walking back and forth as if she were in a conversation with someone.

"I've never seen her like that," said Auntie Rufe.

Donna Cody sat down on a stump and crossed her long legs. She clutched at the fiddle on her lap, looking like a dejected stork.

"So what happened?" asked Sandy Panther.

"I was playing a few tunes, some we learned from Dora and Likens," said Donna Cody. Next thing I knew, she came running over, yelling. Then she waved at me like she wanted me to play, but every time I did, she'd behave like this."

"Guess the best thing is to stop playing," said Auntie Rufe. "But that's a shame."

"Why should she carry on that way?" said Sandy Panther belligerently. Turning to Old Mother: "What you got against her fiddlin'? What, maybe you need a little banjo to warm it up?"

Old Mother stopped for a minute, looked sideways at Sandy Panther, and then spat on the ground and walked off.

"Guess she likes banjo even less'n the fiddle," said Sandy Panther.

Auntie Rufe told them more about Old Mother over lunch, which, like many people they'd met, she called "dinner." No one knew Old Mother's real name, though various conjectures had floated about. She had been living there for several months and had appeared out of nowhere.

"Do you take in strangers, ma'am?" asked Donna Cody.

"Takes in kin, that's for sure," said Sandy Panther. "Took me in when Daddy left and Momma wasn't about to deal with no baby or any of the other kids, I guess. And after Granny died."

"Sandy Panther," said Donna Cody, "that is terrible. You never told me about this."

"Lots of things you don't know," said Sandy Panther quietly.

"Sandy's grandmother taught her how to play an old banjo her grandfather had made. Groundhog skin and catgut. I've got it around here somewhere," said Auntie Rufe.

"That thing," said Sandy Panther, perking up.

"But then, you take in all kinds of folks, don't you, Miss Blechard?" said Viv Smythe softly. Auntie Rufe shot her a look, but she replied that yes, she did.

"How do you do that?" asked Donna Cody. "And why? Is this a charitable organization?"

"It's a story that should be told, Joan," said Viv Smythe.

"Please tell, Auntie," said Sandy Panther. "And is your name really Joan?"

"I would love to hear about your history," said Donna Cody.

"Viv Smythe, you are egging them on," said Auntie Rufe, glaring and laughing at the same time. "Well, then. Miss Smythe is correct about my name, and she knows some of my family up north."

"You've got relatives up north?" said Sandy Panther.

"Sure do. But I met Viv in college."

"*College?*" Sandy Panther was stupefied.

As Auntie Rufe talked, Donna Cody noticed that her accent shifted a little into something different, crisp, northern. It turned out that Auntie Rufe had grown up in a settlement school, where her mother had taught until her death.

"She figured she could make everyone more Appalachian than they already were," Auntie Rufe said. "She meant well and she did well."

Donna Cody said, "But we heard all about the settlement schools and how good they were. Dora and her folks said—"

"Naturally they were good!" snorted Auntie Rufe / Joan Blechard. "They were good in a high-toned way, but lots of the women who started them weren't from here, hadn't grown up here with folks, had their own ideas. My mother felt that everyone needed to speak as if they'd grown up with the Queen of England. Naturally, I talked like the other children, so I got in plenty of trouble.

"But the public schools came in, and then folks didn't need the settlement schools anymore, or so they thought. Some of these institutions dried up—lucky my momma died before she saw that. But others became colleges."

"Who was your daddy, Auntie?" asked Sandy Panther.

"Never knew," said Auntie Rufe. "He passed in the Spanish flu. But his people were well off. Some of them helped us out. And they sent me to college. But they weren't too pleased when I came back here. There were all these folks traipsing through the mountains looking for folk songs and taking pictures, making everyone dress in dirty old clothes as if they didn't have their Sears catalogs and know what a washing machine was."

"What Joan won't tell you is that she has been helping folks out here for a long time," said Viv. Auntie Rufe looked uneasily at her hands. "She's made a place of refuge for those who don't want anything from churches or the government, for those who need shelter, or food, or need to hide. Some folks might call you the Appalachian Socialist. No criminals, are there?" she asked.

"Depends," said Auntie Rufe enigmatically. She did not look at all pleased at being called a Socialist.

"And here I thought everyone was friends and family. How did you get to doing it?" asked Sandy Panther. "And how can you keep doing it?"

"Now Sandy, you know better than that," said Auntie Rufe brusquely. "Everybody puts their fair share in."

"You always think of the money, Sandy Panther," said Donna Cody, sniffing.

"I did not even mention the word," said Sandy Panther. "Seems to me you're the one always thinking about it. But it's funny how I never knew all this stuff."

"You never asked," grinned Auntie Rufe. "And that is enough on this subject."

Chapter 52: Final Things.

There's a little piece of cornbread lying on the shelf
If you want any more you can sing it yourself!

— "Groundhog" as sung by your author's father, traditional

The tension between Old Mother and Donna Cody only grew as the days passed. Sandy Panther would jump into the middle of it things and just make them worse. Finally, one day, after the girls had helped out with cleaning up after breakfast and had picked beans until their hands were green, they decided they would play a bit while Auntie Rufe, Viv, and Frances were canning. Frances was looking frowsy and ready to move on. Viv Smythe kept questioning everyone about everything. Nearby, Carden Wade Goodman was sketching in his journal.

As the bright, happy notes cascaded out, Old Mother came running in, snatched the fiddle and bow from the astounded Donna Cody, and began sawing away. It sounded terrible, but it was interestingly terrible. Viv Smythe was over with her tape recorder in a flash. Sandy Panther tried to keep up with it but finally gave up.

"I can't tell what you're doing," she said.

"I'm a crooked fiddler," hissed Old Mother, never missing a beat except that the beats changed with almost every other note.

"Better humor her," said Donna Cody to Sandy Panther. "We have to be polite to her even if she can't play." Then, turning: "That's nice, Old Mother," she said condescendingly.

"Shah, you don't know anything, fiddler girl!" spat Old Mother, but she put the fiddle and bow down carefully and then put her hands on her hips. "You ain't from here, you don't know nothin' about it."

Everyone was watching this strange musical fight. Donna Cody's face crumpled and she sat down. Sandy Panther jumped up.

"Now gol dang it to heck, you hold on, old lady. You for sure ain't *my* mother, and—no, Auntie—she's been so mean to Donna Cody. Now listen, I know she's not from our parts and doesn't always understand things, but she is one of the best fiddlers I've heard, and I've heard a lot! She can be pig headed, I know, oh Lord, do I know. We have certainly had some rough times. I will not deny it. but she has gone around recording and learning, and she never stops.

"But Old Mother, or whoever you are, and all you folks laughing at Donna Cody, she can't help it that she wasn't born down here. Look at Mr. and Mrs. Goodman. Look at Miss Smythe. You all aren't from here, but you love the music and you love the people who play it—well, at least most of 'em. You don't look down your noses or try to change things 'cept maybe for the better. And Donna Cody, she's pure of heart. She loves the music to pieces. And I love playing the old tunes with her.

"But right now, I think it's time for her to head home and me with her and we're gonna make our record and move on. I have a number to call. I have places to go. And that's that."

Everyone was astounded at this oratory, especially Donna Cody. Old Mother stomped off, and they never saw her again. The goats were inconsolable for days, constantly giving voice to their heartbreak.

Viv Smythe began clapping, with Carden Wade Goodman and Frances joining in. Some of the others who had gathered clapped as well. The boy in the chinos and blindingly white shirt was taking notes.

Auntie Rufe smiled.

Donna Cody blushed. She was not used to receiving an encomium from Sandy Panther. Even stranger, she was speechless—a condition she seldom experienced.

The next day Viv Smythe agreed to record Donna Cody and Sandy Panther. "While you two aren't exactly in my line, I will make you a tape and you can go from there," she said. "Perhaps you will record again in a studio. Meanwhile, until my batteries run out—"

"I'll take it," said Sandy Panther. "This should get me somewhere." With an appreciative audience around them, the two of them launched in. They played and played, with some false starts, running out of tape at one point, but Viv had more. Everyone agreed that they made a lively blend, that mysterious sum that is bigger than its musician parts, the banjo and fiddle grown together like the famed rose and the briar.[34] Sandy Panther took the tapes and packed them into her banjo case.

But soon after that Donna Cody was listless again. The dogs hung around her as animals will do sometimes, wanting to make things better. She and Rockandy (and often Blue) would sit and snuggle and sleep. She had never gotten all the way well, and, surprisingly, she realized she was pining for home.

A few days later, Viv Smythe bade everyone farewell.

"How you going to walk all that way back?" asked Sandy Panther.

"I believe I have a ride," Viv Smythe said, nodding at Carden Wade and Frances Goodman. "Haven't you noticed? It's been cold in the mornings. The season's turning, and I'll be heading back up to the Big Apple for a little. I'll look for Dora and the boys. Maybe we can head over to visit you, Donna Cody."

"But you were all going to come back with us," said Sandy Panther.

"We have discussed it at some length," said Carden Wade Goodman. "We think that enough time has passed and that you are close enough to home to make it. I suggest you get in contact with Marvin's father, if he will permit it. I believe he is more than competent."

"A lawyer?" said Donna Cody. "Why would we need a lawyer?"

---

[34] As in "The Ballad of Barb'ry Allen."

"Donna Cody, even you can see that your escapade with the prisoners—"

"Oh, *that*. But oh, you have been such good friends to us. I will miss your company! Mr. and Mrs. Goodman, I hope I can visit again and play with and record your wonderful neighbors."

"My dear Donna Cody," said Frances, putting an arm around her. "You are welcome anytime. And you too, Sandy Panther," she said, turning to her in time to put any jealousy to rest.

Soon after, they all waved goodbye as the Goodmans left with Viv Smythe. There were tears, hugs, and more promises. No one likes to believe there can be a last time you see a person, or even a place.

The last night, Sandy Panther stayed up late with her Auntie Rufe. If you had been nearby, you would have heard an exclamation.

The night had been cold, with a rime of frost. A bright but more brittle, more distant sun hung in a blue sky streaked with high cirrus clouds, and a tang of woodsmoke drifted through the woods. Auntie Rufe hugged both Donna Cody and Sandy Panther hard and admonished them to return. They both promised they would. Other folks wished them good luck or ignored the whole thing, depending. The boy with the chinos waved goodbye. They had never heard him speak once.

They walked down to the bridge, shooed Rockandy and Blue onto it, called goodbye one last time. They all climbed into the Rambler. And they were off.

The drive home was a blur to Donna Cody even though she was doing the driving. Once you decide to go home, that's what you're thinking about. The trip seems shorter. You want to go faster. You don't notice what's going on around you because you're seeing another place.

They wound around out of the valleys and soon found themselves on a big highway headed northwest. All the other drivers still passed them, or when they couldn't, honked and cursed while Donna Cody wandered over by the middle line in the road or sped up just enough to prevent them. Everybody knew where they were going and that they had to get there as zoomingly fast as possible. There was no way to get lost on this road. Exits were clear. Nobody wanted to be where they were, only somewhere else.

Donna Cody tapped out tunes and argued only halfheartedly with Sandy Panther, who, annoyed, finally sat in silence, applying her makeup and sulking. She was sad and didn't want to admit it to herself.

At a bank, Donna Cody cashed her last traveler's check, and they stayed in decent motels that would allow dogs inside or they sneaked them in or the dogs slept in the Rambler. They bought food and ate it while they drove. And before they knew it, they were turning in at the little Craftsman's driveway. The maple in the front was beginning to flame, the gardens looked only a bit more ragged than usual, with the soft colors of the autumn crocuses and asters holding forth. The native witch hazel tree was beginning to put forth yellow flowers, with the leaves yellowing to the color of the flowers. Their spicy fragrance drifted into the Rambler's window. Donna Cody turned off the engine and sighed, and both of them sat there for a minute, not saying anything.

Soon, though, Mabel peeked out the back door. "Miss Donna!" she squealed, hustling down the back stairs. "Miss Sandy!" And then it was all a flurry of riotous barking, hugs, laughter, all the talk and catching up and hurrying in of belongings and the whirl of home. Donna Cody hugged Mabel for a long time.

It was after baths, dinner (Mabel's finest fried chicken, greens, and biscuits, pure bliss) that everyone truly began to catch up.

"I thought you were off to those civil rights marches," said Donna Cody to Mabel. "You know, I would like to join you."

"You'll have to talk to Duncan about that," she said. "He calls me on Sundays like a good boy who loves his mama. He's been in the marches, met lots of folk, almost got bit by one of them terrible dogs even. I worry about him all the time."

"I do too, Mabel!" said Donna Cody.

"I haven't heard you sayin' nothing about it," said Sandy Panther.

"Well I do. I just didn't speak to you about it," said Donna Cody. "But what happened, Mabel? Why did you leave?"

"I'll tell you something I don't need," said Mabel, "and that's more men telling me what to do, whether they're black, white, or purple. Specially if you wasn't with your husband, they told us we were glory-seeking, as if some of them men wasn't! And there was some hanky-panky, I'll tell you. And I reckoned I needed to get home anyway and shape things up. I figured you would be back eventually. But I sure do miss Duncan around the place. I can't keep up with all the weedin' and all the cleanin'."

Donna Cody felt bad. She assured Mabel that she would help. It was obvious that Mabel was dubious about Donna Cody's weeding and cleaning capabilities.

"We'll just see, Miss Donna," she finally said.

Later that night, in spite of the chill, after everyone had washed dishes and Mabel had gone home to bed, Donna Cody and Sandy Panther lit a fire in the back yard and sat around playing and shivering. Rockandy and Blue lay on blankets. Sandy Panther sucked contentedly on a cigar in between tunes. They talked about their whole trip and played tunes about boats and lovers and 'shine and farewells.

When they paused for a quiet moment, looking up at the stars, Donna Cody said, "Now, Sandy Panther. What are you going to do? I know I promised we would make an album. Do you think those tapes will do for that? Can you make me some copies?"

"I think they'll have to, Donna Cody. And I'll try to get copies. I have somewhere I need to be."

"Where is that?"

"Oh, just somewhere. You'll see. But listen: I've got something to tell you. You can't get riled now."

"What?" with great suspicion.

"OK, then, you know that last night down at Auntie Rufe's? You were sleepin', but my auntie—I'm still gonna call her that no matter what—she told me, happened to mention, that Old Mother—you remember her—"

"How could I not?" said Donna Cody. "What?"

"Auntie Rufe said she had told her that once her name was Dulse or Dulcie. Dulcie Tobey, she thought maybe. That one you kept hoping—"

"No, no, no, no, no!" Donna Cody jumped up, holding her fiddle and bow and spun around like, as Sandy Panther put it, a crazy person. A dog barked in the distance. Rockandy and Blue sprang up, sniffing the air.

"I've got to go back and find her! I will find her if it's the last thing I do. So close, so close."

"Wish you good luck," said Sandy Panther with a sigh. "She's gettin' up there and even crazier than you. And remember, she didn't even like the way you fiddled."

Sandy Panther petted the dogs and calmed them down; they were jumping up and down, all around Donna Cody, barking and yipping.

"But her tune. If only I'd played her 'Chickalielee Daisy-O' at her."

"She probably wouldn't have even liked it. Probably couldn't remember it anyway. You remember when she played your fiddle?"

"But she told me how to play. Why didn't I listen to her?" wailed Donna Cody.

Sandy Panther, heartlessly, watched and smoked for a while. Finally, she said, "And another thing."

"What now?" said Donna Cody, who was now shivering and sitting curled up with her long legs twisted around each other.

"I need to make a long-distance call on your telephone if that's all right."

"Sure, but who to?"

Sandy Panther fished a card out of her pocket. "This guy, the one in the Caddy who gave me a ride, said to call him if I wanted to get famous. It's been fun, Donna Cody, but it's time for me to move on and keep playing. You'll have to keep Blue with you." But she hugged Blue to herself. Rockandy came over and jealously but sweetly licked her pant leg.

Donna Cody wrote a check to Enoch Jenkins in Sullivan's Hollow. The check was eventually cashed.

A few days later, a plane ticket came in the mail for Sandy Panther. It was for Los Angeles.

Duncan came home a week later after calling his mother and discovering Donna Cody was back. He had seen great and terrible things. He used some language that upset his mother and then he apologized. The state of the Rambler's grill horrified him, and he and Donna Cody had their first real fight over it. But they also had long talks together. Mabel noted with alarm that they soon became inseparable. She worried, especially when Donna Cody proposed reckless good deeds that Duncan seemed interested in pursuing.

About a year later, Donna Cody received some new cassette tapes in the mail with no note from a Los Angeles address. She found it was the recordings of her and Sandy Panther that Viv Smythe had made at Auntie Rufe's. She was gratified at how good they sounded, though she was currently distracted by some tunes she had recently learned with C. C.

A few years after that, Mabel came running into the house and dragged Donna Cody and Duncan over to her house. There, on the television set, was Sandy Panther in a tight shirtwaist dress and her long dark hair in braids, made up to the hilt and sporting a fake mole next to her mouth. She was playing with all her might and singing some song Donna Cody had never heard of but didn't like. As she ended, she spun the banjo around, handed it off to someone and began juggling some balls someone was throwing out to her.

"Never knew she could do that," said Duncan, staring.

Donna Cody talked a lot about Dulcie Tobey and finding her. However, one day, she heard Mabel singing as she'd always done, over across the yard in her own house, but she was playing a guitar. Donna Cody ran over and knocked on the door. That was the beginning of Mabel's recording career and eventual tours of college stages and festivals around the world. She met up with Sandy Panther more than once, but Sandy Panther was doing less as a musician and more as a film actress. Every now and then a huge box of fruit would arrive from Los Angeles.

Duncan Watkins and Donna Cody lived in sin until the state finally allowed them to miscegenate legally. They celebrated their legal married state at Aunt Jane's old church, where the new pastor rejoiced with them and the deacon's wife and her flock rose to occasion. Even after the marriage, everyone still called Donna Cody Donna Cody.

Rockandy and Blue lived out their years in peace and contentment except sometimes when they both seemed to be waiting for someone to come through the door. Donna Cody speculated that they missed Sandy Panther. Duncan was skeptical.

Donna Cody went to the university where her Aunt Jane had taught and received all sorts of degrees (to the delight of her otherwise scandalized mother). She continued to visit C. C. Leggett and Edna, and wrote her dissertation on him. It is now a classic in folklore studies. She made it down to Dog Lick Hollow and Auntie Rufe's one more time, but later, that place was disbanded.

More often, Donna Cody made it back to Wandering Creek: recording, playing, and arguing with all and sundry, but especially with Carden Wade Goodman. He wrote a science fiction / fantasy novel in which a tall and skinny heroine defeats hordes of Cthulhu-like monsters through her fiddle playing. In a film adaptation, however, the heroine was blonde and curvaceous and she "played" "Orange Blossom Special" on a fiddle with silver strings. Nevertheless, as Carden Wade Goodman churned out more books, he developed a small but dedicated cult following, which, if not financially advantageous was certainly consoling. Frances wrote scripts for a new show that featured two policewomen hunting down supernatural enemies and aliens. She also wrote three literary novels that won wide acclaim. Nevertheless, she and Carden Wade Goodman lived together amicably.

At home, Duncan and Donna Cody began to be visited by streams of raggedy-looking young people who wanted to know about something they called *old-time music*. Her fiddling left some of them breathless, but she sent them south, east, and west to find the players so that she could get back to playing, reading, and writing.

Duncan gardened, cooked, invented an electric car (with some help from Marvin) to which he sold the rights and lost a lot of money. Marvin turned out to be good at making money. As the world grew scarier, he worked harder with Duncan. His wife did not appreciate this and left him, taking their three children. Brokenhearted but determined, he moved into

Mabel and Duncan's old house and remodeled it to suit himself. Donna Cody had never needed his father's talents with the law.[35]

Mabel moved into Aunt Jane's old house with Duncan and Donna Cody. She helped with the children when she wasn't touring. They didn't allow her to clean, though she sneaked it in sometimes. She sang the children her songs, and they loved her.

Dora became the chanteuse of the Old Town Rounders and made them even more famous. She wrote a lively yet sweet book about an idyllic growing-up, one that did not jibe with what Donna Cody and Sandy Panther had seen, but was beautifully enhanced by a famous children's book illustrator. The dream of the farm, of land, of all that was not machines was reviving by then, and the book sold well. However, she also wrote fierce songs like "Stand Up to Your Man" and occasionally played a funky electric guitar that could moan like a train whistle, issuing a challenge to the whole country music world.

Dora and Josh ran into Marcy Mellow one night at a benefit. She was still fierce and ready for anything. They ran into Sandy Panther when they were music consultants and performers for a film about the Appalachian coal wars. They managed to get Donna Cody in on some of the consulting, and there was general joy and sadness and talk together about how dark the days were growing.

"I wish it were that we're getting old, that everything just looks bad to old folks," said Dora.

---

[35] An industrious scholar found a mention of the incident with the prisoners. Apparently, due to some embarrassing details that came out about Mr. John, the whole thing was dropped. Miss Evans became a well-respected trial court administrator for Nob County.

"Even in the worst, we must fight for the best and for the beauty still in the world," said Donna Cody, who had only grown more sententious over the years. Still, her heart was right, she knew a lot more and respected what she did and didn't know, and so, she was loved. She had always meant well.

Viv Smythe would suddenly appear at Duncan and Donna Cody's, give them a copy of her latest production, get into long discussions with Donna Cody, and then disappear again.

The Richards children became doctors and teachers and social workers, even Maritrue. They all came home regularly to visit. Likens went on to become an engineer but also an activist. He was especially revered or despised because he wrote clearly, fiercely, and plainly, with as little jargon as possible. Maritrue, of all people, finally took on the farm, fought the coal companies, and married a heroic union organizer who was eventually shot and killed. She soldiered on, took care of her parents, and never gave up hope. Her siblings helped her out as much as they could. But her children—alas, there were some stories full of pain and grief.

Mandy Morgan finally tracked Donna Cody down. Their misunderstanding was settled in about five minutes, the rattle remained in its place, and they then spent several days playing, singing, and talking. Donna Cody recorded her and took notes and wrote a somewhat pedantic book about the musical mores of the old shantyboaters.

Albert and Vera prayed and loved and died in a terrible car accident, but Donna Cody and Sandy Panther never knew this.

Fred Jones prospered and was hated by many. He died old and rich, as did his Uncle Lamar.

Donna Cody and Sandy Panther's cassette was copied and passed around a little in the late sixties. There is only one copy left now that is playable, and it sits in a private collection. Many people, however, learned the tunes on it, though they have undoubtedly changed them, as all good players do. No one knows what happened to Viv Smythe's original tapes. Years later, Donna Cody finally typed up a list that named and dedicated some of them. The tune list is as follows:

- "Porter's Reel": Dedicated to Professor Jane Porter. Source: C. C. Leggett.
- "Diddly Bo Diddle": Dedicated to Mabel Watkins. Source: Mabel Watkins.
- "The Beloved Waltz": Dedicated to Duncan Watkins. Source: Traditional.
- "Chickalielee Daisy-O": Dedicated to C. C., Edna, and Buster Leggett. Sources: C. C. Leggett and Dora Richards.
- "Blessed and Busy": From the singing of Mrs. Mary Jane Stout. Source: The Buckeye Harmony.
- "The Panther Strut": Banjo solo. Source: Unknown.
- "The Little Dutch Boy": Dedicated with apologies to Mr. Rotmensen. Source: Traditional.
- "We Must All Fade Away" and "Jericho Jubilee": Source: Albert and Vera Love.
- "Cole's Pot's a-Boil": Source: Mandy Monroe.
- "The Cave of Yunwiya": by Donna Cody.
- "Our Time Here Is Sweet": Dedicated to Dora Richards and Josh Coshinsky and to all the Richards. Source: Dora

Richards.

- "Solly's Cave": Dedicated to Maritrue Richards. Source: The Richards Family.

After incredible personal sacrifices that I won't even mention, I found an account of Donna Cody's third big collecting trip. It is rumored that she found Dulcie Tobey again. Much research remains to be done sorting Donna Cody's personal papers and notes.

Epilogue

As a friend of mine[36] reminded me, "We have to remember what's going to happen." And so, dear readers, we must.

---

[36] Thanks, Moe Bowman.

Acknowledgements

"There is no book so bad. . .that it does not have something good in it."
—Miguel de Cervantes Saavedra

A web of people nurture and inspire art, even (maybe even especially) if they don't know it. This book is dedicated to Debbie Spiegelman, whose love and belief in goodness and potential waters plants of all kinds, including mine. I'd be remiss if I didn't add Stephen Wade, Kerry Blech, Allen Hart, Jim Ketterman, and Chris Cooper for years of ongoing musical joy, inspiration, and some vigorous riding of hobby horses. Add Carthy Sisco, an old-timer with a magical fiddle. Add Helen White, dear friend and most excellent of psychopomps.

Bertram Levy had an idea for a fiddle festival in Port Townsend. The Festival of Fiddle Tunes opened doors for me that would otherwise have remained closed. Thanks to him, Peter McCracken, and our dear departed Warren Argo and all the staff who work so hard to give us the gift of the music.

Barbara Taylor edited content. Her scholarly acumen helped me expand Donna Cody's monologues and gave me a broader vision of musical and folkloristic conundrums. She caught many inconsistencies and a fair share of lazy thinking. And she plays a mean fiddle (among other instruments). Deep thanks, Barb. All the mistakes and dumb stuff are mine.

Kate McLaughlin, former Microsoft buddy and visitor to that infamous den of editors in the famed Voodoo Lounge, copy edited this book and saved me from countless errors. Any mistakes or other deficiencies need to be laid at the usual suspect's door, and it's not hers.

Nancy Merrill, artist magnifique, agreed not only to beta read but to create the brilliant cover art. She continually inspires and encourages because that is what she does. Her belief in this book made all the difference.

Anthea Lawrence provided support, housing, and expertise on publishing and all things book. My deepest thanks. Check out her books on Amazon under her pen names: Anthea Sharp and Anthea Lawson.

Much additional gratitude and many thanks to:

- Victoria Josslin, Sheila Blech, Dixie Llewellin, Vicki Scannell, Pam Gray, Nancy Merrill, John Hatton, Randi Winter, and Scott Marckx, who were beta readers and provided me kind yet forceful feedback. In addition, Victoria, thank you for the loan of your house when I had to go hide and write.

- My children, Phoebe and Philip, for their patience through all the years of their mother's musical and literary enthusiasms.

- My parents, for playing the right records at the right time and for having hallways of books in a big old house.

- All the singers and players out there for whom music is a prayer, a party, and a necessity.

- Miguel de Cervantes Saavedra.

- Finally, but most importantly, my soul's strength, source of unending love and great fiddling, as well as some great editing, my dear Scott. Going far beyond the call of husbandly duty, he read through this ms. *twice*. He is my prince.

- And our beloved T-Lou, who inspired the delightful character of Rockandy. May he be waiting for us someday.

- If I forgot you, forgive me, and tell me so that I can put you in the next printing. I apologize to everyone from whom this book was extracted. Writers have their own methods of pillage, and not all of them are good.

Jeanie Murphy grew up in New England and went to Beloit College and Portland State University, where she received her BA and MA in English. She has worked as a strawberry picker, life guard, library page, factory hand, apple picker, banjo instructor (if you can call that *work*), technical editor, and English instructor. She is now retired but not retiring. She has an album on CD Baby called *The Time's Been Sweet* in which she plays the banjo. She has published a few minor things here and there and plays music in a band called *The Possum Carvers* or *The Glutton-Free Loafers* depending on what kind of music they're playing. This is her first novel. She lives on the Olympic Peninsula.

You can contact her at donnacodyfiddler@gmail.com
If you find errors, I'd love to know about them for the second printing!

65156655R00208

Made in the USA
Lexington, KY
02 July 2017